THE ENDEARMENT

LaVyrle Spencer is the author of many top selling novels, both historical and contemporary, with over fifteen million in print. A recent title, *Forgiving*, went straight into the *New York Times* bestseller lists and confirmed her place as one of today's most successful writers of romantic fiction. She lives in Stillwater, Minnesota, with her husband, Dan.

LAVYRLE SPENCER

The Endearment

HarperCollins*Publishers*

HarperCollins*Publishers*
77-85 Fulham Palace Road,
Hammersmith, London W6 8JB

Special overseas edition 1994
This paperback edition 1996
3 5 7 9 8 6 4

Previously published in the USA by
Jove Books 1990

ISBN 0 58621695 2

Printed and bound in Great Britain by
Omnia Books Ltd, Glasgow

To my cherished friend, Ellen Anderson Niznik, whose mama and papa, in the long ago, held hands and walked over to the church steps to sit in the sunset . . .

HISTORICAL NOTE

During the years immediately preceding Minnesota's declaration of statehood, while it was still considered the frontier, few women ventured into her depths, particularly not north of St Anthony Falls. Frontier life made the woman pay too dearly for her place in the North Country. Although newspapers in the East carried tempting descriptions of all the Minnesota Territory had to offer men, along with open invitations to settle there, no such invitation was extended to women. Instead, those newspapers ran articles discouraging women from that rough, untamed land. Thus, most men who came as pioneers to pluck a living out of the wilderness of the Minnesota Territory came, at first, womanless.

And so was necessitated the practice of sending for women, sight unseen.

And these were called 'mail-order brides.'

1

Anna Reardon had done the unforgivable. She had lied through her teeth to get Karl Lindstrom to marry her! She had intentionally deceived the man in order to get him to send her passage money to Minnesota as his mail-order bride. He was expecting her to be twenty-five years old, an able cook, an experienced housekeeper, a willing farm worker and . . . a virgin.

Furthermore, he was expecting her to arrive alone.

The only thing Anna hadn't lied about was her looks. She had accurately described herself as whiskey-haired, Irish, about as tall as a mule's withers, on the thin side, with brown eyes, flat ears, a few freckles, passable features, all her teeth and no pox marks.

But the rest of Anna's letters were a passel of lies good enough to finagle the unsuspecting Lindstrom into sending her fare, enabling her to escape Boston.

Still, lie though she had, those fabrications had not come easy for Anna. They were dictated by a desperate, homeless girl, written by her youngling brother and had lain like a hair shirt upon Anna's conscience ever since. Indeed, every time she recounted her lies, she was punished by a dull pain in the pit of her stomach until now, only minutes away from meeting Karl Lindstrom, Anna had a stomach-ache the likes of which she'd never suffered before.

The pain had gotten worse and worse all through their long and tedious trip west, a trip that began a month ago after the ice floes had broken up on the Great Lakes. Anna and her brother, James, had travelled throughout June by train from Boston to Albany, then by canal boat to Buffalo. There they'd boarded a lake steamer bound for a mudhole called Chicago, a town that in 1854 consisted of not more than a plank road leading from the boat landing to a hotel. Beyond lay the wilderness country that Anna and James had crossed.

A teamster drove them to Galena in the Illinois Territory, this leg of the trip taking an entire week while mosquitoes, weather and the bumpy ox-cart trail joined forces in making everyone miserable. At Galena, they boarded a steamboat for St Paul, where they transferred to an ox team that took them the few miles to St Anthony Falls.

Alas, compared to Boston, the town was utterly disillusioning – not much more than a smattering of rough-hewn, unpainted buildings. It made Anna wonder what to expect at the outpost settlement of Long Prairie where she was to meet her future husband.

For more than a month now, she'd had nothing more to do than watch miles of earth and water slip by and worry about what Karl Lindstrom would do when he learned of her countless deceits. Her nerves shattered, Anna wondered why she'd ever thought she could get by with such a scheme in the first place.

One lie would be apparent immediately – James. Never had Anna told her future husband that she had a brother for whom she felt responsible. She had no idea what the man's reaction would be when presented with an adolescent brother-in-law along with his bride-to-be.

The second of Anna's lies was her age. Karl Lindstrom had stated in his advertisement that he wanted an ex-perienced, mature woman, so Anna knew beyond a doubt that had she admitted she was only seventeen, Lindstrom would've known she was greener than spring corn! And so, instead, Anna had told him she was twenty-five, the same age as Lindstrom himself. Anna figured any woman of twenty-five would have the practical experience a man out here needed in a frontier wife. But Lord help her when he found out different!

For the first time in her life Anna Reardon wished she had some wrinkles in her skin, some crow's feet about the eyes, maybe some fat around her waist – anything to make her look a little older than seventeen! He'd take one look and know the truth. And what would he say then? Take your brother and pack yourselves straight back to Boston? With what? thought Anna.

What would they do if Lindstrom left them high and dry out here in the middle of nowhere? Anna had been forced once to earn passage money – she'd had to get James to Minnesota without Lindstrom knowing – and she shuddered now at the memory, the knot in her stomach growing sickeningly fierce. Not again, she thought. Never again!

She and her brother were completely at Lindstrom's mercy. It helped calm Anna's roiling stomach to wonder if Lindstrom might've told a few lies of his own. She had no guarantee he'd been truthful with her. He'd told her all this stuff about his place and his plans for the future, but what bothered her was that he'd said so little about himself. Maybe because there wasn't much to tell!

He'd written endlessly about Minnesota, Minnesota, Minnesota! Apologizing for his lack of originality and his inadequate English, Karl had instead quoted newspapers, which were trying to entice immigrants and settlers to this untamed place.

Minnesota is better than the plains. Here is a spot where one can live in rude but generous plenty. Here there are trees for fuel and building materials. Here, too, wild fruits grow in profusion, while game of all kinds range the forests and prairies; lakes and streams swarm with fishes. Noble forests, fertile prairies, hills and sky-tinted lakes and streams provide well their yields of necessity and beauty.

These descriptions, Karl wrote, had reached even as far as his native Sweden where a sudden explosion in the population had caused a land shortage. Minnesota, sounding so much like his beloved Skäne, had lured Karl with its invitation.

Thus, he crossed the ocean, and hoped his brothers and sisters might soon follow. But neither brother nor sister nor neighbour had come to alleviate his loneliness.

How idyllic it had sounded when James read to Anna all Karl said about Minnesota. But when it came to describing himself, Lindstrom was far less adept.

All he'd said was that he was Swedish, with blond hair, blue eyes, and that he was 'pretty big.' Of his face, he'd said, 'I do not think it would make milk curdle.'

Anna and James had both laughed when he read that, and agreed that Karl Lindstrom sounded like a man with a sense of humour. Riding now toward her first meeting with him, Anna fervently hoped he was, for he'd need it sooner than he knew!

In an effort to dispel her misgivings, Anna again began to wonder what Karl Lindstrom would be like. Would he be handsome? What would be the timbre of his voice? The bent of his disposition? What kind of husband would he be – considerate or unkind? Gentle or rough? Forgiving or intolerant?

This, above all, worried Anna, for what man would not be angry to learn that his wife was not a virgin? At the thought, Anna's cheeks burned and her stomach grew worse. Of all her lies, this was the greatest and least forgivable. It was the one she could most easily conceal from Karl Lindstrom until it was too late for him to do anything about it, but the one that made her break out in a cold, clammy sweat.

James Reardon had been made a willing accomplice in his sister's scheme. As a matter of fact, he was the first one

12

who found Lindstrom's ad and showed it to Anna. But because Anna couldn't read or write, it had fallen to James to pen the letters to Lindstrom. At first it had been easy to write a glib description of the kind of woman they thought Lindstrom wanted. Yet as time went on, James realized they were becoming caught in a web of their own making. Repeatedly he had argued that they should at least let Lindstrom know he, James, was coming along. But Anna had won. She had insisted that if Lindstrom learned the truth, their hopes of escaping Boston would be lost.

Riding now atop the packing crates, barrels and sacks, James wore a deep furrow between his brows. Bouncing along the ill-kept government road, he worried about his fate should Lindstrom hold Anna to her promise to marry but be unwilling to accept James in the bargain. He frowned into the lowering sun, a worn hat pulled low over his eyes, a fringe of auburn hair showing above his ears, the lines of worry too deep for such a boyish face.

'Hey,' Anna said, reaching out to lightly rap one of his knuckles, knuckles that seemed to outproportion the length of fingers, 'it's gonna be all right.'

But James only stared toward the west as before, his head resting against the side of the wagon, bumping there as the wheels thudded into each pothole. 'Oh yeah? And what if he sends us packin'? What'll we do then?'

'I don't think he will. And anyway, we agreed, didn't we?'

'Did we?' he asked, giving her a brief glance. 'We should've told him I was coming, Anna. We should've told him that much of the truth.'

'And end up rotting in Boston!' Anna replied for the hundredth time.

'So, we end up rotting in Minnesota. What's the difference?'

But Anna hated it when they argued like this. She

13

tweaked a bit of hair on his arm. 'Aw, come on, you're just getting cold feet.'

'And I suppose you aren't,' James returned, refusing to be humoured. He'd seen the way Anna'd been clutching her stomach over there. Her face crumpled a little, making him sorry he'd started arguing again.

'I'm just as scared as you,' she finally admitted, all pretence of brightness now gone. 'My stomach hurts so bad I feel like I could throw up.'

There was absolutely no doubt whatsoever in the mind of Karl Lindstrom that Anna Reardon would be every bit as good as she sounded in her letters. He took her words at face value. He paced back and forth in front of Morisette's store, looking east for sign of the approaching supply wagon. He polished his boot tops on the backs of his calves yet another time. He removed his small-billed, black, woollen cap and thwacked it against his thigh, eyed the road, and settled the hat back on his fair hair. He tried whistling a little between his teeth, but became critical of the notes, and stopped. He cleared his throat and jammed his hands into his pockets and thought of her again.

He had taken to thinking of her as his 'little whiskey-haired Anna.' It did not matter that she'd said she was tall, nor that she said she had trouble controlling her hair. Karl pictured her as he remembered all the women from back home – pink-cheeked, vigorous, with a becoming face framed in blonde, Swedish braids. Freckles, she'd said. Passable, she'd said. What did that mean – passable? He wanted her to be more than passable, he wanted her to be pretty!

Then, feeling guilty at placing too much value upon such a superficial thing, he took up pacing again, telling himself, 'So, what is in a face, Karl Lindstrom? It is what is inside that matters.' In spite of himself, Karl still hoped that his Anna might be comely. But he realized beauty was much

14

to expect when she would be able to help so much on the farm.

The only thing that worried him was the fact that she was Irish. He had heard that the Irish had short tempers. Living where they would, so far from others, with only each other, would turn out to be a fine fix if she proved to be quick to anger. He himself, being Swedish, was an amiable fellow – at least he thought himself so. He did not think his temper was anything to put a woman off, although sometimes, looking in the mirror, he worried about his face doing so. He had told Anna it would not make milk curdle, but the closer he came to meeting her the more he fretted. Yet he knew beyond a doubt she'd love the place.

He thought of his land, much land, so much more than in Sweden. He thought of his team of horses, a rare thing here where most had oxen, which cost a full two hundred dollars less than his beautiful Percheron team. He had named them the most American of names – Belle and Bill – in honour of his newly adopted land. He thought of his sod house, which he had cleaned so meticulously today before leaving it, and of the log house already begun. He thought of his grainfields ripening in full sun, which only two short years ago had been solid forest. He thought of his spring, his creek, his pond, his maples, his tamaracks. And even though he set small store by himself or his appearance, Karl Lindstrom thought, yes, I have much to offer a woman. I am a man with plenty.

Yet he dreamed of having more.

He pulled Anna's letters out of his deep pants pocket and studied the script again with great pride, thinking how lucky he was to be getting a woman who was lettered. How many men could claim a thing like that? Here, a man was lucky to have any woman, let alone a lettered one. But his Anna had learned her letters in Boston, and so could teach their children some day. Touching the coarse paper upon which she had written, thinking of her hands touching it – those hands he had never seen – and of the children they would one day make together, a lump clotted his throat. Thinking that no more would he have only his animals to talk to, only his own solitary company at mealtime, only his own warmth in the bed at night, he felt his heart beat crazily.

Anna, he thought, my little whiskey-haired Anna. How long I have waited for you!

Anna peered around the backs of the half-breed drivers as long as she dared, before hiding behind them, wiping her palms on her hand-me-down dress and telling James to alert her when he saw what he thought was the store.

'I see it!' James croaked, stretching his neck while Anna tried to shrink lower in the wagon.

'Oh nooo,' she moaned under her breath.

'There's someone standing out front!' James said excitedly.

'Is it him? Do you think it's him?' Anna whispered nervously.

'I don't know yet, but he's looking this way.'

'James, do I look all right?'

He glanced at her garish, royal blue dress with its ruffled skirt. James didn't much care for it. It revealed too much of her breasts, though she'd done her best to make tucks to draw its bodice protectively closer to decency. But he answered, 'You look fine, Anna.'

'I wish I had a hat,' she said wistfully, touching her flyaway locks, absently smoothing them while her inadequacies loomed ever more obvious.

'Maybe he'll buy you one. He has one. It's a funny little cap like a pie plate with a bill.'

'Wh . . . what else? What does he . . . what does he look like?'

16

'He's big, but I can't make out much. The sun's in my eyes.'

Anna's eyes slid closed. She clasped her hands tightly between her knees and wished she knew how to pray. She rocked forward and backward, then resolutely opened her eyes again and took a deep breath that did nothing whatever to stop the quivering in her stomach.

'Tell me what he looks like as soon as you can make him out better,' she whispered. One of the Indian drivers heard the whispering and turned around questioningly. 'Just drive!' she said testily, flapping an impatient hand at him, and he faced front again, chuckling.

'I can see now!' James said excitedly. 'He's awful big, and he's wearing a white shirt and dark britches tucked into his boots and – '

'No, his face! What does his face look like!'

'Well, I can't tell from here. Why don't you look for yourself?' Then James, too, sat down so he wouldn't be caught gaping when they pulled in.

At the last minute Anna warned, 'Remember, don't say anything about who you are until I have a chance to talk to him. I'll . . . I'll try to get him used to me a little bit before he has to get used to you.' She dusted at her skirt and gave it a useless fluff, then looked down at her chest and placed a trembling hand there, hoping he would not notice the patch of skin she couldn't quite cover when she'd altered the dress.

James swallowed hard, his youthful Adam's apple looking pronounced in his gangly neck. 'Good luck, Anna,' he said, but his voice cracked in the way it did so often lately. Those unexpected falsettos usually made the two of them laugh, but neither Anna nor James laughed now.

As the wagon approached, Karl Lindstrom suddenly wondered what to do with his hands. What will she think of these hands, such big, clumsy things? He jammed them into his pockets and felt her letters there, and grabbed onto

17

one of them for dear life. His ears seemed suddenly filled with the sound of his own swallowing. He could see the two drivers clearly now. Behind them bobbed two other heads, and Karl fixed his sights on one of them, trying to make out the colour of its hair.

A man, Karl thought, should not appear to be shaking in his big Swedish boots when he comes to meet his woman. What will she think if she sees my fright? She will expect a moose like me to act like I know what I am doing, to be sure of myself. Calm down, Karl! But the trembling in his gut could not be talked away so simply.

The wagon slowed, then stopped. The Indians secured the reins, and Anna heard a deep voice say to them, 'You are here in good time. You have had a good trip?' The voice had the faint musicality of a Swedish accent.

'Good enough,' one driver answered.

Footsteps came slowly around the rear of the wagon bringing a broad, blond giant of a man. In that first moment she felt like her whole body wanted to smile. There was a boyish hesitation before his mouth dropped open just a little. A big, callused hand moved up in slow motion to doff the little pie-plate hat from his wheat-coloured hair. His Adam's apple bobbed once, but still he said nothing, just stood smashing that poor cap into a tight little twist in his two outsized fists, his eyes all the while locked on her face.

Anna's tongue felt swollen, and her throat wouldn't work right. Her heart was clubbing the bejesus out of the wall of her chest.

'Anna?' he spoke at last, charming her by his old-world pronunciation that made of the word a warmer thing than it had ever been before. '*Onnuh?*' he questioned again.

'Yes,' she finally managed. 'I am Anna.'

'I am Karl,' he said simply, and up went his eyes to her hair. And up went hers, also, to his.

Yellow, she thought, such very yellow hair. All this time

she had wondered, imagined. Now here it was, the one thing that had had colour in her thoughts of him. But she found her imagination had not done it justice. This was the most magnificent blond hair she had ever beheld on a man. Thick and healthy it was, with a hint of curl at the nape of his neck and around his face where tiny beads of perspiration formed.

Her hair, Karl found, was indeed the colour of rich, Irish whiskey, as when the sun glances through it and lights its depths with shafts of sienna. It flew free in scarcely manageable wavelets; there were no Swedish braids in sight.

When his glance went wandering, so did her hand, to touch an unruly lock at her temple. The way Karl was staring, Anna wished once again that she had a hat. Then suddenly her hand dropped down and self-consciously clutched her other as she realized what she'd done, touching her hair as if frightened to have his gaze rove over her.

Once again their eyes met, his the colour of the Minnesota sky, hers like the darkest brown stripes in the agates he so often plowed up from his soil. His glance dropped to her mouth. He wondered what it would look like when she stopped biting her upper lip. And just then it slipped free of her teeth, and he beheld a lovely mouth with the curve of a leaf, sweet but unsmiling.

And so he smiled a little himself, and she tried a shaky one in return. She was afraid to smile as wide as his appearance merited, for he was as handsome a man as she'd ever seen. His nose was perfectly straight, and symmetrical, with fine nostrils like halves of a heart. His cheeks were long, and just concave enough to make him look young and eager. His chin bore a shallow cleft, and his lips – still fallen open as if he too was having difficulty breathing – were beautifully sculptured and bowed up at crest and corners. His skin held the richness of colour put there by the sun.

Guiltily, Anna dropped her gaze, realizing how freely she'd allowed her eyes to travel his face.

And Anna thought, no, he would not make milk curdle.

And Karl thought, yes, she is much more than passable.

At last Karl cleared his throat and settled his little cap back on his head. 'Come, let me help you down, Anna, but pass me your things first.' When he reached, his arm filled his white sleeve as fully as fifty pounds of wheat fills a grainsack.

She turned and reached beyond James who had sat through all that feeling like an eavesdropper – for all they'd hardly spoken to one another. When Anna got to her feet, she found her muscles stiff and unreasonable after the long ride, and feared Karl would find her clumsy and graceless. But he didn't seem to notice the hitch in her hip, only reached up his large hands to help her over the heckboard. His shirt-sleeves were rolled up to the elbow, exposing thick, sturdy forearms. His shoulders, too, filled his shirt until it was taut against his skin. When she braced upon them, she found them like rocks. Effortlessly, he took the distance from her leap, then his two wide hands lingered at her waist.

His hands are so big, she thought, her stomach going light at his touch.

Karl felt how little there was to her, and at closer range his suspicion was confirmed. She was no twenty-five years old!

'It is a very long ride. You must be very tired,' he said, noticing that – young or not – she was very tall, indeed. The top of her head came nearly to the tip of his nose.

'Yes,' she mumbled, feeling stupid at being unable to think of more to add, but his hands were still on her waist, the warmth of them seeping through and touching her, while he acted like he'd forgotten they were there. Suddenly, he yanked them away.

'Well, tonight you will not have to sleep beneath a

wagon. You will be in a warm, safe bed at the mission.'
Then he thought, fool! She will think that this is all you
can think of – bed! First you must show concern for her.
'This is the store of Joe Morisette I told you about. If there
are things that you need, we can get them here. It is best if
we do the trading now because in the morning we will start
early for my place.'

He turned and walked beside her, watching the tips of
her shoes flare her flouncy skirt out. She wore a dress that
was not to his liking. It was sheeny, and too bright, with
gussets at the breast as if made for an older woman of far
fuller figure. It was an odd thing, with too much ruffle and
too little chest, ill-suited for a place like Minnesota.

He was suddenly sure she wore it to make herself appear
older. She could not be more than eighteen, he guessed,
watching her askance as she walked a step ahead of him
toward the store. There was a hint of breast camouflaged
within the tawdry bodice, but what did he know of such?

She moved through the door ahead of him and he saw
her from behind for the first time. There was nothing to
her. Oh, she was tall all right, but far too thin for Karl's
taste. He thought of the poles upon which his mother's
green beans climbed, and decided the only thing this Anna
of his needed was a little fattening up.

Morisette looked up as soon as they entered, calling out
in a robust French accent, 'So, she is here and the bride-
groom can stop his nervous pacing and whiskey drinking!'

You have a big mouth, Morisette, Karl thought. But
when Anna turned sharply and glanced back at Karl, she
found him red to the ears. She'd seen enough whiskey
drinkers in Boston to last her a lifetime. The last thing she
wanted was to be married to one.

Must I deny such a thing to her right here before
Morisette? Karl wondered. No, the girl will just have to
learn that I am honourable once she has lived with me for
a while.

Anna gazed around the store, wondering what he would say if she told him she would like to own a hat. Never had she owned a new hat of her own, and he *had* asked her if there was anything she needed. But she dared not ask for anything, knowing James still waited outside, thoroughly unnoticed by Karl Lindstrom. A hand at her elbow urged her toward the storekeeper. The swarthy French-Canadian wore a ready smile and a somewhat teasing grin.

'This is Anna, Joe. She is here at last.'

'But of course it is Anna. Who else could it be?' Morisette laughed infectiously, flinging his palms wide. 'You have had quite a ride up the government road, eh? It is not the best road, but it is not the worst. Wait until you have seen the road to Karl's house, then you will appreciate the one you have just come down. Do you know, young lady, that the newspapers warn women not to come here because the life is so hard?'

It was not at all what Karl would have had Morisette tell Anna. He did not want to scare her away before she even had a chance to see his wonderful Minnesota and let it speak for itself.

'Yes, of course, I've . . . read them for myself,' Anna lied. 'But Karl thinks there is no place better to settle because there is so much land and it is so rich and . . . and there's everything a man could want here.'

Morisette laughed. Karl had filled her head already, he could tell.

Pleased with her reply, Karl answered, 'See there, Morisette, you cannot scare Anna away with your foolish talk. She has come this far, and she is here to stay.' Anna's heart grew a little lighter. So far she seemed to be passing muster, seventeen or not, wrinkles or none.

'And so the good *père* is marrying you at the mission?' Morisette asked.

'Yes, in the morning,' Karl said, looking at the back of

Anna's shoulders where those tumblecurls were rioting over her collar.

Just then the half-breed drivers came into the store, each with a barrel hoisted on his shoulder. One of them set his load down with a thud, then said, 'That boy stands in the road as if he is lost. Did you not tell him this is the end of the run?' There was no doubt that he was directing his question to Anna. But she stood dumbstruck.

'What boy?' Lindstrom asked.

Seeing no way out, Anna looked him square in the eye and answered, 'My brother, James.'

Baffled for a moment, Karl stared back at her, the truth dawning on him even as Morisette and the drivers looked on. 'Ya, of course ... James.' Lindstrom stalked to the door, and for the first time looked fully at the lad who had been the other passenger on the supply wagon. Karl had been so intent upon Anna that he'd scarcely realized the boy was there.

'James?' Lindstrom spoke, trying to make it sound as if he'd known all along.

'Yes?' James replied, then amended it to, 'Yes, sir,' wanting to create a good impression on the tall man.

'Why do you stand in the road? Come in and meet my friend, Morisette.'

Surprised, the boy's feet seemed rooted momentarily, then he jammed his hands in his pockets and entered the store. When he passed before Karl, the man noted some similarity between the boy's looks and Anna's. The lad was gangly and thin, too, with similar colouring, but the freckles were missing, and the eyes, although large like his sister's, were green instead of brown.

Karl expertly concealed his surprise, moving about the store methodically, loading supplies on his wagon out front. James and Anna explored the shop, catching each other's eye now and then, quickly looking away, wondering at Karl's reaction or lack of it. They were both

23

amazed at how unconcerned the man seemed to be with James being here. He just went about calmly loading supplies onto his wagon, bantering with Morisette.

When things were firmly lashed on behind the pair of blinking Percherons, Karl came back inside, announcing that it was time to leave. But Anna noticed he did not repeat his offer to buy her anything she needed. He bid goodbye to Morisette and took Anna stiffly by the elbow to guide her outside, but there was a pressure there that warned her this new husband-to-be was not as complacent as she'd thought earlier.

2

Anna thought Karl would dislocate her arm before he let go of it. Without a word he herded her along, Anna taking two steps to every one of his, but he ignored all but her elbow with which he finally pushed her up to the wagon seat. She ventured a peek at his face, and his expression made her stomach take to quaking something awful. She rubbed her misused shoulder socket, wishing more than ever that she had written the truth in all those letters.

Karl's voice was as controlled as ever as he spoke to his horses, gave them a cluck and started them up the road. But when they were around a bend, beyond earshot of the store, the wagon lurched to a sudden halt. Lindstrom's voice bit the air in a far different tone than he had used thus far. His words were as slow as always, but louder.

'I do not air my arguments before Joe Morisette down at his store. I do not let that tease Morisette see that Karl Lindstrom has had a fast one pulled on him. But I think this is what has happened! I think you, Anna Reardon, have tried to take in a stupid Swede, eh? You have not been honest and would make a fool of Karl Lindstrom before his friend Morisette!'

Her back stiffened. 'Wh . . . what do you mean?' she stammered, growing sorrier by the minute.

'What do I mean?' he repeated, the accent more pronounced. 'Woman, I am no fool!' he exploded. 'Do not take me for one! We have made a bargain, you and me. All these months we make the plan for you to come to me, and not once do you mention your brother in your letters! Instead, you bring a little surprise for Karl, huh, that will make people laugh when they know that it is the first time I have heard of my bride bringing an extra passenger I have not been expecting!'

'I . . . I guess I should have told you, but – '

'You guess!' he shouted, totally frustrated. 'You do more than guess! You *know* long ago you are planning this trick on me, and you probably think Karl Lindstrom is such a big dumb Swede that it will work!'

'No, I didn't think that at all. I wanted to tell you but I thought once you saw James, you'd see what a help he'll be to you. James is a good, strong boy. Why, he's almost a man!' she pleaded.

'James is a stripling! He is another mouth to feed and another set of winter clothes to buy.'

'He's thirteen years old, and in another year or two he'll be full-grown. Then he'll be twice the help that I'll be.'

'I did not put the advertisement in the Boston paper for a hired boy, I advertised for a wife.'

'And I'm here, aren't I?'

'Ya, you sure are. But you, plus this brother, is more than I bargained for.'

'He's a good worker, Lindstrom.'

'This is not Boston, Anna Reardon. Here an extra person means extra provisions. Where will he sleep? What will he wear? Will there be enough food to feed three during the coming winter? These are things a man must consider in order to survive here.'

She pleaded in earnest now, words rushing out. 'He can sleep on the floor. He has enough clothing for one winter. He'll help you raise extra crops during the summer ahead.'

'The crops are already in the ground, and you were supposed to help me tend them. I only needed one – you.'

'I *will* help you. Just think of how much more three of us could raise! Why, we'd have so much – '

'I told you, the crops are already in! Right now I do not even think it is the crops I am concerned with. It is the fact

26

that you have lied to me and what I must do about that. Never would I willingly choose a liar for a wife.'

Anna sat smitten into silence. There seemed no argument against that.

James, who had gotten onto the wagon without a word, spoke up at last. 'Mr Lindstrom, we didn't have any choice. Anna thought that if you knew I was part of the deal you'd turn her down flat.' James's voice cracked from tenor to soprano, then back again.

'And you think right!' Karl exploded. 'That is exactly what I would do, and I am thinking I might still do just that!'

Anna found her voice again, but fear made it tremble. Her eyes were wide in her too thin face, and they sparkled with threatening tears.

'You . . . you wouldn't send us back? Oh, please don't send us back.'

'When you lie to me, you break our agreement. I do not think I am responsible for you any longer. I did not bargain for a wife who was a liar.'

He sounded so self-righteous, sitting there all sated and healthy-looking, so obviously well-fed, that Anna's temper suddenly flared.

'No, you don't have to bargain at all, do you!' she lashed, then gestured with hands thrown wide toward the earth in general. 'Not when you have your precious Minnesota to yield all its *nectar* and *wood* and *fruit*!' Her voice fairly oozed with sarcasm. 'Not when you're warm and fat and cosy! You wouldn't know the first thing about going cold and hungry, would you? I'd like to see you that way, Karl Lindstrom. Maybe then you'd find out how easy it is to lie a little to improve your station in life. Boston would teach you quick how to be a blinkin' artist at lying!'

'So you make a habit of lying? Is that what you are saying?' He glared at her then, finding her cheeks pinked beneath their sprinkling of freckles.

'You're damn right,' she cursed with fierce intensity, looking him square in the eye. 'I lied so I could eat. I lied so James could eat. First, we tried it without lying, but we got no place fast. Nobody wanted to hire James 'cause he was too skinny and undernourished. And nobody wanted to hire me because I was a girl. Finally, when trying for an honest living didn't work, we decided it was time to try a little dishonesty and see if it'd work out better for us.'

'Anna!' he exclaimed, disappointed as much by her cussing as by her lying. 'How could you do such a thing? There have been times I have been hungry, too. But never have I been hungry enough to make lies. Nothing makes Karl Lindstrom into a liar!'

'Well, if you're so almighty honest, you'll keep your half of the bargain and marry me!' she spouted.

'Bargain! I said the bargain is broken by your deceit. I paid good money for your passage. What of that? Can you return it to me? Can you do that, or have I been fool enough to get you here and end up with no wife and no money?'

'I can't pay you back in money, but if you'll take us, both of us, we'll work hard. That's the only way we can pay you back.' She looked away from the genuine shock in Karl Lindstrom's eyes, the kind that comes from gentle rearing where black and white are clearly defined.

'Mr Lindstrom,' James interjected, 'I'll pay my way, too, you'll see. I'm stronger than I look. I can help you build that cabin you're planning on, and I can help you clear land, and . . . and plant it and harvest it.'

Karl's eyes bored straight ahead between Belle's ears. His jaw was so taut it looked swollen.

'Can you manage a team, boy?' he snapped.

'N . . . no.'

'Can you handle a plough?'

'I've never tried.'

'Can you lift a logging chain or handle a flail or fell with an axe?'

28

'I . . . I can learn,' James stammered.

'Learning takes time. Out here time is precious. Our growing season is short and the winters are long. You come to me unskilled and expect me to make you teamster, logger and farmer all in one summer?'

Anna began to see the shortsightedness of her plan, but she couldn't give up now. 'He learns fast, Lindstrom,' she promised. 'You wouldn't be sorry.'

Karl looked at her sideways, shook his head despondently and studied his boots. 'I am already sorry. I am sorry I ever had such an idea, to send for a wife through the mail. But I waited two years thinking there would be other settlers coming, other women. In Sweden there is much talk about this Minnesota, and I believed other Swedes would follow me. But nobody comes and I can wait no longer. This you know, too. This I think you have planned to use against me to get your way.' He sounded sad.

'Maybe I did, but I thought you'd see that an extra person would be useful.' Anna picked at a piece of loose cuticle while she said this.

There was another point Karl wanted to make, but he did not know how to say it without seeming to be a man of great sexual demands. He could not imagine taking a wife to bed in the same room with a brother. If he said as much, Anna would undoubtedly be horrified. All he could do was tiptoe around the issue by saying, with his eyes now on Belle's neck, 'I live in a house of only one room, Anna.'

Anna quit picking at her cuticle. She felt her face warming, understanding fully what Karl implied. His courteous way of implying they would need more privacy touched her. He was different from any man she had ever met. She'd never before met a human being who was totally good, but it looked as if perhaps Karl Lindstrom was. That goodness filled her with self-recriminations that she could not have come to him a better person herself.

29

Had Karl dared to look at Anna that moment, he would have seen a faint blush beneath her freckles. But he did not. He stared absently, preoccupied with another disillusioning thought. Suppose Anna had been wily enough to reckon on using their lack of privacy to keep her from performing the duty that some wives – he'd been told – found distasteful. This, of course, he could not accuse her of, especially not in front of the lad.

Karl only wanted to take his new wife to his little home, which was waiting in readiness for their return. There he would have had time and privacy to woo her as in any normal courtship. Ah, thought Karl, what a strange way we have come together, Anna and me.

Within the heart of Karl Lindstrom fell a heavy sadness. How he had looked forward to this day, thinking always how proud he would be when he took his little whiskey-haired Anna into his sod house for the first time. He would proudly show her the fireplace he had built of fieldstone from his own soil, the table and chairs he had fashioned of sturdy black walnut from his own trees. He remembered the long hours spent braiding buffalo grass into ropes to restring the log frame of the bed for her. How carefully he had dried last season's corn husks to make the softest tickings a woman could want. He'd spent precious hours collecting cattails, plucking their down to fill pillow ticks for her. The buffalo robes had been aired and shaken and rubbed with wild herbs to make them smell sweet. Lastly, he had picked a sheaf of sweet clover, its fragrance headier than any other, and had lain it on the spot where their two pillows met, in the centre of the bed.

In all these ways Karl Lindstrom had sought to tell his Anna that he prized her, welcomed her and strove to please her. Only now that she was here, he found her a liar, perhaps not worthy of his lofty concern, a liar who brought a brother who would be sleeping on the floor on the night Karl Lindstrom took a bride to his bed for the first time.

Karl pondered long and silently, while Anna and James held their tongues. At last, unable to bear the strained silence any longer, Anna bit the inside of her cheek and said, 'You keep me and I won't lie no more.'

Karl looked at her finally. There was the stain of guilt upon her skin, which in itself was pleasing to him. It told him she did not lie without feeling small at getting caught. Her cheek had turned the colour of the wild roses that graced Karl's land in June. And, just like coming upon one of them unexpectedly at a turn of the trail, coming upon that rosy colour in Anna's cheeks now made him want to pick it and take it home with him.

He was a man to whom loneliness was a dread thing. Again he thought of awakening to find the bloom of her cheek on the pillow of cattail down beside him, and his own face felt warm. He found he had been studying her golden freckles, too; they seemed to lessen the severity of her guilt. They made her look utterly innocent. In that moment he thought of her lies as childish tales, told by a youngster to turn things her way.

'You promise me that?' he asked, looking straight into her eyes. 'That you will not lie to me anymore?' His voice was soft again, disarming.

'I promise, yes,' she vowed, matching his steady gaze with a steadiness of her own, matching his quiet tone, too.

'Then I want you to tell me how old you really are.'

Her eyes dropped, she bit her lip, and Karl knew he had her cold again!

'Twenty,' she said. But the colour in her cheeks had deepened to the heliotrope hue of the prairie thistle blossom, which Karl had never desired to pick and take home.

'And if I say I do not believe you?'

She only shrugged her shoulders, but avoided his eyes.

'I would ask your brother to tell me the truth, but I see that the two of you are in cahoots together with this pack of lies you have cooked up for me.' The gentle tone of his voice did not deceive her this time. Beneath it was an iron stubbornness to get at the truth.

Anna threw up both hands at once. 'Oh, for heaven's sake! *All right.* I'm seventeen! So what!' She glared bravely into Karl's face, her sudden spunk making him want to smile, which he carefully did not do.

'So what?' he repeated, raising his eyebrows, leaning back relaxedly – a cat playing with a mouse before sinking his teeth in. 'So I wonder if you are the cook and housemaid that you said you are.'

She puckered up her pretty mouth tight and sat staring stonily ahead.

'Do not forget, you said you are done with lying,' he reminded her.

'I said I'm seventeen. What more do you want?'

'I want a wife who knows how to cook. Can you cook?'

'A little.'

'A little?'

'Well, not much,' she spit, 'but I can learn, can't I?'

'I do not know. How will you learn? Will I have to teach this, too?'

She elected not to answer.

'How much housework do you know?'

Silence.

He nudged her. 'How much?'

She jerked her arm away. 'About as much as I know about cooking!'

'Can you make soap?'

No answer.

'Can you make tallow dips?'

No answer.

'Bake bread?'

No answer.

'I guess that you have never done much farming either, or gardening or caring for a house.'

'I can stitch!' was all she'd say.

'Stitch . . .' he repeated, quite sarcastically for Karl Lindstrom. 'She can stitch,' he said to the wagon wheel. Then Karl began talking to himself in Swedish, and that really riled Anna, for she couldn't understand a word he said.

At last he fell silent, studying the wagon wheel, his head turned away from her. She sat ramrod still, her arms crossed over her chest.

'I reckon you should've waited for those Swedish girls to come to Minnesota, huh?' she asked sourly, taking her turn at staring down the horses' necks.

'Ya, I think I should have,' Karl said in English. Then he muttered, once more for good measure, 'Seventeen and she knows nothing but how to stitch.'

He mulled silently for some time, then finally turned to face her, wondering how a man of his age could take to bed a child of seventeen without feeling like a defiler of innocence. His eyes flickered down to her breasts, over to James, then back to Anna's face. 'There seems to be a lot you do not know how to do.'

'I can damn well do anything you set me to, seventeen or not!' But she prayed her face was not flushed.

'You can sure cuss real good, but I don't need no woman to cuss.' He wondered how he'd survive the rest of his life with her Irish temper. He wondered how he'd survive another year or two womanless. All he said was, 'I must think.'

'Sir . . .' James began, 'Anna and me –'

'*Do not disturb me when I think*,' Karl ordered. James and Anna looked at each other out of the corners of their eyes. They thought he'd set the horses to walking, but he continued to brood in silence. It was his way, the way his father had taught him, the way his grandfather had taught his father. He spent time meditating a situation first, pondering before making a decision, so that when he tackled a problem, he almost always solved it. He sat quiet as a stone while the birds twittered, soft evening talk as if putting their young ones to nest for the night.

The summer evening imposed itself on Anna, and she thought how bird-talk wasn't often heard in Boston. There, at this time of day, came the music from the taverns opening for the evening. Already Anna found she preferred the birds. In his letters Karl had said there were more birds here than anyone could name. She wondered now if she'd ever get the chance to try.

'Anna!' he said, making her jump, 'you must tell me now what other lies you have told. I think I am entitled to know if there are any more.'

Anna felt James jab her in the side with his elbow.

'I didn't tell any other lies. Heaven's sake! What more could there possibly be?' Oh, she sounded so convincing she thought she should be on the stage.

'There better not be more!' he warned. But still he did not give a clue what else he was thinking. He picked up the reins, started the horses on their way again and drove to the mission.

He pulled the horses up before the pair of log buildings with well-worn earth between them. The larger building had a crude cross atop the door, while the other had none. It was the school, Anna knew.

'I have much thinking to do yet,' Karl said. 'We will sleep here tonight as planned, and I will seek the wisdom of Father Pierrot to guide me. In the morning I will decide about everything – whether to keep you or send you back to Boston on the next Red River cart train that comes through.'

Suddenly Anna realized the significance of the term, 'Father.'

'*Father* Pierrot?' she inquired. 'Is this a Catholic mission?' Already her mind was racing ahead, wondering how she'd get out of this one.

'Yes, of course. In my letters I told you we would be married here.'

34

'But . . . but you never said it was Catholic.'

'Of course it is Catholic. Are you worried that Father Pierrot will not be willing to witness our marriage because I am Lutheran and you are Catholic? It is all fixed and Father has received a special dispensation from Bishop Cretin to witness the vows we will speak ourselves. But think no more about it because perhaps we will say no vows after all.'

Anna was not sure which prospect scared her more, being sent away, or having Karl unearth her other deceptions.

Karl jumped down, tied the reins, then helped Anna alight. But this time, when he put his hands on her thin waist, he could not help recalling what she'd said about his always having plenty to eat. She was reed-thin.

They were greeted at the door of the smaller building by Father Pierrot himself. 'Ah, Karl, what a pleasant thing it is to greet you, my friend. And this must be Anna.'

'Hello, Father.'

Anna bobbed her head while the dark-haired priest broke into an even deeper smile. 'Do you know how this young man has been waiting for you? Each time I see him, all he can talk of is his Anna. His little whiskey-haired Anna. I thought if you did not get here soon, he would abandon that place he's always bragging about and run looking for you.'

Irreverently, Karl thought, you, too, Father, have a big mouth, even if you are a man of the cloth! Karl had been raised to have great respect for the clergy. It was natural for him to radiate toward the friendship of the only cleric within a hundred miles, no matter what denomination he was.

'Do I brag, Father?' Karl inquired.

'Oh, do not look so worried, Karl. I enjoy teasing you.' Eyeing James, the priest next asked, 'And who might this young man be?'

'James, sir,' the boy replied, 'James Reardon.'

'He's my brother,' Anna declared forthrightly.

'Your brother . . . mmm . . . Karl neglected to tell me you had a brother. This is good news. Minnesota can use strong young settlers like you, James. It is not a bad place for a boy to grow into a man either. Do you think you will like it here, James?'

'Yes, sir,' James quickly answered, 'but I have lots to learn.'

Father raised his head and laughed. 'Well, you pick a good man to come to, son. If you have any doubts about Minnesota, this big Swede will soon put them out of your head.'

Karl suddenly cleared his throat and said, 'I must tend my horses, Father. You will perhaps like to talk to Anna and James about Boston and the East.'

'Can I help you?' James asked immediately.

Karl looked at the lad, so stringy, so lean, so young, so eager. Karl found himself not wanting to have the tug of the boy's willingness influencing his decision regarding Anna. 'You go with Father and your sister. You have had a long trip, and it is not over yet. You rest.' The look in the boy's eyes seemed to ask, but will the rest of my trip take me back to Boston or forward to your place? Karl looked away, for he did not yet know the answer.

Watching his broad shoulders going through the door, Anna felt a sudden longing to please him for James's sake. James had never known a father, and this man would be the best influence a boy of his age could possibly have. When Karl was gone, the image of his sturdy back lingered in Anna's mind.

An Indian woman served a delicious mixture of corn and meat. Anna and James fairly wolfed supper down. From across the table Karl now studied Anna more thoroughly. Her face was appealing enough, but he truly disliked her dress, and her hair seemed wild and disorderly, nothing

36

like the neat coronets of braids he was used to on Swedish women.

Anna looked up unexpectedly and caught him watching her. Immediately, she slowed her eating.

But the word 'hungry' stayed in his mind, just as she'd said it earlier. Her shoulders were peaked beneath her dress, and her knuckles were large on otherwise thin hands, making him wonder just how hungry she had been in Boston. The boy, too, was painfully thin, with eyes that looked too large for their sockets. Karl tried to dismiss these thoughts as he ate his meal, but again and again they forced their way upon him.

After dinner, Father Pierrot asked the Indian woman to prepare pallets for his three guests on the floor of the schoolroom.

This done, the woman returned and led Anna and James to their beds, while Karl stayed behind to talk to Father Pierrot.

Brother and sister found comfortable makeshift beds of straw and buffalo robe, and they settled down drearily to worry about what was to become of them. It was quiet and dark, the night rampant with unspoken thoughts.

Finally, James asked, 'Do you think he'll send us back?'

'I don't know,' Anna admitted. He could tell by her voice that she was really worried.

'I'm scared, Anna,' he confessed.

'So am I,' she confessed.

'But he seems like a fair man,' James put in, needing some hope.

'We'll know in the morning.'

Again silence fell, but neither of them was remotely sleepy.

'Anna?' came James's small, worried voice.

'What now?'

'You shouldn't have lied to him about the other things. You should've admitted them when he asked.'

'About what other things?' she asked, holding her breath for fear he knew her worst, most unforgivable secret.

But he only listed the others. 'About not knowing how to write, and that I was the one wrote those letters, and where we lived.'

'I was afraid to tell the truth.'

'But he'll find out. He's bound to find out.'

'But he'll find out too late, if we're lucky.'

'That ain't right, Anna.'

Anna stared up into the darkness above her, feeling tears gathering in her throat. 'I know. But since when's right ever worked on our side?'

No, James admitted to himself, right had never been on their side at all. Still, he didn't think two wrongs made a right either. He knew what a shock it must've been to Karl Lindstrom to see him arrive today with Anna – a kid Karl hadn't even known existed! And then poor Karl learned that Anna was only seventeen instead of twenty-five, and that she couldn't do a blame thing around the place. James acknowledged that Karl had taken it all better than most men would have.

'What'd you think of him, Anna?' he asked quietly.

'Oh, shut up and go to sleep!' she exclaimed in a choked voice. Then she buried her head in her arms to stifle a sob as she thought of the bald look of innocent expectation that had greeted her on Karl's face. And of how he had helped her down from the wagon at first, and offered to buy her anything she needed in the store. Oh, she liked him all right. But at the same time she was scared to death of him. He was, after all, a man.

3

'Father Pierrot, I must speak to you as a friend as much as a priest. I have a problem regarding Anna.' The two had settled in Father's little sitting room at the rear of the school building, companionably smoking fragrant pipes of Indian tobacco.

'Ah, Karl, I could tell you were troubled as soon as you arrived. Are you having last-minute thoughts?'

'Ya, I am, but not in the way you might think.' Kàrl sighed. 'You know how many months it has taken to get Anna here. You know I have prepared a good home for her, and I have plans for an even better one. I have been much more than ready for a wife for some time now. All this time I have dreamed of her coming. But I think I have been a little foolish, Father. I dreamed her to be something she is not. I find out today she has lied to me about many things.'

'Was it not a risk you took, courting her by letter?'

'Ya, a risk it was. But still, not a good way to begin married life. I think I do not want a wife who is a liar, yet I want a wife, and she is the only one available.'

'About what has she lied, my friend?'

'The first is a lie of omission. This brother James was a complete surprise to me today. She did not tell me of him. I think she knew I would not want a lad of that age living with us when we are newly married.'

'Would you send them back because of this?'

'I threatened to do just that, but I do not think I could stand the loneliness for another year while I try to find another wife. Forgive me, Father . . . I should perhaps not speak of it, but I am already twenty-five years old. I have been alone since I left Sweden, two years already. I am eager to begin building a family. There have been times, especially in the winter when I am snowed in for days at a time with nobody for company when I . . .' Karl cupped the bowl of his pipe in a big hand, rubbing the glossed wood with a large thumb, watching the slow curl of smoke rise from it. He remembered only too wrenchingly the emptiness of those winter nights.

He looked up to find the eyes of his friend upon him, and laughing sheepishly, Karl leaned his elbow on a knee and rested his chin in his palm. 'You know, Father, sometimes I bring the goat inside to keep her from freezing in the bad blizzards and so I have somebody to talk to. But poor Nanna, I think she grows tired of hearing her foolish master pining for human companionship.'

'I understand, Karl. You need not apologize for your needs. There is no dishonour in wanting a wife for long winter nights, and for beginning a family. Neither is there dishonour in wanting to begin married life with time to get accustomed to each other in privacy.'

'But I feel small for resenting the boy.'

'What man wouldn't?'

'You would not, Father, if you were in my place?' Karl was reluctant to think a priest could feel such human failings.

'I think perhaps I would. On the other hand, I would weigh it against the boy's value to me in this wilderness. He could be more than a helper. He could, in time, be a friend, perhaps even a buffer.'

'What does this mean, Father – buffer.'

'Let me put it to you this way, Karl,' the priest said, sitting back with a philosophical air. 'Do you think that if you marry Anna, all your troubles will be magically over and she will be all those things you dreamed she'd be? I think not. I think that – beginning as strangers, as it were

40

– the two of you will cross swords many times before you truly know and accept each other for what you are. Sometimes in the crossing of swords it is good to have a third party to act as conciliator or mediator, or as I said before, just a plain friend.'

'This I had not thought of before, but I see you are wise. It is almost like you heard Anna's temper flare today, to say nothing of my own.'

'You had words, you two?'

'Ya, words. But the lad was there, so I think we both said less than we maybe thought.'

'Aside from the fact that the lad came unannounced, what do you think of him?'

'He seems eager to learn and has promised to work hard.'

'The boy could do worse than end up with you as a teacher, Karl. Under your tutelage I believe young James would learn quickly. Had you thought there might be reward in teaching him, too?'

The two puffed at their pipes in companionable silence again. Karl thought of all the priest had said about the boy. The idea of having the lad to teach, to nurture, became an inviting challenge. Karl thought of the log house and all it would take to erect it, imagined himself and the lad working side by side, bare-chested in the sun, imagined the first . . . then second, then third – tier of logs going up, and the two of them bantering as they worked side by side skidding, notching. He could teach the lad much about building and about woods, just as his papa had taught him.

'Karl?' A lazy curl of smoke floated upward with the word.

'Hm?' Karl replied absently, quite lost in thought.

'There is something I must ask, but I ask it to make you think realistically about all of this.'

'Ya, well ask, then.'

'Have you been considering sending the girl back because you are disappointed in what you saw when she arrived?

41

I think you must consider this aspect of marrying her equally as much as all the others. You brought her here sight unseen, with high hopes. If you find her repugnant, it could bring much difficulty to your marriage. You must look at this realizing you are a human being, Karl. As such, you are subject to doubt and scepticism. Maybe even outright dislike. I think you are a man whose principles would speak louder than his dislikes, though, and would keep her with you out of duty, if you thought you were obliged to do so.'

Karl was learning a new side of Father Pierrot tonight, a human side that Karl deeply needed. 'Oh, no, Father, I truly do not find her unattractive, only a little thin. But her face . . . she . . . I . . .' It was difficult for Karl to express to this priest the feelings that had swept over him when he'd first seen Anna, when he had taken her hand in his to help her down from the wagon, or the feeling of her slim hips and waist as she jumped down. It was difficult for Karl himself to equate those feelings with anything but lustfulness. Naturally, he did not wish to appear crude before his friend, this priest.

'My eye is pleased, truly, Father, but I have tried to use good reason. It should not matter to me if her looks please me, I should instead – '

'But of course it should matter!' the priest interrupted, jumping to his feet. 'Karl, don't turn fool on me now. If you do, it will be for the first time since I've known you. You will look at the woman for many years if you marry her. What fool would not want to be pleased with what he sees?'

Karl laughed. 'You surprise me, Father. In the time I have known you I would not have thought you to be a man with such sympathy when it comes to matters of the heart.'

Father, too, laughed. 'I was a man first, a priest second.'

Karl now looked his friend straight in the eye, all laughter faded. 'Then I admit to you I am pleased by her appearance.

42

I am perhaps too pleased. Perhaps I will not use good judgment about her other lies.'

'Tell me,' the priest said simply, sitting down again.

'She is only a child. I was expecting a full-grown woman of twenty-five. But Anna lied about this, too. She is only seventeen years old.'

'But did she not make the choice of her own free will to come here and be your wife?'

'Not exactly. I think she and the boy were destitute. I was their last resort. Yes, she came to be married, but I think it was the lesser of two evils.'

'Has she told you that?'

'Not exactly in those words. She has begged me not to send them away, but while she is begging I see how very young and scared she is, and I do not think she realizes all that is entailed in being a wife.'

'Karl, you are placing a burden of worry on yourself that perhaps is not necessary. Why not let her be the judge of whether or not she is old enough to marry?'

'But seventeen, Father . . . She has admitted she knows almost nothing about being housekeeper and cook. There would be much I would have to teach her, too.'

'It would be a challenge, Karl, but it could be fun with a spirited girl.'

'It could also be a mistake with a spirited girl.'

'Karl, have you considered why she lied? If she and the boy came to you as a last hope, I can see why she felt the need to lie to get here. I do not condone the lies, Karl, not at all. But I think perhaps they are forgivable, perhaps her circumstances make them so. I think you must ask yourself if she could not, underneath, be an honest woman who was forced into lying by her circumstances. Perhaps, Karl, you are judging her too harshly for your own good.'

'You leave me much to consider, my friend,' Karl said, rising and stretching. 'All my life I have been taught what is right and what is wrong, and I have been warned that the path runs narrowly. Never before have I had to consider circumstances that lessen the degree of wrongness. I think you have helped me tonight to look at things from another person's viewpoint. I will try to do this.'

He paused, glanced across the room toward the doorway. 'Anna and the boy have had plenty of time to get themselves settled for the night. I think I will join them and finish my considerations there.'

'Sleep well, Karl,' the priest wished.

Karl scraped the ashes from his pipe. 'You know, Father,' he said thoughtfully, 'she has assured me these are the only lies she told, and made me the promise never to lie to me again. That promise is worth something.'

Father Pierrot smiled, placed a hand on Karl Lindstrom's shoulder and understood how a man of his nature would be torn by uncertainty at a time like this. Most men who had lived alone for two years on the frontier would not stop to think of anything but their own need for a woman, both in and out of bed. But Karl was a man of rare quality, rare honesty. Anna Reardon would be a lucky woman to marry such a man.

It was dark, dusty and dry in the schoolroom. Karl found his empty pallet and stretched out on his back with both hands behind his head. He thought about all Father Pierrot had said, and for the first time, and guiltlessly now, would have allowed himself to consider Anna as a woman. But he could not do this; he found he thought of her as a child instead. She was tall, but so thin it gave her a look of almost boyish callowness.

Her wide-eyed fright at times today made him think of her as a green young girl who perhaps did not even know what was the duty of the marriage bed. In some ways this pleased him, but in others it frightened him, too. It was one thing to take to bed a woman of twenty-five who knew what to expect. It was quite another to bed a child of

44

seventeen whose luminous dark eyes might burn up at him in fear when she learned what was expected of her. She seemed so frail her little bones might snap were he even to hug her against his chest.

But even as he thought this, the hair on his chest prickled teasingly. He ran his hand over his shirt, sliding it across the breadth of his chest. It was a wide chest. His arms were thick and fully muscled from using the axe all his life. His thighs were heavy, long from knee to hip. He had the tall, muscular stature of his father. Always before, he had taken for granted what women thought as they looked at him.

Now, for the first time, as he thought of Anna, he realized that to a girl, perhaps his size seemed frightening. Perhaps he did not please her. It struck him quite suddenly that tonight he had been selfishly concerned with what he, Karl, thought of her, Anna. Perhaps he should have given equal time to wondering what she thought of him! Yes, she had pleaded with him not to send them back. But had she pleaded with him out of fear? Penniless and scared, what else would the girl do when threatened with abandonment in the middle of the wilderness?

He thought once again of his sod hut, of the bed he had prepared for her with the most honourable intentions. He tried to imagine what she would think when she saw that sheaf of sweet clover. His own heart hammered with uncertainty now. Perhaps it had been a stupid blunder to prepare the bed in so obvious a manner for her coming, as if the only thing on his mind all these months was getting her into it! She would see the full, plump tick, the freshly stuffed pillows, the clover meant as a welcome only, and she would shy away like a foolish spring colt shies from a rabbit, never knowing the rabbit could not and would not do it harm.

Anna, he thought, what should I do with you? How can I send you away? Yet how can I ask you to stay? And if I do, how far we have to go together, and how much we have to learn of one another.

He awakened in the morning when the sunlight was but a promise. It was the time when day hesitates before nudging the night away, the pale light tiptoeing into the room with scarcely the strength to threaten the shadows that lay heavily upon Anna as she slept on her side, facing Karl. She had an arm tucked beneath her ear, her chin tucked down childishly upon her chest. She wore a look of such innocence, that again he wondered if he were doing the right thing.

But his mind was settled. He had thought well and long about what was right, for both of them, and within the heart of Karl Lindstrom beat the conviction that together, he and Anna and the boy could make this thing work. They must make a marriage in which this unfortunate beginning was forgotten. If it took patience on his part, it would take courage on hers. If it took forgiveness on his part, it would take humility on hers. Each of them, he was sure, would need to have strengths the other lacked, for this was the foundation of a marriage.

Anna had, so far, shown the kind of strength many women lacked. Just coming here, braving it the way she had, with the boy she was responsible for, meant she had determination. A quality like that could be priceless here.

Karl rolled from his pallet, fully dressed, and knelt down on a single knee beside Anna. He had never before awakened a sleeping woman, except for his sisters and mother, and wondered if it were too intimate to touch her arm and shake her gently. Her arm lay relaxed over the buffalo robe, thin and long. He could see pale freckles upon the back of her hand. Despite the thin light, he saw more freckles dancing across the bridge of her nose, across her cheeks. Childishly she slept, unaware of how he studied

46

her, and he thought it was somehow an unfair thing of him to do.

'Anna?' he whispered, and saw her eyelids move as if she were dreaming. 'Anna?'

Her eyes flew open. In the instant she awoke they took on the look of startled wariness already so familiar to Karl. She stared at him for a moment, gathering her senses. He could tell by her expression the moment in which recollection stirred and she remembered where she was and who he was.

Because she looked so young and helpless and wary, he asked, 'Did you know you have sandman in your eyes?'

She continued to stare at him as if surprised speechless. She blinked and felt the grit grinding against her eyelids, knowing it was there because she had been crying last night before going to sleep.

'It is time you get up and wash them out. Then I want to talk to you,' Karl said.

The boy awoke at the sound of Karl's voice, so the man stood and spoke again. 'Time to get up, boy. Let us leave your sister to get herself together.' Then he stalked from the room.

'Anna?' James croaked, a little disoriented, too.

She rolled over to look at him. 'You sound like a bullfrog this morning,' she teased.

But he didn't smile. 'Did he say what he decided?'

'No. He said he wants to talk to me. That's all. He's coming back as soon as he gives us time to get up.'

'Hurry, then, let's get ready.'

But although James scurried from the room, Anna lay for a moment, hesitant to leave the warm protection of the buffalo robes, wondering what Karl planned to do with her and James.

She thought of the curious words he'd used as he awakened her. They were gentle words, those used with a child. Perhaps he was usually a kind man whose temper had been tested in an extreme way yesterday by all her and James's revelations. Perhaps, given the chance, given time, Lindstrom would be less fierce and fault-finding, perhaps even gentle, as he'd been a moment ago. But when she thought of awakening in the same bed with him where he could note more than just the sandman in her eyes, Anna shivered.

She arose and tried to whisk the wrinkles out of her dress, rinsed her face and tied her hair back. A knock on the door told her Karl had returned, and she glanced up from where she knelt, gathering up the heavy buffalo robes.

He apparently had washed his face and combed his hair. He wore his little strange cap again. He came to stand beside her, gazing down at her wide, brown eyes that always wore that too open look whenever he came near.

'How did you sleep, Anna?'

'Fi . . .' But her voice croaked almost as James's had, and she cleared her throat before trying again. 'Fine.' Her hands lay idle on the furs, as if she'd forgotten what she was about.

His simple question was meant to put her at ease, but he could see she was tense and apprehensive. It broke his heart to think that she might be this way because of him. He knelt down on one knee upon the buffalo robe she'd been folding. 'Anna, I did not sleep so well. I spent a long time thinking. Do you know what I learned while I thought?'

She shook her head no, saying nothing.

'I learned that I thought only of myself yesterday, and of what I wanted in a wife. Selfishly, I did not consider your opinion of me. All the time I think only of what Karl thinks of Anna, never what Anna thinks of Karl. But this is not right, Anna. Today, this must be a decision that both of us make, not just me.'

She studied his golden arm braced across one upraised knee, knowing he studied her face while he spoke.

'We start out backward, Anna, yes? First we agree to

marry, and it is only after this that we meet each other. And when I meet you, all I can do is get angry because you have lied to me, without considering why it was you lied. Father Pierrot made me see I must understand your side and realize you had to get out of Boston where things were bad for you and the boy.' He studied the freckles on her cheeks and saw the pink glow beneath them, and could feel the thrum of his heart in strange places in his body. He wished she would raise her eyes. It was hard to read her feelings when she avoided looking at him.

Anna's heart skittered and leapt in her breast at his unexpected gentleness and selflessness. Considerateness of this sort was foreign to her. She wanted terribly to meet the blue depths of his eyes, but had she done so, she thought she might start crying. She could only stare at the strong, brown hand draped over a wide kneecap as he went on speaking.

'Anna, it is not too late for you to go back. It is not too late for either of us to change our minds. I thought that now you have met me, maybe . . . maybe you might not want to get married. Knowing how young you are and how you had to think of some way for you and the boy to live, I see you had to act quick, but maybe you think now you made a mistake, now that you see Karl Lindstrom. I think, Anna, that I must give you two choices. I must promise you first that if you want to go back, Father Pierrot and I will find a way to get you to Boston safely. Only if you are very sure this is not what you want, then I must give you the second choice to marry me.'

The callus on his thumb grew wavery. Anna felt the tears form upon her lashes and quiver there, just short of dropping. 'I told you, I have nobody to go back to, no place to go back to.' Still she did not look up at him.

'Father and I will try to think of something else if this is what you want. Some place for you to go and live here in Minnesota.'

'Your place sounded pretty good to me,' she braved timorously.

Yes, she was afraid of him. He knew it now because of the tremble in her voice.

'You are sure, Anna?'

She nodded at the buffalo robes.

'In that case, a girl should have the right to say she has been given a proper proposal of marriage, and that she truly had a choice in the matter, *after* she has met the man, not *before*.'

Now she did look up. Her eyes flew to his face, so close above hers. His intense eyes had never left hers, were only waiting for her to raise her glance to his. Those eyes were liquid blue, shining with sincerity. She wondered how many girls had gazed into them and found them as heart-stopping as she did at this moment. The lashes were darker than the perfectly shaped eyebrows, which beckoned her fingers to trace their curve. That silly compulsion prompted her to close her fist about a handful of buffalo fur, to keep it from doing such an outrageous thing.

'*Onnuh* . . .' he began, and during the long hesitation before he continued, she wanted to say, yes, yes, I am *Onnuh* now, say it once more just like that. And as if he heard her thought, he did. '*Onnuh*, if I am not what you thought I would be, I will understand. But if you think that we could forget this poor start we had yesterday, I promise I will be good to you, *Onnuh*. I will take both you and the boy with me.'

Slowly one big hand went up to slide the cap from his hair, the old-country courtesy tearing at her heartstrings. He reached to take her elbow in his free hand. The warmth of his flesh, the look of need she read in his eyes, the feather touch upon her elbow, all combined to make Anna feel light-headed and dizzy.

'*Onnuh* Reardon, will you marry me?'

She felt like she had awakened in the midst of some

fantastic dream, to find this handsome blond giant kneeling upon one knee to her, rubbing her inner elbow with his thumb, an expression of intense hope and promise upon his sun-bronzed face.

Anna's lips fell open, a quickly drawn breath told the secret mingling of emotions she was experiencing: relief, fear, and – yes – a new, beating exhilaration that made her breasts seem tight and brought a film of perspiration to the palms of her hands.

'Yes,' she breathed at last.

Karl smiled, a relieved tilting of the corners of his lips. He glanced at her hair once, then gave her elbow a light squeeze of reassurance.

'Good. We will make this our beginning then, right here. And everything else is forgotten, right?'

'Yes,' she agreed, wondering wildly if she should confess the rest to him here and now. Yet she was terrified lest he withdraw his proposal and the security it offered. She gave him a wavering smile.

'We will make a good start . . . just Karl and Anna . . .' Then, with a full wide smile, he added, 'and James.'

'Karl and Anna and James,' she repeated, almost like a vow.

Karl stood before her then. As she looked up, she noticed for the first time what straight teeth he had. Has he no flaws whatsoever? she wondered. Anna became ever more aware of a feeling of inferiority as she compared herself to him.

'Come,' he said nicely, 'I will help you roll up these robes, then we will go tell Father Pierrot the decision is made and we are ready.'

Outwardly, Father Pierrot beamed as he shook their hands with great enthusiasm, saying, 'I have every confidence that you will build a good and lasting marriage.'

Inwardly, he was troubled. Although he had led Karl to believe he'd received a special dispensation from the diocese to act as a witness while these two spoke their own vows, this was not altogether true. Bishop Cretin had sympathized with the couple's plight, but had adamantly refused, saying such dispensation must come from the Holy Father himself in Rome and could take one to two years to get. Father Pierrot found this attitude hard. After all, he was not asking to perform the Sacrament – this he knew would be entirely out of the question!

So Father Pierrot had faced the dilemma of which dictates to follow, those of Holy Mother the Church or those of his own heart. Surely, it was a more Christian act to witness the sealing of vows between two such well-meaning souls and sanctify the union than to send them away to live in sin. This is the frontier, argued Michael Pierrot, the man within the ordained priest. This is the only church within a hundred miles, and these people have turned to it and to me with the best of intentions.

Michael Pierrot's human side was swayed also by the fact that Karl Lindstrom was a good friend. Their relationship surmounted any differences of faith. Leading the way toward the humble sacristy, the priest thought of this marriage as wholly right, perhaps the most fitting he might ever perform.

'Come, Anna, I will hear your confession now without delay, for I know you are both anxious to be on your way.'

Totally taken off guard, Anna came up short behind the black cassock. 'My . . . my confession?' she blurted out, appalled.

'Yes, Anna, come,' the priest said as he continued into the incense-scented vestry.

Anna's legs seemed to have turned to mush. She had instructed James to tell Karl that they were devout Catholics, knowing that the man wanted a wife of Christian bent. Never had Karl told her in his letters this mission was Catholic. If he had, she would obligingly have told him she was some other religion, to avoid having to prove

52

Catholicism. As it was, she was now entangled in another lie.

'But can't I just . . . I mean . . . well, I don't want to go to confession.'

'Anna,' the priest chided, turning around, 'forgive me for being direct, but last night Karl and I talked. He said you admitted telling him lies. These are sins, my child. You must confess them, so you will be in a state of grace before entering the state of marriage. Surely you know this.'

Of course she didn't know this. All she knew about the Catholic church was that it was warm inside St Mark's, and they refused no one entry there.

'But . . . but I've told Karl I'm sorry and I've promised I won't lie any more. Isn't that enough?'

'It is not enough for a Catholic. You know that confession is necessary, Anna, to cleanse the soul.' The priest truly didn't understand her reluctance.

She fidgeted and shifted from foot to foot, refusing to look at him while Karl, too, wondered at Anna's hesitation. With growing trepidation, Anna realized the only confession she would be making here today was the truth. She bit the inside of her lip, clasped her hands tightly behind her back, then, big-eyed and brave, admitted, 'I'm not a Catholic.'

Karl couldn't believe his ears. He took her by the elbow – it seemed to Anna that her elbow was certainly being over-worked lately – and forced her to look up into his face. 'But Anna, you told me you were Catholic. Why did you tell me this?'

'Because you said in your advertisement that you wanted a God-fearing woman.'

'Another lie, Anna?' Karl asked, dismayed anew.

'That's not a lie, that's the truth. You said you wanted the truth, so I gave it to you this time. But what does it matter anyway, as long as we're going to be saying our vows ourselves?'

Caught now himself by the half-truth he had let Karl believe, Father Pierrot suffered pangs of remorse. What was he to do? If he witnessed the union, he would be liable for excommunication should his bishop ever learn of it. At this point the priest was wishing that Long Prairie boasted just one justice of the peace, so he could send these two to get themselves legally married without all this confusion.

But the staunch Irish girl looked her betrothed in the eye and kept a stiff upper lip. 'Well, if it's still all right with you, Karl, it's all right with me.'

This was all too much for Karl. He had spent most of the night carefully reflecting in order to decide it was the right thing to marry Anna. Now another of his delusions about her lay shattered. He was acutely embarrassed to have this newest lie come to light in front of Father Pierrot. Karl found he could not abase himself further by standing there and arguing. And the day was moving on. So much time had been wasted already on this trip, it was folly wasting more, and there were no other churches nearby. But a godless woman! thought the beleaguered Swede. What have I gotten into?

'It does not matter,' Karl said tightly, and everyone in the room could see it mattered a great deal. 'We will be married as we agreed.' He turned to his friend in the black robes.

Father Pierrot hadn't the heart to say, no, Karl, I cannot witness this marriage after all, nor record it in my books. The strength of the vow rests within the heart, he thought, not in witnesses nor penned words. If these two were ready to accept each other, he would not stand in their way.

Anna felt a flood of relief wash over her as the ceremony was agreed upon. Her knees were weak. Her tongue stuck to the roof of her mouth. She squeezed her eyes shut and silently promised the man beside her that she'd make it up to him, one way or another.

But Karl's heart was heavy as he stepped to the altar. He had, in his own halting way, achieved his amnesty with her this morning. Peace should be the feeling in a man's heart as he spoke his vows, not this resentment that now lay coldly inside. It is difficult enough to promise love, Karl thought, when the one you promise it to is a stranger. To promise it with such a feeling of foreboding is less than good.

Father had donned his surplice, alb and stole, and the time was at hand.

'James will be our witness,' Anna said, wishing to please Karl in some small way. Karl, she could see, was very dissatisfied with her. He avoided her glance, and studied the distance as if ruminating the deepest of thoughts. Also, when he'd last spoken, his voice had become devoid of its usual musicality. It told her in no uncertain terms that he was displeased.

The pair stood so stiff and erect that Father Pierrot felt certain things must be said. He could sense the animosity, which had sprung up so quickly. Karl's mouth was pursed, and Anna stared at the little bouquet of lemon lilies and wild roses at the feet of St Francis of Assisi.

'Anna,' he began, 'I speak to you first, and I speak with the hope that you will take to heart everything I say. You are young, Anna. You are taking on a grave responsibility when you marry Karl here. The two of you have a long life ahead of you, and it can be a good life if you work to make it so. But goodness must be built upon mutual respect, and this respect must stem from trust. Trust, in return, must spring from truthfulness. I believe you have done what you thought necessary to get here to Karl. But henceforth I caution you to be truthful with him in all ways. You will find him to be understanding and patient. This much I know of him. But you will find, too, that he is rigid in his honour. I caution you once more always to tell him the truth. When you make your vow here to love, honour and obey, I ask you to add in your heart that you, Anna, will always be truthful with Karl.'

She looked up at him with her girlish face and said guilelessly, 'Yes, Father, I was.' Father Pierrot could not help the tiny curve of his lips at her reply. He noted, too, the way Karl glanced briefly sideways.

'Good. So be it. And Karl, there are things not expressed in the vows, about which I must caution you. It falls onto your shoulders to protect Anna and provide for her. In your case, here in the wilderness, and with the added responsibility for James, this job is a far greater one than for most men.' Karl glanced at the boy, and the priest saw a perceptible softening of Karl's expression. 'The wilderness is new to them, and there will be much they have to learn. Patience will be required of you time and again. But you have the gift of knowledge to give them. You must be teacher as well as protector, father as well as husband, almost from the start. If at times this task falls heavy upon you, I ask you to remember that on your wedding day you silently added the vow of patience.'

'Yes, Father.'

'And while it is not written in the vows either, there is an old adage I firmly believe in, which I would repeat here and ask you both to remember on days when perhaps you have not seen eye to eye. "Never let the sun set on your anger." There will be disagreements between you, and these cannot be avoided – you are human beings with much to learn about each other. But differences incurred during the day become lodged in stubbornness if held throughout the night. By remembering this, you will perhaps not cling to your opinions when it is long past the time you should have conceded or compromised. Will the two of you remember that?'

'Yes, Father,' they said in unison.

'So be it. Then let us begin.'

Father Pierrot began praying.

The soft tonal inflections of Latin brought back to Anna the memories of nights she and James had sheltered in St Mark's. Nights when all the rooms above the tavern were busy and they were told to get out and not show their faces till the last customer had staggered home. Anna tried to push the hurtful memory aside, but the priest's flowing Latin brought back the anguish all over again, the anguish of huddling in the scented dusk – beeswax, incense, candle-lights – vowing that she would find a way out of a life where, since her mother's death, nobody cared whether Barbara's brats lived or died.

They'd hung on, she and James, by the skin of their teeth, but all the while Anna was determined to get them away from the hopeless situation somehow. Well, she was doing it now. She and James would never go homeless again. Never would they be chased away by the 'ladies' and their 'gentlemen' customers. But knowing what she'd done to get here, knowing that she was duping a man who truly didn't deserve it, an engulfing guilt washed over her.

She felt her hand taken into the large hand of Karl Lindstrom, felt the calluses of labour there, felt the firm grip that told of his intensity, and she knew beyond a doubt that this big, honourable man would never, never understand a thing like she'd done. His palm was warm and dry and as hard as oak. The way he squeezed her knuckles she thought they might shatter in a moment, but his grip told her he meant all he promised here today. She found herself looking up into blue eyes, then watching sensitive lips speaking the words from the book Father Pierrot held open upon his palms. Karl's voice came lilting, and she watched his mouth, memorizing the words as best she could.

And the long months of hoping, dreaming and planning for this day would become part of the fabric that wove Karl to Anna in the words he spoke aloud. Nor would the thoughts, which had so long lived in Karl Lindstrom, now be denied their part in all he promised.

'I Karl, take thee, Anna . . .' *My little whiskey-haired Anna . . .*
'for my lawful wedded wife . . .' *How I have waited for you . . .*
'to have and to hold . . .' *Not yet have I even held you, Anna . . .*
'from this day forward . . .' *Forward to this night, and tomorrow and tomorrow . . .*
'For better, for worse . . .' *In spite of everything, I know I could do far worse . . .*
'for richer, for poorer . . .' *Ah, how rich we can be, Anna, rich with life . . .*
'in sickness and in health . . .' *And I will see this thin hand grow strong . . .*
'till death do us part.' *These things I promise with my life – these things and the promise of patience, as Father, my friend, said.*

As Anna's eyes roved over Karl's face, a shaft of golden sun came through the open door, gilding his features as if nature itself bestowed the blessing Father Pierrot could not. In the tiny outpost mission of Long Prairie only wild-flowers adorned the altar. Only the cooing of mourning doves provided song. But to Anna's ears and eyes it was as fine as any cathedral hosting a hundred-voice choir. She could feel the beats of their hearts joined where her slight, pale hand rested in his wide, dark one. As she took her turn at vows, Anna felt a willingness she had certainly not expected when she'd thought of this moment through the dreary winter, waiting to come to an unknown husband.

'I, Anna, take thee, Karl . . .' *Forgive me, Karl, for tricking you . . .*
'for my lawful wedded husband . . .' *But James and I didn't know what else to do . . .*

58

'from this day forward . . .' *Never again will we be homeless . . .*

'for better, for worse . . .' *I promise I will never, never tell another lie . . .*

'for richer, for poorer . . .' *Riches we do not need. A home will be enough . . .*

'in sickness and in health . . .' *I'll learn all I said I knew . . .*

'till death do us part.' *I'll make up for everything, Karl, somehow I promise I'll make up for everything.*

She saw Karl swallow and detected a tremble in his eyelids.

Then, still squeezing her hand, he looked at Father Pierrot. 'There is no gold ring, Father. I could not afford gold, and there was nothing else at Morisette's store. But I have a simple ring because it doesn't seem right without a ring.'

'A simple ring is fine, Karl.'

From his pocket he extracted a horseshoe nail curled into a circle. It was on his lips to say, I'm sorry, Anna, but she was smiling down at the ring as if it were burnished gold.

Anna saw Karl's hands shake, and her own, as she extended her fingers and he slid the heavy iron circlet over her knuckle. He had misjudged in bending it, and she had to curl her fingers quickly to keep it from slipping off. Then Karl's hand recaptured hers again. Gently, he spread her fingers and lay the banded hand upon his open palm, the fingers of his other hand lightly touching the ring as if to seal it upon her flesh for life.

'Anna Reardon, with this ring I make you my wife forever.' His voice cracked faintly upon the last word, bringing her eyes up to his once more.

Then she put her free hand over his and the ring, and said into his eyes, 'Karl Lindstrom, with this ring I accept you for my husband . . . forever.'

He looked down at her turned-up freckled nose, her pretty, waiting lips. His heart became a wild thing within him. Now she is really my Anna, he thought, suddenly timid and eager all at once.

Fleetingly, Anna's eyelids quivered, and she felt his hold upon her hands tighten a fraction of a second before he bent to kiss her lightly, forgetting to close his eyes as he brushed her lips uncertainly, then straightened again.

'So be it,' Father Pierrot said softly, while bride and groom nervously cast about for something upon which to settle their gazes. Anna's turned to her brother, and the two hugged quickly.

'Oh, Anna, Anna . . .' he said.

She whispered in his ear, 'We'll be safe now, James.'

He squeezed her extra hard. 'I'll do my part.' But he looked at Karl as he said it, though it was Anna's hand he still held.

'I know,' Anna said, now looking at Karl.

Father Pierrot surprised her by warmly embracing her, then planting a congratulatory kiss on her cheek. 'I wish you health, happiness and the blessing of many children.' Then, turning to Karl with a firm handshake of four hands instead of two, the priest said emotionally, 'And the same to you, my friend.'

'Thank you, Father. It seems that I already have one of those things.' Karl looked meaningfully at James, who smiled broadly.

'Yes,' Father Pierrot said, shaking James's hand in a manful way. 'Now, young man, it will be your job to see that these two do as I have ordered. There may be times it will be the hardest job of all.'

'Yes, sir!' James replied, and everyone laughed.

'So be it, and so it is done. Now all that remains is for you two to put your signatures on the document, to be witnessed by James here and myself. Then you may be on your way. You have a long ride ahead.'

Karl turned, placing Anna's hand in the crook of his elbow, then reached to include James, who stood uncertainly. 'We have a long ride ahead, eh, James?'

'Yes, sir!' the boy beamed.

'But we go together, you and Anna and I.'

While Father led them once again to his tiny rooms at the rear of the school building, Anna moved beside Karl, her hand on his solid arm, worried sick once again. Father produced ink and quill, then dipped the tip and handed it to her, indicating the parchment on the desk.

'You may sign first, Anna.'

But Karl was right there, smiling broadly, watching her. She didn't know how to write her name!

'Let Karl sign first,' she said ingeniously.

'Very well.' Agreeably, Karl carefully placed his name on the paper.

She stood behind him, eyeing the back of his neck while he formed the letters. She glanced at James, who shrugged covertly in reply. Anna exchanged places with Karl and made a grand X on the paper while he looked over her shoulder.

And so quickly was the next deception exposed.

He saw her make the mark, and was naturally surprised, knowing she was a lettered woman. But she smiled brightly into his face in an effort to disarm him.

But Karl was not disarmed. And so, he thought, I learn one more truth about Anna. But he did not let Father Pierrot know what little drama was being acted out here. Instead, he took Anna's arm stiffly, steered her toward the door and led her out.

'Wait here. I must get the wagon,' was all he said. Then he stalked off, leaving her with James.

'Anna, I didn't know what to do,' her brother sympathized. 'I couldn't sign that one for you. I told you we shoulda told him.'

'It's all right. At least now he knows.'

61

'But why didn't he say anything? Maybe he's not too mad about it.'

'Oh, he's mad all right. He nearly cracked my elbow leading me out of there, but I promised never to lie to him again and I'm never going to. But I didn't promise to tell him every lick of truth about myself all at once. I'm not sure he could take it all in one gulp.'

'I'll rest easier when he knows it all,' James said.

Anna looked at him sharply, wondering again if he suspected anything about how she'd earned money for his passage and his clothes. But just then Father Pierrot came out with a bundle of food for their journey, and Karl appeared with the wagon. It was time for fond farewells, handshakes and the ride into their uncertain, married future.

4

They had not travelled a mile up the road before Karl
pursued the subject which could not be avoided. But he
drove his team, and when he drove his team he was not
one to raise his voice, so he spoke now with stilted patience,
glowering at the reins that stretched ahead of him through
the checkrings.

'I think you have more to tell me, Anna. Do you want
to tell me now?'

She peeked sideways. Sure enough – that jaw bulged out
like a rock. 'You know already, so why make me tell you?'
she asked her lap.

'It is true then? The letters were not written by you?'

With a shake of the head she answered no.

'And you do not know how to read or write?'

Again she shook her head negatively.

'Who wrote the letters?' he asked, recalling all the times
he had touched them, lingered over them, thinking of his
Anna's hands having touched them first.

'James.'

'James?' Karl looked across Anna to the boy who stared
straight ahead. 'You set the boy to writing deliberate lies
because you could not write them yourself?'

'I didn't *set* him to writing them.'

'Well, what would you call it, teaching a young boy like
him such lessons?'

'We agreed, that's all. We had to get out of Boston and
find a way to live. James was the one who found your
advertisement in the paper and read it to me. We decided
together to try to get you to marry me.'

'You decided together to get Karl Lindstrom to marry a twenty-five-year-old woman, a good Catholic girl who could read and write and teach our children to read and write, who could cook and make soap and garden.'

The two guilty parties sat silent.

'And who will do that, Anna? Who will teach our children to read and write? Am I supposed to take the time to come in from the fields and teach them?'

His casual reference to *their children* brought roses to Anna's cheeks. Still she answered, hopefully, 'James can teach them.'

'James, you said, is to be my helper in the woods and in the fields. How can James be in two places at once?'

She had no answer.

'How is it that James learned to read and write, but you did not?' he asked.

'Sometimes, when our mother got a fit of conscience, she'd make him go to school, but she didn't see any girl needing to know her letters, so she left me alone.'

'What kind of mother would only send a boy to school now and then, when she had a fit of conscience? Conscience over what?'

This time James saved Anna from lying or revealing the full truth. He burst in. 'We didn't have much, even before Barbara got sick and died. We lived with . . . with friends of hers most of the time, and I had to go out and try to find work to help. I guess she thought I was kind of young to be out working, and sometimes she'd get . . . well, sorry, kind of. That's when I'd have to go to school. I managed to go enough to learn to read and write a little.'

Puzzled, Karl asked, 'Barbara? Who is Barbara?'

'That was our ma's name.'

'You called your mother *Barbara*?' Karl could not conceive of a child calling his mother by her given name. What kind of mother would allow such a thing? But since neither of them answered, Karl pressed on. 'You told me there was no work for you in Boston and that is why you needed to get away.'

'Well, there wasn't. I mean . . . well – '

'Well, what, boy?' Karl demanded. 'Which is the truth? Did you work or not?'

James took a gulp of air and braved it, in a strange falsetto. 'Mostly I picked pockets.'

Karl was stunned again. He looked at the fledgling's profile, trying to imagine a boy that young doing such a dishonest thing. Then he glanced at Anna, who sat sullenly staring at the narrow road ahead.

'Did your mother know this?' he asked, watching Anna's face carefully for signs of lies. But there was no sign, just a resigned sadness that expressed age far older than her actual years.

'She knew,' Anna said. 'She wasn't really much of a mother.'

Something in her tone of voice melted Karl. The resigned way she said it made him suddenly sorry for both of them, having such a mother. Karl thought of his own mother, of the warm and loving family she had raised, teaching the value of honesty and of all the old beatitudes. Father Pierrot had been right to admonish him that he must be prepared to be their teacher. It seemed he would have to make up to both Anna and the boy all the teaching that this lax mother of theirs had not bothered to instill in them. Now more than ever Anna seemed but a child to him, a wayward child much like her brother.

'Here in the wilderness you will not find many pockets to pick,' Karl said. 'Here, instead, there is much honest work to keep a boy's hands busy from sunup to sundown. It is a good place to forget that you ever learned how to pick pockets.'

Brother and sister both turned and looked at Karl at the same time, then with growing smiles, at each other, realizing they'd once again been forgiven. Anna ventured a brief study of Karl's profile, the nose so straight and Nordic, his burnished cheek, his bleached hair curling like a sun-washed wave over his shell-like ear, his lips that had brushed her own such a short time ago. Oh, he was magnificent in every way, it seemed. And she wondered how a person came to be so good. What manner of man is this, she asked herself, who faces each new hurdle and moves past it with such forbearance?

He turned a ghost of a glance down at her. In that moment she could have sworn she saw a smile aborning upon his lips. Then he scanned the woods on his far side.

Some weight seemed to turn to warm, summer-scented air and drift away from Anna's shoulders like a dandelion seed in the wind. She clasped each knee, and smiled at the rutted road. For the first time, she looked around, fully aware of the surrounding beauties.

They were passing through a place of green magnificence. The forest was built of verdant walls, broken here and there by peaceful embrasures where prairie grasses fought for a stronghold. Trees of giant proportions canopied above saplings vying for the sky. The sky was embroidered with stitches of leafy design. Anna leaned her head way back to gaze at the dappled emerald roof above.

Karl eyed her arched throat, smiling at her childish but pleasing pose. 'So what do you think of my Minnesota?'

'I think you were right. It's much better than the plains.'

'Far better,' Karl seconded, pleased by her answer. Suddenly, he felt expansive and glib.

'There is wood here for every purpose a man could name. Maples! Why, we have maples aplenty, and they are filled with nectar such as you will find no place else.' He pointed, stretching a long arm in front of Anna's nose. 'See? That is the white maple, a hundred feet of wood and twelve gallons of sap every year. And such grains it has – fiddle-back, burl, birds-eye, leaf ...' He chuckled deep in his throat. 'When you cut into a maple it is always full of surprises. And hard . . . why, it can be polished to shine like still water.'

Anna had never thought about trees as anything but trees before. She was amused at his rapport with them. They drove a little farther before he pointed again.

'See that one there? Yellow locust. Splits as smooth and true as the flight of an apple falling from a tree. And that chestnut there? Another smooth splitter, to make boards as flat as milk on a plate.'

They passed through a little patch of sun just then. Anna shaded her eyes and peered up at Karl. He looked down at her piquantly cocked head, the squint, the crinkled-up nose, the cute smile. He found it all thoroughly delightful, and was pleased she didn't seem to find this subject too profound nor too boring.

Anna searched all around, with a sudden intuition of how to please him. She discovered a new variety, pointed and asked, 'What's that one?'

Karl followed her finger. 'That's a beech tree.'

'And what's it good for?' she asked, following it with her eyes as they came abreast of it.

'Beech? The beech you whittle. It takes to the carving knife like no other wood I know. And when it is rubbed smooth, no wood is prettier.'

'You mean you can't carve just any old wood?' James interjected.

'You can try, but some will disappoint you. You see, some people don't understand about trees. They think wood is wood, and they ask of some trees things they cannot do. You must ask a tree to do what it does best, then it will never disappoint you. And so I split the locust, carve the beech and make boards from pine and chestnut. It is the same with people. I would not ask a blacksmith to bake me a pie, would I? Or a baker to shoe my horse.' Karl tipped a little grin their way. 'If I did, I would perhaps have to eat my horseshoe and tack the pie to my horse's hoof.'

James and Anna laughed gaily, making Karl feel truly clever and more optimistic than ever before about this family of his.

'Tell us more,' James said. 'I like hearing about the trees.'

Anna looked up, studying Karl's jaw while he constantly played his eyes back and forth as they jogged up the road. She thought that she had never seen a person so alert while looking as if he weren't.

'Soon we will come to the oaks,' he continued. 'Oaks like to grow in groves. The white oak makes shingles that will keep a roof tight for fifty years. You must think of that – fifty years! It is a long time, fifty years. Longer than the life of my *morfar* who – '

'Your *what*?' Anna interrupted, crunching up her face.

'My *morfar*, my mother's father. He taught me much about trees, as he did my *far* . . . my father, too. My *morfar* gave me my first lessons in riving.'

Anna digested the idea of being taught to love the land and its fruits by a grandfather. 'But your . . . your *morfar*?' It sounded ridiculously English to Anna, but Karl nodded approvingly at her attempt. 'He is dead now?'

'Yes, he died years ago, but not before he teaches me much of what he has learned about the woods. My *mormor*, she is still alive in Sweden though.'

A wistful note had crept into Karl's voice. Anna wanted more than anything to lay her hand comfortingly upon his forearm. He seemed lost in thought, then momentarily glanced over his shoulder, as if sorry he'd burdened them with his memories or his lonesomeness.

It's all right – Anna smiled the tacit message, then urged, 'Go on . . . I interrupted. You were talking about the oaks.'

'Ya, the oaks . . .' Again he looked glad, and Anna liked him better that way. 'Do you know that when you rive shingles from oak, there are natural and beautiful grains

68

which catch the rain and send it running in channels as true as the course of a river over a falls? It's true. But when I need fence rails I use red oak. Once I made an axe handle of white oak, but it was not good. Too hard. Hickory is best for axe handles, but this I do not have here. But ash does almost as well. It is light and strong and springy.'

'Springy?' James asked, mystified at the idea of wood being springy.

'It must be, to absorb the shock from the hands when it strikes the tree trunk.'

'What other kinds of trees do you have?'

'Not too many dogwood here, but one here and there. With dogwood I make gluts and mauls. Willows I split into withes. Elder is for shade and beauty.' Karl smiled. 'We must not forget that some trees are given to us for nothing more than shade and beauty, and if this is all we ask of them, they are happy.'

James smiled crookedly. 'Aw, Karl, trees can't be happy.' He leaned his elbows on his lap and peered around Anna at the blond man, who only grinned as if he knew something special. 'Boy, Karl, you sure know a lot about them though,' James said, sitting up again and looking around in a wide arc, wondering how a man could ever learn as much as Karl knew. And Karl was only twenty-five!

'Like I said, I learn from my *morfar* and my *far* in Sweden, which is much like Minnesota. That is why I came here instead of Ohio. Also, I learn from my older brothers. We have all worked with wood since we are much younger than you are now. I think we get a late start teaching you, eh, boy? You will have to learn twice as fast as Karl did.'

But James detected a teasing lilt in Karl's voice, which made him all the more eager. 'So tell me more about the trees,' he demanded almost giddily, getting caught up in the magic of learning, already catching the contagious love that flowed from Karl to the woods.

'Here are the pines, the best friend the axeman has.'

'Why?'

'Because they save him trouble. Most trees have sapwood and heartwood that must be cut away before he can make boards. But the pine has only bark to strip off, then there lays the wood, ready to make a batch of fine board. Have you heard of the brake and froe, boy?'

'No, sir,' James replied, eyeing the lofty pines, which swayed with fairy-wing tips into the blue firmament above.

'I will teach you about them. They are the tools of shingle-making.'

'When?'

Karl laughed a little at the boy's impatience. 'In time. First comes the axe, and when you have mastered that you will be able to carve your way to survival in any forest. A man worth his salt can survive with no other tool but his axe in the deepest wilderness nature ever made.'

'I never used one.'

'Can you shoot a rifle, boy?' Karl asked, with a sudden change of subject.

'No, sir.'

'Do you think you could if you had to?'

'I don't know.'

Something made Anna look sharply at Karl now. The tone of his voice had not changed, but something told her that the last question was not as casual as the others had been. Sure enough – Karl's eyes shifted watchfully from side to side.

'What is it?' Anna asked, a tingle fingering its way up her spine.

'Boy, climb into the back,' Karl said calmly but intensely. 'There is a rifle there. Get it, but be careful. It is loaded.'

'Is something wrong?' James asked.

'Your first lesson in this woods is that when I tell you to get a rifle, you move as if your life depended on it, because most often it does.' James scrambled to the rear of

70

the wagon without further ado, even though the words had not been harsh or critical. They were spoken with a quiet evenness while Karl cautiously continued to scan the woods. 'Now come back up here, but point that rifle well away from our heads while you are climbing.'

James did as he was told, quickly this time.

'What is it?' Anna insisted, growing nervous now.

'That smell,' Karl answered. 'Do you smell it? It is the scent of cat.'

She sniffed repeatedly, tasting only the pleasant aroma of the pines. 'I don't smell anything but pines,' she said.

'At first it was the pines only, but now there is the smell of cat, too. There are cougars in these woods. They are wily, and leave their scent where the pines can disguise it. So we must be wilier and be ready if one of them stalks us. Keep your eyes on the trees ahead. When we break into the oak grove, we must be most cautious. The branches are high, and the cougar can perch there in wait to pounce on anything that moves below.'

He spoke as calmly as he had when discussing the attributes of the trees that grew here. Even so, ripples of fear threaded through Anna's blood. She realized suddenly how totally dependent she and James were upon this man's knowledge of the woods.

'The gun will kick if you must shoot it, so remember to pull the stock up tight against your shoulder before you pull the trigger or you will end up with bruised bones. It is a good rifle. It is a Sharps breechloader – the best, made right here in America – Windsor, Vermont. It will not fail you, but you must learn to use it properly. Once the lever is raised, you have sheared off the end of the cloth cartridge, leaving the powder exposed. She's got no flint, boy. She doesn't need it with that percussion cap, so you are holding a live thing in your hands right now. When you are holding it, that means you are respecting it. Now lift it to your shoulder and sight along the barrel. Get used to the feel of it there, and do not be afraid to fire it if you must.'

The gun was sleek, simple, only the thumbnotch of the hammer breaking its long, smooth line as James lifted it to his shoulder. Anna heard his breath coming in short jerks, and sensed both excitement and fear emanating from him. She wished Karl would take the gun himself, but no sooner had the thought appeared than he said, 'If you must fire the gun, be ready to hold tight, because at the report, the horses will panic. I can control them, but it is best if I keep the reins. Are you all right, boy?'

'Y . . . yessir.'

The horses nickered and Karl soothed them, 'Shoo-ey, Belle. Shoo-ey, Bill. Easy does it.' There was a jingle of harness, as if the horses understood and nodded their agreement. Again Karl cooed, 'Eeeasy.' Then he spoke to James. 'Ease up on that gun, boy. You are wound up as tight as a three-day clock. When you do not know what is out there and you do not know how long you must wait to find out, you can get so tense that nothing works when you want it to. Relax a little and let your eyes do the guarding as much as the gun.'

'But . . . but I never saw a cougar before,' James said, swallowing.

'We do not know if it is cougar. Could be lynx. If it is cougar it will be golden brown, like a nicely turned pancake, with a long graceful tail. If it is lynx he will be buff gray, spotted and harder to see up there in the dark green leaves. Sometimes we see bobcat here, too, with just a stub of a tail and reddish brown. He is much smaller than the cougar, but is harder to spy.'

There was a sudden popping sound. Anna jumped!

'It is only acorns popping beneath the wheels,' Karl explained. 'We are in the oaks now. You can see what I meant about the high branches.' James noticed the way Karl scanned left, then right, then above, studying the woods constantly. Karl sat upright, his entire body taut with caution. 'Lots of oak woods here in Minnesota, and plenty of acorns for the pigs to eat. They grow fat and good on acorns. The trouble is pigs are too stupid to stay at home, and sometimes they wander off into the woods and get lost. Then we must go in search of them.'

'Why don't you fence them in?' James asked.

Anna thought the two of them had gone crazy, talking of pigs and acorns at a time like this.

'In Minnesota we build fences to keep the animals out, not in. The woods are so rich with foods for livestock, we let them wander wherever they will. It is our own vegetable garden that must be fenced in, so the greedy pigs will not eat up our winter supply of food. I have seen pigs root up an entire turnip patch in short time, and eat the whole thing. Oh, pigs love turnips! If a family loses its turnip crop, it could mean much hunger during the winter.' There was a subtle relaxing of Karl's posture. Both James and Anna sensed it before the man said, 'It is all right now. You can rest easy.'

'How do you know?' inquired James.

'By the squirrels. See the squirrels?'

Anna looked but didn't see any squirrels. 'Where?' she asked, squinting.

'There.' Following Karl's brown finger, she at last saw a bushy tail lithely leaping through the oaks. 'The squirrels hide in their nests when cats are near. When you see the squirrels busy scampering free through the oaks, the threat is gone. Still, you will hold that gun for a while yet, but rest it on your lap now, boy. You did fine.'

A thrill of pride such as he'd never before felt filled James's chest. The exhilaration caused by the danger was something new to him, too. It was totally different from anything he had experienced in his life. To hold the gun like a man, to be trusted enough by Karl to do this, to feel that if danger approached he would have been their defender – all this created a blossoming sense of maturity in the boy.

'And so you have learned your first lesson about the woods,' Karl noted.

'Yessir,' James replied, his cheeks puffed out.

'So, tell me what it is you have learned.'

'To be careful in the pines because the cats use them to cover their scent. That the oaks are pretty good places for cougars to perch. To watch the squirrels and keep the gun ready till they show up again. And . . .' James had saved the best for last, 'that a lot of loud talking helps keep a prowling cat at bay.'

Anna was amazed! Without it being said in so many words, James had learned such a lesson only from Karl's example. She had never before realized her brother was so quick-witted.

As if he read her mind, Karl praised, 'You are quick with your wits, boy. Do you think your sister is as quick?' He glanced at Anna momentarily.

She cocked her head quite saucily his way, then aside to find more squirrels while she said, 'She's quick enough to learn she'll probably have the insufferable job of chasing pigs through the woods when they need rounding up, and she'll be eating lots of turnips, which she despises.'

For the first time Karl laughed without holding back. It was a sonorous, baritone sound that pleased and surprised Anna, and made James laugh, too. There had been so much strain between Karl and Anna, it was a relief to hear this first billowing laughter.

'In that case,' Karl said, 'we had better check the wild hops, so while James and I are eating turnips, his sister can eat bread, eh, James?'

'Yessir!' James agreed eagerly, then made them all laugh again by adding, 'What for?'

Karl explained that hops were necessary for making yeast. Each summer he came to this spot to pick enough hops to last the entire year. 'I think these are the longest hops in the world. I also think they will not be ready – it is early yet – but we will check them just the same, as long as we are passing. It will tell me when to come back for the picking.'

Karl pulled to a stop at a point in the road that looked no different from any other.

'How do you know where to stop?' Anna asked.

Again he pointed. 'By the notch,' he answered. 'I know enough to start looking for it just beyond the oaks.'

A wide, white gash showed on a tree trunk, telling Karl the whereabouts of the hops, which could not be seen from the road. He led them into the brush, the gun cradled in the crook of his arm. He took them into fragrant shade, holding back branches now and then, turning to watch Anna dip her way through the thick press of elderwood, with its pink flowers that would turn to black berries come fall. She bent and led with her elbow, sidetracked a branch and looked up unexpectedly into blue eyes that were waiting for her to pass.

'Be careful,' he said.

Quickly she looked away, wondering when was the last time anyone admonished her with the simple phrase that meant so much more than it said. 'What are these?' she asked, distracted by her thought.

'Elderbrush.'

'And what is elderbrush good for?'

'Not much,' he answered, walking along behind her. 'In the autumn it berries, but the fruit is much too bitter to eat. Why should we eat bitter berries when there are plenty sweet ones to be had?'

'Like what?'

'Many,' he answered. 'Strawberry, raspberry, blackberry, gooseberry, pincherry, grapes, blueberry. Blueberry is my favourite. I have never seen a land with so much wild fruit. The blueberries grow to the size of plums here. Oh, there are wild plums, too.'

They arrived at the place of the hops then, twining vines

that clung to the elderbrush and cascaded from it in grape-shaped leaves. Although they were not coning yet, Karl seemed pleased. 'There will be plenty of hops again this summer. Perhaps my Anna will not have to eat turnips after all.'

For so long he had thought of her as 'my Anna' that the term had slipped out without warning.

Anna flashed him a quick look of surprise, but she felt the heat creep up her cheeks.

Karl quickly concerned himself with the hops again. He picked a large, perfectly formed leaf, saying, 'Here, study it well. If ever you find another like it, mark the spot well. It would save time if we did not have to come this far for the hops. Maybe you will find some nearer to our place.'

Our place, she thought. She peeked up to find a band of deeper colour rising from his open, white collar. She stared at the hollow of his throat. Suddenly, his Adam's apple jumped convulsively. He was playing with the leaf, staring at it, twirling it by its stem as if he had forgotten he'd picked it. She reached out a palm, and Karl twitched as if waking up. Guiltily, he laid it on her hand. Her eyes lingered on his for a moment longer, then she dropped them again and smoothed the leaf.

He was beguiled by her freckled nose. Standing there studying his Anna while shadows dappled her brow, he pictured his sod house and the sheaf of sweet clover lying on the bed in welcome. His chest tightened like new rawhide. Why did I dream up such an idea, he wondered miserably. At the time it seemed gracious, but now it just seems foolish and misleading.

'I think we had better go,' he said softly, glancing briefly at James who was exploring big beige mushrooms. Karl suddenly wished that the boy were not here at all so he could touch Anna's cheek.

She glanced up then. Her heart started thumping and she immediately took up leaf studying again.

Karl cleared his throat and called to James, 'You pick a leaf, too, boy. It will be your second lesson.' Then he turned and led the way from the woods, while thoughts of freckles on Anna's perky little nose dotted his mind.

5

It was near day's end before they finally swerved off the main road and turned into a trace where the trees formed a closer tunnel overhead. Here there was room for only one wagon to scrape through the infringing forest. The underbrush pressed so close that the horses sometimes snuffled when the weeds touched their noses. The horses made the harness sing again, throwing their great heads in exaggerated nods of recognition. 'Ya, you are impatient. You know we are nearly home, but I cannot let you run away with us. Slow down.'

Neither Anna nor James had ever heard a person speak to beasts as if they were human. Unbelievably, Bill angled a blinker at the sound of his name. 'The lane is as narrow as it was yesterday,' Karl said, 'so slow down, Bill.'

In a way much like the horses, James and Anna raised their heads, sensing home, wondering what it would be like. Karl had announced this was his land, and already every leaf, limb and loam took on greater importance to her. It even seemed to smell more pungent, of things burgeoning, ripening while others decayed, adding their own secret scent of nature's continuing cycle.

This is my road, thought Anna – my trees, my wild-flowers, the place where my life will be joyous or sad. Come winter, the snows will seal me in with this man who speaks to horses and trees. Her eyes tracked over everything as fast as they could take it all in. The space broadened and before them lay the home of Karl and Anna Lindstrom, this place of plenty about which the bride had heard so much.

There was a wide clearing, with a vegetable garden

planted within a split rail fence. Anna smiled to see how sturdily the fence was built so their pigs would not root up Karl's turnips. Turnips! she thought . . . yukk!

The house lay off to the left, a nearly rectangular dwelling made of large cubes of sod, pasted with mortar of white clay and buffalo grass. A stone chimney ran up its side, and it had a roof of split logs, covered with blocks of sod. It had two small windows and a plank door against which a large length of wood was wedged. Anna's heart sank as she looked at this place where Karl had already lived for two years. It was so tiny! And so . . . so crude! But she could see his eyes scan it to make sure all was as he'd left it, the look rife with the pride of ownership. She must be careful not to hurt his feelings.

Beside the sod house stood the most enormous woodpile Anna had ever seen, its rank and file as straight as if a land surveyor had shot it with his transit. She marvelled that the hands of her husband had chopped all that wood and piled it so precisely. There were smaller buildings, too. One looked to be a smokehouse, for it had a clay chimney sticking out of its centre. The enclosure for the horses was made of vertical split wood, its roof of bark secured with willow withes. Anna experienced a queer thrill of pride because already she knew that withes were cut of willow. But, looking around, she knew suddenly how much – how very, very much – she would have to learn to survive here and be any help to Karl.

The clearing extended to the east to include tilled patches where new corn, wheat and barley sprang up. Directly opposite where the road entered, a broad avenue had been cleared of trees, and upon it lay a double track of logs with their bark removed, running up a gentle slope like a wooden railroad track, disappearing into the trees around a wide curve in the distance.

Never did Karl Lindstrom leave this place without returning to it filled with wonder and pride. His sod house hovered in welcome, the vegetables seemed to have grown immeasurably in two such short days, the corn clicked in the wind as if asking where he'd been while it had been busy growing, the barn seemed impatient to gather in Belle and Bill between its bark walls. The skid trail beckoned like the road to his dreams.

It was difficult for Karl not to throw his chest out and crow like a rooster upon seeing his place again. His place? No, their place now. His heart beat with gladness at the sight of it, and at last he let Belle and Bill have their heads and hurry the last fifty yards to the barn. When he stopped them just short of it, their heavy hooves pawed the earth, impatiently. And suddenly it was far easier for Karl to speak to his horses than to face Anna.

Suppose she does not like it, he thought. He jerked the brake home, tied the reins to it. It will not seem to a woman what it seems to me. She will not feel the love with which I have done all this. She will perhaps see only that it is very lonely here for her with nobody near enough to be a friend to her except the boy and me.

To the horses he said, 'I think maybe you will be jealous because I make you wait, but first I must take Anna and the boy to the house.' She saw Karl nervously wipe his palms upon his thighs, and read the silent plea for her approval in his eyes. Softly, he said, 'We are home, Anna.'

She swallowed, wanting to say something to please him, but all that she could think of was if the outside of the house was so miserable, what was the inside going to look like? She might spend the rest of her life there. And if not that long, at least her wedding night, which was fast coming on.

Karl's eyes skittered to the house. He was remembering that sheaf of sweet clover and wishing to high heaven he had never put it there! It was a stupid move, he was sure now, made when he had thought to please her. It was meant as a symbol of welcome only, one which spoke not only from the heart of the man, but from his land and his home, which had no voices of their own.

But would she know his intention? Or would she perhaps see the clover as only a decoration of a bed and the eagerness of the man to take her to it? There was little he could do about it now. It was there, and she would see it as soon as she walked in.

He leaped from the wagon, while James went off the other side and gawked at the surroundings.

Anna stood up, again finding Karl waiting to help her down. As usual, his shirt-sleeves were rolled up to the elbow as he raised his arms to her. She avoided his eyes and let herself swing down to his grasp. The touch of his hands on her waist made the coming night loom up before her in a formidable way. She would have turned quickly from Karl, but he gently held her, the butts of his hands resting lightly on her slim hipbones. He glanced quickly at the boy, but James was paying little attention to them.

'Anna, do not be afraid,' Karl said, dropping his hands. 'It will be good here, I promise you. I welcome you to my home and to all that is mine. All of it is yours now, too.'

'I have a lot to learn and to get used to,' she said. 'I probably won't be good at much and you'll be sorry you brought me.'

There were things that Karl, too, had to learn and he thought with racing heart of the coming night. But, he thought, this we will learn together. 'Come, I will show you the house, then I must tend Belle and Bill.'

He wished he could take her into the house alone, but the boy was running toward them. It was his home, too, and he was eager to see inside.

Crossing the clearing, Anna noticed a bench beside the door with a bucket on it, a leather strop hanging on a peg above, apparently where Karl did his washing and shaving. There was a stump beside the woodpile where he must do the chopping.

He walked just behind her. When they reached the door, he leaned around her to remove the chunk of wood wedged against the outside of the door. 'It keeps the Indians from stealing everything in the place,' he explained, and walked to the side of the house to fling it toward the chopping block. 'Indians have a curious sense of honour. If you leave and they discover you gone, they will take whatever they can lay their hands on. But if you place the block of wood before the door to tell them you are gone, they would not take so much as a wild plum from the bush beside your door.'

'Are there many Indians around here?'

'Many. But they are my friends, and you need not fear them. One of them is taking care of my goat while I am gone. I will have to go fetch her.'

But he'd avoided taking Anna inside as long as he could. He reached for the latchstring. She'd never seen such a thing before. It hung outside the door, leading from a small hole in the puncheons, tied to the latch itself which was on the other side. When he pulled the string, she heard the klunk as a heavy oak bar lifted, then the door swung open. He leaned with the door, his shoulder blade against it, letting both Anna and the boy pass in front of him.

The interior was dark and smelled of musty earth and wood smoke. She wondered how he had stood it to live in such a burrow for two years! But he quickly found a tallow candle, his flint and steel, while she stood waiting to see what was beyond the arc of fading afternoon light created by the open door.

She heard the scratch as the tinder lit, then the candle flared. She saw a wooden table and chairs with pegged legs; another bench like the one outside; a curious thing that appeared to be a section of tree trunk on four legs; a fireplace with its iron cauldron suspended above the dead ashes, brass containers hanging on hooks, various earthen-

82

ware dishes on the hearth; barrels raised off the floor on wooden slabs; dried foods hanging from the ceiling; an earthen floor with fresh swirls telling her he'd swept it last thing before he left.

Karl stood expectantly, watching her glance from one thing to the next. His throat filled with heartbeats as he saw her slowly turn in the opposite direction and find the bed. He wanted to reach out and take her slim shoulders and say, 'I meant it as a welcome, nothing more.' He saw her hand go up to her throat before she looked quickly away to his clothing hanging on pegs behind the door, then to the wooden trunk nearby.

James turned, too, to eye the bed, and Karl longed more than ever to snatch up the sheaf of sweet clover and run outside with it. Instead, he excused himself, saying, 'Belle and Bill are anxious to be free of the harness.'

When he was gone, James explored the place further, saying, 'It's not so bad, is it, Anna?'

'It's not so bad if you're a badger who expects to live in a burrow. I don't see how he could live here all this time.'

'But Anna, he built it all by himself!' James was intrigued by everything, examining the set of the stones in the fireplace, the way the legs of the table were set into the puncheon boards, the windows covered with waxed sheets of opaque cloth that let in only negligible amounts of light. While Anna wondered how anyone could possibly mistake them for windows, James seemed pleased by everything. 'Why, I'll bet this place is as snug as a rabbit's nest in the winter. He's got these walls so thick that no snow or rain could ever get in.'

She took their rolls of clothing and laid them on the bed and began untying them, trying to pretend she wasn't crestfallen. James charged out the door saying he was going to help with the horses. She sat down on one of the chairs and clasped her hands between her knees, staring at the bed across the room, at the flowers that were drying there on their stalks. Something at once inviting and foreboding flooded her veins at the sight of them.

She thought about Karl, his first displeasure with her, his later acceptance and forgiveness, his hesitancy at times, his seeming kindness. She imagined him picking these flowers all alone, getting this hut ready for her. She remembered how he had slipped and called her 'my Anna' and it raised goose bumps on her skin. She shivered and hugged her arms, still wondering about the clover, the sight of it somehow prompting a surge of guilt in her.

This was not a man who took a wife lightly to his bed with no thought of what it all meant. His word of welcome by the wagon came back to her now, telling her again how he felt about sharing all that was his. These were words of a man who was doing his best to please, who offered all that he had as a kind of dowry to his bride. But the only dowry she brought was deceit.

Already she knew how her lies had disillusioned Karl, and how very difficult it had been for him to accept her in spite of them. Thinking of lying with him, of his discovering the one lie she was most afraid to reveal, she knew with unerring certainty that a man like Karl Lindstrom would be totally unable to accept a used wife.

He came in with a barrel on his shoulder, filling the doorway with his bulk before leaning to set it on the floor, then turning to find her huddled on the chair.

'Anna, you are shivering. I will light a fire. It is always cool in the place. The sod keeps it so. Why do you not go outside where it is warmer?'

'Karl?' she asked hesitantly. His head snapped around.

She realized it was the first time she had used his first name. 'Don't you have a stove?'

'I have never needed a stove,' he answered. 'The fireplace is good and I can do everything with it – cook, keep warm, dry herbs, heat water, make soap, melt wax. I have never thought too much about a stove. Morisette sells them, but they cost dearly.'

She wondered how in the world she was going to use that black pit of a fireplace when the little she suspected of how to cook was all based upon doing so on an iron stove like everybody had back East.

He studied her a moment. He himself liked a fireplace. For the long, dreary nights of the winter there was nothing so heartening as blazing flames to stare into, especially a fire kindled of logs from one's own land. How many times he had envisioned this night when he would bring her here, his Anna, and of building up the fire high, and by its light laying her down on a buffalo robe before it. Yes, he thought, a house should have a fireplace. A house with love should have a fireplace.

'So you want a stove, Anna?' he asked anyway.

She shrugged. 'A stove would be nice.'

'Perhaps in the log house we will have a stove,' he offered. She smiled then and he felt better. 'Come,' he said. 'You can gather the woodchips for kindling while I bring in the logs.' He took down a willow basket and handed it to her, leading the way outside.

James called from across the clearing, 'Hey, Karl, what's all this stuff in your garden?'

'A little bit of everything,' he called back. He liked the sound of the boy's voice calling him Karl.

'What's all this stuff here?' James called.

'Those are turnips.'

'*All these?*'

'All those. But do not say it so loud. You will make your sister want to run away.' He smiled sideways at Anna, and she realized how hard he was trying to put her at ease.

'I can tell the peas and beans and stuff,' James said proudly.

'Did you see the watermelon there at the end? Do you like watermelon, boy?'

85

'Watermelons? Really?' With arms flapping, James went to the far end of the vegetable plot. 'Hey, Anna, did you hear that? Watermelons!'

Karl laughed and continued watching as James explored the garden. 'It does not take much to gain that one's interest, does it?'

'I guess not. He seems as happy as you are to be here.' But she made no mention of her own feelings as she started to pick up wood chips and place them in the basket. The fragrance of freshly chopped wood seemed to hang around Karl Lindstrom all the time. She recalled the way he had spoken of the trees on their ride home, and the woodsmell seemed right.

Inside the cabin, Karl knelt with his back to her, a small hatchet in his hands. He shaved curls of wood off one of the pieces he'd brought in. They were much the same colour as the hair at the back of his neck, which she studied. He finished, then reached up to her for the basket. Again, his eyes lingered on her in a way that made her mind stray to bedtime. He took a small scoop and cleaned the ashes from the fireplace into a pail. He found a large chunk of charcoal at the bottom of the ashes and carefully placed it aside as if it were quite precious.

Anna watched all this from behind, observing the play of muscles as he reached up for the scoop, leaned forward to use it, swivelled at the hips toward the pail, pivoted on the balls of his feet to take the charcoal up, straightened, then knelt again with a cracking of knees. He turned abruptly to look up at her, and she wondered if he knew she'd been wondering what the muscles beneath his shirt looked like.

'Hand me the candle,' he said.

She reached to put it in his outstretched hand. Their fingers carefully avoided touching.

He pivoted again toward the fireplace, readjusting the fleecy mound of wood curls. It kindled and flamed under

Karl's watchful eye. He added chips. He squatted before the growing fire, unmoving, lost in thought, elbows braced upon knees. The blaze before him brightened and turned his hair to the colour of flame.

Anna stared fixedly at the spot where his shirt disappeared into the back of his pants.

'You can put your things in the trunk,' he said, not turning around.

'I don't have much.'

'What you have you can put there. There is room for them, and the trunk will keep them from getting damp. You can put the boy's things in it, too.'

He heard her move, heard the lid of the trunk squeak open. He arose, the fire now burning satisfactorily. He turned to find her laying her clothing into the trunk, partially hidden by the door.

'Would you like me to show you the spring?' he asked. 'I have a wonderful spring, and there is watercress growing near it.' Such a foolish thing to say, Karl told himself. Why do you not say what it is you want to say about the spring? But if I mention washing, she might think I am criticizing her – or worse – she might think I want her clean for bedtime and this is the only reason I bring up the spring.

'I've never tasted watercress before. What's it like?' The clothes were all in the trunk and she had to stand up fully now and act as though her mind were on what she was saying.

'It tastes like . . . like watercress,' he ended, then laughed nervously. 'A little like collard, a little like dandelion, but mostly like watercress. Sweeter than other greens.' Karl picked up the chunk of charcoal and took it with him outside, saying, 'Come, you have to see my spring.'

'Hey, Karl,' James hollered, 'where's all this water come from?' He was already studying the bubbling flow that came from beneath the walls of the springhouse.

'It comes from deep in the earth. It runs all year long,

no matter how cold the weather gets. We are lucky. Never will we have to chop holes in the ice of the pond for water, or melt down snow or ice, which takes much time.'

'You mean all we have to do is come right here and have a cold drink, any time?'

'Ya, that is so, boy,' Karl said proudly, hoping Anna, too, would be impressed with this spot he had chosen for their home. 'This is a springhouse. Open the door and look inside.'

It was built of wood, with a latched door that swung on hand-carved wooden hinges. When James opened it, he was surprised at how very cool it was inside. The soft sand around the spring had been hollowed out, shored up and formed a wide bowl in which earthen jugs and crocks were partially submerged. The crystal-clear water purled with a whisper around the jugs, then wended its way out below the walls again. In one corner was a leather bag hanging above a pail where Karl placed his chunk of charcoal.

'What're you saving that for?' James asked.

'This is my lye leach. The water drips from the bag onto the charcoal, and slowly lye is made. The bag is empty again, so I must refill it.' He stooped to do so. 'With it we make soap and tan leather and many other things. You could be a help to me if you would check the water bag when you come in here, and always keep it filled and dripping. But I must warn you, there are times when we must test the lye to see if it is strong enough. Then I must find a prairie chicken egg and float it. When it sinks, this tells me the lye is ready. The lye in the cup will look so much like tea a person could not tell the difference. Never leave it in that cup. If it was mistaken for tea and somebody drank it, this would be a disaster.' The bag was again filled and hung. The regular plops of the dripping water accented the constant music of the spring, the smell of the damp wood.

'Gosh, Karl, did you think this up all by yourself?' James asked, taking in the entire structure.

'No. My father taught me this, too, how to make a springhouse, when I am only a tad like you.'

'In Boston we got water from out back in barrels where they came and filled them every other day or so. Seems like it never tasted fresh. This water's the best I ever had. Hey, Anna, come and try some.'

James passed the dipper to his sister, while Karl looked on expectantly. It was water such as she'd never tasted in her life. It was so icy it hurt her teeth, making Karl laugh when she grabbed them with her fingers to warm them. But that didn't stop her from drinking again and again while Karl watched with pleasure in his eye.

'It's good,' she said, when she'd finally drunk her fill.

'It is plenty close to the house, and even closer to where the new log house will be. Enough good, fresh water, and close enough to the house that a lad has little excuse for not keeping clean with it, huh? I think maybe it is time we filled a couple of these buckets and let the water lose its chill for later. What do you say, James?'

'You mean for washing?' the boy asked.

The tone of his question made Karl ask, 'Do you object to washing?'

'Well, I never been much for bath-taking,' James admitted.

'Such a reply for a tadpole. Anna, what have you taught the lad? In Sweden a boy learns right from the start that in all of nature, animals clean themselves to keep healthy. A boy must do the same.'

But James said, 'Anna's not much for baths either.'

'She's not?' Karl said before he could stop himself. He was beginning to realize that a lad of thirteen could be an embarrassment to an older sister. 'Well, when you have only a barrel in your backyard it is a problem. Here there is no such problem. There is the spring here, and the pond and the creek. Plenty water for everything.'

Anna could have kicked James into the spring! It was true she hated baths, but did he have to spew out the fact to Karl first thing?

'Come. Fill yourself a pail, boy, and take it back to the house. Tonight we will baby you a little bit and heat the water. Most times I will not warm it up. It is refreshing, and makes you want to work hard to get warm fast.'

With filled pails they trudged back to the house, and the subject of baths was blessedly dropped. Anna, however, was well aware that Karl was outside at what she'd guessed to be the washbench. He shaved before supper while she explored things around the kitchen end of the house, peeking inside barrels and tins and crocks. There were odd-looking foods, some of which Anna could not identify. Others held basic staples.

She heard a yelp outside and realized that James must be following Karl's suit. They both came in, shiny-faced and combed, making her realize she would surely be expected to wash as well. But there was no privacy, and she had no inclination to let the icy water touch her skin.

Their supper was simple. Karl laid it all on the table, showing Anna where things were kept. They had cold meat, which he brought from a crock in the springhouse; bread, which he said he baked himself, although Anna couldn't for the life of her figure out where; cheese he'd made from his own goat's milk. Anna had never eaten goat's cheese before, and found it sweet and full-flavoured.

Naturally, James again brought up what Anna would have avoided. 'You don't expect Anna to know how to make cheese, do you, Karl?'

'No,' he answered, avoiding her eyes. 'But I will have to teach her. It is not too hard. There is a corner of the chimney that keeps the milk just warm enough to curdle good and slow. In the morning I will walk to get my goat from my friend, Two Horns. Then we will have fresh milk for breakfast. Have you ever milked a goat, boy?'

'Never,' James answered. 'Are you gonna teach me?'

'First thing in the morning. Maybe Anna would like to learn, too.'

Then again, maybe Anna would not, thought the one in question, while her brother went on with his questions. 'Why do you keep a goat? Why not a cow like everybody else?'

'Cows are truly expensive here, and they like to stray away into the woods like the pigs. Then you must find them each day when it is time to milk them. Goats are like pets. They do not stray as far, and they are good company.'

'I never thought about a goat being like a pet before.'

'Goats make maybe the best pets of all. They are loyal and quiet and do not eat much. During the winter blizzards, there were many times when I was grateful for the company of my Nanna to listen to me talk and never complain when I tell her how impatient I am to have neighbours, and how I miss my family back in Sweden and how I think spring will never come. Nanna, she just chews her cud and puts up with me.' His eyes strayed to Anna as he spoke, then back to the boy.

'Is that your goat's name – Nanna?'

'Ya. You will love her when you meet her.'

'I can't wait! Tell me about the rest. Tell me what else we're gonna do tomorrow besides milk the goat.'

Karl laughed softly at the boy's eagerness, so like his own since he had come here. 'Tomorrow we begin felling trees for the log house, but by the end of the day I do not think you will be as pleased as you are right now.'

'Will Anna help, too?'

'That is up to Anna,' Karl said.

She looked up quickly, anxious to be included in anything that would get her out of this dingy cabin and into the sun. 'Could I, Karl?' she asked, fearing he meant to leave her to watch goat's milk turn into cheese on the chimney corner. But Karl read only happiness into her question.

'Anna will help, too,' Karl said. 'Even for three the work will be hard.'

'So we were right, and you'll be glad I'm here,' James boasted a little.

'Ya, I think so. Tomorrow I will be glad you are here.'

But tonight was a different matter. Even though Karl enjoyed talking with the boy, he was ever aware of bedtime drawing near. The fire was spitting and settling. Karl stretched his legs out toward it, forcing himself to relax back into his chair. From his pocket he fished a pipe and leather pouch.

Anna watched his movements, learning something new – he smoked a pipe.

He filled it slowly, while he and James talked about the cabin and all it would take to build it. The smell of the tobacco smoke drifted lazily, and James leaned his chin more and more heavily upon his hand. Now and then Karl's gaze moved toward Anna, but she would look quickly away toward the fire. There, on the hob, hung the black cauldron Karl had filled with water after supper.

James revived when Anna arose to clear away their few dishes, but soon he nodded heavily once more.

The squeak of Karl's chair called out as he got up, saying, 'The boy will fall off his bench soon if I do not make a bed for him. I will go to the barn and bring back a forkful of hay.'

She turned her eyes to Karl, trying not to look skittish and seventeen. 'Yes,' she said.

He left her standing gawkily, and within minutes returned, bringing a wooden fork laden with sweet-smelling hay. 'It grows wild in the meadows,' Karl said, looking squarely at Anna, then back down to his chore of piling it high and spreading it with a buffalo robe.

James dove for the shakedown immediately, while Karl leaned on the fork and watched him. 'Do you think you have time to take your shoes off before you sleep, lad?' James doggedly removed his shoes.

Again Karl's eyes met Anna's briefly, and he said, 'I will take the fork back where it belongs.' When he left, she turned and stared at the pot of water, tested it quickly and found it was getting warm much too fast.

'Anna?' She jumped at the softly spoken word and turned, unaware that Karl had returned.

'Yes?'

He realized they had never had a chance to talk alone, to acquaint themselves with each other. Wildly, he searched his mind for something to give them time to do so. A woman should not jump so when she hears her man's voice, he thought. 'Would you like a cup of tea?'

'Tea?' she repeated stupidly, then quickly added, 'Oh, tea . . . yes.' The relief was evident in her voice.

'Sit down. I will make it for you. I will teach you how.'

She sat, watching him move about the room, now and then casting an anxious glance at her brother who was snuggled comfortably on his makeshift bed. At last Karl brought their two cups to the table and pushed hers over to her.

'Rose hips,' he said quietly.

'What?' She looked up, startled.

'The tea is made of rose hips. First you must squash them in the cup, then add the hot water.'

'Oh.'

'Have you never had tea of rose hips before?'

'The only tea I ever had was . . . well, tea. Real tea. But not too often.'

'Here there is little real tea or coffee either. But rose hip is almost better. When winters get long, rose hips will keep you from getting scurvy.' Achingly, he wondered why he rambled on about rose hips. But his tongue had a mind of its own. 'Wild mulberry hips will do the same, but they are not so plentiful here as rose.' She took a sip of her drink. 'How do you like it?'

She found it delightful, which gratified him.

'Anna,' he said, leaning on an elbow across the table from her, 'there is so much here in Minnesota, I cannot tell you how good a life we will have. Why, I could walk out into the woods right now and pick you more herbs for tea than you could remember by morning. There is wild strawberry, chamomile, basswood, salsify . . . Have you ever tasted comfrey, Anna?' She shook her head no. Karl promised, 'I will show you how to make comfrey tea. Comfrey is so good I grow it in my garden. I will show you, too, how to dry it. You will love comfrey tea.'

'I'm sure I will, Karl,' she said, realizing all of a sudden that he was just as nervous as she.

'I have so much to show you, Anna. Have you ever caught a bass on a line and felt him fight you so hard the line would cut your hand if you let him take it through your palm? You will love to fish, Anna, and so will the boy. In Skåne where I grew up, my papa and I fished much, and my brothers, too. Here there are as many fish and more than in Sweden, and wild fowl and deer and elk. Anna, I have seen an *elk* in my woods! I did not know what it was, but my friend Two Horns told me. It was magnificent. Did you ever imagine a place with so much? In the autumn when geese fly south from Canada, there are battalions of them. So many a man can bring down one with each shot. And the way things grow here, Anna, you will not believe it. Potatoes grow to be the size of squash and squash grow to the size of pumpkins and pumpkins – '

Suddenly Karl stopped, realizing he was rambling on about his favourite subject, quite carried away by it. 'I think I chatter on like the squirrels,' he said sheepishly, dropping his eyes to the tabletop only to find her hands tense upon her cup.

'It's all right. You had forgotten to mention the squirrels anyway.' Her reply brought smiles to both of their faces before she again dropped her gaze to her cup and said quietly, 'It's very different here from Boston. Already I'm beginning to see the difference. I think it'll be good here for James. He seems to like it already.'

A moment of silence went quivering by before Karl quietly asked, 'And you, Anna . . . how about you?'

They studied each other across the table while the fire lit a single side of each of their faces, the far sides cast into complete shadow. And so it seemed to Karl and Anna, as if only half of what each was, was illuminated for the other to see so far. There was yet much that remained in shadow, but only time would bring it to light.

'It . . . it takes some getting used to . . .' Anna dropped her eyes. 'But little by little I think I am.'

He wondered what she would like for him to say, what was the best way. After some time he could only think to ask, 'Are you tired, Anna?'

She looked sharply at James, but he was still. 'A little,' she answered uncertainly.

'The water is warm.' Of course it was warm. It was hot enough to have steeped rose hip tea. Together they looked at the pale threads of steam rising from the kettle. 'But I have only homemade lye soap.'

'Oh, that . . . that's fine!' she said too brightly. He made no move to leave and she sat glued to her chair.

'The basin is on the bench outside. I will fill it for you.'

'Thank you.'

He took the kettle from the hook and went outside.

By the time she followed him out, he was gone somewhere into the dark. She washed herself faster than she ever had in her life. In spite of how she hated baths, she had to admit it felt more than tolerable to be rid of the travel grit. She glanced toward the clearing, but there were only fireflies skipping in the dark. From the barn came a gentle nicker, then all was quiet.

She slipped back into the house, found her nighty in the trunk, put it on and stood uncertainly, looking first at James asleep on the floor, then at the bed. Resolutely, she crossed to it, flung the buffalo robe back and put one knee on the mattress. But she stopped still at a crackling noise – cornhusks filling the mattress. My God! What is that! Gingerly, she moved her knee and the crackling sounded again. There was nowhere else to go. So with her mind set, she scampered the rest of the way in and pulled the robe up to her neck.

The door moved, its shadow widening, then narrowing on the sod walls, before Karl closed it with the wooden thud of the latch falling into place. Carefully, he drew the latchstring in. He came to the side of the bed, no longer able to ignore the sheaf of sweet clover, which still lay where he'd placed it yesterday morning. Her eyes followed him as he leaned to pick it up from beside her head.

'This is sweet clover,' he said dumbly.

'It smells good,' she choked.

'There is no sweeter smell in all of Minnesota.' Then he swallowed. 'Oh, Anna, I meant it as a welcome, but after I left it here I thought perhaps I should not have done so. I thought . . .' He looked down at the clover in his hand. '. . . I thought it might scare you.'

'No . . . no, it didn't.' But her body was shaking so beneath the buffalo robe, its nap of hairs was trembling.

He turned and went to the fireplace and thrust the stalk of sweet clover into it. She watched it flare, brightening the room momentarily, throwing Karl's silhouette into sharp relief. Hands on hips, he studied the fire while she studied his back. Then he bent to bank the coals, sending sparks popping their way up the chimney. He hesitated, kneeling there in thought, while the room's illumination waned to

96

a gentle glow. But there was no more to be done, nowhere to go but to bed. He ran a hand through his hair.

Her eyes stayed fixed on the pale fireglow as he returned to the side of the bed and, with his back to her, slipped from his clothing and into the spot beside her. The husks crackled. The ropes creaked. The tick readjusted to his weight, and she found a new force threatening to roll her in his direction. She tightened her shoulder muscles to keep it from happening.

They lay on their backs, staring at the logs of the ceiling. At last Karl turned his face to her, studied her profile, then whispered, 'Look at me, Anna, while there is still enough light left to see by.'

She did, wide-eyed and undeniably frightened, re-membering that other time. She tried to focus on Karl Lindstrom's face, but only the scalding memory of Saul McGiver came to her, and with it dread and shame.

'It is hard for me to believe you are here at last,' Karl whispered. 'The way we started – I want to forget all that. I want to do things right with you. I want this to be right.'

She was afraid even to swallow, let alone talk.

He wondered if she knew his turmoil. He found her hand and brought it to his chest and pressed it palm down upon his hammering heart, surprising her.

His heart is going crazy just like mine is! she thought disbelievingly.

'You are so young, Anna. Seventeen . . . no more than a child, when I had expected a woman.'

'Seventeen is . . . is old enough,' she whispered in a strained little tone.

'Do you know what you say, Anna?' He wondered if she truly understood.

She wondered if she truly understood. She said what she felt compelled to say to a husband who had all rights to her. Knowing what her duty was, she had answered as she did. But she did not know what Karl's response would be.

Memories of the past and fear of the future gripped her. As long as they talked, nothing else happened, so she went on, 'I know lots of girls who got married at seventeen.' But she really didn't. She only knew lots of slatternly women who – at thirty, thirty-five and forty – had long ago given up hope of marrying out of their profession.

'Anna, in Sweden things like this are not done – two strangers agreeing to marry as we have done. If we lived in Sweden and I could meet you first in the village, I would buy for you a silk hair ribbon and maybe tease and laugh with you a bit. You would have a chance to say to yourself, "yes, I think I like getting a silk hair ribbon from Karl" or "I will take no more hair ribbons from Karl." But if you took the ribbons with a smile and tucked them into your little hanging pocket on your waist belt, I would next take you to meet my *mor* and *far* so you could see for yourself where I come from. I had always thought to court a girl in the way I remember my brothers doing in Skäne.' He rubbed his palm over the back of her hand, remembering, while his heartbeat thundered on.

Anna's only opinion of men in this element – in bed – was tainted too vividly by growing up where she had, among people with whom flesh was a business and nothing more. But slowly the realization was dawning that Karl was just as uncertain about this as she was, that his heart was hammering not solely from arousal, but in hesitancy, too.

'I used to imagine something like that,' she admitted, 'when I was younger.'

'Ya, I think all girls do. I thought to marry a golden-haired girl whose braids were pulled up beneath a small white starched hat with deep pleats, and who wore her embroidered apron on Midsummer's Eve, with the laces tied criss-cross upon her waist girdle. Our families would be there, and there would be dancing and laughter, much laughter.' His voice had grown reminiscent, wistful.

Anna somehow found herself, too, growing wistful. But the dancing and laughter, she had observed in her tender years, were nothing of which she wanted a part. She had not observed them in such a heartwarming setting as Karl's homeland. She had never had a starched hat, nor a girlish apron and cross-ties. She had never been courted by young swains on the village green, nor had she been given ribbons or smiles or invitations to their homes to meet their mamas and papas. She was not a girl given to fits of self-pity, but at the moment she was fighting the urge to indulge in it.

But Karl was handsome and earnest and sincere, and the murmur of his voice in the gloaming made it somehow easy for Anna to voice some of her girlhood dreams.

'I thought to get married in St Mark's. I always felt good in St Mark's. Sometimes I would dream of marrying a soldier in high boots and braids, with epaulettes on his shoulders.'

'A soldier, Anna?' He knew he was far from a soldier.

'Well, there were always soldiers around Boston. Sometimes I'd see them.'

It grew still – both the nightshadows and Karl's hand grew still.

'There are no soldiers here,' Karl said, disappointed.

'There are no blonde braids either,' she said timorously, surprising her husband once again.

Karl swallowed. 'I think I can get along without blonde braids,' he whispered. Beneath Anna's hand his flesh rose and fell more rapidly.

Despite his seeming gentleness, she was afraid to give him the reply he sought, even though a soldier in epaulettes was at this moment the farthest thing from her mind.

He rolled onto his side, facing her. 'I think I go too fast, Anna. I am sorry.' He lifted her hand to his mouth and kissed its palm – warm lips, soft breath for the briefest moment touching her – then laid it on the pillow between them, quite where the sweet clover had lain before. 'But I have been alone so long, Anna. There has been no one to talk with, no one to touch, no one to touch me, and at times I thought I would die of it. I would sometimes bring the goat inside, when the blizzards blew fierce in the winter, and to her I would talk, and often I talk to my horses. And to touch their velvet noses is good, or to stroke the ears of the goat, but it is not the same. Always I dream of the day when I have more than the animals to talk to. More than the bleat of my goat for an answer.'

Again, he took her hand to his lips, but differently this time, as if its warmth were the cure of him. The way he placed her fingers upon his lips, then moved the hand upward as if to wash himself with its touch, she felt glorified and undeserving. He whispered throatily, 'Anna, oh Anna, do you know how good just your fingers on me feel?'

Then he pulled her palm against the length of his long cheek. It was warm, smooth, and she remembered its appearance as her hands fitted its contours. Her fingertips brushed his eyebrow and, for a moment, his closed eyelid, and she felt a faint quiver there that made her yearn for light so she might see such a surprising vision as a man who held deep-pent emotions within.

'I never knew . . . You never told me all these things in your letters.'

'I thought I would scare you away. Anna, I do not mean to scare you. You are such a child and I have been alone too long.'

'But I made the agreement, Karl,' she said, determinedly.

'But you shake so, Anna.'

'So do you,' she whispered.

Yes, Karl thought, I shake from a little eagerness, a little timidity, maybe a little fright of scaring her off. It was his first time, and he wanted it to be by mutual consent – but more – by mutual love. He could wait a while to earn those things from her, but he had been alone too long to take away nothing with him this night. He reached to curl a hand around her neck, stroking her chin with his thumb, filled with wonder at the softness of her skin after feeling only his own for so long.

'Would it be all right if I kiss you, Anna?'

'A man doesn't need permission to kiss his own wife,' she whispered.

But he took it – slow-leaning on an elbow beside her, grazing her lips with the thumb, wishing she was not so afraid.

Anna lay rigidly, waiting for the bad part to begin. But it didn't. Everything was different about Karl. Different, the way he waited and touched her gently first, as if assuring her he meant well. Different, as he leaned so slowly closer, making the corn husks rustle in hushed tones. Different, as he hovered on an elbow, pausing, giving her time with his thumb still on her lips to say no. Different, as he touched his lips to her lightly, lightly.

There was no force, no fight, no fear, only a light lingering of flesh upon flesh, a blending of breaths, an introduction. And her name, 'Anna . . .' whispered upon her mouth in a way no person had ever before spoken it. His fingers slid into her hair at the back of her head, tenderly, not clutching, while she understood new things about this man. Patiently, he waited for some sign from her. It came in the tiniest lifting of her chin, bringing her lips closer to his. Again, his lips touched hers, warmer, nearer, a little fuller, letting her ease into the newness of him.

For the first time ever, Anna found a willingness to let a man know this much of her. But when he moved his hand slowly to her ribs, she stiffened, quite unable to control the reaction. He raised his mouth from hers, anxious to do the right thing with her, for he could feel the way her forearms were tightly guarding her chest.

'Anna, I would not hurry you. We have time now, if we did not have before.'

Reprieved, Anna nevertheless felt silly and inadequate. Her heart raced wildly while she searched for the right thing to say. He still hovered above her, and she felt his warm breath caressing her face. He smelled of clean shaving soap and tobacco, but he had tasted faintly of rose hips.

How can I be afraid of a man who tastes like roses? she thought. Yet she was. She knew very well what it was that men did to women. This man, with his might, could do it with tolerable ease, should he choose. But instead, he backed farther away, so she could no longer feel the touch of his breath on her nose.

'I . . . I'm sorry, Karl,' she said, then added, shakily, 'and thank you.'

Disappointment swept through Karl's veins. But he touched her jaw with the back of a callused index finger, a brief, reassuring brush upon her downy flesh.

'We have plenty time. Sleep now, Anna.' Then he lay back on his own side of the bed, but unrelaxed, for now he knew what her skin felt like.

Anna rolled onto her side facing the wall, curling her spine and tugging the buffalo robe up securely between shoulder and jaw. But a strange feeling crept over her, as if she'd done something wrong but she wasn't sure what. She felt much like just before she started to cry. Finally, she rolled slightly backward, looked over her shoulder and whispered, 'Goodnight, Karl.'

'Goodnight, Anna,' he said thickly.

But for Karl it was not a good night. He lay stiff as a board, wanting to leap from the bed and run into the dewy damp night air and cool off, talk to his horses, dip his head in the icy basin of water in the springhouse – something! But he lay instead like a ramrod – sleepless – for now he knew the feel of her skin, the taste of her tongue, the tug of her diminutive body making its furrow into the other half of the husk mattress. How long, he wondered miserably. How long? How long must I court my own wife?

6

In the morning Karl was gone to fetch his goat before James and Anna awoke. By the time he returned, they were up and dressed and already making nuisances of themselves. They heard a bell tinkling, and looked at each other hopelessly through the billowing smoke. Anna fanned her hand before her eyes and nose uselessly.

'Oh, no. I think he's back,' she wailed.

'It's a good thing, too,' James observed.

A moment later Karl stepped to his doorway. 'What are you two doing? Burning our house down?'

'Sod doesn't – ' Anna coughed. 'Sod doesn't burn.'

'And so I am a lucky man or I would be homeless by now. Have you ever heard of a damper?' Of course they'd heard of a damper. All the cast-iron stoves had dampers in their pipes, but they hadn't considered that Karl's fireplace would have one. He stepped to the smoking mouth of the fireplace, made the necessary adjustment, then herded the two of them outside while the air cleared.

'I can see I will have to watch you two every minute to keep you out of trouble,' he said good-naturedly.

'We thought it'd help if we got the fire going.'

'Ya, it would help if you built a fire instead of a smudge. But you will come in handy when the mosquitoes need chasing away.'

Karl, it seemed, was prepared to practise the patience he'd promised to exercise. 'Tonight I will teach you to build a proper fire. Now, come and meet Nanna.'

James took to the goat at once, and there seemed an answering friendliness in the animal.

'Nanna, this is James,' Karl said affectionately, folding the goat's ear backward. 'And if he milks a goat like he builds a fire, I would run back to the Indians, if I were you,' he whispered into Nanna's ear.

Anna laughed, and at last Karl looked directly at her, his hand still toying with the soft, pink ear. Smiling, he said, 'Good morning, Anna.'

'Good morning, Karl,' she replied, her eyes sliding back to his fingers, which scratched affectionately as the animal nudged and bent her head for more. But while he scratched, Karl's eyes stayed on Anna.

'Can you make biscuits?' he asked.

'No,' she answered.

'Can you milk the goat then?'

'No.'

'Can you fry salt pork and make corn mush in the drippings?'

'Maybe. I'm not sure.'

'Now we are getting somewhere!'

And this is how it became James's job to milk the goat in the mornings, once Karl showed the boy how. And to Anna fell the chore of cooking mush in drippings, while Karl brought water from the springhouse for the horses, for use in the house and for washing outside.

He washed at the bench by the door. From the beginning it intrigued Anna how he would strip off his shirt and suffer the freezing water without so much as a shiver. Karl brought out his straightedge razor and honed it on the strop while the boy eyed his every movement.

'Does it hurt to shave, Karl?' he asked.

'Only if the blade is not sharp enough. A sharp blade makes all cutting easier. Wait till I show you how to sharpen the axe. Everywhere a logger goes he should carry his stone and use it perhaps once each hour. I have much to teach you.'

'Oh boy! I can't wait.'

'You will have to. At least until we finish your sister's cornmeal mush and salt pork.'

'Hey, Karl?'

'Ya?'

James lowered his voice. 'I don't think Anna ever cooked that before. It'll probably be pretty bad.'

'If it is, you must not tell her so. And if your first sharpening is bad, I will not tell you so, either.'

It was bad, all right. The poor salt pork had had the life fried out of it, and the cornmeal was lumpy. Amazingly, Karl made no comment. Instead, he talked of what a beautiful day it was, and of how much he hoped to get done and of how pleasant it was to be eating his meal with company. But Karl and James seemed to be enjoying some private little joke Anna was not asked to share. Still, she was pleased the way Karl seemed to be accepting her brother.

It was a jewelled day of brilliant colour – blue of sky, green of tree, bedazzled by gilt the sun lay upon them. The sun had not yet topped the periphery of the clearing before the three went out. From hooks above the mantel Karl withdrew his broadaxe, handed the hatchet to Anna. James proudly accepted the rifle once again.

'Come,' he said. 'First I will show you the place where our cabin will be.' He stalked across the clearing to the basework of stones laid in a rectangle of some sixteen by twelve feet. As he stepped to the foundation, he placed a foot upon one of its stones and pointed with the sharpest tip of his axe. 'There will be the door, facing east . . . due east. I have used my compass, for a worthy house should sit square with the earth itself.'

Turning his head toward Anna, he stated, 'No dirt floors in this house, Anna. Here we will have real plank floors. I have hauled the stones from the fields and along the creek, the flattest I could find, to hold the foundation logs.'

Then he turned, flipped the axe up until the smooth, curved ash handle slipped through his hand. Pointing again with it, he said, 'I have cleared that path and put down the skids from here to the tamaracks.' The double track of skinned logs led away like a wooden railroad track running north into the trees. 'On my land I have the straightest virgin tamarack anywhere. With logs that straight we will have a tight house, you will see. No half-timbers for us. I will use the whole log, only flattened a little to make it fit tight so the walls will be thick and warm.'

Skids and half-timbers meant nothing to Anna, but she could see by the density of the forest what it had taken him to clear that wide skid path.

'Come, we will harness Bill and Belle and get started.'

As they walked toward the barn, Karl asked, 'Have you ever harnessed a pair, boy?'

'No . . . nossir,' James answered, still looking over his shoulder at the skids.

'If you want to be a teamster, you must first learn about harnessing. You will learn now,' Karl said with finality. 'Your sister, too. There could come a time when she might need to know.'

They entered the barn, and Karl spoke in soft greeting to the animals. Nearing them, he patted them on rump, shoulder and finally on their wide foreheads, giving each horse a scratch between the eyes. It was a small building, and the space was narrow.

'Get over,' Karl said to Bill. But the horse stood contentedly, waiting for more scratching. 'Get over!' Karl repeated more sternly, wedging his body between the animal and the wall, giving Bill a solid slap that commanded but did not hurt. Bill moved over, while Anna marvelled at the man's assuredness in putting his mere body between the awesome bulk of the horse and a solid barn wall.

Karl seemed unconcerned, confident. To James he said,

'A horse who does not know what "get over" means, needs a wider vocabulary.' But even as he said it, a smile tugged his cheek, and his big hands smoothed the horse's hide affectionately. 'Remember that, boy. And remember that you talk to a horse with more than words. Your terms are only as good as your tones. Tones say much.

'Hands talk most of all. A horse gets to trust a man's hands first, and the man himself second.' All the while he spoke, Karl's hands rode the horse's hide, resting on the withers, gliding over the shoulders, patting the flanks, returning to the high poll. He looked Bill in the eye as he said, 'You know what I am talking about, ya, Bill?'

He led the horse near the wall where the harnesses hung on two thick wooden pegs. 'A horse is nearsighted, did you know that, boy? This is why the horse shies away from movement that is a ways off – because he cannot see it clear enough to trust it. But you show him what it is, up close, and he rewards you by being still.

'First comes the collar,' Karl went on. He lifted the flanged leather oval. 'This one is Bill's.' At his name, Bill jerked his head and Karl spoke to the animal. 'Ya, you know I am talking about you. Here is your collar, my curious friend.' Patiently, he showed the animal the leather before placing it over the horse's head, all the while instructing the two novices. 'You must make sure never to get the collars mixed up, for if you put the wrong one on a horse, he gets a sore neck and shoulders. A horse gets used to his own collar, just as you get used to your own shoes. You would not give a marching soldier someone else's boots now, would you, James?'

'Nossir, of course not,' James answered, his eyes never leaving Karl as the man buckled the collar beneath Bill's neck, then slipped it firmly back against the Percheron's massive shoulders.

Sliding his big hand between the horse and collar, he said, 'It should fit snug. Make sure it is not too tight, for if it presses against his windpipe, the horse will choke. If it is too long, it will rub and chafe the poor boy and cause shoulder galls.'

From two hooks on the wall, Karl withdrew the first harness, his muscles straining as he lifted it down. Approaching Bill from the left, Karl seated the hames on the collar, buckled the hame strap, walked to the horse's flank, adjusted the breaching seat. Then he walked forward again to connect breast strap to hame. Never did he move without first running his hand ahead of him along the horse's flesh or pacifying Bill with low words. The animal stood motionless, only a slow blink of his eyes indicating he was even awake.

Karl instructed the watching pair in the same tone of voice with which he spoke to Bill. Instruction and lulling words blended into a feeling of serenity. Next, he adjusted the belly band, and through it all, Anna found she was mesmerized by the gentle movements of his hands upon horseflesh, his voice in the animal's ear, in her own. She found herself thinking of the coming night, of what it would be like should be handle her as he now handled the horse.

She came to with a start, realizing that Karl had put the bit into the horse's mouth. As he led the reins through the various checkrings, he was asking her if she thought she could do all that.

'I . . . I don't know. I suppose if I could lift that heavy thing down from the wall, I could do the rest.'

'I will have to feed you well to put some muscle on your bone,' Karl said. She found he could look at her in an amused way that made his comment playful instead of critical.

But James was confidently boasting, 'I think I could do it, Karl! Can I try?'

With a silent chuckle, Karl turned the job of harnessing Belle over to the lad. James struggled beneath the weight of the harness, but with a little help from his teacher, made surprisingly few mistakes in dressing the horse in its loggingwear.

'You have a quick memory,' Karl complimented, when the boy had finished. James beamed at Anna as if he'd just invented the craft of harnessing.

Next, Karl patiently explained the why and wherefore of attaching the round oak singletree to the two smaller doubletrees. In the exact centre of the doubletree went the clevis, and finally they were ready for the massive logging chain. It was an enormous thing.

Again, Anna realized the power behind the man as Karl hefted a coil of it and dragged it over to attach to the clevis. He knelt down, securing the slip hook up into a link of the chain. 'When you are going out empty like we are now, never let the slip hook dangle at the end of the chain. It likes to catch on roots, and the horses can be hurt that way.' He rose, touching the nearest warm flank again. 'Always, the horses must be your first consideration. Without them a man is powerless here.'

'Yessir,' James responded.

Karl's eyes touched Anna momentarily, and she gave a soldierlike salute, repeating, 'Yessir!'

Karl smiled. She seemed a game thing, in spite of her narrow shoulders and willow thinness. Today she wore a dress no more suited to outside work than yesterday's had been. She would soon learn. Once the work began, she would realize that simple clothes suited best, and would choose differently.

Meanwhile, the moment Karl had dreamed of during the long winter alone had come at last – the time of turning toward his trees, husband and wife together, to work in the sun toward their future. The three of them headed out into the Minnesota morning. They walked behind the team in the heightening sun, up the skid path. The horses, with their nodding gait and long stride, set the pace. With sleeves rolled up to the elbow, Karl held the four reins, leaning backward from the waist against the tug and strut of the horses. There was a look of oneness about the man and his team, each of them well-toned and thick-muscled, with a big job to be done.

Anna, long-legged though she was, had to stretch her steps to keep up. Her long skirt swept the morning grass and soon was wet to the knees. She ignored it, listening, smelling, tasting the day. The morning had a music of its own, played out by the awakening wildlife, the squeak of leather, the chink of chains, the clop of the horses' hooves. The dew was still heavy, and the earth redolent with summerscent. There was the ever-present mustiness of leaves decaying, and the crisp flavour of vegetation renewing itself. Birch, beech, maple, black walnut, elm, poplar and willow burgeoned with life.

Karl pointed and named each tree, saying, 'A wood for each purpose a man could have,' as if he could never get over the bounty he owned, no matter how often he measured it.

'It's funny,' Anna mused, 'I always thought before that wood was just wood.'

'Ah, how much you have to learn. Each wood has a personality. Each tree has a trait that makes it . . . like a man, an individual. Here in Minnesota, a man need not worry that he will not have the proper tree for each need.'

They came to the place of the tamaracks, tall, spindly pines with scaly trunks and tapering tips swaying into the morning clouds. 'And these are my tamaracks,' Karl said with pride, looking up. 'A full sixteen feet of log before the taper begins,' he boasted. 'See what I mean? The best. Will a sixteen-foot cabin be big enough for you?' He eyed Anna sideways, wondering if she believed he could build her a house so big.

'Is that a big one?' she asked, leaning, also, to look at the top of the tamaracks.

'Most are twelve. Some fourteen. It depends upon the

trees. Here, where a man has tamaracks ... here a man has plenty.' Again Karl paused. 'More then plenty.'

Dropping her gaze down the tamarack trunks, Anna found Karl's eyes upon her. Something warm and expectant fluttered through her limbs, making her concur. 'Plenty,' she said softly. 'Sixteen feet will be plenty.'

Karl suddenly glanced at James, as if remembering he was there. 'And plenty work. Come, boy, I will show you how to fell a tree.'

He took the broadaxe and approached a tamarack, walked in a full circle around it, gauging, reckoning the course of its fall, glancing up, then back down, checking it for weighty limbs. After some deliberation, he said, 'Ya, this is a good one. It is a perfect fourteen inches in diameter. Remember that now, boy. It will make your task easier if each tree is the same size. Before you start, you must consider the wind.'

James looked skyward, saying, 'But there isn't any.'

'Good! Now you have considered it. If there is wind, we must allow for it with the very first cut of the axe.'

Anna watched and listened with only half an ear as Karl patiently explained the rudiments of tree-felling. She was far more taken by the effect Karl was having on her brother.

James doted upon his every word, even unconsciously imitating his wide-legged stance as the pair gazed up the towering trunk and planned the course of the fall. And when James asked a question, Karl's boot scraped aside pine needles to clear a small spot on the forest floor. He broke off a sturdy twig and knelt down to make a rude drawing in the dirt.

Anna smiled as James again imitated the big man, kneeling on a single knee, leaning to brace an elbow on the other in manly fashion. But James's thin back looked all the thinner when posed beside Karl's as the pair hunched forward, studying the sketch. It showed the placement of the notches, which Karl called 'kerfs.' Karl explained that the first kerf they'd make would be on the opposite side of the tree from the direction of its fall.

Anna's attention to instructions suffered further as Karl reached to point, causing the back of his shirt to stretch so tightly it looked as if it would split up the centre. Her eyes followed it downward to his waist, mesmerized by the sight of a tiny width of exposed skin where the shirttails had shinnied up. Karl's hips were narrow, but his thighs bulged, kneeling down that way.

He swivelled half around. Anna's eyes darted toward the tamaracks.

Just then James surprised Karl by pronouncing the word 'kerfs' and asking where they should go and how deep they should be. Karl grinned at the boy, then lifted his glance to Anna while he teased and taught in one and the same breath.

'I know from cutting down many trees – many, many trees – in Sweden with my papa and brothers, and right here before you came. It takes much practice to know these things.'

What patience he has, admired Anna. Even his voice and pose were patient, as well as the expression on his face. Even if she could read and write, she thought, any child would be luckier to be taught by a man like him. She herself had little tolerance. James's face radiated pure pleasure as he studied the rude sketch, committing Karl's instructions to memory.

Karl stood up, using the axe handle to push himself. When he moved, it was with easy grace, always with the axe an integral part of his pose. Anna was beginning to understand that where the man went, the axe went. He used it as a natural extension of himself.

The tool was terribly heavy, but even so Karl now held it straight out by the end of its handle, measuring the distance between himself and the bole of the tree as he took up a spraddled stance at a right angle to it. As he held the extended axe the veins along his inner elbow stood out like blue rivers, disappearing into a shirt-sleeve rolled up just above the elbow. The powerful muscles of the forearm appeared to have square edges as he poised. He explained that the first cut must be perfectly horizontal, at waist level, and he took a slow-motion swing, demonstrating. He swivelled at hip and shoulder, the muscles beneath his shirt tensing one by one while Anna watched, realizing what strength lay within the man's well-toned body.

Karl raised the axe and let its handle slip through his palm until the poll rested against the rim of his hand. He pointed with the honed edge. 'Now take your sister over there. When a tree comes down, it can be a killer if you underestimate it. The trunk can snap and jump farther and faster than even a spry boy like you could get away from.'

He turned his blue eyes on Anna, and she dropped her own and quickly followed James.

Once they were a safer distance away, Karl called across the cleared space words he had been hearing since he was only a tadpole. 'A man who is worth his salt should know exactly where a tree will fall. Some say that you can set a spike in the ground and a worthy Swede can drive it clear in with the trunk of a falling tree.'

He smiled teasingly, spotted a gnarled root and pointed at it, again with his axe. 'See that root on that oak over there? It will break in half where it humps up out of the ground.'

Again, he turned toward the tamarack. From his first movement, something magical happened within Anna. He hefted his axe, swung, first left, then right, while she looked on. With a fluid movement, he wielded the tool in perfect rhythm, his right hand slipping down to meet his left at the exact moment of impact. In a grace born of long practice, he shifted the bite of each swing, left and right, left and right, sending woodchips flying high into the air. The rhythm never slowed, and Karl's eyes never wavered from the trunk of the tree. The axe made a whistling song as it cut through the air, a thud of percussion as each measure ended with steel meeting wood.

It was impossible for Anna and James not to look up as the deepening kerfs set the tree atremble. A tremble of sorts began, too, in Anna's belly. The man, the axe, the motion, the tree – all created a dizzying spectacle that heightened her heartbeat and made her hold tightly to her stomach with both hands. There began the final anguished cracking, and slowly the scaly trunk tilted.

Karl placed the axe poll against it, gave a push, then backed off himself. He glanced over to see his two, with their chins in the air. Anna clutched her stomach, while the boy had his hands clasped upon the top of his head in a sort of ecstasy. The head of the axe slid to rest against Karl's hand as the bole shuddered, hesitated, then gave way with a final popping of bark and core, until there came the roar of limbs and foliage as the tree plunged downward with a magnificent, resounding crash onto the needle-strewn earth.

There followed the small nicker of the horses, then the mightiest stillness Anna had ever heard. She looked at Karl through the dust motes caught in shafts of sunlight, and found him watching her with a small smile on his face. He stood at ease, Karl and his axe, as if it had been someone else who'd chopped down that tree – relaxed, one knee bent, fingers curled around the axe handle, a film of barkdust settling upon his shoulders, a sprinkling of tamarack twigs drifting down near him.

And everywhere ... everywhere ... the stunning fragrance of tamarack – sweet, fresh and vital.

Before she could control it, the full sensation of what she had witnessed flashed in Anna's eyes. For perhaps the first time in her life she had seen a thing of total beauty. For that brief moment, Karl Lindstrom read it in her face and knew she felt what he felt when the tree hit the earth, landing with its farthest tip upon the gnarled root of the oak – satisfaction.

James broke the spell to come back to Karl, leaping, arms flapping, exclaiming, 'Wow! That was really something! When can I do that?'

Karl laughed in his slow way and nudged the boy lightly in the stomach with the poll of his axe. 'I think you will not fell many before you are asking when you can stop. Right, Anna?' He was reluctant to break the feeling of affinity he'd sensed between the two of them.

'How many can *you* do before you stop?' she asked, coming nearer, still awed by what she'd seen.

'As many as I must,' he answered, 'while my two helpers take care of smaller branches and pulling the logs down the skid trail. Now we must trim the tree and do the bucking.'

'Bucking?' James ventured.

'Chopping the tree into the length we want.'

Together they set to work using axe and hatchet to trim the scraggly branches from the tamarack. Anna was assigned the task of dragging the branches away to form a scrub pile.

When the tree was stripped, Karl measured it by axe lengths, marked the sixteen-foot spot with a small notch, then mounted the trunk at that spot. Grasping his axe, he bounded up to a stance upon the rough bark. He stood with feet perfectly balanced, about half an axe handle's width apart, the notch halfway between his boots. This time he talked between swings, explaining to James that the two kerfs he would cut, one on each side of the log, must form a perfect forty-five-degree angle to one another.

The axe went soaring and swooping again and again. With each stroke Karl bent lower, lower, lower, until he was doubled over at the waist, chopping so near to the ground. Then, with the agility of a monkey, he turned, scarcely needing to curl his toes to keep abreast of the log as the opposite kerf was honed away with precise strokes. He leapt from the tree, leaving behind the severed sections, each with a perfect V-shaped tip.

Four more trees were felled and bucked. 'A good logger does not raze the forest, but only thins it,' Karl explained. 'Therefore we take one tree from here, one from there and one from over there.'

The logs trimmed and ready now for skidding. Karl demonstrated the proper technique of lifting, bending the knees rather than the back. With a powerful effort he raised the end of one log off the earth, and James slung the heavy chain beneath it.

When the team was brought over, Karl instructed, 'Attach the load close to the singletree, boy, like this, then the skidding is easier for the horses.' Accompanied by the chink of chain as the big hook fell into a link, Karl warned, 'But when you do this yourself, you must stand to the side as you work. Only a fool gets between his team and the load.'

Then Karl gave a single command and the horses lugged the log toward the top of the skid trail to be deposited. Even as they moved, Karl instructed the lad who matched the big man step for step, stretching his youthful legs unnaturally to do so. 'When you are skidding, you must think ahead before giving the command to turn. Always keep the draft angle wide, out of consideration for your horse-flesh. The straighter the course, the easier the work is for them.'

Heading the horses back for a second log, Karl's voice changed; nothing more than a faint cluck set the team on the move. But when their load was heavy, Karl spoke to them in melodic tones. '*Eee-easy*, now.' And the tractable animals flexed their huge shoulders, leaning into their burden with muscle wrought patiently, as ordered. And so it was for each new log – advice for the boy, an order for the team, each treated with respect to individual intelligence and ability.

Never in her life had Anna seen James this happy. He absorbed every word Karl spoke, kneeling when Karl knelt, rising when Karl rose, watching when Karl demonstrated, striding when Karl strode. When, at last, Karl handed James the reins, telling him to take the team to the next log, the boy looked up with anxious uncertainty in his eyes.

'Really, Karl?'

'Really. You want to be a teamster, do you, boy?'

'Yessir . . . but – '

'The horses must learn to get used to you, too. Now is as good a time as any.'

James wiped his palms on his thighs.

'I will be right beside you,' Karl assured him. 'Just hold the reins like I showed you and do not pull on them. Bill and Belle know what to do. They will teach you as much as I will, you will see.'

The boy took the sweat-smooth leathers into his smaller hands, cooing, '*Eaaasy now*.' With the horses' initial steps, James's eyes grew wide.

But Karl spoke reassuringly to the boy, much as he did to Belle and Bill. 'You are doing good, lad, let them have their heads . . . Ya . . . good . . . Now rein left . . . light, light . . . good.' By the time the horses drew nigh the next log, James was smiling. His chest jutted in satisfaction.

Karl, too, seemed pleased. 'You will do good as long as you remember *never* ride the logs, and *never* walk beside them once we start skidding down the trail and the logs ride sideways. If the end of a log strikes a tree, it can swing away and crack your legs like they were no more than kindling. Only walk behind the load!'

'Yessir, I'll remember.'

More instructions were necessary as the load of logs was bound with a chain at each end, then towed down the skid trail to the cabin site. They went down together with the first load. Karl allowed James to handle the reins, showing him the correct speed and the importance of avoiding

117

stumps, which edged near the open way and were hazardous to both horse and driver. He also explained how the downward slope had been kept gentle to avoid the risk of a load sliding into the horses' hocks.

When the logs were dropped at the clearing, Karl watered the horses, saying that a hot horse should never be fed icy water. Instead, he used water he'd drawn that morning. Next, the horses were fed – hay before grain – then watered again. Finally, the animals were allowed to rest, while the three went inside for their noonday meal.

After dinner, James took the team out empty and headed back up the trail. He pleased Karl by remembering to hook the gaff into the links before starting. Karl and Anna came behind, he sweat-stained, bearing his axe and gun, she pink-nosed, bearing a basket in which to collect woodchips and carrying the hatchet.

'You're a fine teacher, Karl,' she said, watching his boots whisk the grass with each step, unable to look him in the eye.

'The boy is quick and willing,' Karl replied modestly, looking ahead.

'I've never seen him quite so happy,' Anna peeked up at Karl.

'No?' His blue gaze fell on her face, which moved beside him in his noontime shadow.

'No,' she said, thoughtfully. 'He's never been around a man before.'

'What about his father?' He gave Anna a sidelong look, but she quickly turned her gaze to James and the horses.

'James never knew his father.'

'Did you?'

She flashed him a quick eye before admitting, 'Me neither.' Then she bent down, never breaking stride, and whisked up a little stick and started fraying its end with her fingernail.

'I am sorry, Anna. Children should know their fathers.

I myself could not have come here and started such a life without the wise teachings of my own father.'

'And now you teach it all to James,' she said reflectively.

'Ya. I am lucky.'

'Lucky?' she questioned.

'What man is not lucky who has learned so much and can keep all these good ways alive forever by passing them on to another willing pupil?'

'And so I am forgiven, Karl, for bringing him and not telling you before?'

'You are many times forgiven, Anna,' he said, stalking along beside her, wondering if he had ever really resented the boy.

'And you really enjoy teaching him?'

'Ya. Very much.'

'He learned a lot this morning. So did I.'

'It has been a memorable morning. The teaching has been part of what made it so.' Then, looking from the thin shoulders of the lad who drove the team ahead of them, to the glorious woodland surrounding them and, lastly, to Anna's face, he finished, 'The morning in which we have begun building our log house.'

His face wore a look of serenity, the look of a man who knows where he's been, where he is and where he's heading.

To Anna, who'd never been blessed with such knowledge, the look spoke loudly of the inner peace garnered from the simple knowing of one's self. No, Anna thought, I do not know who my father was. I do not know where I came from. I do not know where I'll be headed once Karl learns my secret. But now is mighty good. Yes, now is mighty good, she thought, walking beside her husband to continue their work in the sun-strewn day, woodchips once again flying and perfuming the air, the song of the axe careening back to them from the green forest walls around them.

7

The trio melded into a routine of chopping, trimming, hauling, hitching and driving as the day wore on. The sun was high upon their shoulders. Karl stripped off his shirt and worked bare to the waist.

Anna had difficulty keeping her eyes from sliding time and again to the golden head, the tanned torso, the lean hips, the flexing arms. He performed with a fluidity akin to a dance. He was tapered like the tamaracks themselves, from shoulder to hip. The muscles in his arms bunched and hardened with the flow of his work, the cords of his neck stood out. The veins of his arms became defined each time he poised with the axe at its apex above his head. From behind, she watched his shoulder muscles gather in ridges at each fall of the blade, relax with the release, then hunch again.

He would bend to brush away some errant woodchip or branch, leaning on the axe handle, one foot balanced behind him. And Anna would find her eye drawn to the spot where the shadow of his spine widened and disappeared into the back of his britches. Sometimes, without warning, he would turn and find her watching him, and she would quickly lower her gaze from the sparkle of sun off the gold hairs of his chest and the line where it tapered down his abdomen.

'Are you tired, Anna?' he would ask. 'Are you hot, Anna? Have a drink,' he would say. Always she glanced down the skid path, away from him.

Soon another tree would go crashing down, and the two would find themselves enjoying the exhilaration of the moments just afterward. Always their eyes met then, if only briefly, before they found themselves working side by side, he with the axe, she with the hatchet, removing branches, while James continued to skid with the team.

Then Karl straightened from his task, saying, 'Your cheeks will be burned. Here, take my hat.' He plopped his soiled straw hat on her head, carrying with it the smell of him.

'I had a straw hat once,' she said, concentrating on her chopping. 'One of the women at – someone I knew gave it to me, but it was almost a goner when she decided she was done with it.' She whacked another branch off, then added, 'It had a pink ribbon around the crown.'

'Hats with pink ribbons are scarce here in Minnesota.'

'Doesn't matter,' she said. 'I'll get along.' She started dragging a load of branches to the scrub pile.

He noticed the dark rings beneath her arms and said, 'There is a deep spot in my creek where we can all go to cool off at the end of the day.'

'How deep?' she asked, wondering just what he meant by 'cool off.' Wearing what?

'Over your head.'

'I can't swim.'

'I will teach you.'

'How cold is it?'

'Not as cold as the spring.'

'Oho! It better not be!'

'You will try it then?'

At last she stopped tugging at the branches and looked over at him. 'We'll see.'

'You really do not like to bathe, then?'

Embarrassed now, she lunged again at a bough. 'It's just that we never had to before. I mean, nobody ever made us. There was nobody to tell us what to do.'

'What about your mother?' Karl asked, amazed.

Anna gave a tug that sent her quick-footing it in reverse to keep from tumbling. 'She couldn't have cared less,' she said expressionlessly.

By the time Anna and James made their last trip down the hill, the shadows had lengthened and their strides had shortened. They stumbled along after Karl, who still strode sure and long and vigorously.

Looking at the wilted pair of helpers, Karl laughed. 'Go to the house, you two, but do not start any fires. I will come in as soon as I have seen to the horses.' He knew how tired they were after the day they'd put in.

The fire-making and supper-making fell to him. He showed James the proper way to build a blaze, then showed Anna the proper way to build a stew. Alas, the two observed him listlessly, nearly asleep on their chairs. When the venison and turnips and wild onions were bubbling away on the hob, Karl could not help laughing again at his sapped companions.

'If I do not do something quick to keep you two awake I will be eating all that stew by myself. And I have had my fill of solitary meals. Come!' He nudged each of them. 'I think it is time we went for that swim.'

The two sat disconsolately, while he gathered up clean clothing and flannels for drying. 'Come along. Get your dry things and follow me.'

'Karl, you're a merciless mule!' Anna complained, feeling a rush of intimacy in the criticizing.

'Ya, I am,' he smilingly agreed. 'And you, Anna, are a musty one.'

Shamed, she could only follow him, ordering James to do the same.

The trail followed the bank of the creek, a narrow footpath worn by Indians and animals in the long past. The creek was a purling brook that bubbled over stones in some spots, ran smooth in others. In most places it could be leaped in a single bound. The spot to which Karl led them had had the help of the beavers in creating a serene pond above a dam. Maidenhair and bracken ferns brushed their knees, while beneath the thick press of fronds, feather-grass sprang up. The smooth water was dotted with wild violets, shaded by tall virgin elms that stepped back to give sprawling black willow bushes first chance at the stream's edge.

The last thing in the world Anna wanted to do was climb into that frigid water. 'Do you do this every day?' she asked Karl.

He was already stripping off his shirt. 'Every day in the summer. In the winter I use my bathhouse where I sweat myself clean like in Sweden.'

'Do you have some kind of fetish for cleanliness?'

He stared at her, shirt hanging in his hands, while she stood without making any move to remove her clothing. 'A person keeps clean,' he said simply.

'Yes,' she agreed lamely.

'Why do you not – ' He felt suddenly shy. 'Why do you not go put your things in the willow thicket there while James and I get in?'

Mutely, she turned and headed for cover.

'Come on, James,' she heard after two splashes. 'We will hide behind the beaver dam while your sister gets in.'

She shucked down to her shift and crept out of hiding. The two were gone; all their clothes lay in heaps.

Anna hesitated. A toe in the water confirmed her sus-picion. It was freezing! A person keeps clean, she said to herself, grimacing as she took the hated plunge.

At her shriek, laughter sounded, then James called, 'Come on in, Anna. It ain't so bad once you get used to it and move around some.'

She sat down, screamed again. 'James Reardon and Karl Lindstrom, you're both a pair of liars and I hate you!'

For an answer came a big laugh answered by calls from

birds perched nearby, watching these foolish humans who removed their plumage before bathing.

'I'm in now, you can come out!' she called. When Karl and James emerged and moved toward her, she had no choice but to dip in up to her neck. She didn't want either one of them seeing her puckered nipples through the flimsy shift.

'James, you little traitor!' she teased. 'You never liked bathing any more than I did.'

'It's different when you can get clear in.' His head disappeared, popped up with a big grin on it. 'I dare you to duck under, Anna!'

'Oh yeah?' Gamely, she dipped, only to come up sputtering and shuddering. Eyes still closed, she playfully nagged, 'I hate your pool, Karl Lindstrom! Can't you heat it up for me?'

'I will go down and ask it.' He flipped his feet, dove and with a flash of white skin was gone. He emerged across the way and yelled, 'Sorry, Anna. The beavers do not agree. It is as warm as it is going to get.'

He struck out in long, even strokes, effortlessly swimming the distance to her. 'Come, I will take you to where the ledge angles down, then we will swim back toward shore. Do not be afraid.'

He took her hands under the water and pulled her slowly off her feet. She glided, mouthing water. He smiled at the way the droplets clung to her eyelashes and hair.

'Don't take me too far,' she begged.

'Do not worry. Do you think I would risk you now that you are here?'

'Maybe!' she sputtered. 'What are you going to do with a woman who can't cook stew?'

'There are uses I can think of,' he said quietly, so James could not hear. His mouth, like hers, was halfway beneath the surface. They bobbed, weightless, holding hands and learning each other's eyes, with eyelashes stuck wetly

124

together, hair swept back in furrows and skin jewelled by occasional runnels.

'How about a woman who cannot bake bread?'

'She can be taught,' he burbled, the water lapping about his lips.

'Or make soap?'

'She can be taught,' he repeated.

'To make it or to use it?'

'Both.' And he opened his mouth, took in a mouthful of water and spit it right between her eyes.

'You big Swedish bully!' she yelped, coming after him. But he was gone like quicksilver to the deep near James.

'Be good and I will come and teach you to swim,' he backtalked.

'Why? I don't like your miserable pond, anyway!'

But a serious look came over his face. Then he pointed just behind her, asking James, 'Is that a snapping turtle?'

Poor Anna almost broke her neck wrenching around. Her hands dug wildly at the water as she scrambled to get out. On her way up the bank, her pantaloons sagged, revealing one white cheek before she snatched angrily at them and turned with hands on hips, bellering, 'Karl Lindstrom, see if I come in there again! That wasn't funny!'

But Karl and James were slapping the surface of the water in disgusting merriment, falling over backward like fools, while Anna fumed. She sat miserably on shore, hugging her arms, shivering while the two took up surface diving, racing and exploring the outer perimeter of the beaver dam. Stubbornly she sat until Karl swam toward her. 'Come on, Anna. I won't tease any more.'

She crossed her arms over her chest. Her nipples were like spearpoints now.

'Should I come and get you?' he threatened, taking one more step. Her eyes dropped to the level where the water sliced across his hips, revealing the hollows just below the hipbones.

'No! I'm coming!' She leaped up and plunged in, venturing farther than before. Karl taught her to roll on her back and flap her hands at her sides, like a fish using its fins. But lying that way with his arm slung beneath her back, her breasts became islands with no more than a cloud-thin veil of clinging cotton to disguise their darker centers. She quickly flipped onto her stomach again.

Anna and Karl bobbed out to the ledge and swam toward shore many times. Once, heading back out, she overshot the shallows and panicked when her feet touched nothingness. Karl grabbed her from behind with one swift flexing of his steely arm, and again her feet touched sand. But his arm lingered long after she was safe, spanning her ribs, touching the bottom of her breasts, pulling her back against his nakedness below the water.

Then James came near, and Karl released her. The trio broke for shore.

When Karl announced their stew must now be done, Anna was surprised to find she had forgotten her tiredness while they were frolicking. They each went their separate ways to dry and dress, then met back on the path to walk home. On their way they were accompanied by night peepers and frogs who'd tuned up to orchestrate dusk.

Fragrant aroma greeted them at their door. Karl enjoyed supper, especially watching Anna and James polish off enough food for a pair of grizzlies. Before the bowls were emptied for the last time, James drooped and wilted, then his sister followed suit. Karl scooted them off to bed.

With full night fallen, Karl lit his pipe and wandered out to the barn. Belle and Bill, their great breaths pumping slowly, shifted contentedly, thumping hello in their stalls. They knew who entered, knew a oneness with their visitor. His gentle hand stroked the wide heads between the eyes. Finally, when the pipe coals turned pungent, dying away, came the deep voice. 'She is a spunky one, my Anna. What

126

do you think, Bill? Not as easy to break to the halter as your Belle, here.'

In the dark sod house Karl lay aside his pipe, then his clothes. He settled into the enveloping cornhusks. Automatically, he reached out to encircle the slumbering Anna. He pulled her into his curve, knowing at once content and want. He thought about her breasts and how they had looked in the water. They lay now so close above his arm. All he need do was shift his arm slowly, slide his hand upward and he would be touching her breast at last. How badly he wanted to caress her, to know that first feel of her.

But she slept in utter exhaustion while Karl's sense of fairness rankled. When he explored Anna for the first time, he wanted it to be a shared thing. He wanted her awake, aware, receptive and responsive.

He could hold off. He had waited all this time to ease his loneliness. What they'd shared today – the three of them – would be enough for now. That and the feel of her sleeping body curved against his belly, the texture of her hair where he pressed his face against it upon her back.

8

Anna awakened to a myriad sounds: bird-song so involved it became tuneless chatter, the crack of the axe, male voices, a short spurt of laughter. The bed beside her was empty. So was the pallet on the floor. The cabin door stood open, beckoning the long sun to cascade across the floor in a welcome rush of gold. She clenched her fists and stretched, lynxlike and twisting, savouring the goodness of everything – the sounds, the sun, the snugness.

Arising, she found a blanket had been strung up across one corner to act as her dressing room.

When Karl came inside, he saw only her backside. He eyed it appreciatively as she poked her head around the drape to investigate her niche of privacy.

'Good morning, Anna.'

She whirled around to find him smiling at her, sunshafts at his back, hugging a burden of firewood against his chest. In his other hand was the axe again, looking ever so right.

'Good morning, Karl.' She stood with bare toes curled against the dirt floor, her nighty wrinkled, her hair in terrible disarray.

Karl couldn't have been more pleased with her appearance.

Suddenly, Anna realized that they'd both been stupidly smiling at one another, he with perhaps thirty pounds of wood on his arm, she with a blanket pulled across her front. She looked at the rope from which it hung, patted the cloth to make it wave a little and asked, 'Did you remodel your house for me?'

He laughed and answered, 'I guess I did.' Then he went to the fireplace with his load.

'Thank you,' she said to his strong back as it bent, sending the wood clattering.

He turned, his eyes flicked momentarily over her breasts, then back to her face. 'I should have thought of it yesterday, with the boy here and all.'

Having followed the path of his eyes, she grew flustered, so asked quickly, 'Were you teaching him to use the axe?'

'Ya, on something a little smaller than a standing tamarack.'

'How did he do?

James sailed in just then, answering her question. 'Look-it, Anna! I split nearly all the wood Karl brought in.'

'Nearly all?' Karl repeated, with a cock of his head.

'We-e-e-ll . . . half anyway.'

All three laughed at once, then James asked, 'Which pail should I use for the milk?'

'Any one from the springhouse.' Karl nodded toward it.

Before James darted away again, excited, eager, he bubbled, 'You were right, Karl. Nanna came home all by herself to get milked, and she came right up to me and nuzzled my hand as if she knew I was the one who'd be taking care of that job from now on.'

Within Anna grew the realization of what this place, these duties, this man, meant to a boy of thirteen, and just how good it would be for her brother to grow to manhood learning a life such as this. 'He's awful happy, Karl,' she said, knowing no other way to express it.

'So am I,' Karl answered, turning to look over his shoulder at her from where he hunkered to his fire-making again.

As she slipped behind the drape, Karl found himself intrigued by the sight of her bare feet peeping below it and lost track of what he was supposed to be doing. He watched her nightgown fall in a heap around her ankles. The blanket billowed here and there. Anna's feet turned around toward the trunk, which was also behind the blanket now. Then she seemed to balance on a single foot.

'Ow!' Anna heard from the direction of the fireplace.

'Karl? What's wrong?'

'Nothing.'

'Then why did you say "ow"?'

'I think there will be a little skin burning with the kindling, that's all.'

Anna's hands fell still. *Karl* made a mismove with his axe? she thought wonderingly. *Karl*? Then, looking down at her bare feet and the space between the floor and the blanket, she smiled widely to herself.

When his fire was started, he called, 'Do you know how to build a pancake?'

'No.'

'You will after today. I thought I could give up these kitchen duties once you came, and be a woodsman instead. But I think I must teach you how to make pancakes first.'

Anna grimaced. She herself already liked the woods far better than the kitchen, but she buttoned the last button and stepped out to meet her domestic fate.

'So, teach me how to build a pancake,' she ordered in an affected tone of command.

'Annuuuh!' he exclaimed when he saw her, drawing out her name. 'What is this you wear?'

'Britches.' She flapped her hands.

'Britches? Ya, I see it is britches but ... but you are a woman.'

'Karl, my skirts were wet to the knees before we got halfway out to the tamaracks yesterday. And they caught on the branches and made me trip, and got pitch all over them from dragging across the scrub. And ... and they made my work harder, so I decided to try on a pair of James's britches. Look!' She spun around. 'They fit!'

'Ya, I see, but I do not know what to think. In Sweden

130

'no lady would be caught hiding in her pantry in britches.'

'Oh, fiddle!' she snapped lightly. 'In Sweden I'll bet there are so many men to build your houses the women don't have to help, right?'

'Ya, that is right,' he reluctantly admitted. 'But, Anna, I do not know about these britches.'

'Well, I know. I know I'm not tripping over soggy skirts. Besides, who's gonna see me except you and James?'

He couldn't actually think of a logical argument. He had thought her dresses inappropriate. But britches? He could not resist asking, 'I suppose in Boston there was no one to stop you from running loose in britches any time you wanted either?'

She looked sideways at him, then away. She found the still-rumpled bed and made herself busy flipping the covers smooth. 'I did pretty much as I pleased there.'

'Ya. I think you sure did. And it did not please you to learn pancake batter?'

'Here I am,' she flipped her hands palms up, 'ready to learn. But I'm not promising just how much I'll like it.'

Karl explained that he had to adapt his mama's recipe for filmy, light Swedish pancakes because he had to do without eggs here.

He looked so utterly ridiculous, her great big Karl, standing there at the table, mixing up pancakes, she could not help teasing him. Throughout the lesson she refused to be serious, while he instructed her in odd measurements.

'Two palms full of flour.'

'Whose palms? Yours or mine?' she kidded him.

'Two pinches of salt.'

'I might have to borrow your palms and your fingers when it's my turn, because yours are a different size than mine.'

'Enough saleratus – leavening – to fill perhaps the half shell of a hazelnut.'

'And if I've never seen a hazelnut?' she asked

131

mischievously, eliciting his promise to show her one soon, and an order to straighten up and pay attention, though he tried hard to hold a straight face.

'A lump of lard the size of two walnuts or so.'

'Now – walnuts – at last, I know! It is the first useful measurement you have given me.'

'No eggs,' he said hopelessly. 'No chickens, no eggs!'

'No eggs!' she exclaimed, pretending chagrin. 'Whatever shall I do? I'm sure my pancakes will be tough as calluses without any eggs!'

He was having the utmost difficulty getting through this without kissing her teasing little face. He promised that soon they would hunt for prairie chicken eggs. Then came goat's milk.

'Enough to make it the right thickness,' which she observed at extremely close range, getting her head in his way so he could not see, telling him ignorantly when she thought the batter was 'just right.'

The eggless pancakes proved sumptuous fare, indeed, especially when topped with syrup, which Karl explained proudly, was tapped and boiled down right here just this spring, from his own maples, which he promised to show her soon.

Anna was forced to miss the harnessing of the horses that morning, for she was left behind to clean up the dishes and scour the wooden pail from the goat's milk, using the disgusting yellow lye soap, which burned her skin. It was becoming increasingly apparent to Anna why a man needed help out here in the wilderness. Who in his right mind would not want someone to take care of these unpalatable household tasks?

But once again free of the cabin, her spirits blossomed. Outside was where she loved it best, with the wind lifting her hair, and the horses snorting and tossing their heads impatiently, and James pleased because he'd helped with the harnessing again today and had remembered everything quite clearly, and Karl seizing up his axe and the five of them all heading out to the tamaracks again.

They flushed a covey of grouse that morning, and Karl brought down one of the elusive darting birds with a single shot, laughing when he lowered the gun to find Anna squatted down in terror with her elbows over her ears.

'It is only a grouse,' he said, 'my little brave boy in britches.'

'Only a grouse? It sounded like a hurricane!'

'Next time you hear it, you will know it is only wings, and you will not need to hide like a mouse.'

The ease with which Karl brought the bird down convinced Anna that he was a practised marksman, along with everything else. He gutted the kill immediately. At noon he completed the dressing of the bird, while James watched and learned, and Anna gagged.

Karl beamed with pride when he showed her where he kept his wild rice. It, too, was harvested off a slough on his own land in the northeast section. He set the rice to soak in boiling water, promising them a delightful supper. Later he taught them how to stuff the grouse with the musty-smelling rice, and how to wrap it all up in damp plantain leaves and plunge it into the coals along with yams wrapped likewise. He showed them how to sweeten the yams with maple syrup. Their meal would be truly delicious when they returned from their swim.

Anna was less tired that night, and also somewhat less unwilling to dip into the cold water. While Karl and James stood in chest-high water, throwing pink rocks into the drop-off, concentrating hard on just where they'd have to dive to retrieve them again, Anna took an enormous breath, glided underwater from behind Karl and bit him on the ankle, touching nothing else of his skin. Karl yelped. Anna heard him clear underwater, and came up howling and sputtering, the sand all awhirl where Karl had jumped and kicked at the underwater menace.

'Oh, Karl, you're so funny!' she gasped. 'Scared of a little fish that doesn't make half the commotion of a bunch of dumb ruffed grouse!'

But one glance at Karl, and she knew the play war was on. He crouched. He narrowed his eyes menacingly, and lowered his face till it rode the water like a crocodile, only his eyes showing as he glided silently in pursuit. She backed away, hands spread to fend him off.

'Karl ... no, Karl ... I was just teasing, Karl!' She thrashed wildly, laughing and screaming, trying to get away from him.

James hollered, 'Git her, Karl! Git her!'

'James, you little turd! I'm your sister! You're supposed to be on my side!' she yelled, clumsily ploughing water. She looked over her shoulder and found she was getting nowhere fast.

'Git her, Karl! She called me a turd!'

'I heard her. Do you think a woman with such a nasty tongue should be punished?'

'Yeah! Yeah!' cheered the disloyal James, loving every minute of it.

'Traitor!' she badgered while Karl advanced, a feral gleam in his eye. Suddenly, he disappeared. Anna turned a circle, but the surface was broken only by little ripples. 'Where'd he go? Karl? Where are – '

Like a whale surfacing, Karl lunged up and out of the water, catching Anna with a shoulder behind her knees, pitching her high in the air while the forest reverberated with her shriek. She flopped butt-up and landed with an ignominious splat! Up she came, with hair every place but where it should be, to the tune of James and Karl guffawing in great camaraderie.

'I think I just made a new kind of sea monster!' Karl pointed at Anna, who was coming on with fingers gnarled, snarling beautifully through the mop of dripping hair. Karl feigned helplessness when she caught him with both hands from behind his waist and wrestled him off his feet. She got the worst of it, naturally, for she went down backward and Karl sat on top of her. Under the water her arms slipped down on his water-slicked body and came into contact with more than just his belly. Swiftly, he turned in that liquid world, caught her against his chest and together they shot up like geysers, laughing into each other's faces.

'Oh, Anna, my little sea monster,' he said, 'what did I do before you were here?'

They all went to bed at the same time that night, in the room flavoured with tobacco smoke and fellowship. When the cornhusks quit rustling, James's voice came lazily. ' 'Night, Karl. 'Night, Anna.'

'Goodnight, James,' the two wished together.

Then Karl found Anna's hand and made patterns on its palm with his thumb. At last he pulled her nearer, making her roll on her side to face him, while he did likewise. 'Are you tired?' he whispered very near her lips.

'No,' she whispered back, thinking, no, no, no, no, no! I'm not at all tired.

'Last night I was disappointed you went to sleep so fast.'

'So was I,' she whispered, thrilled by his simple words and the feel of his hard thumb softly brushing. Her heart beat in double time while the palm of Anna's hand grew hot where Karl stroked it. They lay so still, with eyes wide open, noses almost touching, breathing upon each other.

James sighed, and Karl's thumb stopped moving. His breath warmed her face. With a slight movement, he touched the tip of his nose to hers. Silently, he let the touch speak for him while feelings of greater need coursed through his body. His grip on her hand became almost painful. A hint of movement brought Karl's lips lightly to hers.

Do that again, Karl – harder, she thought, while her heart hammered wildly. They lay unmoving, childlike, knees to knees, nose to nose, lips to lips, breath to breath, absorbed in the growing feeling of goodness at such simple nearness.

'Today was so good, Anna, having you and the boy here. I . . . I feel such things,' he whispered.

'What kind of things?'

'Things about all three of us,' he whispered hoarsely, wishing he knew better how to tell her what he meant. 'Working together on the logs – it is good. Eating together, swimming. I feel . . . I feel full, Anna.'

'Is . . . is that what makes it? Working together and all the rest?' She nudged his thumb aside so hers could stroke his palm. Briefly his warm breath stopped falling upon her face, then she heard him swallow.

'You feel it, too, Anna?'

'I think so. I . . . I don't know, Karl. I just know it's different here from Boston. It's better. We never had to work before. Working here, helping you . . . I don't know. It doesn't really seem like work.' She wanted to add things she didn't know how to say, things about his smile, his teasing, his patience, his love of this place, which somehow had started to seep into her, even the sweet peace of weariness last night, a satisfied weariness she had never before known. But these were things she yet only sensed but could not put voice to.

'For so long I dreamed of you being here to help with the cabin. Now it is just like I thought it would be. Going out all together in the morning, working all day, relaxing together in the evenings. I feel . . . how good it is to laugh again, to laugh with you.'

'You make me laugh so easy, Karl.'

'Good. I like to see you laughing. You and the boy, too.'

'Karl?'

'Hm?'

'We never had much reason to laugh before. Here, though, it's different.'

It pleased him that he should have provided this nicety, one he had not consciously sought to provide. He felt her admission was more than a simple statement of enjoyment, sensed it as her invitation for affection. Soundlessly, he moved, taking a piece of her upper lip between his, tugging lightly at it, as if to say, come nearer.

She obliged, and their mouths met softly, each of them slightly open, hesitant, hopeful, yet infinitely childish in their slowness, their willingness to let the other move first. There had been only that chaste kiss the first night. But this kiss had been born on the rising sun, had been foretold by their first 'good mornings' while Karl stood holding an armload of wood and Anna stood holding her curtain. Through the day the certainty of this kiss had grown, enriched by their teasing and good humour and their growing sense of familiarity with each other.

He slowly straightened his knees to move nearer. This time he took her lips fully, undemandingly at first, but his wet, warm tongue came seeking, riding upon the seam of her lips as if dissolving some sugar stitches he tasted there. Dissolve them he did, feeling beneath his tongue a first opening of her own mouth. Emboldened, he cradled the back of her neck, pulling her into the kiss, using his tongue to tease her away from passivity. What Karl waited for was some first sign, a movement, a touch of encouragement. His exploration touched a response in Anna and she, too, straightened her legs.

Cautiously, she laid her hand upon his cheek. Never before had she caressed him in any way. The touch of her hand upon his skin raised an ardour in Karl that became difficult to control. Beneath her palm Anna felt his cheek muscles stretch as his mouth widened. His tongue entered her mouth more forcefully while she felt the strokes of it through her palm and his cheek.

Never had Anna experienced kissing as an enjoyable thing. Now was awakened in her the knowledge that things like this could be different from the way she had always thought them. About this there was nothing sordid or ugly. There was no compulsion to push this man away, no crawling of skin, no stinging of tears. There was instead a feeling that he honoured her, and thereby honoured the act upon which they embarked. She sensed in Karl the unfolding wonder he experienced in taking her nearer fulfilment one slow step at a time. Anna felt herself unfolding, too, like the petals of a flower until the full beauty of the blossom is revealed.

With a slow relaxing of muscle, he lowered his chest across hers, resting there upon her breast to see what she'd do. But she only laid her hand on the bare skin of his shoulder blade, testing again the rightness of what she felt, training her hand to move down the ridge beneath her palm. How well she remembered it after watching it flex in the sun these two days.

Karl collapsed with his face buried in the pillow he'd filled for her with cattail down, basking in the first tentative exploration of her hand upon his back. Needing more, he arched away, freeing her pinned hand. But when she didn't seem to understand what he needed, he found the hand there beneath him and nudged it onto his shoulder, then settled down upon her, his face lost once more in the pillow beside her head.

Anna could not help vividly recalling the expression on his face when he had told of bringing Nanna inside the house for company during winter. She remembered, too, the way Karl's hand had toyed with the goat's ear. She had never known before that men needed simple touching.

The years of aloneness slid away with each pass of her hands along his skin. Their hearts, pressed tightly together, spoke of the human need both had harboured for so long. Within Anna, to whom such a feeling had also been denied for long years, a desperate voice warned she could lose all this warmth that radiated to her once Karl carried this act to its climax. But it was a good thing to feel so at one with another human being. She could not stop her hands from playing upon his back just a little longer.

'Oh, Anna, what you do to me,' he said huskily, suddenly raising up, pinning her down with both hands on her arms. 'Do you know what you do to me?' he whispered with a kind of vehemence that warned her she had perhaps already gone too far. But at Karl's movement, the cornhusks rustled, and they heard James make a sound as he rolled over. Karl's head jerked up in alert.

They waited a moment before Anna whispered, 'I think I know, Karl, but . . .' She had received the reprieve she needed, from James. She was confused herself, liking everything so far, still afraid to let it go further. 'Karl, I wish . . .' Never before had she felt such dread of hurting someone's feelings. It was a new thing to Anna, this concern she had for Karl. She knew she must pick her way carefully. 'It's only been three days. I feel like each day we've gotten to know each other a little better, but I think we need more time.'

He'd done the thing he most wanted to avoid: he'd pushed her too fast. By now Karl liked Anna so much, and felt she liked him, too. Still, he tried to look at it from her point of view. She was perhaps afraid of being hurt. For this Karl could not blame her. 'I should not have pushed you this way,' he admitted. 'I only thought to touch you, but I find it is hard to hold back.'

'Karl, please don't be so hard on yourself. I liked it and it's all right you touched me and kissed me. I'm only getting to know you better when I return the touches, like any woman wants to know her husband. Please understand, Karl . . .'

She wondered exactly how to say what she meant. She wanted him – yes – yet she wanted to put off the time of consummation because she feared afterward he would find her repugnant, and that would be the end of this interlude of adjustment she was so enjoying.

Also, Anna wanted more time to be wooed. It had nothing to do with whether or not she was a virgin. She was a woman, and as such had had dreams of soldiers with braids and epaulettes. How could she make him understand that braids and epaulettes mattered little, but that she wanted the joy of anticipation to go on a while longer? She wanted to be courted when she was already married. How absurd it sounded, even to her. Still, she had to try to explain.

'Do you know what I want?'

'No, Anna, what?' He thought he would give her anything if she would only not deny him interminably.

'I want some more days like today ... first. I want laughing and teasing and looking at each other across the way and ... oh, I don't know. The things we'd have done if we had met in Sweden and you had bought me that hair ribbon, I guess. All girls want that sort of thing, like we talked about the other night. Do you understand, Karl?'

'I understand, but for how long do you want such a thing?' The intensity was waning from his voice, and she thought perhaps she had succeeded in keeping from alienating him.

'Oh, a little while, Karl. Just a little while for you to be my suitor instead of my husband. A little while to enjoy getting to know each other.'

'So you like some teasing and some ...' Karl could not thing of the right word.

'Flirting?' she filled in.

'A true American word – flirting.'

'Yes, Karl, maybe I do. For both of us.'

'You are a strange girl, Anna, writing letters to me to agree to be my wife sight unseen, now demanding me to flirt with you. What am I to do with such a whiskey-haired girl anyway?'

'Do as she asks,' Anna said coquettishly, something quite new to her.

'You will have your way, Anna. But before you do, let me have another kiss like the last one. Just one.'

9

If Anna wanted flirting, she got it in subtle ways during the following days. Karl could do things in the most off-hand manner, making her turn red, or away, or look quickly to see if James saw. Karl could draw his over-size red handkerchief out of his hip pocket and dry his neck and chest in the sun, never laying an eye on Anna, but knowing full well she watched his every shimmering muscle.

Anna could bend to pick up a load of branches and point the hind pockets of James's britches at Karl in as equally an innocent manner. He could remove his straw hat – she had taken time to stitch a sunbonnet for herself, realizing Karl needed his hat – and wipe his forehead with his forearm, then squint at the sun and say, 'It is hot today.' Guilelessly?

Anna didn't think so.

Raising the hair from the back of her neck, she would agree casually, 'It sure is.'

In the pond their frolicking became sensitized by more frequent brushing against each other, under the guise of dunking, learning to swim, being teacher and student.

Those sun-splashed days in the tamaracks were harbingers of more to come. But one day when the three awakened to rain, the tamaracks were forgotten for the time being. Karl checked the grey drizzle after breakfast, lit his pipe thoughtfully, then went to the barn to fetch a pitch-fork and dig worms. Soon afterward he and James left with fishing poles in hand.

Anna was alone in the springhouse washing vegetables, displeased at being left behind. She muttered to herself and threw the beans from pail to pan in irritation. Beans! she silently griped. I'm left to clean beans while those two go off to fish bass!

Suddenly the light from outside was dimmed even more. Anna looked up and screamed. A bunch of Indians stood crowding around the doorway of the springhouse, sombre faces impassive while she jumped up and spilled green beans everywhere. They all had oiled hair, pulled back into braided tails, and were dressed in fringed buckskin.

The one nearest the doorway smiled in a toothy grin at the sound of her fright. They all acted like they were waiting for her to step outside. What else could she do? She squelched her fears and stepped into the misty day.

'Foxhair,' Toothy Grin grunted.

She stood in the drizzle, wondering what to do, while they all stared at her hair. Should she act as if it were totally natural to stand in the rain carrying on a conversation with an Indian, or stalk off toward the cabin where they were sure to follow?

'Anna,' she corrected. 'Anna Lindstrom.' The name surprised even her.

Toothy Grin shot a curious glance to one of his friends who had the face of an old buffalo on the body of a young deer.

'Foxhair,' Toothy Grin repeated, nodding now.

Buffalo Face grinned. He had magnificent teeth for such an ugly face. 'Foxhair marry Whitehair, together make baby striped like skunk kitten.'

They all laughed in great amusement at this.

'What do you want?' she snapped. 'If all you've come here to do is make fun of my hair, you can leave! If you want to see my husband, he's not here. You'll have to come back another time.' She was trembling in her britches, but she was damned if she was going to let them come sneaking here into her own yard and ridicule her!

'Tonka Squaw!' one of them said, in a tone she could

have sworn was approving, although why was beyond her guess.

'What do you want?' she asked again, none too gently.

'Tonka Squaw?' one Indian asked Buffalo Face. 'How you know she squaw?' They seemed to be amused by her britches, all pointing and jabbering in their unrecognizable jargon while eyeing her clothing. She grew angrier by the moment at being talked past like she wasn't even there.

'Talk English!' she spit. 'If you're going to come around here, you can just by-damn talk English! I know you know how because Karl told me!'

'Tonka Squaw!' one said again, with a broad grin.

'Spit fire!' another said.

Then they laughed again at her britches.

'Well, if you weren't all so rude, I'd invite you inside to wait for Karl, but I'll be darned if I'll have you in when all you came to do is laugh at me!'

She spun and headed for the cabin, and they all silently followed. In the doorway, she turned to challenge them. 'Anybody who comes in here had just better forget about my britches and keep his smart comments to himself!'

But in they came, right behind her. Silently, they squatted and sat cross-legged on the floor before the fireplace. She wondered what she was expected to do to entertain them.

She decided the best course of action was action. She would pretend to be very busy preparing dinner, and maybe they would get tired of watching her and go away. She had struggled once before through the making of a kind of mince cake, baked in the spider instead of in an oven. She struggled to remember the ingredients Karl had taught her, and in her preoccupation thought she was probably ruining it entirely. But she didn't care. Anything to look busy and distract the Indians. But they muttered among themselves, now and then breaking into laughter, as if what she did were the funniest thing in the world.

She began mixing the cake ingredients, found the mince

144

made of pumpkin and vinegar and put the crock on the table while she reached for a clean spoon. Turning around, she found an Indian, with a nose like a beaver, reaching into her jar with his bare hand. Without thinking, she whacked him a good one across the knuckles with her wooden spoon.

'Git!' she spit at him. 'Where are your manners? You don't come into my house and reach your big dirty hands into my mincemeat and eat it behind my back! Sit down and keep out of my way and maybe, just maybe, I'll give you some cake when it's done! Meanwhile, keep your hands where they belong!'

Beaver Nose's companions had a jolly good laugh at that one. While he held his smitten knuckles, the others held their sides and rocked in raucous laughter, repeating over and over, 'Tonka Squaw, Tonka Squaw.'

'Quiet! You're no better than him,' she warned the rest brandishing her spoon, 'you all came in here uninvited!'

She tended to her cake-mixing, discomfited by having five Indian men sitting and watching her. So far they seemed to respect her spunk. As long as it worked, she'd keep it up. She had no other defense against her fear anyway.

She knew before the batter was done she'd made a mess of it again. But she went about putting it on the spider to fry into cakes as if it were an epicurean delicacy. The Indians watched her and mumbled as if intrigued by this involved cooking method. The little patties were flatter than Beaver Nose's nose, but she couldn't stop now. She fried away until all the batter was cooked. Such as they were, she ceremoniously put all the cakes on her largest wooden platter, and said, 'Now, if you will be patient, I'll make some rose hip tea for you.'

She set the platter on the table, keeping a corner of an eye on the Indians, lest they reach out for one of her sad confections before she bid them do so. Hungrily, they eyed the cakes, but not one of them made a move toward them, remembering the fury of her spoon on Beaver Nose's knuckle.

She mashed and steeped the rose hips, all the time remembering that Karl said rose hips prevented scurvy, wondering why in the world she was keeping the disease from befalling this group that had won her wrath. When the tea was steeped, she had a problem of where to find enough containers to serve all five Indians at the same time, but she would by-gum do this thing right!

She went to the doorway, stopped and turned an admonishing finger at the sitting men. 'Don't you dare touch those cakes till I get back!' Then she ran to the springhouse to get the dipper and a couple of small, empty crocks.

She came back to the sound of their guttural mumblings, and made a big show of putting rose hip tea into the dipper, the two crocks and her three mugs. She was darned if she'd drink out of that dipper herself. She handed it to Buffalo Face, since he was the one who had poked fun at her britches. Let him drink out of the dipper! She was a lady and would drink from the mug, britches or not!

This, then, was the sight that greeted Karl and James when they returned from the creek, dripping, but bearing a stunning catch of widemouth bass. Anna reigned supreme, the only one of the group sitting on a chair. At her feet were five oily-haired, buckskinned Indians, drinking rose hip tea, of all things, and eating the most miserable-looking mince cakes Karl had ever seen in his life – eating them and nodding in appreciation as if they were angel's food!

Anna turned startled eyes to him as he entered. He could almost see her shoulders sag in relief at his appearance. He wondered how long the Indians had been there.

'Whitehair! Hah!' one of the Indians greeted.

'Hello, Two Horns,' Karl replied, 'I see you have met my wife.' It was Karl's best friend, Two Horns, that Anna had

146

insulted by making him drink his tea from the dipper. But he didn't seem to mind.

'Tonka Squaw!' Two Horns said again.

'Tonka Squaw!' they all chimed in, if you could call all that guttering 'chiming.'

'Yes, she is,' Karl agreed, smirking and cocking an eyebrow, raising Anna's temperature a notch.

'Tonka Squaw dress like Whitehair. How you know she squaw?'

Karl laughed. 'I know by what is inside.'

So, thought Anna, Tonka Squaw means a woman who wears britches! Just wait until I get you alone, Karl Lindstrom!

But they were all laughing at Karl's remark. The ominous look on Anna's face told him he'd been a little precipitous in making jokes about her britches before his friends.

'I have fish. You will all stay for supper,' Karl said.

Oh, great! thought Anna. I've been entertaining his rude Indian friends all afternoon. So what does he do but make sure I have to put up with them through supper, too!

'Anna can throw a few more potatoes into the fire,' Karl added.

That's just what Anna did. She was downright huffy by this time. She stomped out to get more potatoes from the root cellar. She knew the Indians loved potatoes and the white wheat bread so different from that which the Indians themselves made of corn. She returned to thrust the potatoes into the coals, not even bothering to wrap them in plantain leaves. She wasn't going to get all soaking wet gathering up plantain for the benefit of a bunch of outspoken Indians!

Karl had begun cleaning the fish on the tabletop. The Indians expressed their disapproval of this, adding heat to Anna's already fiery anger. 'Why Tonka Squaw not clean fish? Whitehair sit and smoke pipe with his friends.'

'Anna is not very good at cleaning things,' Karl

147

explained, embarrassing her further. 'She has never learned how to clean fish anyway. These are the first fish we have had since she has been here.'

'Bad start to marriage,' was the general consensus among the group.

Anna gathered that no self-respecting Indian would be caught dead cleaning fish when he had a wife to do it for him. She began to resent Karl a little less for not expecting her to perform that loathsome duty. She went to the springhouse for water, came back and conceded to wash each fillet after it was scraped free by his knife.

The Indians had taken James into their circle, already having dubbed him One-Who-Has-Eye-Of-Cat because he had green eyes, something new to them. When they brought out their pipes, they included James in their offer to smoke.

'Oh no, you don't!' Anna objected. 'You're not teaching him any of your bad habits at his age. He's still a growing boy.'

They saw the way James withdrew the hand he'd been reaching toward the pipe, and once more nodded in approval, saying 'Tonka Squaw.' But when it was time for the frying of the fish, they became amused at the big white Swede whose woman did not even know a simple thing like that. Nevertheless, they ate their fill, relishing in particular those potatoes. The only potatoes they usually ate were wild ones, not nearly as delicious as these the white man cultivated.

When the meal was over, Anna was left to clean up while the men sat around with their pipes again. She wondered if the Indians would ever leave, for she was getting sick and tired of being called Tonka Squaw at every move she made, and having her britches closely scrutinized and being criticized because she didn't perform all the duties these big bullies let their women perform.

But they left at last, long after dark, and she wondered how they would find their way home in the blackness. Karl bid them goodbye at the door, and they all raised their palms to him. They did the same to James, but never gave Anna so much as a glance, which nettled her to a snit again, after it was she who'd invited them in in the first place!

Karl came back inside and could tell she was in a lather, so left her alone. He and James talked about the Indians, Karl saying he'd known all along they'd come around to have a look at his new squaw sooner or later.

She flounced into bed and faced the wall, really puckered now because Karl had called her a squaw! She'd had enough of it from those redskins!

When the fire was banked and the cabin dark, Karl laid down beside her. Instead of taking her hint and leaving her alone, he leaned over her shoulder to whisper into her ear, 'Is my Tonka Squaw upset with her husband?'

In a forced whisper she sizzled, 'Don't you dare call me a squaw one more time! I've had about all of it I can stand for one day! You and your big bully Indian friends!'

'Ya. We are some big bullies, calling you Tonka Squaw. Maybe you do not deserve it, after all.'

Now he had her wondering. She turned her face a little his way, asking over her cold shoulder, 'Deserve it?'

'Ya. Do you think you do?'

'Well, how should I know? What does it mean?'

'It means Big Woman, and it is the highest compliment an Indian can pay. You must have done something to make them think you were really tough.'

'Tough?' At last her pent-up emotions of the afternoon and evening began evaporating. 'Karl, I was so scared when I saw them standing in the door of the springhouse that I threw beans all over forty acres!'

'So that's why those beans are covering the springhouse step.'

'I was scared,' she repeated, seeking his sympathy now.

'I told you they were my friends.'

'But I never saw them before, Karl. I didn't know who

they were. The one with the toothy grin made fun of my hair, then Two Horns poked fun at my britches. All I could think to do was put them in their places for being so rude to me . . . and in my own home, too!'

'I thought as much. You just are not used to their ways. The Indian respects authority. When you put them in their places, you fix yourself in yours, and they look up to you.'

'They do?' she asked, surprised.

'So they call you Tonka Squaw, Big Woman, because you make them behave, when Indian men are used to having their own way with their women.'

'They are?'

'They are.'

Anna couldn't help laughing. 'Oh, Karl, do you know what I did? I smacked old Beaver Nose so hard with my wooden spoon that before the end of the night he had black and blue marks on his knuckles.'

'You did such a thing, Anna?' he asked, amazed at this wife of his.

'Well, he stuck his dirty hand right in my mincemeat pot!'

'So you smacked him with your wooden spoon?'

'I did. Oh, Karl, I did,' she giggled now. 'That was an awful thing to do, wasn't it?' Her giggling grew louder at the thought of her own temerity.

'It seems you are the kind of squaw those Indians would like to have, but make sure they don't! One who keeps her men in line!'

'Oh you!' Anna spouted. 'You just forget about calling me Tonka Squaw, right this minute. I like *Anna* just fine, no matter what kind of squaw I am!'

'Tonka,' Karl reiterated.

'Well, you might have thought I was enjoying it all, but let me tell you I was plenty scared. Besides, I was put out with them for teasing me about my britches and my hair.'

150

'They teased you about your hair, too, Anna?' Karl asked now.

'Yours and mine both, I gather.' Too late she realized she had led herself toward a subject that would better have been avoided.

'Well, what did they say?' Obviously, Karl was eager to hear the rest.

'Nothing.'

'Nothing?'

'Nothing, I said.'

But in the dark, he leaned and teased at her earlobe. 'When you say it is nothing, I know it is something. But maybe something you do not want your husband to know.' Anna stifled a giggle as he lightly nipped her jaw.

'Something like that,' she admitted.

'How would you like to gut the fish the next time I bring the catch home?' he teased. 'You would just love it, I bet.'

He could feel her cheeks round up in a smile against his teasing lips.

'How would you like a rap on the knuckles with my spoon? After all, it is Tonka Squaw you are threatening.'

'I am not very scared, as you can tell.' He was whispering against her cheek now. 'That is not why I am shaking.'

'Why are you shaking then, Whitehair?' she whispered back.

His hand came seeking.

'I am shaking with laughter at those foolish Indians who think I have such a Big Woman.' His hand found her breast. There was scarcely a spoonful of it.

She grabbed his hand and took it to her mouth, saying, 'I guess I'll just have to prove those Indians right.' Then she bit it.

When he yelped out loud, James asked what was going on up there.

'Tonka Squaw is just trying to prove she is more tonka than she really is.'

'One of the reasons I first got mad at your big red friends was because they made themselves at home without asking,' she informed Karl merrily.

He got her good and tight this time in a mighty hug that subdued her. The cornhusks were carrying on something awful as the two of them scrapped and rolled, laughing and teasing. They ended in a kiss, with Karl saying into her ear, 'Ah, Anna, you are something.'

'But not tonka?' she whispered, knowing that the bosom pressed against his chest was anything but ample.

'It does not matter,' came his voice in the dark. And Anna smiled happily.

In the morning when they got up they found two pheasants hanging on their door. How the Indians had shot them before sunup remained a mystery. But Karl explained the Indians had chosen this way of thanking Anna for her hospitality. It was, too, their tribute to her, their approval of 'Tonka Woman,' their welcome and their utterly predictable sense of honour. The Indians never took anything without giving something in return.

10

Anna and Karl had been married for two weeks. They found they were compatible in countless ways, but disparate in others. Like all newlyweds, they revealed pieces of themselves to each other daily. Perhaps the similarity they found most enticing was their appreciation of fresh, healthy teasing, which went on daily.

The chief shortcoming Karl found in Anna was the way she hated all domestic work. If she had her way, she'd be outside from sunup to sundown and let the housework go to the devil. When she had to stay behind to perform household tasks, she tended to sulk, and often gave him the honed edge of her Irish tongue just to let him know she didn't appreciate this aspect of wifehood.

If there was one thing that bothered Anna about Karl, it was only that he was too perfect. Silly as it sometimes sounded, even to herself, it rankled her that beside him she must seem nearly ignorant. Anna had yet to find the thing Karl could not do or figure out how to do or couldn't teach either James or herself how to do. He had every virtue a man could possibly have: he was loving, patient, gentle . . . oh, the list went on and on in her mind until sometimes, beside him, she felt positively inadequate by comparison.

But Karl never complained. When her temper flared, he soothed her with his own good humour. When she became irritable at her own incapacities, he patiently told her there was much to learn around a house and it would take time. He took precious hours out from the cabin work to teach the never-ending lessons Father Pierrot had admonished him to teach, even though Anna knew how badly Karl wanted to devote all his time to the raising of the new house.

But above all, at bedtime Karl practised more patience than any new wife had a right to ask of her husband, and Anna knew it. The flirting and innuendo could not go on endlessly. It came to a head one night after they'd had a particularly carefree session in the pond where Anna had been even more playful than usual. In bed, later, she was still feeling sportive and coquettish.

'Know what, Karl?' she whispered.

'What?'

'I've never kissed you.'

'But we have kissed every night.'

'You've kissed me every night. Now it's time for me to kiss you.' She'd been thinking about it, about what it would be like to be the instigator. But she knew she'd better be careful. Any active move on her part raised ever-greater response in Karl as the days went by.

Karl was totally surprised, wondering what impish thing she could think of next. 'Come then, kiss me and I'll be good.' He lay back with both arms crossed behind his head. Anna amazed him further by sitting up on her knees beside him. Although it was dark, he pictured her there, childlike, kneeling beside him in her nighty with those freckles dancing across her nose. If he thought of her that way, as a child, perhaps he could make it through one more night of the torture he now suffered at this time each day.

Thankfully, she gave him only a childlike peck. But she braced both hands on his chest to do it. After the peck, they stayed there.

I am playing with fire, thought Anna, but it is such fun. His skin was bare, warm, covered with a fine mat of hair. Beneath her palms she could feel the thrum of his heart, and for a moment she was confused. Did she want him to make love to her or not? Times during the day, watching him with the axe or stroking the horses or splashing water

154

over his neck she often quelled the desire to reach out and caress his beautiful flesh.

In the dark he was only a shadow, a voice, but a warm shadow, a throaty voice. By now she knew the colour of the skin concealed by darkness, the shine of the hair resting on the pillow so near her. She need not even touch them to remember them, but the memories tempted her hands, and they strayed lightly across the rises of his chest while she spoke.

'Karl?'

'Hm?'

How could a single syllable sound so strained, she wondered.

'What did you think when you first saw me?'

'That you were too young and too thin.'

She tugged at a couple of hairs, and he winced, but kept his arms behind his head. 'Do you want an old, fat wife?' she teased.

'In Sweden girls are a little plumper.'

'A little plumper, huh?' She felt him shrug apologetically, and promised with mock sincerity, 'I'll try to get fat for you, Karl. I think I can do that quite fast, the way I've been eating. But it will take me awhile longer to get old.'

In the dark he smiled. 'Have I married a girl who will tease me to death?'

She pushed against his chest one time, as if it were a lump of dough she was kneading. 'Yes, a skinny, young tease I am. I will tease you mercilessly.' She sat back on her heels, but left her palms lightly on his ribs, for she could tell more about him by what was going on beneath her touch than ever she'd seen in broad daylight.

Karl chuckled softly, pleased as usual by this bent of hers toward humour. Again it grew quiet, and Karl battled to keep his tongue from asking what he'd always thought was supposed to be of little importance. Lately though, since she had played this game of keeping him at bay, the question had grown significant, until now he could not help asking.

'What did you think when you saw me?' His low voice sounded slightly hoarse.

She remembered that first day, his face appearing around the wagon, the large hand sliding his cap from his head in slow motion, the look of boyish wonder upon his handsome features as his eyes wandered over her for the first time. She remembered that her heart had raced then just like it did now.

'That you lied,' she answered softly.

'Me!'

'Yes, by making less of your looks than you should have in your letters to me.'

Her finger brushed against his nipple. It was as hard as a pebble, and with a start she thought, do men's get hard like that, too? Quickly, she slid her fingertips away from it, wondering if it was hard because he was aroused or if it was that way all the time. Her own breasts were puckered so tightly they hurt.

A swell of self-satisfaction washed through Karl at Anna's last words. And the tiny things she was doing to his chest . . . Ah, she does find me pleasing, he thought. But then, feeling guilty for the thought, he said gruffly, 'It is what is inside that matters.'

'What's inside matters, but other things matter, too.' By the minute these other things were coming to matter more and more and more as Anna's hands played upon Karl.

'What other things?' he couldn't resist asking.

'Size, shape, colours, features, faces.'

'I . . . I guess maybe you are right,' Karl admitted, remembering Father Pierrot's lecture on this subject the night before their marriage.

'I thought so much about what you would look like while James and I were on our way to Minnesota. When I got here and saw you for the first time, I was pleased. I liked what I saw, but I remember being ... well, surprised at your size. It ... well, it rather scared me.'

Her hand sailed lightly across his chest, raising goose bumps up the lengths of both his arms.

'You're a big man, Karl,' she whispered into the dark.

'Like my father,' he got out.

Then, hand over hand, she measured his breadth, burning a path across his skin. 'Seven hands wide,' she counted.

'From using the axe.' Where her touch lingered, his heart thudded dangerously. Still, he did not move, so she slid her hands up to encircle one of his biceps.

'And you're strong.'

Stridently, he whispered, 'I have cleared much land.'

'Like your father?' quietly.

'Yes, like my father,' shakily.

'And is this your father's neck?' she asked, placing both hands around it, falling just short of spanning it, making the hair on the back of it prickle with awareness.

'I guess so.'

'I can't even reach around it. I've wanted to try it for the longest time, just to know what it felt like.'

He thought if she continued this way much longer, she would learn the feel of more than just his neck. But next she found his hair.

'You have such blond hair. I never saw such blond hair.'

'I am Swedish,' he reminded her unnecessarily.

'And do all Swedes think so little of their looks?' she asked, thinking, now, Karl, please, now.

He lay unmoving, stunned by the sensations her exploration invoked.

'I can only speak for myself,' he croaked.

'That your face would not make milk curdle?'

'Ya.'

She found his temple, laid a palm against his long cheek and followed the line of one eyebrow with a fingertip.

157

'What kind of thing is that to say about a face like this? That it would not make milk curdle.'

There followed a long, intense silence, and it seemed as if the thunder of two hearts reverberated off the cabin walls into the trembling night.

'Would it?'

'No, Karl, it most certainly would not,' she whispered, her fingertips passing lightly across his lips, then disappearing.

His chest was so taut he could scarcely find the breath to whisper, 'My mother's face.'

'Your mother is a beautiful woman.' Karl's chest expanded like never before.

Anna knew exactly what she was doing, what was happening to Karl. And she knew, too, that it was unfair. But she had discovered the universal power of femininity and could not resist wielding it. I *am* merciless, she thought. I know what is happening to his body, and I know it can lead nowhere tonight, yet I cannot resist plying him, knowing I have bent him to my will.

Bent him, she surely had, to an angle that would bear little more force before snapping. He had laid all this time with both hands folded behind his head, but now he brought one to her shoulder in the dark, squeezing it forcefully. The grip was like iron before he moved in one smooth flow, coming up, turning her, pushing her onto her back with a kiss that told her he was done with her games.

Oh God, Karl, I thought you would take till morning, she thought.

His mouth was warm, wide, and his kiss hungry. His tongue touched hers, then moved in a circle upon her lips. She felt the soft silken skin of his inner lips beneath her tongue, and deep in her body a pulsing made her lower parts feel ready to burst from want. His tongue washed her teeth, explored the warm crevice between them and her upper lip. The turn of her waist was his undoing as he found it, then moved his hand upward to slake its emptiness and fill his palm with her breast while his other cupped the back of her head.

He rested his lips against the side of her nose as he pleaded hoarsely, 'Anna, do not play games with me this way. I have waited long enough.'

Tell him now, she ordered herself. But it was heavenly being touched at last by him, fully, intimately. The hand that lifted trees, harnessed horses and held an axe as if it were a child's toy now was gentle in its insistence, provoking a yearning in Anna's breasts to be bared to that callused palm. Yes, yes, she thought, just this. For tonight, just this joy of knowing your touch and tingling to it and tasting the sweetness of my body yearning for more.

'Oh, Anna, are you child or woman? You are so warm.' Gently, he fondled her breasts, carried away by touching them at last, feeling her nipples hard and aroused.

'Oh, Karl, I fear I am both. Wait, Karl!'

'No more waiting, Anna. Do not be afraid.' His hand slid down her ribs and kneaded her hip while he covered her mouth with his.

Anna realized she had tricked not only Karl, but herself. She wanted him so badly, all thought of playing him any longer fled, for as she played him, she played herself, and it had become torturous. She grabbed his hand.

'Karl, I'm sorry . . . wait! I . . . I shouldn't have started this tonight. I – it's my time of month.'

His hand stopped kneading, and he tensed away from her. She heard his sharp, indrawn breath before he fell aside with an audible groan, throwing the back of a wrist across his forehead. She thought she actually heard his teeth gritting.

'Why didn't you tell me, Anna?' he asked tightly. 'Why did you start this tonight of all nights?' His displeasure was evident.

She could sense how he'd withdrawn from her with

scarcely controlled anger as he lay back again, arms crossed behind his head.

'I'm sorry, Karl. I didn't realize.'

Only cold silence greeted her.

'Don't be mad. I . . . I don't like it any more than you do.' Defensively, she drew herself over to her side of the bed, fluffed the covers over her chest and pinned them with her arms.

'You knew all the time and still you started this.'

'I said I was sorry, Karl.'

'I have played along with this game of yours for two weeks already. I think I have had enough of it. I do not think what you just did was such fun.'

'Don't be mad.'

'I am not mad.'

'Yes you are, Karl. I won't do anything like this again.'

He studied the blackness above him a long time, obviously put out at her. Finally, he asked, 'How long does this thing last with women?'

'A couple more days,' she whispered.

'A couple more? Two more, Anna?' he asked deliberately.

She was cornered, but could only answer, 'Yes, two more,' realizing that with the words she at last committed herself to a definite time. Two nights from now would be either her doing or her undoing, depending upon what Karl would or would not realize about her past, once they made love.

'All right,' he said now with finality, 'two more days.'

Anna didn't put her fears into precise pigeonholes. She didn't actually think to herself, if Karl realizes the truth about me he'll send me away. Somehow she knew he wouldn't do that. Still, guilt and uncertainty provoked her to arm herself against his possible displeasure. Her only insurance was to prove her worth around the place beyond

160

a doubt, to make Karl think of her as indispensable. That, she admitted, was a lot to prove over the next couple of days.

She began the next morning by attempting to make pancakes. When Karl and James came in from morning chores they found the intrepid Anna ready to pour batter in the griddle.

'So, I can be a full-time logger at last?' Karl asked smilingly, while Anna nervously wiped her hands on the thighs of her britches.

'Maybe,' she quavered, and would have poured the batter into the ungreased spider had Karl not reminded her to lard it first. When she had the cakes baked on one side, then turned them, she realized they looked nothing like his had. These were flat and lifeless. But she served him the first ones anyway, hurrying to pour the second batch for James.

Karl eyed the flat specimens with their wavy edges. Too much milk, he thought, and not enough saleratus. But he ate the helping, then another, kindly withholding criticism. When Anna took her first bite, her jaws stopped. Karl and James eyed each other sideways and tried not to snicker. Then she spit the mouthful back onto her plate with disgust.

'Ish!' she spouted. 'That's like a slice of a cow's hoof!'

The other two at last burst out laughing, while Anna railed at herself in disgust. 'I thought I'd surprise you, but I'm too *stupid* to remember the simplest recipe. It's awful! I don't know how you ever ate so many!'

'It was hard, wasn't it, James?' Karl managed between gusts of laughter.

James curled his tongue out and rolled his eyes upward.

'Don't you dare poke fun at me for failing, Karl Lindstrom! At least I tried! And you can put your tongue back in now, you little brat!' she yelled at her brother.

Karl silenced his laughter at once, but his chest still shook.

'You were the one who said it was like a cow's hoof,' James reminded her.

'*I* can say it!' she snapped. 'You don't have to!' She whisked her plate from the table, turning her back on the both of them.

'Tell your sister not to throw away the leftovers,' Karl whispered loudly behind her. 'We can use them to shoe the horses with.'

But when she whirled on him, he had already made it to the door. The pancake missed his head and sailed out into the yard where Nanna came and nosed at it inquisitively, then – unbelievably! – turned away in disinterest. Anna stood in the door with her hands on her hips, yelling across the clearing at Karl's retreating back, 'All right, smarty, what'd I do wrong?'

'You probably forgot the saleratus,' he called merrily without so much as turning around.

She kicked viciously at the pancake lying in the dirt, then swung back to the door, mumbling, 'Saleratus! A nincompoop forgets saleratus!'

For good measure, Karl turned now, and added, 'And you put in too much milk!' He watched her feisty little backside swivel into the house again. He'd had a sneaking suspicion last night she'd fibbed to him again just to put him off for a while longer. But now he was sure she'd been telling the truth. He had enough sisters to remember their bursts of temper and inexplicable irritability that came and went in mysterious cycles.

Anna was so disgusted with herself she could have cried. After all her promises to try her best to please Karl, look what she'd done! Flying off the handle at him and throwing the pancake like it was his fault. But, oh, those pancakes had been so miserable!

Noon dinner was worse, because it should have been easier. All she had to do was slice bread and fry venison steaks. She volunteered to go back down the skid trail early and get the fire stoked up and the meal begun so it'd be ready when Karl and James brought the load of wood.

Her bread slices were wedge-shaped. The venison, which had looked so appetizing when raw, was charred to a curl on the outside, oozing cold blood on the inside. Nobody mentioned the inept preparation of the food. But the steaks were scarcely touched.

Anna's ineptitude in the kitchen served a purpose after all. She was so furious with herself she worked like a dynamo to get rid of her frustration. That afternoon, because of her excessive energy, she and James kept up, tree-for-tree, with Karl. In the twenty minutes or so it took Karl to fell one tree, Anna could skin another tamarack of its branches, while James could skid a load down the hill from the siding. Time of the month or not, Anna would show Karl she was good for something!

By the end of the day Anna's stomach was growling like a riled hedgehog. Once it chose to growl when she was so near Karl, he heard it and could not resist a little corner-of-the-mouth smile. But he kept on working, bare-chested and amused.

Anna could not stand it any longer. When the next tree went crashing down, she looked at Karl across the roaring silence and, even though it was earlier than usual, asked, 'Karl, could we go back early today?'

'Why?' he asked, already seizing his axe, moving to the next tree.

'Because I'm so hungry I haven't got enough strength to whack one more limb off.'

'Me, too,' James put in from his spot at the far end of the tamarack. Still, he cast a wary glance at his sister while he admitted it.

'Me, too,' Karl said, trying not to smirk.

Suddenly, the humour of the situation struck Anna. All of them working away here while she grumbled and mumbled and was the worst kind of spitfire! She knew she

163

had to be the first one to laugh. It started as a thin, self-conscious giggle, but before she knew what was happening, James chuckled, then Karl. Then a most unladylike snort came through her nose, and all three of them let go fully!

She collapsed in the sawdust in an uncontrollable fit of mirth. Karl stood with one foot on a stump, one hand braced on the axe, hooting at the azure sky, while James came whisking through the branches of the downed tree to Anna's side, where he, too, settled onto his knees in the sawdust. The crows must have heard, for they started up a cacophony of their own from the woods. The trio laughed until their stomachs growled all the more. Anna finally sat up, weak, exhausted in the nicest way. Karl eyed her appreciatively, her hair now salted with sawdust, dark circles of sweat beneath her arms, smudges of bark lichens on her chin. He'd never seen anything prettier.

'I think I was right the first time when I took you for a whelp still wet behind the ears, Anna. Look at you. No wife of mine could look like that, sitting there in her britches with sawdust all over everything.'

But the way he smiled at her, she knew she was forgiven for last night. Making a face at him, she asked, 'Can we go down right now, Karl?'

'Right now?'

'Right this very now!'

'But we should trim and buck this tree first, and – '

'And by that time you will have to bury me! Please, let's go now. I'm starving, Karl, starving!'

'All right,' Karl laughed, pulling his axe from its slice in the stump, extending it toward Anna. 'Let's go.'

She squinted up at this husband of hers, his tanned, smiling face framed by damp, unruly curls near his temples. She wondered how she'd managed to get so lucky. Her heart tripped in gay excitement at the very sight of him, holding the axe in his powerful grip, with that blue-eyed smile slanting down at her. With a coy smile of her own, she grabbed the cheeks of the axe with both hands, and he tugged her to her feet in a shower of woodchips. She came flying to land lightly against him, and he caught her with his free arm, pulling her up against his hip, then laughed down into her eyes as she peered up at him.

James smiled, watching them, then scampered off, saying, 'I'll get Belle and Bill.'

Karl dropped his arm, but raised his eyes to Anna's hair, then reached out to pick a piece of pine from it. 'You are a mess,' he said smilingly, and flicked the fragment away.

She touched her index finger to his temple and followed the track of a bead of sweat that trailed downward at the edge of his hair. 'So are you,' she returned. Then she put the finger to the tip of her tongue, her brown eyes never leaving his, which widened a little in surprise before she coquettishly whirled away.

They started down the hill, the five of them, Anna declaring that the team had never moved this slow before; surely she would fall dead in her tracks halfway to the table if they didn't hustle. But Karl reminded her with a smirk that for safety's sake the horses must not be hurried. She strode half a pace ahead of Karl with impatient steps, making sure her hips swung a little come-hither message into the bargain.

'What are you cooking for supper?' asked the husband behind her.

She fired him a withering look over her shoulder, then faced front again as she scolded, 'Don't be smart, Karl.'

'I think it is someone else who is being smart here, and if she doesn't watch her teasing she will end up doing the cooking yet.'

Anna turned around and skipped a few steps backward while pleading in her most earnest voice, 'I'd do *anything* for a decent meal cooked by somebody else for a change.'

'Anything?' he questioned suggestively, stretching his

steps to gain on Anna, who suddenly whirled around, ignored his innuendo, continuing to march vigorously toward supper.

'Come back here, Anna,' he ordered mildly.

'What?'

'I said come back here. You have sawdust on your britches.'

She stuck her rear out to inspect it as best she could while still downhilling it. But Karl caught up to her, and she felt his hand swipe her seat, sending little shivers of anticipation through her belly and breasts. Then, his sweeping done, Karl left his hand around her waist, pulling her lightly against his hip. With the axe swung over his other shoulder, they walked down to the clearing.

That night they splurged on precious sliced ham because it was the fastest thing Karl could think of. He plucked it down from the rafter of the springhouse where it had been hanging upside down like a bat. He showed Anna how to make red-eye gravy of flour and milk. With it they had crystalline boiled potatoes, which she managed to peel quite nicely for Karl – this first small domestic success filling her with pride.

During the supper preparations, Karl warned her, 'We're almost out of bread. Tomorrow I think I must show you how to bake more.'

Disheartened, she wailed, 'Ohhh, no! If I couldn't handle pancakes, I'll for sure kill the bread!'

'It will take time but you must learn.'

She threw out her hands hopelessly. 'But there's so much to remember, Karl. Everything you show me has different stuff in it. I can't possibly get it all straight.'

'Give yourself time and you will.'

'But you'll be sick and tired of me ruining all your precious food when you have to work so hard for every bit of it.'

'You are too impatient with yourself, Anna. Have I complained?' He raised his blue eyes to hers.

'No, Karl, but I only wish I could learn quicker so you didn't have to do it all. If I could get things right the first time, you could leave me without worrying I'll burn the house down and your supper with it. Why, I still haven't got the spider clean from dinner!'

'A little sand will work it clean,' he advised, non-plussed.

The sand worked beautifully, and she displayed the rejuvenated pan with pride. But later, when the ham was spitting and smelling unendurably delicious, Anna stopped in the door, clutching the bowl of potato parings against her stomach.

'Karl?'

He looked up to find her playing with a curl of potato peeling, twisting it around an index finger distractedly.

'What is it, Anna?'

She studied the peeling intently. 'If I knew how to read, you could write things down for me so I'd be able to cook stuff right. I mean . . .' She looked up expectantly. 'I mean, then it wouldn't matter if my memory's not so good.' Again, she dropped her eyes to the bowl.

'There is nothing wrong with your memory, Anna. It will all smooth out in time.'

'But would you teach me to read, Karl?' Her eyes wandered back to his. 'Just enough to know the names of things like flour and lard . . . and saleratus?'

A soft, understanding smile broke across his face. 'Anna, I will not send you packing because you have forgotten the leavening in the pancakes. You should know that by now, little one.'

'I know. It's just that you can do everything so good, and I can't do anything without you watching every move. I want to do better for you.'

He wanted nothing so badly as to step to the doorway

and pitch the bowl of potato parings aside and take her in his arms and kiss her until the ham burned.

'Anna, do you not know that it is enough for me that you wish this?'

'It is?' Her childish, large eyes opened wide.

'Of course it is.' He was rewarded with her smile.

'But would you teach me to read anyway, Karl?'

'Perhaps in the winter when time grows long.'

'By then I will have burned up all your valuable flour,' she said mischievously.

'By then we will have a new crop.'

She turned with her bowl to leave, happy now.

'Anna?'

'What?'

'Save the parings. We will plant those with eyes and see if the season is long enough to give us a second crop. We will need it.'

She turned to study him thoughtfully. 'Is there anything you don't know, Karl?'

'Ya,' he answered. 'I do not know how I will make it till tomorrow night.'

That evening he showed Anna how to make yeast from the potato water, which he saved from supper, and a handful of dried hops. To this he added a curious syrup, which he said was made of the pulp of watermelons, a plentiful source of sugar. The maple sugar, which he harvested, had too strong a flavour for bread, he said. So instead he boiled watermelon pulp each summer and preserved it in crocks by pouring melted beeswax over it.

With the yeast ingredients set in the warm chimney corner for the night, they all enjoyed cups of the remaining watermelon nectar, a treat Anna and James had never known before.

'Can I have more, Karl?' James asked. Karl emptied the jug into the boy's mug.

168

'It's delicious,' Anna agreed.

'I have many more delicious things to introduce you to. Minnesota knows no end of such delights.'

'You were right, Karl. It really does seem to be a land of plenty.'

'Soon the wild raspberries will be ripe. Then you will have a treat!'

'What else?' James asked.

'Wild blackberries, too. Did you know that when a wild blackberry is green, it is red?'

James puzzled a moment, then laughed. 'It's a riddle in reverse – what's red when it's green.'

'But when it is ripe, it turns as black as the pupil of a rattlesnake's eye,' Karl said.

'Have you got rattlesnakes here?' Anna asked, wide-eyed.

'Timber rattlers. But I have not seen many. I have had to kill only two since I am here. Snakes eat the pesky rodents in the grainfields, so I do not like killing a snake. But the rattler is a devil, so I must.'

Anna shivered. They had not gone for their swim before supper because they'd been in too much of a hurry to eat. Karl suggested a swim now, but the mention of rattlesnakes made Anna opt for the washstand instead. James, too, agreed for this one night he'd put off their swim.

When they were tucked in bed, Anna spoke, in a whisper, as usual.

'Karl?'

'Hm?'

'Have you thought any more about a stove for the new house?'

'No, Anna. I have been busy and it slipped my mind.'

'Not mine.'

'Do you think a stove will make you a better cook?' he asked, amused.

'Well, it might,' she ventured.

But Karl laughed a little.

169

'Well, it might!' she repeated.

'And then again, it might not, and Karl Lindstrom will have spent his good money for nothing.'

A little fist clunked him one in the chest.

'Perhaps we make a bargain, you and I. First Anna learns to cook decent, then Karl buys her the stove.'

'Oh, do you mean it, Karl?' Even in a whisper her voice was enthused.

'Karl Lindstrom is no liar. Of course I mean it.'

'Oh, Karl . . .' She grew excited just thinking of it.

'But I will be the judge of when your cooking is decent.'

She lay there smiling in the dark.

'I'm going to make good bread tomorrow. You'll see!'

'*I* am making good bread tomorrow. You are watching me make it.'

'All right. I'm watching. But this time I'm gonna remember everything,' she vowed, 'just like James does. You'll be going off to buy that new stove before the month is out, you'll see.' She imagined how it would be to own an iron stove, and how glorious it would be to find cooking not a hateful job, to have things turn out right.

'Karl?'

'Hm?'

'How do you bake bread without an oven?'

'In a kiln in the yard. Have you never seen it?'

'No. Where is it?'

'Back by the woodpile.'

'You mean that mound of dried mud?'

'Ya.'

'But it has no door!'

'I will make a door by sealing up the hole with wet clay after the loaves are inside.'

'You mean you want me to goop around with wet clay every time I make bread, for the rest of my life?'

'What I want is for you to come over here and shut your little mouth. I said I would think about the stove, and I will. I grow tired of talking about bread and clay and stoves now.'

So she found a spot to nestle in Karl's arm, and she did what she was told: she shut her mouth. When his kiss found it, she refused to open up. He backed off, tried again in his most persuasive fashion, but could only feel her smiling with lips sealed.

'What is this?' he asked.

'I'm only doing what I promised to do. I vowed to obey my husband, didn't I? So when I'm told to shut my mouth, I do it.'

'Well, your husband is ordering you to open it again.'

And she did. Willingly.

11

The bread-making was a larger undertaking than Anna had imagined, made so mostly by the fact that they were to make fourteen loaves at once, enough for two weeks.

In the morning the hop tea had turned into a crock of effervescent bubbles, which had to be strained through a horsehair strainer into the hollowed-out black walnut log with legs, which Karl called a dough box. Water and lard were added, and much, much flour. Anna got into the act at this point by kneading, elbow-to-elbow with Karl. Before the flour was all mixed in, her arms ached as if she'd been wielding Karl's axe instead of his bread dough. The dough box had a concave cover, also made of hollowed-out wood, and when at last it was in place, the whole thing was left beside the fireplace where it was warm and the dough could rise.

'And now you know how to mix bread,' Karl said.

'Do you always make so much?'

'It is easier in the long run than having to mix dough more often. Are your arms tired?'

'No,' she lied – a little white lie – not wanting him to think her too weak for such a task.

'Good, then let us go see about that tamarack we left lying on its side yesterday.'

The day was different from any so far. Between Anna and Karl there was none of the light banter. There was, instead, a concerted avoiding of eyes, of touch, even of speech.

For this was the day!

They mounted the skid trail behind Belle and Bill. Today

172

Karl took the reins instead of turning them over to James. The familiar reins felt comforting in Karl's palms. The familiar rumps of the horses were good to set his eyes upon when they felt like wandering to Anna. The words of command flowed in gentle but gruff tones to the horses, though Karl found little to say to his wife.

He was attuned to her every motion, though. He need not even look her way to sense each movement, each sound she made. The sigh of her pant legs through the damp morning grass, the quick tilt of her head at the bark of a pheasant, the accented swing of the basket she carried, the natural swing of her hips, the perk of alertness when a gopher caught her eye, the way she watched the small animal as she walked past it, the determination in her stance as she set to work on the branches, the way she raised the jug to her lips when she broke for water, the way she backhanded her mouth after taking the drink, the curl of her back as she bent to fill the basket, the way she put the first chip to her nose before dropping it in, the pause to push her hair back when the nape of her neck grew warm, the way she smiled reassuringly at James when he seemed to be questioning silently, why this sudden change between you and Karl?

Anna, too, knew a sense of content with Karl, as if, suddenly, a tuning fork had been struck in her body and its vibrations matched his as they played out this new movement of a symphony started two weeks ago.

That first movement, with its light allegro-like gaiety, echoed and was gone now, high among the tamaracks. It was replaced by this sensual adagio that caught them in its slowly measured beat. Even Karl's axe seemed to match that slower rhythm, its mellow thud counting away the minutes until nightfall. It was as if Anna stood beside Karl, elbow-to-elbow, as she had earlier.

She knew his every movement, though she never looked squarely at him the entire morning. The brush of his hand

173

upon Belle's haunch, the way it absently eased down to her thigh, the pat on her shoulder before leaving her in favour of curved ash, the squaring of shoulders and that last gaze skyward before hefting the axe for the first time that day, the great breath, the way he held it in his thick chest before that initial fluid swing, then the symmetry of motion, the flash of yellow hair back and forth in the sun as he nodded into each stroke, the rise of chin at the measure of trembling tree, the squint of eye as the bark cracked, the near shudder of satisfaction as it plunged, the one-handed way he unbuttoned his shirt, the rolling backward of shoulders to be free of it, the axe handle leaning upon his groin as he shrugged from the confines of cotton, the shirt flying through the air, his hands flexing wide before taking up the axe once more, making it sing, the sudden silence when James pointed wordlessly, Karl walking with catlike stealth to reach for the rifle and raise it, aiming at the squirrel who perched in mesmerized silence waiting to be their supper, the recoil that scarcely rocked Karl's shoulder, his look of amazement as the butt of the gun slid down to rest beside his foot while the squirrel scampered free, untouched.

And for one of the few times that day, Karl's eyes meeting Anna's, hers falling away, her head turning so she could smile at his missed shot without his knowing.

And all day long their thoughts ranged over parallel themes.

'What will she think of me?'

'What will he think of me?'

'Will she come along swimming?'

'He will want to go swimming.'

'I had best shave again.'

'I had best wash my hair.'

'I wish I had better than lye soap to offer.'

'I wish I had better than homespun to wear.'

'Supper will seem endless.'

'I'll hardly be hungry.'

174

'Shall I go to the barn?'
'Shall I go to bed first?'
'When have two days been this long?'
'When have two days been this short?'
'Will she resist?'
'Will he demand?'
'She is so slight.'
'He is so big.'
'What do women need?'
'Will he be gentle?'
'Will she know it is my first time?'
'He will know it's not my first time!'
'I must wait till the boy sleeps.'
'James, fall asleep early!'
'She will sure want the fire low.'
'James will see in the fireglow!'
'Blast those cornhusks!'
'Oh! Those crackling cornhusks!'
'Should I take off her gown?'
'Will he take off my gown?'
'My hands are so callused.'
'My hands have grown rough.'
'What if I hurt her?'
'Will it hurt like the first time?'
'Will she know all my doubts?'
'Will he know all my fears?'
'There will be blood.'
'There'll be no blood!'
'Let me do it right.'
'Let him not suspect.'

At noon they punched down the dough and Karl showed
Anna how to shape the loaves. He sprinkled the hand-
forged iron pad with cornmeal before placing the first loaf
in it. He said they had enough tamaracks to begin hewing,
so they need not return to the woods that afternoon. If she

wanted, Anna could tend to some weeding in the vegetable garden, which had been sadly neglected lately. Also, those potato peelings needed planting if they were not to dry into uselessness. And the hardwood fire in the kiln would bear tending in readiness for the baking.

So Karl went to his hewing and Anna to her weeding. Alas, Anna could not tell the weeds from the herbs and pulled up Karl's comfrey, so much taller than the rest, and looking ever so unvegetablelike. Unaware of her mistake, she continued on with her task until Karl came to show her how deep to plant the potato parings. Eyeing the plot, then the weedpile, Karl asked, 'Where is my comfrey?'

'Your what?' Anna asked.

'My comfrey. A little while ago it was growing right up along the end of this row.'

'You mean that big, tall, gangly stuff?'

'Ya.'

'That's . . . comfrey?'

Karl again eyed the weed pile, then Anna bent to fetch up the abused comfrey. 'Is this it?'

'I'm afraid so. It was.'

'Oh no.'

Another day they would have laughed joyously at what she'd done. Today they were too aware of each other. Anna shrugged, Karl smiled, not at her face but at the wilted comfrey. 'Comfrey is tough,' he said, reaching for it. 'I think it can survive in spite of your gardening. I will put it back where it came from, but it will need a little drink to get it going again.'

'I'll get it, Karl,' she offered, and scampered away, jumping the vegetable rows, running toward the spring-house while he watched her whiskey-hair fly untethered with each leap and bound, the limp comfrey forgotten in his hand.

She returned with her pailful. Karl dug a hollow, stood back while she poured water in, then knelt on one knee to

176

replace the herb and tamp moist earth upon its roots with the sole of his big foot. Above him, Anna grasped the rope handle of the wooden bucket with both hands, mesmerized by the sight of his bare back and the shallows of his spine diving into the back of his pants. He'd been hewing in the sun before he came over; his shoulders gleamed with a film of sweat. The hair at the back of his neck was wet, curling in rebellion at the heat. He stood up, took the pail from her, lifted it and drank deeply, wiped his mouth with the back of his hand and said, 'I must get back to my hewing.'

She wished she could help with hewing instead of poking potato peelings into the ground. At the same time, it was disconcerting being near Karl today. It was probably a good thing, their working separately.

The sun wore low and the pigeons began moving again. The day cooled slightly as the birds fluttered to the edges of the clearing, then to the roof of the springhouse with throaty clucks and soothing coos. At the spring the chipping sparrows dipped their rust caps for an evening drink. Barn swallows swooped out across the open, darting in blue-grey flashes on their evening pursuit of bugs, cutting sharply to scatter the grey haze of gnats. Dragonflies left the potato blossoms, disappearing somewhere to fold away their jaconet wings for the night. The inchworms gave up their incessant measuring of the cabbage plants, flexed their backs one last time and disappeared within the leaves where the hungry birds wouldn't find them.

Karl, too, flexed his back one last time. The ash handle of his axe slid through his palm and he scanned the first tier of logs, which lay now in place. Anna had gone from the garden to the springhouse.

'Well, boy, what do you think?'

'I think I'm tired.'

'Too tired to take a walk to the clay pit?'

'Where is it?'

'Up along the creek a little ways. We need fresh clay to seal up the kiln.'

'Sure, I'll come with you, Karl.'

'Good. Ask your sister if she wants to come along, too. And tell her to bring an empty pail from the springhouse.'

James thought Karl could have asked Anna as easily as not, but the two had acted strangely standoffish all day long as if they'd had a tiff or something. Anyway, James called, 'Hey, Anna, Karl says do you wanna come with us to get clay!'

She turned from latching the springhouse door. Karl was standing just behind James, watching her.

'Tell Karl yes,' she called back.

'He says to bring a pail.'

She went back in to get it.

Anna carried the bucket, James the spade and Karl the rifle. Karl led the way, explaining, 'The pheasants are feeding now, filling their crops with gravel along the creek bank. I want you behind me if I flush one up.' Both he and Anna remembered how he'd missed that sitting target this morning.

They walked in single file along the worn footpath to the creek. But halfway there they overtook a sluggish porcupine headed the same place they were. He waddled along unconcernedly on stout, bowed legs, sniffing his way with a flat nose until he realized he had company. Then, giving a warning snort, he tucked his head between his front feet and brandished his tail, protecting his barbless little belly.

'Give this fellow wide berth,' Karl warned, leading the way around the quilled rodent. 'It pays to remember we share the woods with him and he likes the salt from a man's hands. He is the reason why I always teach you to hang up our axe at the end of the day. He will eat up the sweaty handle in short time if you let him. It takes a man some time to fashion his axe handle.'

They continued walking and came to where the yellow clay lay thickly at the feet of the willows. There were countless footprints in it. Intrigued, James at once knelt, asking what they all were. He and Karl squatted a long time, inspecting the markings while Karl patiently identified each one. Raccoon, skunk, mouse, otter, long-clawed porcupine. But no rabbit or woodchuck, for they, Karl said, needed only the moisture they took in with the dew-laden leaves of early morning. At last Karl had satisfied all of James's questions. They filled the pail with clay and started back through the emerald caress of the forest light.

When they returned to the clearing, they found the kiln aglow with hardwood coals, which Karl scooped out, leaving only the heated brick radiating within. After the loaves were inserted, he quickly sealed the opening, packing it with handfuls of damp clay, smoothing, shaping, watering, then smoothing again, with the thick yellow rivulets oozing between his fingers, running down the backs of his hands.

There was something sensual about the sight and Anna could not tear her eyes away. She was reminded again of the many times she'd watched his hands stroke the horses, and of the night he had fondled her breast. Something wild and liquid and surging happened within her as she stood above and behind Karl's shoulder, watching the task he performed. She looked down at the back of his neck, his shoulders, which shifted sinuously as he made wide circles on the new kiln wall he was building. She remembered the salt of him upon her tongue from the droplet she had taken from his temple.

Suddenly, Karl swivelled around to glance up at Anna from his hunkered pose. He watched her face turn the colour of ripe watermelon, and quickly she looked aside, then down at her own hands with dirt from the gardening still imbedded beneath the nails.

A thrill of anticipation shot through Karl, and he turned

to give the kiln one last pat. 'We will open it in the morning and there will be fresh bread for our breakfast.'

'That sounds good,' Anna said, but her face had not faded yet, and she studied the barn wall across the way.

Karl stood up and stretched. 'Probably every Indian for ten miles will be here, too. They can smell that bread baking clear across forty acres.'

'Really?' James put in excitedly. 'I like the Indians. Can we go swimming now?'

Karl answered the boy, but watched his wife. 'Anna is afraid of snakes since I mentioned the timber rattlers.'

'No I'm not!' she quickly interjected. 'Yes, I am, but . . . I mean . . . well, let's go. I'm full of the garden anyway.'

Karl controlled an impulse to smile. Nothing made Anna react like a challenge thrown her way. He watched her face carefully while he noted, 'And I am full of our kiln.' But she swung around, away from him, and he could not tell if she still blushed or not.

'Let's go then!' James said, leading the way.

An honest sense of shyness had sprung up between Karl and Anna now. It heightened their anticipation as well as their apprehension at the coming of night.

Whatever must James be thinking? Anna worried, knowing exactly how stilted she and Karl had acted toward each other most of the day. But there was no cure for it. James was given to think whatever he might. But in a way James became the blessing Father Pierrot had predicted. For while they talked *to* him, they communicated *through* him.

As is often true with breathless lovers, it was not the things they did say that mattered, but those they didn't.

'I've never seen a timber rattler at this time of evening. They hunt for food during the day, and they are not swimmers.'

'I'm not the one who's worried about them, Karl. Anna is.'

'If I thought there was danger, we would not be going to the pond.'

'James, slow down! You're walking too fast!'
'It's not me, it's Karl. Slow down, Karl! Anna can't keep up.'
'Oh, was I hurrying?'

'Hey, Anna! Come on out here in the deep part with us!'
'No, not tonight.'
'How come?'
'I'm going to wash my hair instead.'
'Wash your hair! But you always said you hated that lardy soap!'
'Leave your sister alone, boy.'

'You shaving again, Karl? You shaved once this morning.'
'Leave him alone, James.'

'Man! I'm starved after that swim! Pass me the stew.'
'Sure . . . here.'
'Hey, how come you two ain't eating tonight?'
'I'm not very hungry.'
'Me either.'

'Hey, Anna, you sure been quiet all day.'
'Have I?'
'Seems like it. How come?'
'I pulled up Karl's comfrey and I think he's disgusted with me.'
'Is that why you two are mad at each other?'
'I am not mad at her.'
'I'm not mad at him.'

'Help your sister clean up the supper things, James. She's had a hard day.'

'So have I!'

'Just do as I say, James.'

'I'll see to the horses.'

'What in the world is there to see to out there when they're all put away for the night?'

'Leave Karl alone, James.'

'Well, heck, I just asked is all.'

'Get your bed ready, okay?'

In the barn, Karl lit his pipe, but it lay fragrantly forgotten in his hand.

'Hello, Belle. Just came to say goodnight.' Karl stroked the heavy neck and mane, running the coarse hairs through his fingers until Belle turned her giant head curiously. 'What do you think, old girl? Do you think she's ready for bed by now?'

Belle blinked slow, there in the dark. But tonight, her presence and Bill's soothed Karl less than usual.

'Ah, well . . .' the man sighed. 'Goodnight, you two.' He gave them each a pat on the rump, then walked slowly to the house. He took the latchstring in his fingers. He paused thoughtfully, then turned to the washbench and cleaned the smell of the horses from his hands.

Back inside, Karl found James still up. Time moved like the soft-shelled snails on a dewy morning. Anna brushed her hair, while James seemed more interested than ever in erecting log walls. His questions went on interminably. Karl answered them all, but finally arose and raised his elbows in the air, twisting at the waist and yawning most convincingly.

'Don't tell me,' James warned Karl, 'tomorrow is another day . . . I know! But I don't feel sleepy at all.'

Anna's stomach flipped sideways. 'Well, Karl is. And he can't entertain you here all night, so get to bed, little brother.'

At last James hit the floor.

'I will bank the coals,' Karl said. He knelt, heard the lid of the trunk squeak behind him and stayed where he was, poking at the fire, fiddling until finally the cornhusks spoke.

Karl stood up, pulled his shirttails out, stepped over James's feet and slipped into the shadows cast upon his and Anna's bed. Karl wondered if the hammering of his heart might make the ropes creak. Surely a commotion like the one inside him would rock the world!

His entire life had come to this, to lying beside this woman, this girl, this virgin; and his Papa had taught him well and fully how to be a man in this world in all ways but this. Papa had given him a deep and abiding respect for women, but beyond that, little more. From his older brothers Karl had gathered that this aspect of marriage was distasteful to some women, chiefly because it brought them pain, especially the first time. How to make this pleasant for her, this was what Karl wondered. How to lead her slowly, how to soothe her. What is Anna thinking, lying over there so still? Did she put that nightgown on? Don't be asinine, man, of course she put it on! It is no different tonight. Oh, yes it is! How long have I been lying here like a quaking schoolboy?

'Come here,' Anna heard him whisper, and felt him raise his arm to put around her. She lifted her head and his arm slipped close, gathered her in and passed downward along her back. Softly, he rubbed in ever-widening circles through her nightgown. Shivers danced along her spine. Fleetingly, he hesitated at the base of her spine, moved again in gentle motions until he felt her relax a little. Deftly, he had rolled her onto her side until her ear was pressed upon his biceps.

Within her head resounded her own thumping heart. How long had she lain stiffly on her back, telling her locked muscles to relax? Now, slowly, his hand began to achieve what her will had not. Close your mouth, she told herself, or he will hear you breathing like a jackrabbit and know how scared you are. But breathing through her nose was worse. And so, when Karl's lips touched hers, they were already parted.

He pulled her fully into his kiss. Her lips were soft and seeking. Halfway through the kiss he swallowed. Fool, he thought! Surely the boy heard you swallow clear over there! Saliva pooled in his mouth and he was forced to swallow again. But when Anna, too, swallowed, Karl quit worrying about it. And the problem took care of itself.

One-armed he'd captured her, rolled her toward him so her hands rested lightly upon his chest. As the kiss lingered and lengthened, her fingers timidly began to move, as if she'd only now realized his skin lay beneath them. She glided lightly over the silken hairs she'd so often seen in the sun. It felt like thistledown, so softly textured in contrast to the firm muscle from which it sprang. Her tiny movements set his senses on edge, awakening nerves he'd not guessed he possessed. Inadvertently, she brushed his nipple, quickly passing it by. He captured her hand to place it again where the touch had brought pleasing sensations. Again her fingers fanned his chest in butterfly movements of encouragement, while she wondered what it was he waited for.

He waited for her arms to encircle him, to free the breasts she protected so virginally. Finally, he whispered, 'Put your arms around me, Anna.' Her arms found their way, her hands played over his muscled back. Slowly, Karl drew a pattern on her flesh that brought his palm to the gentle swelling of her breasts. Her hands fell still. All of her lay expectant, waiting, waiting, breath falling warmly on his cheek, until his caress found its way like the fall of a feather.

Lightly, he rubbed the backs of his fingers upon the cockled tip. The universe held its breath with Karl and

184

Anna as he slowly eased his touch in search of buttons, finding them, slipping them free, one by one, in slow, slow motions. Don't move, Anna, he thought. Let me feel your warmth. She lay unresisting, receptive to his touch. He smoothed his hand within the loosened garment, riding his palm from the shallows of her ribs upward to rest on her breastbone. He stroked her jaw with his thumb, caressed her neck, encircled it fleetingly, then again rested the heel of his hand just above and between her breasts, savouring the delight of making them both wait, want.

She closed her eyes, sighing as his touch fell upon her bare breast, cupping it, contouring it, making fire build in its nerve endings. In a wonder of discovery his hand roved her skin, so different from his own. Her breasts were soft, like the petals of the wild rose, unbelievably soft. Yet, here, puckered tightly with a contraction so unexpectedly powerful. 'Anna,' he breathed, his lips skimming hers, 'you are so warm, so soft here,' he gently squeezed the resilient flesh; 'so hard here,' he took the firmly aroused nipple to stroke it gently, roll it between his fingers rapturously. 'How I have wondered.'

She lay with her mouth a mere inch away from his, feeling his words on her skin, finding no answer but to lie beneath his touch while he learned the beautiful mystery of man and woman. As if she were his altar, he came to adore in profound awe the goodness of this offering.

Within Anna grew the incredulous knowledge of this man's innate respect for the act upon which they embarked, so that when he soothed her gown from her shoulders there was goodness flowing already between them, even before their bodies joined. He touched her hair, her shoulder, took her hand from behind him and kissed its palm, then pressed her back into the pillows.

Then he leaned to do what he'd thought of for so long; he kissed her breasts, stunning both Anna and himself with sensations that gushed through them. Warm, wet, hungry tongue swooped, swept, stroked. Ardent, eager lips encircled, engulfed, enflamed.

To Anna came an incredible thirst at the tugging of his kiss upon her breast. She knew physical thirst that brought unexpected cravings for cool, flowing water. She knew emotional thirst that brought visions of warm, quivering flesh. It built in a marvellous anguish until her head pressed back of its own accord. Her ribs rose, her back arched, her hands found his hair. He groaned softly as her fingers threaded the strands. Her hands tugged impatiently, then fell to his cheeks to hold their hollows, the better to feel his open-mouthed possession of her flesh. His searching, suckling mouth created within Anna such a confusion of warring sensations. She was at once slaked but thirsty, filled but hungering, sapped but fortified, languid but vital, relaxed but tensile.

His face travelled her body while Anna luxuriated in the leisurely pace he'd set. Beneath his lips he felt her stretching like a cat as he touched the hollow between her ribs. His hands stroked the curve of her waist. As if this triggered some magic, she raised her hands above her head, arching further upward in a languor he had not expected. Her hips were hilled and warm, their hollows small and soft beneath his palm. Slowly, fluidly he stretched himself beside her, finding her lips with his again while the circle of her arms came down to press his shoulders to her.

'Karl,' she murmured, lying in wait until at last he found the mystery of her in treasured folds of warmth.

'Oh, Anna,' his voice came raspy, his mouth buried between the pillow and her ear. 'I cannot believe you.' Hosannas filled his mind at the newness of this woman and her reaction to his touches. He rubbed his ear across her mouth, his touch taken at last within her.

'It's so different,' she whispered. 'I was so afraid.'

'Anna, never will I hurt you.' Glorying in her acceptance, he explored her until his body's forces could be denied no

186

longer. He covered her with the length of his own body, thinking, Anna, Anna, that you should be such as you are! You do not reject me or make me feel callow as I feared. His hips thrust against her of their own accord, bringing a rustle to the room. Fiercely, he cupped the back of her neck, pulling her ear roughly against his throaty whisper. 'Anna, let's go outside . . . please.' He bent his ear to her lips again.

'Yes,' she whispered huskily.

And he was out of the bed, finding his discarded clothing in the dark while she thrust her trembling arms back into sleeves, found buttons, felt Karl's hand reaching to pull her from the bed. At their sounds of departure James's sleepy voice came from the floor.

'Karl, is that you?'

'Ya. Anna and me. We want to talk a while so we are going for a walk. Go to sleep, James.'

They stole barefoot onto the night grass, latching the door behind them, limbs quivering with each step. The liquid moon fell upon their heads like rich cream while they walked, untouching, in disciplined slowness, toward the barn. Anna felt a tugging at her arm and looked up to find Karl's face and hair alight with moonglow, the seam of his lips etched in moonshadow. He stopped and swept an arm around her shoulders, mantling them with the blanket he had hastily pulled from where it hung in the corner as they fled to privacy. Her arms took his broad neck in a tight, clinging loop while he picked her up off the ground, spreading his feet and leaning back for balance. His hastily donned shirt hung unbuttoned between them. She plunged both hands into the back of it, rubbing his high-muscled shoulders while he kissed her throat which arched into the night sky.

'I would have this first time last all night if I could,' he groaned. The curves and planes of her body were pressed beguilingly against his as he held her aloft. 'Just your touch,

187

Anna . . .' She kissed away his words, her hands playing over his back until at last he eased her down. Her toes touched dew, then she and Karl were running toward the barn with hands joined and the blanket flaring behind them.

He tugged her hand in the hay-scented dark, showing her the way. She heard the flip of the blanket, the vague rushing sound of it settling upon the hay. She reached for the buttons of her nightgown, but his hands came seeking, stopping hers, taking her wrists in a commandeering grasp. Relentlessly, he forced them down to her sides, then his fingers plied her buttons.

'This is my job,' he said. 'I want every joy of this night to be mine.' He brushed the gown from her shoulders and found her wrists again and brought them to his stomach. 'Right from the beginning, Anna, the way it ought to be.'

Wordlessly, she did his bidding, with trembling hands, until they stood in naked splendour before each other. Blood beat in their ears. They savoured that moment of hesitation before Karl reached out with strong hands to grip her shoulders and take her against him, drawing her down to the hay, the blanket.

He was lithe and engulfing and impassioned, rolling with her, kissing her with an ardour she had not imagined, everywhere, everywhere. Her arms clung. Her lips sought. Her body arched. Above her he braced, poised.

'Anna, I do not want to hurt you, little one.'

Never had she expected such sensitive and pained concern. 'It's all right, Karl,' she said, gone past thoughts of waiting longer for the final blending of their bodies.

He hovered, quivering, then placed himself lightly in her. He felt her hands seek his hips and wielded her in shallow movements. Again he waited for her sign, slowly, lingeringly. She moved, flowing into his being, gently, thrusting up. Together they found rhythm. Their breaths came in laboured draughts through the dusky night, uttering each other's names. Their motion became ballet, graceful, flowing, smooth, choreographed by the master hand of nature into a synchronization unlike either had imagined. Karl heard the sound of his own moans of pleasure as heat and height built. An unintelligible cry broke from Anna and he stopped moving, agonized.

'No . . . don't . . .' she cried out.

He moved back, stricken. She pulled at him.

'What is it, Anna?'

'It's good . . . please . . .'

She told him, too, with some obscure language of centuries to flex now, until time and tone and tempo reached deeply to bring Anna reason for being. And at her grip and flow, Karl, too, shuddered, collapsed, lowering his head to cradle in exhaustion at her neck.

She held him there, fiercely stroking the damp hair at the back of his neck, wondering if it would be all right to cry, fearing it was not a choice left up to her. For her chest was filled to bursting. A stinging bit in the depths of her nose. The warning glands in her jaws filled. Then, horrified, she burst forth with a shattering, single sob that filled the barn with sound and Karl with alarm.

'Anna!' he cried, fearful at something he'd done to hurt her after all. He fell to his side, taking her with him. But she forced her face sharply aside and covered her eyes with a forearm.

'What is it, Anna? What have I done?' Regretfully, he withdrew from her, stroked the arm she held over her eyes.

'Nothing,' she choked.

'Why do you cry, then?'

'I don't know . . . I don't know.' Truly she didn't.

'You don't know?' he asked.

Silently, she shook her head, unable to delve this mystery herself.

'Did I hurt you?'

'No . . . no.'

189

His big hand stroked her hair helplessly. 'I thought it was . . .' He begged, 'Tell me, Anna.'

'Something good happened, Karl, something I didn't expect.'

'And this makes you cry?'

'I'm silly.'

'No, no, Anna . . . do not say that.'

'I thought you would be displeased with me, that's all.'

'No, Anna, no. Why would you think such a thing?'

But she couldn't tell him the real reason. Unbelievably, he did not seem to know.

'It is I who wondered if I did right. All day long I thought of this and worried. And now it has happened and we knew, Anna. We knew. Is it not incredible how it was? How we knew?'

'Yes, it's incredible.'

'Your body, Anna, how you are made, how we fit.' He touched her reverently. 'Such a miracle.'

'Oh, Karl, how did you get this way?' She clutched him against her almost desperately, as if he'd threatened to leave.

'How am I?'

'You're . . . I don't know . . . you're filled with such wonder at everything. Things mean so much to you. It's like you're always looking for the good in things.'

'Do you not look for the good? Did you not look for this to be good, then?'

'Not like you, I don't think, Karl. My life hasn't had much good in it until I met you. You are the first truly good thing that has happened to me. All except for James.'

'That makes me happy. You have made me happy, Anna. Everything is so much better since you are here. To think that I will never have to be lonely again.' Then he sighed, a pleasured, full sigh, and snuggled his face into her neck again.

They lay silently for some time, basking. She touched the

190

arm he'd flung tiredly across her and rubbed its hair up, smoothed it down. He idled his foot upon the back of her calf, using it to hold her near. They began talking lazily into each other's chins, necks, chests, anywhere their mouths happened to be.

'I thought I would die before this day was over.'

'You too, Anna?'

'Mm-hmmm. Me, too. You too?'

'I worried about the craziest things.'

'I didn't know if I should look at you or ignore you.'

'I worried about those cornhusks all day.'

'You did?'

He nodded his head. She laughed softly.

'Didn't you?'

Again she laughed softly.

'I did not know what I would do if you would not come out here.'

'I was so relieved when you asked me.'

'I will hurry to finish the log cabin, then James will have a loft to himself.'

They fell silent, thinking of it.

Soon she asked, 'Karl, guess what?'

'What.'

'You lied tonight.'

'I?'

'You told James we were going for a walk. You said "nothing makes a liar out of Karl Lindstrom" but something did.'

'And something might again,' he warned.

And something certainly did.

12

James could tell the minute he opened his eyes that things
were okay again between Karl and Anna. For one thing,
today was the first day Karl hadn't risen before Anna and
gone outside to keep out of the way while she got up
and washed and dressed. When James opened his eyes and
stretched to look over his shoulder, he found both his sister
and brother-in-law tucked up in bed yet. They were
whispering, and James thought he heard giggles. A pleasant
sense of security enfolded the boy. It was always terrible
when things were strained between Karl and Anna. But
today, James knew, would be one of those good, good days
he liked best.

Karl was at the moment lying nose to nose with his wife.
He had her by both breasts. 'There is not a handful in both
of these together,' he was whispering.

'You didn't seem to mind last night,' she whispered back.

'Did I say I minded?'

She faked a heavy Swedish accent and whispered, 'If
you-u-u vant a vife *who-o-o* is shaped like a *moo-o-ose*
and has *bu-u-u*-soms like vatermelons, you vill haff to go
back to Sveden. This vun has only *two-o-o* little *blu-u-u*-
berries.'

Karl had to put his face somewhere to stifle the laughter,
so he plunged it into her two little bu-u-u-soms.

'But, Anna, I told you, blueberries are my favourite,' he
said when he was able.

'*You-u-u* don't *foo-o-o-l* me! I know *you-u-u*!'

'A man cannot help having a favourite.'

'Ya, favourite, says this *foo-o-o-l*. He should remember

that if he did not have hands like *sou-u-u-p* plates, they would be *fu-u-u-ll* right now!'

Another spasm of laughter grabbed Karl. Beneath his hands, he felt Anna's breasts bounce with laughter, too. 'And if you were not so busy being smart to your new husband, you might have your hands full, too.' He captured her hand and placed it upon his genitals.

'*Ya, su-u-u-re*,' Anna said, her Swedish accent beautiful by this time, 'like I said, he is a *foo-o-o-l*. Vith the sun up and his brother-in-law on the floor, he vakes up like a ripe *cu-u-u-*cumber!'

Ths time they couldn't keep it quiet any more. They laughed in audible snorts while Karl engulfed Anna in his big, powerful arms and they rolled back and forth, bubbling over with joy.

'What are you two doing up there?' James asked from the floor.

'We are talking about gardening,' Karl answered.

'So early in the morning?' James wasn't misled. He knew things were going to be *great* around here from now on!

'Ya. I was just telling Anna how much I love blueberries and she was telling me how she loves cu – ' The rest of Karl's word was muffled as Anna clapped her hand over Karl's mouth.

Then James heard more giggling, and the cornhusks snapping like they'd never snapped before, and many grunts and sounds of playful battle. But James wisely kept his back to the bed as he got up and went outside to the washbench. He was smiling from ear to ear.

Karl was right; the Indians showed up in the clearing before breakfast, looking longingly at the kiln. What else could they do but invite them to stay for breakfast? Thankfully, there were only three this time, so only one of their precious loaves had to be shared. Karl took his axe outside. Anna, James and the three visitors watched as he rapped on the kiln and broke it open. The fourteen loaves were gloriously brown and still warm.

'Tonka Squaw cook good bread,' Two Horns complimented when he tasted it.

'Two Horns shoots fat pheasants,' she returned. And with her words, peace was made between Anna and the Indians. Karl did not find it necessary to clear up who had made the bread. Instead, he let Anna bask in the Indians' obvious admiration of her. To them she would always be Tonka Squaw, Big Woman, and Karl was proud of her for earning the honorary title. Now that Anna understood the import of it, she was congenial to them.

She found it strange that Karl still said in spite of their friendship the Indians would steal food if the house was left untended. Just as the Indians believed no man owned the birds of the air, they believed no man owned the wheat of the land. If they wanted white bread, they would come in and take it. If they wanted white potatoes, they would come in and take them. But their sense of honour would keep them out if they saw the warning block of wood wedged against the door.

Breakfast with the Indians made for a late start that day, but it didn't matter. The trio were in high spirits, for this was the day the hewing began in earnest, and nothing could rival the excitement they all felt. Anna was glowing. Karl was energetic. James was eager. All in time for the day the actual walls began going up.

Karl brought out his keenly sharpened foot adze and began hewing, explaining the art that seemed dangerous to both Anna and James. Standing upon a tamarack log, Karl used short strokes, which swept toward the toe of his boot. Anna was horrified to realize the blade actually bit into the wood beneath Karl's boot with each swipe. He moved forward a mere three inches after each stroke, making his way along the length of the log to leave behind a creamy, flat surface.

'Karl, you'll hurt yourself!' she scolded.

'Do you think so?' he questioned, eyeing the cleanly hewed wood, then curling his boot toes up. 'A proper adzeman can split the sole of his boot into two layers without touching either the timber beneath it or the toes inside it. Shall I show you?'

'No!' she yelped. 'You and your logger's ego!'

'But it is so, Anna.'

'I don't care. I would rather have you with ten toes than an award for splitting soles!'

'Your sister likes my toes,' Karl said smilingly to James, 'so I guess I cannot prove to her they are in no danger.' Then, to Anna again, he said, 'Come, help James and me roll this log over.'

Together the three of them strained, using braces with which to roll the log onto its flat side so Karl could adze the topside. Then, with no more than six deft strokes, he removed a cleanly rectangular half notch some eight inches from one end of the log. He did the same at the other end, and together the trio worked to raise it onto the foundation. Always there was a perfect fit to receive, a perfect fit to enter.

During those days, as the walls grew higher, Karl made sexual innuendo out of even the fit of the notches. These were days of gruelling work, of sweat-stained clothing, of hot, stinging muscles, but of satisfaction.

Everything to Karl was a source of satisfaction. Whether he was showing James the proper way to drive the blunt side of an axe poll into a kerf to hold it secure for sharpening or measuring the distance between notches by axe lengths or fitting the newly notched log securely onto the last or pausing for a drink of spring water – to Karl the living of life was a precious thing. In all he did, he taught the most important lesson of all: life must not be squandered. A person got from life what he put into it. If even the most arduous labour was looked upon benevolently, it would offer countless rewards.

He would raise one more level of logs, sit straddling the wall up above their heads, slap that log soundly, and say, 'This will be a magnificent house! See how straight these tamaracks lie?' Sweating, hair plastered to the sides of his head, muscles hot and trembling from the massive effort of placing the log just perfectly, he found glory in this honourable task.

Below him, Anna would gaze up, shading her eyes with an arm, tired beyond any tiredness she had ever imagined, but still ready to help raise one more log, knowing that when it was up, she would feel swelling in her chest again, the glorious satisfaction only Karl had taught her to feel.

One day, standing thus, she called up to her husband, 'Oh, this is a magnificent thing all right, but I think it is a magnificent birdcage!' Indeed, it did look like a birdcage. Even with Karl's deeply cleft notches the logs did not quite meet. By now Anna knew perfectly well that all log cabins were made this way, but Karl's infectious teasing had by this time rubbed off on her.

'And I know a little bird I will put inside and keep there and feed her good to try to fatten her up!'

'Like a hen for market?'

'Oh no! This hen is not for sale.'

'Even so, if you want to fatten her up in this cage, you'll have trouble getting her in, since you forgot the door.'

He laughed fully, raising his golden head till the sun caught it brightly against the blue sky. 'Such a smart little hen she is that she noticed a thing like that. Such a foolish Swede I am that I forgot to build a door.'

'Or windows either!'

'Or windows either,' he acknowledged playfully. 'You will just have to peek out between the logs.'

'How can I peek out when I can't get in?'

'You will just have to get in over the top, I guess.'

'That should be easy enough on a roofless house!'

'Does the little hen want to try it?'

'Try what?'

'Try out her birdcage?'

'You mean go inside?'

'Ya, I mean go inside.'

'But how?'

'Come up here, my scrawny little chick, and I will show you how.'

'Come up there?' It looked mighty high from where she stood.

'I have had to look at you in those awful britches all this time. This is the first time I see some advantage in you wearing them. You can climb the walls easily. Come on.'

Anna was not one to waver before a challenge. Up she went! Hand over hand, toe over toe. 'Be careful,' he called down, 'chickens cannot fly!' Twelve logs high she went, and Karl leaned to grab her arm and help her swing a leg over the top of the wall. Of course, she swung the leg out behind instead of before her, almost knocking poor Karl off his perch. But he skittered backward and Anna made it safely up. The world seemed magnificent from this height! She could see the straight rows of the vegetable garden and their corn crop. The wheat lay like a green waving sea below her. The backs of Bill and Belle were so wide! She'd never realized how wide! The roof of the sod hut had a squirrel's nest up against the chimney. The road out of the clearing was so straight and shaded.

From behind her Karl's voice came. 'All this is ours, Anna. Have we not plenty?' He edged forward, put an arm around her waist and drew her back into his spraddled thighs, pulling her tightly till she was forced to lean her head sideways against his shoulder. He smelled of fresh wood and sweat and horses and leather and all things wonderful.

He rubbed her ribs, just beneath her breasts, while she reached behind her to put a hand on his neck. 'Yes, Karl,

I know now what you mean when you talk about having plenty. It has nothing to do with amounts, does it?'

For answer, he squeezed her ribs a little harder, then whispered, 'Come, we will go down inside,' and swung to do so.

Together they climbed down until they stood within the four new walls. The sun coming through the timbers fell upon the interior in bars of light and shadow that angled across their faces, shoulders, hair. It was like a cool, green cathedral with a blue sky ceiling. It was encompassing, private, pungent with the clean, crisp scent of wood. Automatically, they both looked up. Above the walls a fringe of branches swayed lightly in the summer breeze. Instantly, they both looked down. The wind sighed softly through the fretted walls, lazy birds chirped in the elms outside, the gurgle of the brook spoke quietly from the spring. And everywhere were those bands of sun and shadow, crossing Karl's shirtless chest, Anna's freckled face, their humble house where soon would be door, window, fireplace, loft and bed. His arms opened and his eyes closed as she pressed against him. Her arms entwined round his sun-striped body, which sprang to life at her touch against his limbs. Mouths joined, they turned in a slow circle, not thinking about what they did, but answering some need to move with each other, against each other, in harmony with each other.

'Oh, Anna, how happy we will be here,' he said at last against her hair.

'Show me where our bed will be,' she said. He led her to a corner where sticks and leaves and grass were its only furnishings.

'Here,' he pointed, envisioning it. 'And here I will cut the hole for the fireplace. And here will be the ladder to James's loft. And here I will put a dresser. Would you like a dresser in your kitchen, Anna? I can build it of maple. I have already chosen a good maple tree. And I thought of

198

a chair that rocks. Always I have wanted a chair that rocks. With my adze I can hollow out a smooth seat and make spindles for the back of it of willow whips. What a chair that will be, Anna.'

She could not help smiling at him, with him. She thought she would rather have an iron stove than a rocking chair or dresser put together, but did not say so. His enthusiasm was too fine to dampen.

'When can we start chinking?' Anna asked.

'Soon,' he answered. 'First I must bring in the ridgepole from the woods. I have it chosen, too.'

'When will it all be done, Karl? When can we move in?'

'You are anxious, my little one?'

'I am tired of lying to James about all these walks we've been taking lately.'

He hugged her against his chest again, chuckling into her neck, placing his mouth there, tasting salt of her labours, loving it. He dropped his arm to her hips, drew them against his own. Then he placed both hands upon her buttocks and cupped them handily, though there was no need for him to pressure her against her will. Her will was now his own. She had come to love the feel of his body moulded against hers, sought it out as eagerly as he did hers.

'If my Tonka Squaw keeps it up, she will be lying to her brother again and he will know perfectly well this time that we are not going for a walk in broad daylight with a cabin only half built.'

'Since he will know the truth anyway, perhaps this little Tonka Squaw will just go ahead and tell him the truth, that his big, hot-blooded brother-in-law is off to the cucumber patch again.'

His laughter sailed up over the fretwork walls, and hers along with it.

*   *   *

199

The raising of the ridgepole was an auspicious occasion, for it was James's first real chance to prove his mettle as a teamster. It was a tricky business, and as Anna watched his eyes darted time and again to the height of the walls. He pulled in huge gulps of breath, then blew them out exaggeratedly, cheeks puffed, raising the hair off his forehead.

The tamarack Karl had chosen was of necessity a stately old giant longer than any used so far. It lay now in wait beside the cabin wall. Four thinner trees were skinned and shone whitely, leaning up against the topmost tier of logs in the sun.

The great chains were attached to the clevises, and James felt his palms sweat. Never in his life had he wanted to please a man more than he wanted to please Karl today. Wiping his forehead, James again raised his eyes to the top of the cabin, wishing suddenly there were another man here to help Karl, so he could be excused. Yet at the same time, the challenge filled the boy with the will to do his best.

James scoured his memory, recalling every lesson Karl had taught him about the importance of soothing the horse with quiet words before and while it was worked. But his voice cracked to a high falsetto when he tried to speak reassuringly to Belle. The horses were accustomed to working closely, side by side, and were uneasy now at this unaccustomed separation as one animal was attached to each end of the long ridgepole. Only rarely were they asked to respond singly to any command, thus Belle unconsciously swerved toward Bill, and James ordered, 'Haw! Haw!' But nervousness made his voice too sharp.

From across the way, Karl explained. 'Boy, do not forget you are commanding only Belle now, but Bill can hear your orders, too. When you give a command, use her name.'

James swallowed the lump in his throat, going over all the things Karl had taught him – horses have a keen sense of hearing; if you shout at a horse you only shout to relieve yourself; quiet but firm commands are best.

'Keep the reins tight until I give you the nod, then we will start them out together,' Karl instructed. 'Remember, if you let her ease up too much we will lose the ridgepole in a sideslip!'

Unconsciously, Anna balled up her fists, as if the reins were in her hands rather than in her brother's. Her heart beat as quickly as she was sure his did. She spared a glance at Karl. The trust he had in James showed in his casual stance and the relaxed expression upon his face as he turned one last time to reassure the boy.

'How many times have you handled the team, boy?' Karl asked now.

'Lots of times. Every day since I been here.'

'And have they ever let you down?'

'Nossir.'

'And you ever let them down?'

'Nossir.'

'How many are in a team?'

'What?' James's face registered surprise at such a question.

'A team. How many in a team?'

'T . . . two, of course.'

'You handled two overgrown Percherons all this time. Now you have to handle only half as many, right?'

After a hesitation, James replied, 'Right,' even though he realized this was part of the problem.

'A man who can skid a ridgepole into place can do anything with his team.' And with these words Karl squared his stance behind Bill.

Never before had Karl used the term 'man' in regard to James. Hearing it now, knowing that this truly was a man's job, James tried mightily to reflect the confidence Karl placed in him.

The reins seemed greased. The sweat trickled down the

hollow at the back of James's neck while shivers ran up his calves. Belle's haunches looked so massive that no puny hanks of leather could stop that power, should it decide to flesh itself at will. Grasping the reins, James frantically wondered if he could possibly have missed a weak link in the chain somehow when he'd checked it over. Were Belle's tug straps, which bore the vast stress of the load, really thick and unworn? But it was too late to make any further corrections as the chains pulled taut and the slack disappeared with a musical chink.

James looked over at Karl. The big man gave him a great wink. Then came Karl's silent nod, and together the man and boy spoke: 'Get up, Belle. Get up, Bill.' There was a first grating denial, then a clunk, as the ridgepole settled on the green skids. The chests of the Percherons strained in their harnesses, and James took his first step, leaning back, as he'd seen Karl do. The squeak of green wood sang through the clearing, then the groan of the skids as they bent beneath their burden.

'Get up, Belle,' James ordered, as Belle felt the stress build upon her chest. The horse's head arose with the effort, and her step became shorter, higher. 'Get up, Belle. Attagirl, Belle!' The ridgepole – twenty feet of deadly, crushing weight should it go awry – slid steadily, horizontally, skyward.

The horses moved forward and were cut off from each other's range of vision by the cabin. Then the drivers were cut off likewise. Now they could see only an end of the ridgepole, could only envision the rest of it going up level, moving, nearing its mooring, until, when it seemed the lungs of the horses would implode from their efforts, there came the soft thud, and Karl's voice from the other side of the cabin, 'We made it, boy! We made it!'

James forgot himself then, and let out a whoop and a holler and jumped in the air, scaring poor Belle into skittering sideways.

Anna let out the breath she'd been holding and ran forward gleefully, nearly as excited as James by his success. 'You did it! You did it!' she sang, enormously pleased by his ever-growing prowess as a teamster.

'I did, didn't I?'

'With a little help from Belle.'

'A little,' James agreed, but then laughed again. 'Belle, you big old sweetheart!' James exclaimed, and foolishly kissed the rounded side of Belle's belly.

Just then, Karl came around the corner. 'What is this? My brother-in-law kissing my horse!' That brought another round of laughter.

'I did it, Karl,' James said again proudly.

'Ya, you sure did. You could show a thing or two to some Swedes I know about skidding up a ridgepole.' James knew that from Karl there was no higher praise. They both looked up at the pole lying securely in place.

'I was plenty scared though, Karl.'

'Sometimes we must do things, plenty scared or not. To be able to say afterward, "I was plenty scared" makes a man a bigger man, not a smaller one.'

'I didn't want to tell you how scared I was when I took those reins.'

Karl could not help being amused by such an admission. He smiled and nodded. 'And I was plenty scared myself. I always am when a ridgepole goes up. But we did it, eh?'

'We sure did.'

13

The raising of the ridgepole was the catalyst in the nurturing relationship between Karl and James. After that day there developed a compatibility between them such as James had never experienced with another man, and unlike Karl had shared with any but his older brothers.

They found they could speak on more equal terms since James had passed muster as a teamster. The ease with which they worked, learned and taught together created an ease of discourse, too. Soon they found themselves talking of more intimate feelings, memories and hopes.

Karl told James countless tales about his life in Sweden, about the family that had been so close and loving, about the desolate loneliness he had experienced during his two years before Anna and James had come here. Karl even confessed openly how wonderful it was not having to sleep alone any more, to eat alone.

Often they spoke of Anna. There was no doubt in James's mind that Karl loved his sister. The knowledge made for a security that had been lacking in James's life. Warm beneath it, he began unfolding into a man.

Slowly, Karl drew him out about the life he and Anna had known before they came here. But there was only so much James would say. There were gaps he left unfilled, as if they were too unpleasant to remember. One of those gaps was their mother. Whenever she was mentioned, he would withdraw behind a barrier as palpable as the walls of the new cabin. Neither would Anna speak much about her mother.

But Karl learned bits here and there that made him certain

the two did not want him to know about the woman they called 'Barbara.' He did not force the issue, but merely brought the word 'Boston' into his conversations with James now and then as encouragement for the boy to tell anything he wanted about their past.

During this time there were countless chores Karl had to teach James or Anna or sometimes both of them. There was the gathering of wax from honeycombs. Wax, it seemed, was as essential as lye. They would save it till autumn in hopes of killing a fat bear to provide them with plenty of tallow to melt with the wax for candles. It was used also in treating the horse harnesses, in preserving various foods and in medicinal concoctions.

Karl taught Anna how to boil the laundry, rub it on the washboard and hang it over the bushes to dry. The laundry was a very difficult chore for Anna. She complained about the lye soap burning her hands until finally Karl examined them more closely and discovered that she had acquired the malaise commonly called 'prairie dig,' which most newcomers to the plains states contracted. It was a mystery that had no solution but to wait out the itching and puffiness, which made Anna – and soon James – scratch irritably. Karl told Anna it had nothing to do with lye soap, but with digging in the garden. This did not lift her spirits any. Both laundry and gardening were basically her chores.

Karl sought out help from the Indians and did as Two Horns's wife advised. He made an ointment of lard and laurel, hunting for the lance-shaped evergreen branches, then working the dried leaves into a fine powder to be mixed with lard. Anna put this on at bedtime. So did James. At other times they used a weak wash made of the laurel powder and water.

There seemed to be no end to the things a man must learn about horses. The upkeep of the harnesses alone was demanding. They were carefully kept washed clean of sweat, which rotted the leather almost as fast as the urine fumes if the barn was not kept clean. Karl had no forge, so Belle and Bill were not shod. Thus it was necessary always to keep their hooves and feet in tip-top condition. Countless ailments could lame a horse whose feet were not kept clean, whose hooves were not kept trim, or who stood in an unkempt stall.

Karl and James were working over the horses' feet in the barn one day. James, as usual, was leaning close to watch every move the big man made as Karl demonstrated the proper way to grasp the horse's cannon and force the knee to bend. He squatted, holding the giant foreleg in his lap, demonstrating the use of the hoof pick to remove soil and pebbles out of the hollow, spongy part of the hoof called the frog.

'I am very pleased with your progress as a farrier,' Karl praised. 'You have learned it almost as fast as you have learned to drive the team. If I did not know better, I would say you drove many horses before you came here.'

'Nope, never,' said James. Then, remembering something, he quickly added, 'Well, once I did. There was this man in Boston who let me drive his horse and shay just once.'

'And all this time I thought you had never handled a team,' Karl teased.

'Well, it was no team. It was just a single bay. But what a bay! It was one of the most beautiful horses I ever saw, and pulling the fanciest red leather rig in the world. Sometimes, I'd just hang around the livery barn to see if I could catch sight of it. After all that time I got my chance. I never could figure out why Saul let me take her out that day. Up till then he never let me get within a mile of her, even if I offered to lead her to the livery for free. You coulda knocked me over with a toothpick when he ups and says I could take that bay and rig out for a ride.'

Karl continued the lesson and the conversation simultaneously, carefully keeping his questions casual. 'You must see that the frog of the hoof is free of dirt or the horse will develop a disease called thrush. So . . . if you knew this man . . . this Saul, why would he not let you take care of his horse before?'

'Well, I didn't really *know* him, actually. Well, sort of . . . I don't really know. He was a friend of Barbara's and he sort of took to Anna after Barbara died.'

'He was a young man then, Anna's age?'

'No, he was at least as old as Barbara.'

'Once the frog is cleaned out, you must check the hoof wall for cracks.' Karl picked up his cutter, bending, couching the big hoof in his lap. 'But even so, when your mother was gone, this Saul remained your friend?'

'I told you, he was no friend. He never used to like us underfoot when he came to see Barbara. She'd usually send us packing whenever Saul was around.'

'Once the hoof is trimmed, it must be made level with the rasp.' Karl picked up his rasp. 'But that day Saul offered to let you drive his fancy bay and fancy shay, eh?'

'Yup! I took 'er for a sprint around the commons. She was a high-stepper and you shoulda seen the blokes stare. There I came – Barbara's Brat – behind that pretty little bay. It was somethin', Karl, I tell you!'

Barbara's Brat? thought Karl. But he didn't want to interrupt the first insight into James's Boston life. Instead of questioning the queer phrase, Karl only agreed, 'Ya, I bet it was something. Now you watch here and see how I shape this hoof so Bill will balance on it right. What did Anna think of riding behind that high-stepper?'

'Oh, she wasn't along.'

'No? Poor Anna missed out on a treat like that?'

'She acted nervous and said she didn't trust that bay. Said he was too spirited for her taste and sent me off by myself.'

'Anna should have had more sense than to let you take that horse out alone if it was so spirited.'

'She figured I'd be okay, I guess. She said it was too good of a chance for me to miss, so I oughta go without her. That time she stayed behind even though Saul was there.'

The rasp croaked quietly as Karl shaped the hoof. 'Anna, what did she think of this man, Saul?'

'She never liked him much.'

'But he took to Anna, huh?'

'Oh, Karl, are you jealous? That's funny. You don't have to be jealous of Saul. Why, Anna used to run and hide when he came around. She said he gave her the willies.' James smiled at Karl's concerned expression, knowing he had no cause to frown so. Anna had never even *liked* any man before Karl. Of this James was sure.

But Karl was not relieved. He forced a smile and laughed for James's benefit, but the sound was strangely unfamiliar, coming from high in his throat. He tried to picture Anna standing with a man who gave her the willies, a man from whom she had always hidden, while James drove away in the fancy rig. Once he had pictured it, he tried not to.

To all outward appearances, he seemed absorbed in the hoof, studying it critically while he asked, 'I guess he was a pretty rich man, this Saul, huh? That was some fancy rig he owned.'

'I guess. He wore fancy clothes most of the time, too.'

A hot, sick feeling crept through Karl.

'Here, boy, you try trimming this next hoof and I will watch to see you do it right.' But it was not the boy working the hoof that Karl saw. It was Anna, standing beside some dandy named Saul while James drove away.

Karl seemed withdrawn that night. When Anna asked him how James had done at hoof-trimming, he gazed at her vacantly until she had to ask him a second time.

They all went to the pond, as usual, but Karl was not his usual playful self. He swam with singular intense vigour, driving himself back and forth across the deep end of the water, leaving Anna and James to cavort in the shallows if they wanted to. By now Anna could swim out above her head. But when she did and tried to coax Karl into a corner against the beaver dam, he told her to leave him alone tonight; he wasn't in the mood for playing.

In bed later, he muttered something to the same effect, saying he'd had a hard day. He sighed and rolled over, facing away from her. Immediately, she hugged him from behind, settling her lap around his posterior. But he did not take her hand for a long, long time. He only took it when she reached to fondle him, squeezing it then so tightly she had to pull her fingers out of his grip with a sharp sound of complaint. The ointment on the prairie dig was all over his hand and he got up to find a rag and wipe it off his skin, making an unmistakable sound of irritation at the bother.

Anna slept at last, but Karl dozed fitfully. Every time he drifted off, some past comment of Anna's or James's would come tearing through his mind, bringing with it an ulterior meaning. Like pieces of a puzzle, various things fitted into place. But as the picture formed, always it was the vision of Anna standing beside a fancily dressed man as old as her mother, while James rode off in the man's rig.

Guiltily, Karl opened his eyes wide in the darkness to dispel the picture that intimated something about Anna of which he should be shot for thinking! But then again would come James's words, 'he gave her the willies.' Then again, 'that time she stayed behind even though Saul was there.'

By the time dawn was hovering on the horizon, Karl had finally begun the deep search of the thing he had resisted all night long: his memory of the first night Anna and he had made love. It was terrible he should even be suspecting her of such things. Still, he allowed that night to come back fully. Things he'd been too overwrought to see at the time became significant now. Most significantly, three things had been missing from Anna: pain, resistance and blood.

Karl wondered if he was right. How could he know if she suffered pain? Perhaps she had hidden it from him. But he remembered again saying to her, 'I don't want to hurt you, Anna.' What had she said? Exactly what had she said? He thought it had been something like, 'It's all right, Karl.'

Then he remembered something else she had said afterward: 'Something good happened, Karl, something I didn't expect.' He laid his arm across his forehead and found he was perspiring. Another memory came, again too vividly. In the house, before they had run out to the barn, she had said, 'It's so different, Karl . . .' Different from what? he wondered now. Oh God, different from what?

When he could stand the torment no longer, he got up and went out to the barn where Belle and Bill turned inquiring eyes on him. But he did not touch them, only stood with hands in his pockets, staring ahead with unseeing eyes.

'When're we gonna cut out the door, Karl?' Anna asked, just as gay and carefree as ever.

'After the roof is finished,' he answered.

'Hurry, huh?' she said piquantly, tilting her head sideways.

Instead of his usual chuck under the chin or teasing pinch, he turned on his heel and left her staring at James for the answer as to why her husband had become so distant all of a sudden.

James scanned his memory for anything he himself might have done to displease Karl. But there was nothing. He'd come pretty close to giving away their secret about Barbara, but he didn't really think Karl was the kind of man who'd blame them if he did find out what Barbara was. Not Karl. Karl was too good to do a thing like that. Still, James wondered about the conversation in which he'd mentioned Saul. Could Karl be jealous of Saul after all? But it couldn't be that! After all, he'd as much as told Karl that Anna

210

couldn't stand Saul's guts. If anything, that should have put his mind at ease.

Karl's taciturn distraction became more noticeable with each passing day. Anna tried to bring Karl out of his 'drears' as she called it. But he would not be cajoled by her, or persuaded to smile. He made excuses not to make love until one night he changed his mind only to handle Anna so roughly she lay stunned by his lack of tenderness throughout the act. Crushed and hurt, she dared not ask what was bothering him again. She had asked before, but he wouldn't say anything.

Meanwhile, Karl himself was suffering sleepless nights and torturous days. More and more evidence built in his mind against Anna. In his typical way, he said nothing to her, continuing to mull it all over until he had given her every conceivable benefit of doubt. Yet at long last, he could see it no other way than that what he suspected was true. Too many things now fitted, things he had never associated before with Anna's previous life or her mother. Karl realized he could not go on this way, for even his face was beginning to show the ravages of sleeplessness and worry. Dreading it, yet needing it, he must know the truth.

Anna was scrubbing clothes on the washboard in the yard, wearing a pair of James's pants again. Karl could scarcely remember the dress she'd worn the day she came on the supply wagon to Long Prairie. He hadn't remembered until this morning when he'd gone to the trunk and looked while Anna was busy in the yard.

He studied her now as she worked. Her hair was tumbling around her as she scrubbed. Oh, that whiskey hair he had dreamed of during the months alone waiting for her. He pushed the thought aside and quietly came up behind his wife.

'Anna, who is Saul?' he asked simply. He saw her

211

shoulders suddenly stiffen and her head snap up as her hands idled.

Anna felt as if a giant fist had unexpectedly smashed into her stomach. She realized she was clutching the top of the washboard, and forced her hands to move again, dropping her eyes to the tub.

'Saul?' she inquired in what she hoped was a casual tone. 'Who is he?'

'He was a . . . a friend of Barbara's.'

'James says he had an eye for you.'

'J . . . James said that?' Anna's chin was tucked hard against her chest. She had become too intent upon washing.

Karl stepped to her side and grasped her elbow, making her turn so he could see her face.

It was deep scarlet and her chin quivered beneath slightly open lips. Her horrified gaze trembled down to the top button on Karl's shirt, but was drawn inexorably up to his haunted eyes.

'Did he?' Karl asked, his voice strange, hurt.

'I said he was a friend of Barbara's, not mine.'

'What kind of a friend?' His thumb dug into her soft skin.

'Just a friend,' she said, jerking her arm free and turning back to the washbench.

Karl tried to make her look at him by leaning partially in front of her, but she stubbornly kept her eyes cast down and had plunged into her washing once more with frantic energy.

'A friend who sent you and James away when he wanted to be alone with your mother?'

The old pain clutched her stomach muscles. 'Did James say that?'

'Ya, James said that!'

Damn you, James! How could you? Anna's teeth grasped the soft skin of her inner bottom lip to keep it from quivering.

'He also said you were afraid of this Saul ... that he gave you the willies.'

'He did! He made my skin crawl every time I looked at him.' She was scrubbing violently now, her insides repulsed by sordid memories Karl's questions were dredging up.

'And so you sent James away for a ride in his fancy carriage and stayed behind with this man who made your skin crawl? Why?'

She didn't know what to say. What could she say? Please, help me ... James ... somebody, help me make him understand.

But Karl understood only too well. In a steely voice he went on. 'Tell me why a rich man with a fine high-strutting bay horse and red leather shay would let a lad of thirteen take his rig out for a ride after never letting the boy so much as stable the horse before.'

Her eyelids had begun to tremble. 'How should I know?'

'Would you know, then, why this boy's sister would not jump at the chance to ride along when she knew it would mean avoiding the man who makes her skin crawl?'

'Please, Karl ...' Her eyelids slid closed. But this time he forced her to face him fully.

'Anna, rich men like that do not court seamstresses and their orphaned daughters for no reason.'

'He was not courting me!' Anna's eyes flew open and she met his defensively. In Karl's face she read the truth – that he felt as sick about this as she did.

He spoke resignedly. 'I did not think he was courting you – a man the age of your mother, this mother who you call nothing but Barbara. Why did you not call her "mother" like other children call their mothers?'

She would not answer.

'Was it because she was not a simple seamstress? Was it because she did not care to have men like this Saul know she had two children? Was it because it would be bad for her business if they knew?'

213

Anna's eyelids closed. She could not look into the honest face of Karl Lindstrom while he guessed her guilt.

'Was she a seamstress, Anna, or was that a lie, too?'

When she did not answer he went on. 'Where did you get the money for James's passage and those new clothes of his?'

Her cheeks were afire and her stomach hurt so bad she was afraid she would retch on the spot.

Karl grasped her cheeks in the vice of one huge hand. 'What kind of dresses are those you refuse to wear before me?'

As the tears slid from Anna's closed eyes and rolled to wet Karl's fingers where they grasped her cheek, the last and most horrifying truth was revealed. For by now it was evident these questions were already answered. Because they were answered, they need not even be asked.

Still, Karl tried one more halting beginning. 'The first night you and I made love, Anna . . .' But he could not make himself go the full distance of discovering what he did not want to discover. His voice fell still. He dropped his hand from her face, turned away from her and strode across the clearing to the barn, where James was today working on Belle's hooves.

When Karl burst in, James looked up, expecting perhaps a word of praise. Instead, Karl said grimly, 'Boy, I need the truth out of you.'

James looked up from the big, shaggy leg that was cradled in his lap.

'Was your mother a seamstress?'

The rasp hung uselessly in James's hand. His eyes were like saucers. 'Nossir,' he whispered.

'Do you know what she did to earn a living?' The question was fired like a load from a rifle.

James swallowed. Belle's foot clacked onto the floor. 'Y . . . yessir,' he whispered again, this time dropping his gaze to Karl's feet.

Karl could not, need not ask further. How could he force this winsome lad of thirteen to identify his own mother as a prostitute, much less his sister, whom James loved so much better than he ever had the mother?

Karl's voice gentled perceptibly. 'That's all, boy. You got that hoof nice and level. I can tell from here how the hoof is the same angle as the pastern. When you are done with her, you can turn her out to forage for a while. It will be her little treat after standing so still for you.'

'Yessir.' But the word was mumbled, James's eyes still set on the floor.

Anna stumbled through the remainder of the day in a blur of emotions. At first she avoided Karl's eyes, but then tried to catch his glance, only to realize he would not even so much as look at her. In the close confines of the cabin his careful withdrawal cut deeply, for he gave her wide berth, cautiously avoiding even the brush of her clothing against his. She knew self-disgust at having disappointed him so utterly.

By the time dusk fell, Anna's trepidation had spread its tentacles about her, squeezing the life from the small amount of self-confidence she'd slowly gleaned through her days as Karl's wife.

That night when his weight finally joined hers on the cornhusks, not so much as a single crackle sounded. Karl lay rigidly upon his back. After what seemed a lifetime he crossed his arms behind his head. His elbow brushed Anna's hair, and she felt him carefully move further away to avoid even the slightest contact.

After lying beside his stiff form for as long as she could stand it, she realized someone must make the first move toward reconciliation. Gathering up her courage, she turned and lay her palm entreatingly along the underside of his biceps.

As if her touch were now a vile thing, he immediately

jerked away and rolled to face the outside, leaving her stricken, with thick throat and flowing eyes.

Oh God, my God, what have I done? Karl, Karl, turn back to me. Let me show you how sorry I am. Let me feel your strong arms around me, forgiving me. Please, love, let's be like before.

But his withdrawal was complete. She suffered it not only that night, but also during the days and nights that followed. She suffered it in resigned silence, knowing she fully deserved this misery. The days were torture, but bedtime was worse, for the dark held remembrance of their former closeness, the joy they had given and found in intimacy, the passion foregone, gone . . . gone . . .

James knew it had been several nights since Karl and Anna had gone out for their late-night walk, so it surprised him to hear the door opening after they'd already settled into bed. Then he realized it was only Karl who'd gone out. Anna was still there. She turned over and sighed.

Sick at heart for having started this whole thing, James thought he would maybe be able to put things straight. Maybe if he went out and explained to Karl it was none of their fault what their mother had been, maybe if he told Karl for sure how Anna had hated knowing, how she'd vowed to James she'd see he had a better life, maybe then Karl wouldn't be so bitter about it.

James slipped into his britches and out the door. He crossed the clearing to the barn, but once inside, realized that the horses were still tethered outside where he himself had put them that afternoon. He was sure Karl would be with the horses.

He was right. Even from here he could see the outline of Karl, standing beside one of their necks. As he approached on the silent grass, he saw it was Bill by whom the big man stood. The moon picked out the marking on Bill's forehead, and the whiteness of Karl's hair in the night. James saw

216

how Karl had his face buried in Bill's neck, his two fists clutching the coarse mane.

Before James could let Karl know he stood there, Karl's sobs came to him, sounding muffled against the horse and the night. Never had James seen a man cry. He didn't know men cried. He thought he himself was the only boy in the world who had ever cried. But now Karl stood before him, Karl whom he loved almost more than Anna, sobbing wretchedly, pathetically, gripping Bill's mane.

The sound shattered James's bubble of security, which had sheltered him with ever-increasing sureness since he had come to live here in the only home he had ever known. Fearful, not knowing what to do, he turned and fled back to the house, to his pallet on the floor to lie with hammering heart, swallowing back the tears he, too, now wanted to shed, waiting to hear the reassuring footsteps of Karl going back to his bed with Anna. But he didn't cry. He didn't cry. Somebody around here had to not cry.

14

Anna and James worked on the chinking. They made trip after trip to the pit for clay to mix with dry prairie grass. With this they packed the spaces between the logs. Their prairie dig got worse. Karl, meanwhile, continued to work on the roof, using smaller willows for the first layer. These were joined to the ridgepole by boring holes, pegging them in place with small lengths of saplings.

Since Karl had put forth his questions about Saul, there was no more pleasantry at bedtime to break the monotony and lighten the load of the hard-working days. James, ever aware of the distance between sister and brother-in-law, suffered under the strain as much as Karl and Anna. He lay on his pallet listening for the sounds of their whispers, their soft laughter, even for the sounds of the cornhusks trembling secretly.

In her spot beside Karl, Anna felt him turn away from her again and pretended to go straight to sleep. She came to expect the tears, which nightly became her companions, but she swallowed them back and gulped down the threatening sobs until Karl's breathing turned deep and even. Only then did those tears stream down her face, puddling in her ears before wetting the pillow case, until, desperately, she would roll over and bury her face, letting the racking sobs come.

Behind her, Karl was fully awake, his empty arms longing for the Anna he'd known before. But stony Swedish pride held him aloof and hurting.

*   *   *

It was not at all the way Karl had imagined it would be the day he cut the opening for the door. This, he'd thought, would be a time of great celebration – the day Anna and James and I walk into our house for the first time. But she was gaunt and tired, with purple smudges beneath her eyes. James was quiet and plodding, unsure how to act between the two of them. Karl himself was efficient, quiet and polite.

The doorway was opened, facing due east as Karl had promised. But when they stepped inside for the first time, it was not into bands of sun and shadow as before. The roof poles were in place now, and much of the chinking was packed. The only solid light penetrated from the doorway. Inside, Anna found the cabin dismal. Assiduously, she avoided going near the corner where she and Karl had stood kissing, or the spot where he had told her the bed would be.

James put on an interested air, walking around the confined space, exclaiming, 'Wow! It's three times as big as the sod house!'

'More than three times with the loft, too.'

James said, 'I never had a spot of my own before.'

'It is time we get back to work and stop daydreaming about lofts. There is much to be done before we come to loft-building. Are you ready to bring those stones in, boy?'

'Yessir.'

'Good! Then hitch up Belle and Bill, and I will walk out with you and show you where the pile is.'

With a sense of doom, Anna set out with the two of them to help James load rocks onto a carrier bogan, which Karl told them was the bunk and runners of his winter-time conveyance, the bobsled. Karl showed them where his rock pile was, east of the cleared grainfields, then returned to the cabin, leaving them to struggle with their morning's drudgery. Yes, that's what it seemed to Anna today – drudgery. All the beautiful meaning had gone out of their work.

When James drove the bogan back to the clearing with Anna trailing beside, they were both tired and sore.

She dragged herself into the clearing, then to the door of the cabin. It was brighter inside now, for Karl was chopping out a hole for a fireplace.

Sensing she was behind him, he turned and found her staring at his handiwork.

'You're building a fireplace then, Karl?' she asked.

'Ya. A house should have a fireplace.'

And a bride should be a virgin, she thought. Is that it, Karl? So she was doomed to cook and heat water and boil soap and boil clothes using only a fireplace for the rest of her life. So Karl, whom she had not guessed could be vindictive, was getting even with her. She longed to cry out, don't do this, Karl! I had no choice, and I'm sorry . . . so sorry!

Karl, heart swollen in hurt, returned to his chopping, recalling how he'd always thought of the joy of building this fireplace. How he had thought to bring his Anna to it, to lay her before it in the deep of winter when the flames blazed high, to toy with her, to take her body against his, to wrap them both in the buffalo robe later and fall asleep uncaringly, there on the floor.

The stones of the fireplace went up, one by lonely one.

The day came when Karl announced they must drive back to check the wild hops. He announced it to James. He spoke little to Anna now, although when he did, he was always polite. Politeness was not what Anna wanted. She wanted the Karl who had teased and cajoled and been so vocal about her disastrous cooking. Now, though her cooking was no better than before, he made no remarks about it, just ate it stolidly, arose from the table and left with his axe or his gun over his shoulder. He continued teaching her the things she needed to know, but all the playfulness and mirth had gone from the lessons.

So it was to James that Karl announced, 'I think we must go to the wild hops and check them again. If we want bread next winter, we had best go now.'

'Should I hitch up Belle and Bill?' James asked eagerly. These days he tried to do anything he could think of to make Karl smile, but nothing did the trick.

'Yes. We will leave as soon as you have finished milking Nanna.'

When the time came for them to leave, Anna sensed they were not simply heading out to skid a load of building supplies into the clearing. The horses were pointed toward the road for the first time since she had arrived. She stepped to the doorway, staying back in the shadows so Karl couldn't see her. She wondered where they were going. Suddenly, she feared they might leave her here alone, for nobody had said anything to her. Karl had fetched willow baskets and put them in the wagonbed. She saw him turn to James, then James came toward the sod house at a trot. Anna backed away from the door.

'Karl says it's time to go check the wild hops again. He says to see if you're coming, too.'

Her heart sang and cried, both at once. He did not mean to leave her then, but neither did he come to invite her himself. She dropped the scoop in the hod and went with James, hesitating only long enough to close the door behind her.

When she reached the wagon, Karl was already perched on the seat. He glanced back at the house, and Anna's hopes that he would reach a hand down to help her up were dashed. Instead, while she climbed aboard one side, Karl clambered down the other, walked back to the woodpile, got a stout log and braced it against the door.

'Why didn't you remind me, Karl?' she asked, wondering if she would ever learn to be the kind of wife he needed. She couldn't even remember a simple thing like bracing the wood against the door.

'It does not matter,' he said.

Dismally, she thought, no it doesn't matter. Nothing matters any more, does it, Karl?

The wild hops were ripe this time. The heavy stems clung to their supporting trees with hooked hairs, each vine twining in the clockwise direction peculiar to the hop plant, which Karl explained was one way to identify it. The yellow-green flowers were crisp, papery, sticky, bearing hard purple seeds. They all picked, filling the baskets until they had harvested what they needed and more.

'We'll be eating an awful lot of bread this winter, from the looks of it,' Anna said.

'I will sell most of the hops. They bring in fair money,' Karl explained.

'At Long Prairie?' she asked.

'Ya, at Long Prairie,' he answered, giving her no clue as to when he intended to make the trip.

When the baskets were overflowing and the three were ready to go, Anna bent to touch a newly sprouted growth, stemming up near the mother plant. Karl had called the sprouts 'bines.'

'Karl? Since there are no hops on your land, why don't we try taking a bine and starting some there?'

'I have tried it before. They have not lived for me.'

'Why don't we try it again?'

'We can, if you want to, but I brought nothing to dig it up with.'

'What about your axe? Couldn't we chop it out with that?'

Karl's expression was horrified. 'With my axe?' He sounded appalled at the thought of his precious axe digging into the dulling grains of the earth. 'No man willingly sets his axe in the soil. An axe is made for wood.'

Feeling stupid, she looked at the bines, saying, 'Oh,' in a small voice. But she knelt down, determined to get a plant

222

some way. 'I'll see if I can dig one up with my hands then.'

Surprisingly, he knelt beside her, and together they tunnelled, trying to reach the bottom of the root. It was the closest they had worked together in days, and each was conscious of the other's hands, burrowing and scraping to free the root of the hop bine. There was in Anna a desperate need to please Karl in some small way. If the root were to take hold and grow, she knew it would be like giving Karl a gift.

'I'll water it every day,' she promised.

He looked up to find her kneeling there with other promises in her eyes. Then he looked away, saying, 'We had better pack this root in some moss or it will dry up before we reach home.' He went in search of moss, leaving Anna with the promise dying in her eyes and her heart.

James came back from a trip to the wagon with a basket. 'Did you get one up?'

'Yes, Karl helped me.'

'It probably won't grow for you if it didn't grow for him,' James returned.

James's heedless opinion made Anna feel like crying. He's probably right, she thought. Still, it cut her to the quick to realize James was so devoted to Karl he scarcely spent time caring about what she felt or boosting her spirits like he'd always done in the past.

Karl returned with moss, packed it around the root, then arose, saying, 'It is best you take two, Anna.'

'Two?'

'Ya.' He seemed self-conscious all of a sudden. 'Hops grow in both male and female plants. The one you picked is a female, but if you take one male, too, you will have a better crop if they decide to grow.'

'How do you know this is female?' she asked.

His eyes met hers momentarily, wavered away, then he stepped nearer to show her the remaining few cones that hung on the mother plant. 'By the catkins,' he explained.

Reaching out a fingertip he touched the nubbin. 'The female's are short, only a couple inches long.' He stepped to another plant that clung to a nearby tree and reached to stroke a panicle remaining there. It was about six inches in length. 'The males are much longer.' Then quickly he turned, picked up a basket and left her to dig up a male bine by herself, if she would.

Resolutely, she freed the second bine and took it to the wagon, carefully avoiding Karl's eyes. She wrapped it in the moss with the female, while Karl waited patiently for her to board the wagon. Come hell or high water she would make those two plants grow!

When they had travelled more than halfway home, Karl pulled the horses to a stop. 'I have made up my mind to have cedar shingles,' he announced. 'Although the trees are not my own, I do not think this land is owned by anyone else, so I would be taking nobody's timber. It will take no more than a single tree to make shingles for the entire house, and I will have it down in no time.'

To Anna, all conifers looked the same. But once Karl started chopping, she smelled the difference. The cedar fragrance was so heady she wondered if one might become intoxicated by it. Again, she was watching the beauty and grace of Karl's body as he wielded the axe. She had not seen him do any felling since they had become estranged. It moved her magically, creating a longing in the pit of her stomach for this fence to be mended between them.

Suddenly, she realized that Karl had slowed his axefalls, changed the rhythm somehow, which was something he *never* did!

He took two more swings, and each was answered by an echo. But when he stopped chopping, the echo went on. He stood alert, like a wild turkey cock at the cluck of a hen. He twisted his head around, thinking he was hearing things, but the chopping continued somewhere off to the north.

224

Anna and James heard it, too, and poised in alert.

'Do you hear that?' Karl asked.

'It's just an axe,' James said.

'Just an axe, boy? Just an axe! Do you know what this means?'

'Neighbours?' ventured James, a smile growing on his face.

'Neighbours,' confirmed Karl, 'if we are lucky.'

It was the first genuine smile Anna had seen on Karl's face in days. He hefted the axe again, this time forcing himself to keep his own measured beat, forcing himself not to hurry, which tired a man and only slowed him down in the long run.

The answering echo stopped momentarily. The trio imagined a man they had never met, pausing in his felling to listen to the echo of Karl's axe making its way through the woods to him.

The far-off beat joined Karl's again, but this time as a backbeat, set evenly between Karl's axefalls, and the two axemen spoke to each other in a language only a man of the woods understood. They measured their paces into a regularity that beat out a steady question and answer, back and forth.

Clack! went Karl's axe.

Clokk! came the answer.

Clack!

Clokk!

Clack!

Clokk!

The wordless conversation drummed on, and Karl worked now with a full smile on his face. When he stepped back to watch the cedar plummet, Anna felt the same exhilaration she'd felt the first time she witnessed the spectacle.

Karl's eagerness affected her, too. When the roaring silence boomed in their ears, his eyes were drawn to her, as always. He found her beaming in the scented silence and could do no less than smile back.

Into their silence started the other woodsman's axe.

'He heard!' James said.

'Get a basket and take the cedar chips,' Karl said, 'while I buck the tree. Cedar chips are good for keeping the bugs away. A few in the trunk will keep the moths out. Hurry!'

Never since she'd known him had she seen Karl Lindstrom hurry. But he did now. She hurried, too.

While she was picking up the chips, Karl again surprised her by suggesting, 'Try sucking on a chip.'

She did. So did James. 'It's sweet!' Anna exclaimed, amazed.

'Yes, plenty sweet,' agreed Karl, but he was thinking of the sweet sound of the distant axe.

It took little doing to find the source of the sound. There was a new road carved in such a way that the hazelbrush had hidden it from view when they'd passed it earlier in the day. Now, approaching it from the other direction, it was clearly visible. Led, too, by the sound of the axe as they neared, they were as metal shavings to a magnet.

And so it was that they came upon a stocky, middle-aged man working his stand of tamarack along his newly cleared road. They pulled the wagon to a halt while the man let his axe poll slip down to rest against his hand, just like Karl did when he stopped chopping. He pushed back a small woollen cap much like the one Karl owned. Then, seeing Anna, he removed the cap and came toward the wagon.

Karl alone alighted, walking toward the man with hand already extended. 'I heard your axe.'

'Ya! I heard yours, too!'

Their two outsized hands met.

Swedish! Karl thought.

Swedish! Olaf Johanson thought.

'I am Karl Lindstrom.'

'And I am Olaf Johanson.'

'I live perhaps four, five miles up this road here.'

'I live a few hundred rods up this road here.'

Anna watched in amazement as the two greeted each other with disbelief at finding another Swede so close by. They laughed aloud together, pumping those big, axemen's hands in a way that raised a response of happiness within Anna, for she knew how deeply Karl had missed his countrymen.

'You are homesteading here?' Karl asked.

'Ya. Me and my whole family.'

'I hear other axes.' Karl looked off in the direction of the sound.

'Ya. Me and my boys are clearing for the cabin.' Johanson's Swedish accent was far more pronounced than Karl's.

'We have been raising our cabin, too. This . . . this is my family.' Karl turned to the wagon. 'This is my wife, Anna, and her brother, James.'

Olaf Johanson, with hat still doffed, nodded his head repeatedly, coming to shake their hands before donning the little wool thing again.

'Oh, my Katrene will be happy to see you-u-u! She and our girls, Kerstin and Nedda, have been saying, "What if there are no neighbours or friends?" They think they will die of loneliness, those three. How could a person die of loneliness in a big family like ours?' He finished with a chuckle.

'You have a really big family?' Karl asked.

'Ya. I have three overgrown boys and two daughters, maybe not so overgrown, but pretty big girls, I tell you. We will need a big cabin, that is for sure.'

Karl laughed, overjoyed at the news.

'Come, you must meet my Katrene and the children. They will not believe what I am bringing home for dinner!'

'You will ride in my wagon.'

'Su-u-ure!' Johanson agreed, climbing aboard the load of cedar. 'Wait till they see you! They will think they are dreaming!'

Again Karl laughed. 'We cut down a cedar tree for shingles, but I think we have cut it from your land. I did not know you had settled here or I would have asked first.'

'What is one cedar tree among neighbours, I ask you!' Olaf boomed vibrantly. 'What is one cedar among so plenty?' His hand swept, gesturing toward the woods.

'It is a good land, this Minnesota. It is much like Sweden.'

'I think it is better, maybe. I have never seen such tamaracks.'

'They make a wall straight, all right,' Karl agreed.

By the time they reached the narrow clearing where the axes were still ringing, the two men were in their glory.

There was a canvas-covered wagon in the clearing, and evidence of the family's having lived by roughing it since they'd arrived. There were homewares scattered around an open fire, furniture looking hapless out in the elements, makeshift pens to hold an assortment of animals. Trunks, bedding and clothing were airing on the earth, draped over wagon wheels or strewn over bushes.

A woman was stirring something in a pot that hung on a tripod over the fire. Another was climbing down from the back of the covered wagon. A girl about James's age was sorting blueberries. At the edge of the clearing, three broad backs were swinging axes. Everyone seemed to stop what they were doing at once. Olaf called and waved to the entire assemblage, bringing them all from far corners to stand around the wagon as it pulled to a halt.

'Katrene, look what I have found for you,' Olaf bellered, climbing down over the back of the wagon. 'Neighbours!'

'Neighbours!' exclaimed the woman, wiping her hands on her copious apron.

'Swedish neighbours!' Olaf bellered again, as if he were responsible for the existence of the nationality.

Indeed, the clearing was filled with Swedish. Everyone seemed to be yaa-ing and ooo-ing at once. Everyone except Anna and James, that is. At last Karl broke away from the eager handshakes to reach up and help Anna down.

'This is my wife, Anna,' he said, 'but she does not speak Swedish.'

Sounds of pity issued like a swoon.

'And this is her brother, James.'

There was no doubt of the welcome, although it irritated Anna the way they all broke into the foreign language she could not understand. But to her and James, they spoke English. 'You will stay here and have dinner with us. There is plenty for everyone!'

'Thank you,' Anna returned.

Olaf introduced his entire brood, from oldest to youngest. Katrene, his wife, was a rotund woman who chuckled gaily at everything she said. She looked much like Anna imagined Karl's own mother looked, from past descriptions Karl had given. Katrene was braided, aproned, apple-cheeked and jolly, and had dancing eyes that never seemed to dull.

Erik, the oldest son, seemed to be about Karl's age. Actually, he seemed like Karl in many ways, but was a little shorter and not quite as handsome.

Kerstin, the oldest daughter, came next. She was a young replica of her mother.

Then came Leif and Charles, strapping young men of perhaps twenty and sixteen years.

Last came Nedda, fourteen years old, who made James's voice go falsetto when he said hello to her.

Anna thought never in her life had she seen a more robust bunch of people. Pink-cheeked and vigorous and built solidly, even the women. Blond heads, all, nodded and beckoned the newcomers near the fire to have a seat on the felled logs that were the only chairs there. Excited voices exchanged news about Sweden with Karl, who reciprocated with bits about Minnesota.

While the conversations went on, Anna and James were left to listen to the unintelligible jargon and smile at everybody's enthusiasm. She glanced around the circle at all the blond heads. One in particular caught Anna's eye, making her self-conscious of the way her hair flew at will, untethered, around her head.

The oldest daughter, Kerstin, turned to stir up the smell of tantalizing food cooking in the big cast-iron pot. From behind, Anna watched the head with those flawless braids that looked stitched onto Kerstin's scalp, they were so painfully neat. The braids came away from a centre part, ended like the wreath of a Roman goddess in a flawless coronet at the back of her head. Kerstin wore a meticulously clean dress and apron, which she protected from the fire when she leaned over to stir whatever it was that smelled so delicious in the pot.

Anna, in her brother's britches, felt suddenly like a tomboy. She hid her hands behind her back. They were filthy from digging up the hop bines. Kerstin's hands were as clean as her dress. She moved efficiently around the fire, obviously knowing what she was doing with food.

It was unbelievable what materialized for the meal! Where it all came from, Anna was wont to guess. There was Swedish crusty rye bread that had Karl drooling in no time. *Limpa*! went up the hosanna! Butter! There was actually butter, for the Johansons owned several cows. The stew pot produced the most delicious sausage Anna had ever tasted, and though Katrene said it was made of venison, it was nothing like any venison Anna had ever had. It was spicy and rich and full of flavour. They had barley cooked in the meat juices, and a tempting pan of cobbler dumplings steamed atop wild blueberries, crowned with rich cream.

Karl was dipping into his second dish of cobbler when

Katrene chuckled at him, asking, 'You like that cobbler, Karl?'

Already it was Karl instead of Mr Lindstrom!

'Kerstin, she made that cobbler. She is some cook, that Kerstin,' Katrene crooned.

Anna had all she could do to keep the smile pasted on her face.

Karl nodded in Kerstin's direction, acknowledging her talent politely, then went back to eating again.

Nothing would do but that Karl share their harvest of hops with the Johansons. He gave Katrene a whole bushel.

When the meal was done and the three Johanson women began making motions toward dish-washing, Anna offered to help, but they declined, saying she was their guest and they would have no such thing. Today they would only enjoy each other's company. There seemed to be no question that any help Karl wanted to give them with his axe would not be turned down. But the following day, of course. Today they would make a holiday. They all agreed that when they lit into cabin-raising, there would be a building standing in record time. 'Like in Sweden,' they all said, happily deciding that once the Johansons' cabin was livable, they would pitch in together to complete the loft and roof and floor over at Karl and Anna's place.

They ended up staying for supper and left for home with the promises of returning early the next day to whip the cabin up. Katrene waved them away with her apple cheeks rounded in their usual smile, shouting something to Karl in Swedish.

'What did she say?' Anna asked.

'She said we should not eat breakfast before we come tomorrow because she will be making Swedish pancakes with lingonberries they have brought from Sweden!'

The joy in Karl's voice brought such a pang of jealousy to Anna, she didn't know what to do with it. It didn't help any when James added, 'Boy! I hope they're as good as that blueberry cobbler was. That was really something, wasn't it, Karl?'

'Just like my mama used to make,' he said.

'Where'd they get the berries?' James asked.

'They grow all over around here. Why, there is a thick patch of them up on the northwest section of my land, but since we have been so busy with our cabin, I have not been up that way to check them. I suppose they are ripe, too.'

'Gosh, Karl, could Anna make cobbler with our berries?'

'I do not think it would be quite the same without that rich cream from Olaf's cows.' Then he added, 'I had forgotten how much sweeter is the milk from the cows than from goats.'

'If Nanna could hear you, she'd probably stop giving out, just to get even,' James teased.

Karl laughed. 'Ya. That Nanna, she is one smart goat. But I do not think she is quite that smart.'

'Are we going back tomorrow for sure?' James asked, clearly anxious to do so.

'Ya. Of course we are. Just like in Sweden it will be one for all and all for one. With our help the Johansons will have their cabin up in two or three days.'

'Two or three days!' James sounded disbelieving.

'With six men and two teams, it will rise like hop yeast,' Karl predicted.

'I just hope it doesn't go up too fast. I sure like eating at their place,' James said with enthusiasm. 'I can't wait to taste them lingonberries.'

'Ya. You will love them. They taste like Sweden.'

At those words Anna vowed that no matter how delicious Swedish pancakes and lingonberries were, she would definitely not like them!

When they went to bed, Karl spoke to Anna, something he had not done in bed since their falling out. 'It is wonderful to have neighbours again, and wonderful to hear Swedish.'

232

'Yes, they were nice,' Anna said, feeling she must add something.

'I will be going early in the morning to help them with their cabin. Are you coming along, Anna?'

He didn't say, be ready early in the morning, Anna. Or, we must leave early in the morning, Anna. But, are you coming, Anna? Half of her wanted to screech at him that he could go alone to his Swedish-speaking friends, who could make him laugh and smile when his wife could not. But she was too lonely to face a day without anyone for company, too jealous of the entire Johanson family already to entrust Karl to them for the entire day without her.

'Of course I'm coming. I wouldn't dream of missing Swedish pancakes and lingonberries!'

Karl detected a sarcastic note in her voice, but attributed it to nothing more than her usual shortness whenever the subject of cooking came up.

Again, Anna promised herself that if those pancakes were so light they floated off the griddle to her plate unaided, if the lingonberries were so flavourful they made her drool in her dish, she would absolutely not admit she liked them!

Yet she did – the very next day.

The morning meal at the Johansons' was a success. The pancakes were eggy and light and delicious, and the berries were the perfect complement to Katrene's superb cooking. Anna found she couldn't help but tell Katrene so. No matter how jealous of their Swedishness Anna was, it was impossible for her to dislike any of the Johansons. They were indeed a joyful family to be around. Even the capable Kerstin had a guileless charm.

Laughter, Anna was learning, was as common to these Swedes as liking lingonberries. Swedes seemed to laugh in all they did. Teasing, too, was natural, even between the two elder Johansons. Among the sisters and brothers, of course, it ran rampant. Undoubtedly, Nedda took more than her share when James was around, but she accepted it with rosy blushes that made everyone the more gay.

Work, too, came as naturally to these blond giants as breathing. If Anna had been mesmerized by the sight of Karl with his axe, she was hypnotized by the sight of all five men – Olaf, Erik, Leif, Charles and Karl – swinging axes and adzes as if they were shooting bugs away. During the following two days Anna saw a cabin-raising done in the tradition of a bunch of hard-working, companionable Swedes.

They meshed like cogs of a gear as they worked, skidding, hewing, notching, raising, sometimes two logs going up at once on opposite walls. Karl, she was to learn, was a master shingle-maker and took great pride in tapping shingles off the cedar heartwood with his maul and froe nearly as fast as they could be hauled up to the roof and pegged on.

Leif, at age twenty, was a close second to Karl, and between the two of them, the shingles quite flew to the roofpoles!

Erik, it seemed, had a touch with heartwood, and could size up a piece of heartpine with a deadly eye of accuracy. When he drove his wedge into the piece, it split into planks that looked as if they'd been smoothed by running water for fifty years.

Olaf saw to the cutting of the fireplace hole and the door space.

To James fell the task of rock-hauling again. But Nedda worked with him, and he seemed to enjoy his job immensely.

Anna and Kerstin gathered mud for the daubing, for now Anna was allowed to help, too. Katrene did the cooking, and supplied the workers with the water bucket and dipper periodically, bringing it around to inspect the progress and add her lilting Swedish comments to the feeling of goodwill already there.

At the end of the first day, Charles produced his fiddle, and they danced in the clearing while the orange and purple blended in the west behind the trees. Olaf and Katrene cut delightful steps. Kerstin danced with her brothers, and so did Nedda. It took some persuading on her part to get James to give it a try. Olaf and Leif both tried to persuade Anna to dance, but she declared she'd never been taught how and wasn't as brave as her brother, though she wanted ever so much to learn. But she wanted to learn with Karl, not with Olaf or Leif.

Karl danced with all the Johanson women. When he paired off with Kerstin, Anna continued clapping to the fiddle, forcing herself to bite back the storm of emotion that sprang up whenever the two spoke to each other. Watching them spin gaily around the firelit clearing laughing, with Kerstin's full skirts flitting high as she lifted them, Anna again felt dismay at this newest talent she discovered in Kerstin, which she herself lacked.

Even after Anna had turned Karl down, Erik at last made her try it, pulling her out into the festivities with the others. She really didn't do half bad, although she felt far from feminine, swooping around the circle in her britches. She wished she had a dress like Kerstin's, but resolutely refrained from wearing the inappropriate ones she owned.

The work on the cabin went on the next day, and at the end of it the floor was completely laid. The fiddle was tuned again, to christen the new house with music and dancing. This time, Anna participated whenever invited to do so. Karl asked her to dance many times, but she felt clumsy when she compared herself to any of the other women there, particularly Kerstin, who could pick up her skirts and laugh without reserve while she spun and cut figures with her light steps.

Karl danced with Kerstin no more often than he did with any of the others, but it seemed to Anna that each time she looked up, Kerstin was bobbing around in the crook of Karl's arm. At the end of one particularly carefree jig with a fast-paced rhythm, everyone was breathless and laughing as they twirled an end to the song. Anna glanced over Olaf's shoulder to see Karl whirling Kerstin, his arms locked around her, until her feet left the floor and her skirts went sailing. She was laughing unabashedly as he released her. Then she reached to pat her forehead and straighten a wisp of hair that wasn't even out of place.

'Oh, Anna,' she said, coming to take Anna's arm, 'that Karl is some dancer. He wears me right out!'

Anna bit her tongue to keep from saying what had crossed her mind. 'Ya! He used to wear me right out, too-o-o!'

That night Anna lay awake a long time after Karl was sleeping soundly. She rehashed everything about the last two days with the Johansons. Each word between Karl and Kerstin took on an increasingly personal note. Each compliment Karl paid Kerstin's cooking rankled mercilessly. Each memory of that last whirling hug became more intimate. There was no doubt about it. Beside Kerstin, Anna felt as inferior as a ragweed in a rosebed.

Well, she thought angrily, if he wants his perfect, plump Kerstin, let him have her! I'll be damned if I'll stand by and watch while he fawns over every move she makes. They said they'll finish in a short day's work tomorrow and they don't need me anyhow, so why should I go and get in their way anyway? Even when I'm there, I might as well be a stump, for all the attention I get. They talk Swedish around me as if I *am* a stump! Nothing more than the useless stump left when they're done chopping down their precious tamaracks! Well, I might be as useless, but I don't need to stand around and let them lean their big Swedish boots and their precious Swedish axes on me!

15

The following day, Anna woke early enough to prepare breakfast for Karl and James. She did it before they could protest. Let them eat my cooking whether they like it or not! They can just do without their lingonberries for one morning! Anna threw a baleful eye at James. He was rarin' to go. Seems he's hooked on one of the Swedish lovelies, too, Anna thought bitterly, making herself all the more miserable.

When Karl said, 'Hurry up, Anna, we must get going,' it wasn't quite as satisfying as she'd thought it'd be to answer, 'I'm not going today.'

'Not going?' To his credit, Karl sounded dismayed. 'Why not, Anna?'

'I think I had better stay home and tend to my weeding. The vegetables are getting lost out there. Anyway, there's not much left to do on their cabin, so you won't even miss me.'

'Come on, Karl!' James called from the wagon. 'Hurry up!'

'Are you sure, Anna?' Karl asked. 'I do not like to leave you here alone, Anna.'

She needed to show him she was just as capable as the capable Kerstin Johanson . . . even more so, staying all day without a man to depend on for every ounce of protection. 'Don't be silly, Karl, I've got the gun, haven't I?'

It was the longest day of Anna's life. She cried and dried up, dried up and cried, until she thought she would kill the poor vegetables with salt tears! She worked fiendishly, but all day she bludgeoned herself with images of Karl and

Kerstin. She imagined him nodding to Kerstin to tell her how good her blueberry cobbler was. She imagined him telling her how he loved her golden braids, so neatly wrapped upon her fine, Swedish head. She even imagined the two of them speaking together in Swedish, and felt a greater anguish at not being able to share his beloved language with Karl. Time and again, Anna remembered Karl calling her 'my skinny little hen,' and she berated herself for her thinness. There was little Anna could do about her thinness or her wretched cooking, but at least she could take a bath! If Karl wanted his women smelling like lye soap, so be it!

She bathed, then waited, but the sun was still far above the horizon. It was then, with the sun just beginning to filter through the western treeline, when Anna had the splendid idea of how to please Karl.

She would find his precious blueberry patch and pick him blueberries till he got hives from them! Bolstered by the idea of a way to keep busy till he returned, and at the same time do *something* right, she grabbed a wooden pail and took off, following the familiar path to the beaver pond and heading north along the creek until she reached the shallows where she crossed, heading northwest in search of berries.

She kept a close eye on the sun, gauging its descent, knowing when it rimmed the horizon, she had better start for home so she'd be there when Karl and James returned.

Not twenty minutes from the creek she found the berries. They were fat and purple and thick as the mosquitoes that hovered above them. Never in her life had Anna suffered mosquitoes like this! She swatted and slapped, and still they stung her faster than she could swoosh them away. At last she was forced to move out of the thicket for a while. But Karl wanted blueberries, and she was determined he'd have them. She moved from thicket to thicket, continuing to pick

238

until her pail was nearly two-thirds full and heavier than she'd imagined mere blueberries could be.

The sun was as low as she'd decided she should let it get before starting back. She heard the gurgle of the creek and headed for it. The mosquitoes were coming out worst than ever now as evening drew on. But she tried to ignore them, carrying her bucket and following the meandering stream toward home, until she reached a sharp curve that took the creek northward.

On her way out to the berries, she had not passed this bend in the water! Well, with the sun at her right, she ought to be going in the proper direction. But when she retraced her steps, she came to a fork where this creek met another, and they both seemed to be flowing due north. Their own little creek flowed south by southwest!

The pail became leaden, the sun slipped down, dusk came on. Anna picked a willow switch to keep the mosquitoes fanned off herself as best she could. The tree frogs started up, and the mosquitoes kept it up. Finally, Anna thought she could stand neither the singing nor the stinging one more minute! By the time she admitted she was abysmally lost, the western sky was tinted with only a faint hint of orange, making the stark silhouettes of the trees loom like threatening black fingers.

Karl and James returned from the Johansons expecting to find woodsmoke rising from the chimney and a pleasant supper warm on the hob. But the ashes were scarcely warm, and there was no sign of supper cooking. Karl walked out to the vegetable garden, found it freshly weeded. He walked to the new log house and stepped inside. It was dark, for the sun was gone. He could see nothing in the far corners.

'Anna?' he called. 'Are you in here?' But there was only the soft tittering of the birds, chirping through the partially opened chimney hole. 'Anna?'

He met James in the clearing. 'She's not in the spring-house,' James said. 'I checked.'

'There is still the barn.'

'She's not there either. I searched there, too.'

Karl's heart began hammering harder. 'She might have gone down to the pond.'

'Alone?' James asked disbelievingly.

'It is the only other place I can think of.'

They grabbed the gun and headed for the pond. Why hadn't Anna taken the gun if she went out alone into the woods? It was feeding time for the wild animals. Karl knew the pond was the likeliest place to come upon any number of various creatures drinking – creatures with claws and teeth and horns and – But at the pond there were no animals. There was no Anna.

He could think of no place she might be. Sadly, he headed back down the trail for home. James was on the verge of tears. He walked ahead of Karl and kept peering into the darkening woods on either side, hoping to see his sister appear out of the shadows. By the time they reached the cabin, the sun had fully set, and there was a scant hour of dimming light left by which to see.

'Would she have walked out along the road toward Johanson's?' James asked hopefully.

'We would have seen her if she was headed that way to join us.' Karl's eyebrows were blond question marks of worry.

'What's the other way up the road?'

'Nothing. It is only the trail that goes all the way to Fort Pembina in Canada. Why would she go that way?'

'Karl, I'm scared,' James said, his eyes wide with bewilderment.

'When you are scared is the best time to keep your wits about you, boy.'

'Karl, I know Anna's been crying a lot lately.'

Karl felt like James had taken a hot poker and branded

him in the middle of his chest. He gritted his teeth together and stared. 'Be quiet and let me think.'

James did as he was bid, but it didn't settle his nerves any to have Karl pacing back and forth, rubbing his forehead and saying absolutely nothing. Karl built a fire, knelt before it staring. At last, when James thought he wouldn't be able to stand the silence another second, Karl leapt up and exploded, 'Count the buckets!'

'What?'

'Count the pails in the springhouse, boy! Now!'

'Yessir!' James ran out the door while Karl sprinted to the barn to see if there were any pails there.

They met in the clearing again, and it was almost full dark by this time.

'Four,' James reported.

'Three,' said Karl. 'There is one missing!'

'One missing?'

'If she took a pail, she must have gone to get something. What? A load of clay for chinking? No, we have already been down to the clay pit. Berries? No. She does not know where any berries grow – Wait!'

They both thought of it at once.

'You told us blueberries grow on the northwest corner of your property.'

'That's it! Get the team back out, James, and ride to the Johansons. If Anna is lost in the woods, it will take every person to find her. These woods are deadly at night.'

Karl rigged a flare of cattails for James to take along, lit it and handed it to him, ordering, 'Get the Johansons back here as fast as you can. Tell them to bring guns and flares. Hurry, boy!'

'Yessir!'

Knowing there was no sense in going out alone, that one man could do little against these wilds, Karl forced himself to remain calm while waiting for James to return with the Johansons. In the meantime he continued binding the

241

cattails into slow-burning torches the search party could carry through the woods. He tied them into clusters of eight, so each member of the party would have a supply to sling on his back. At last James returned with the Johansons.

They wasted no time on questions, except for those Karl needed to answer to make sure nobody else got lost while hunting for Anna.

'We will quarter the creek,' Karl explained, meaning they would walk at a ninety-degree angle to it. 'Walk fanned out with only the distance of the torchlight between us. Never get so far away you lose sight of the torches next to you. If your torch goes out, signal the person next to you. If you find Anna, pass the word along the line. When we have gone as deep into the woods as I believe she could have gotten, I will fire a single shot. That means everybody turns to his right and walks eight hundred paces before turning back toward the creek again.'

'Do not worry, Karl,' Olaf said, 'we will find her.'

'Everybody take ashes from the bucket and rub them on your face and hands,' Karl ordered, 'or the mosquitoes will eat you alive. When you get to Anna, you will have to use your own face and hands to rub ashes on her. She will be in bad shape from bites, I fear.'

They followed Karl and James into the woods, along the babbling creek, deeper and deeper, until Karl gave the instruction to fan out. They quartered the creek, walking in the buzzing night with only the far-off torch flickers to brave fearful hearts.

Each of them thought of how it must be for Anna somewhere out here alone, with no ashes to protect her from the vicious mosquitoes, no torchlight to remind her there were others within shouting distance, no gun to protect her from the nocturnal prowlers ranging the forests. They strained their eyes and ears, called out until their throats were raw, their voices hoarse.

Karl and James searched with frantic pictures in their minds of Anna hurt, Anna crying, Anna dead.

Karl berated himself for leaving her home alone today when he should have insisted she come along. He thought of the cleanly weeded garden, and swallowed hard at the lump in his throat. He thought of their estrangement and the reason for it, and of how long it had been since they had made love. He thought of James saying earlier, 'I know Anna's been crying a lot lately, Karl.' He knew Anna had been crying a lot lately, too.

Why hadn't he done as Father Pierrot so wisely advised? Why had he not talked this thing over more fully with Anna when he had the chance? Instead, he had not only let the sun set on his anger; tonight he had also let it set on Anna, lost somewhere in the woods with all this enmity between them. And if he never found her again, or if it was too late when he found her, it would be entirely his fault.

Anna, where are you? I promise I will try to work this thing out of my system, Anna, if you are only here and safe. At least we will talk about it and find some way to work at forgetting it. Anna, where are you? Anna, answer me.

But it was not Karl who found her. It was Erik Johanson. He found her not by spying her running toward the torchlight in the woods, but by spying the red eyes of the wolves, by hearing their nipping yaps ahead of him long before their eyes pierced the night.

The wolves were circling the tree where Anna perched in terror, afraid her numb limbs would give out, afraid she would fall asleep and tumble down. Underneath, the jaws snapped and the canine mewls told her the animals were still trying to get to her by leaping at the tree trunk. There were only three of them.

When Erik bared his own teeth and whirled his torch

above his head, the wolves retreated. Still, all three hovered until Erik jabbed at a pair of red eyes with his torch, and at last they slinked off like shifting shadows.

'Over here!' Erik shouted to the search party members nearest, then raised his eyes and arms. 'Anna, are you all right?'

Before she could answer or slip down the tree to him, she saw one of the wolves advancing again toward Erik and she shrieked his name.

He swung about sharply, stabbing at the hungry, glowing eyes, singeing fur upon the beast who thought his threat empty. At the smell, the animal withdrew farther into the woods to join the other two before they disappeared into the blackness for good.

By this time another torch had come to help ward off the attackers, then another. Karl had stationed himself in the centre of the flank, so by the time the word got to him, four other torches were there and Anna had been safely brought down from the tree.

Karl came into the circle of torchlight to find a sobbing Anna clutched in the strong arms of Erik Johanson. Tears streamed down her face, rinsing it clean. Thin rivulets of tears and ashes washed down her skin. Erik had done as instructed, had used his own face and hands, rubbing them upon Anna as soon as he found her. But she had clutched Erik about the neck in a locked grip, which she would not relinquish.

Erik looked across her head as Karl came into the torchlight, helplessly bound by Anna's arms, not knowing what to do or say. Karl was smitten with mental pictures of Erik's cheeks and hands rubbing his Anna's face. His stomach turned curiously tight, and he wanted to shout at Erik to get his arms away from her.

'She seems to be all right,' Erik assured him, then his voice became gentler as he spoke near Anna's ear. 'Anna, Karl is here now. You can go to Karl now.'

But Anna didn't seem to hear, and if she did the words weren't registering. She clung to Erik as if her life depended upon him.

Karl watched with heart so utterly relieved that the sudden release from fear caused his stomach to tremble. James came plummeting out of the woods to fling himself against Anna, hugging her from behind with his face against her back, fighting away the tears. And all the while Anna clung to Erik Johanson.

Kerstin saw the way Karl hung back, strangely reluctant to take his wife from her brother's arms. It confirmed the suspicion she'd had all along that all was not right between the Lindstroms.

At last Karl spoke. 'Anna, you are going to choke poor Erik.' But it was Karl who sounded like he was being choked. He approached, waiting for her to turn to him.

At the sound of his voice, she did. He saw her ash-smeared face wavering in the torchlight while she, too, saw his. When his familiar voice came from behind the grey mask, she whimpered, 'Karl?'

'Yes, Anna.'

And still they hesitated. She stood forlornly, like a ragged, dirty waif, her face smeared and ashen, puffed beneath the grey from bites and from crying. Her hair was an explosion of whiskey strands and blueberry twigs. In the torchlight her red-rimmed eyes were frighteningly enormous. Her tears rolled silently and plopped off her cheeks onto her shirt, making dirty blobs where the garment hung loosely on her thin frame. She struggled to hold her chest still, but could not breathe without shuddering. The back of one hand came up and swiped at her nose, then dropped down forlornly.

Never in her life had Anna wanted a person to touch her . . . just touch her . . . as badly as she now needed Karl to. Bitten, abject, frightened, penitent, she stood before him, her insides trembling, her limbs quaking, knowing she had fallen short of his expectations again.

'You have given us such a fright, Anna,' Karl said tiredly, but relieved.

Between sobs she choked pitifully on her words. 'I wa . . . wanted to p . . . pick you suh-hum blueb . . . berries . . . fo . . . hoar your . . . suh . . . hupper.'

At her wracked appeal, Karl was overcome by pity. Opening his arms, he clutched her against his thick chest, with James somewhere in the hug, too, and Karl's hard, cold rifle pressing into the back of Anna's head, pulling her hard against him.

'The wol . . . wolves . . . ca . . . came . . . Karl,' she sobbed, 'a . . . hand . . . I – '

'It's all right, Anna. It's all right,' he soothed, but she went on.

'And the . . . mos . . . mosque . . . heetoes . . . were . . . s . . . so bad.'

'Shh, shh.'

'I just wa . . . haunted to . . . get . . . s . . . some blue . . . berries for you, K . . . Karl.'

'Anna, you don't have to talk now.'

'The p . . . pail . . . spilled, K . . . Karl.'

He squeezed his eyelids tight shut. 'I know, I know,' he said, rocking her.

'But . . . but the blue . . . blueb . . . berries.'

'There will be more.'

'The creek . . . it flowed north and . . . and I . . . I couldn't – '

'Anna, Anna, you are safe now.'

'Oh, Karl, I'm . . . s . . . sorry. I'm s . . . sorry, Karl.'

'Yes, Anna, I know.' The tears were gathering on the rims of his eyes.

'Don't l . . . let . . . me . . . g . . . go, Karl. I'm s . . . sorry.'

'I will not let you go. Come, Anna, we must go home now.'

But she would not give up her grip. She sobbed out of control against his neck until he finally handed his rifle to James and picked Anna up in his arms.

Encircled by the torches, he carried her home. Before they got there, she was asleep in his arms, though her hold around his neck was as tight as ever. In spite of his stature and physical condition, Karl was in a quivering state himself by the time they reached the cabin.

Everyone hovered after Karl had laid Anna down on the bed, wanting the best for both of them, hesitant to leave for fear they might yet be needed. Karl assured them they had done more than enough, and once outside thanked them all with handclasps and squeezes.

Before going Olaf suggested, 'Karl, perhaps we should not come tomorrow to help with the cabin. We can wait and come the next day. Anna is in a bad state and maybe would like to rest one day. You spend the day with her until she feels better, and we will come the next day.'

Katrene advised, 'You put a thick saleratus paste on those bites so Anna will not feel so awful.'

'Ya, Katrene. I will do as you say. And I think you are right, too, Olaf. One day more or less will not matter. We will finish the work on my cabin day after tomorrow.'

'We will all be here then, don't you worry,' Erik assured him.

Each Johanson made a comforting comment as the family parted.

Charles said, 'You rest now and take it easy tomorrow, too. You can use it.'

In Swedish Katrene said, 'Now do not forget – saleratus will take away that itching.'

Karl smiled and promised he would not forget.

Leif said, 'I sure hope she's all right, Karl. We'll all be thinking about her till we see you again.'

Olaf said, 'We will be here with sharp axes, bright and early day after tomorrow, boy.' He clapped a big paw around the back of Karl's neck, much as he might to one of his own sons.

Erik lingered. 'I am sorry you were not the one to find her, Karl.' His eyes said, she was not thinking of who she clung to, think nothing of it, my friend. Karl's eyes rewarded the young man with a tired smile, telling him he must not worry about it.

Kerstin came last. She laid her hand upon Karl's forearm and looked directly into his troubled blue eyes. She, too, spoke in Swedish.

'Karl,' she said, 'Mama is right about saleratus, but I think saleratus will not fix all that is wrong with Anna. I can see there is something that needs fixing in her heart. Whatever it is, I think you could help her fix it, Karl.'

'We have not been married long, Kerstin,' he muttered. 'There are things between us we are still getting used to.'

'I will not say more now. I can see you are troubled, too, Karl. Just remember, differences cannot be overcome if they continue to be held inside.'

Her words were essentially the same as Father Pierrot's.

'I will remember. Thank you, Kerstin.'

Nedda was the only one not to bid goodbye to Karl, for she and James had strolled near the barn when the others crowded outside the tiny sod house. In the soft late-summer night they stood beneath the starshine. A whippoorwill called a repetitious song from the dark of the trees. Bats swooped and darted, squeaking in mouselike voices, while the cheep of the ever-present crickets scraped away like fiddles with single strings.

Nedda bravely put her hand over the back of James's where it lay on the top rail of the fence. 'I am happy we found her. I did not know before how terrible it would actually be to lose a sister or brother.'

'I didn't either. Anna and me, we been together all our lives. I mean, she's just always been there takin' care of me.

I never stopped to think how horrible it would be without her.'

Nedda removed her hand from his, but watched his face. 'Where's your mama and papa, James?'

'Our ma is dead and our – ' He swallowed, making the sudden manful decision to trust Nedda with the truth, no matter what she'd feel. He had seen his and Anna's lies hurt Karl enough. For himself now, he chose to be straightforward right off and avoid the long-reaching tentacles of lies. 'We never knew our pa, Anna and me. And you might as well know the truth, Nedda. It's a pretty sure bet we each had a different pa. See, our ma really was never too glad to have either one of us. That's why Anna and me had to stick together so close, else we wouldn't have anybody.'

Nedda was stricken by the idea of a mother who didn't want her children. 'I guess Anna's awful special to you, huh?'

'Ya, she sure is.' James didn't even realize that his answer sounded like Karl's might have. 'I mean, golly, it's almost more special when somebody isn't your full blood and they still . . . they – ' James couldn't finish. He was recalling all the times Anna had bundled him protectively off to St Mark's, or promised she'd find them a better life. He remembered how she had refused to leave him behind to come here to Karl. He thought, too, of her recent misery, helpless to find any answer for it himself.

'I guess what you say is Anna's not even your whole sister but she loves you like as if she was. Ya, James?'

He scuffed at nothing with the toe of his boot, looked down with a strange uncomposed feeling upon him. He nodded his head. He thought for a moment, then asked plaintively, while looking up at the stars, 'Nedda, what makes people who love each other not want each other to know it?'

'You mean your ma?'

'No, not her! I never cared a fig about her. It's Karl and

Anna I'm talkin' about. There . . . there's something wrong between them and I'd give anything to fix it, but I don't know how. Heck, I don't even know what it is.'

'Do they fight?'

'That's just it. No!' James sounded frustrated. 'If they did, maybe they'd straighten it out. Instead, they just treat each other – I don't know what to call it. Polite, I guess. You know how your ma and pa laugh and he pinches her and everything?'

'Ya, but my papa is a big tease.'

'Don't you see? That's how Karl and Anna used to be when we first came here. See, they've only been married since the beginning of summer. They seemed to get along so good and then I said something and – ' He swallowed, thinking he would give anything if he could take back the truth he'd revealed when he thoughtlessly spewed out all he had to Karl. 'I think I caused all this trouble between them because I told Karl something one day that he can't forget.'

'About Anna?'

'No. That's why I can't figure out the whole mess. It was about our ma. She was . . . She was a . . .'

'A what, James?'

'A prostitute,' he finally got out, waiting for Nedda to run in shocked disapproval back to her family.

Instead, she remained steadfastly beside him. 'I don't know what that is.'

'But Nedda, you're a year older than me!'

'I still don't know what it is. My English is not so good yet. Some words I haven't learned.'

He searched for some way to say it.

She sensed his struggle and said, 'It doesn't matter, James.'

'Well, it matters to Karl. And if he didn't know, I think everything would still be okay between him and Anna. At the same time, I just can't believe he would hold it against her if he didn't like our ma. He's a fair man. He just wouldn't do that.'

'You really like Karl, don't you?'

'Almost as much as Anna. He's . . .' But it was impossible to encapsulate all he felt for Karl. 'He gave us the only home we ever had. I just wish whatever is between him and Anna would get straightened out so they'd be happy again.'

'It will, James, I just know it will.'

He turned to look at her face squarely. 'Thanks for listening anyway, and for coming to help us find Anna.'

'Don't be silly.'

'I guess . . . I guess I did look pretty silly, how I acted when we found Anna, but, golly . . .' He felt sheepish to have had Nedda see him clinging to his sister's skirts like such a baby.

But then Nedda said something quite wonderful that made him forget how he'd clung to Anna and cried.

'You know something, James?'

'What?'

'I'm kind of glad all this happened.'

'Glad?'

'Ya. Because you rode all that way to our house in the dark by yourself.'

'It's not that far,' James said in a hushed pride.

'In the dark alone it is,' she insisted.

'So, why are you glad?'

'Because now that you did it once, you can do it any time – come over, I mean.'

'I can?'

'Sure. You don't have to wait for Karl and Anna to come. See you day after tomorrow, James.' Then she was gone to join her family, and Karl bade them goodbye at their wagon.

When the Johansons left, Karl clapped a big hand on James's shoulder. 'You did a man's job tonight,' he praised.

251

'Yessir,' James replied, so much more in his heart he was unable to say.

They stood a while in silence before Karl added, 'She is a cute little thing, that Nedda.'

'Yessir,' James said again, swallowing. Then he wisely offered, 'I'd like to go out and see to Belle and Bill tonight if you don't mind, Karl.'

'I do not mind. Just make sure you do not smoke any pipes out there like I do. Your sister would not like it.'

'Don't worry. I just got some thinking to do.'

'I will leave the latchstring out.'

'Goodnight, Karl.'

'Goodnight, boy.'

Anna watched Karl as he entered. He walked to the fireplace and stood facing it. He cradled both of his cheeks in his hands, dug his fingertips into his eyes, then sighed heavily as he rubbed his hands downward and dropped them from is cheeks. His shoulders drooped.

'Karl?'

He whirled around. 'Anna, you are awake,' he said, coming to the bedside.

'I have been for some time now. All the while you and Kerstin were whispering in Swedish outside. What were you talking about, Karl?'

'About you.'

'What about me?'

'She said you will need some saleratus for those bites.'

But Anna didn't believe him. Tears sprang to her eyes. 'I am nothing but trouble to you, Karl. I'm even trouble to the Johansons.'

'They are good people. They do not mind.'

'But I mind, Karl, I mind. I never should have come here.' She lay on her side, watching his knees as he stood beside the bed.

He did not know what to reply. On one hand was a

great engulfing sympathy for her. On the other, that great engulfing hurt she had caused him. Yes, it was still there. He longed to go back to the days before he had guessed the truth.

'It is too late to think of that now,' he said. 'Your face is still all streaked with ashes, Anna. You had better wash it before you fall asleep again. There is warm water for you.'

She struggled to sit up, and he came to take her by an elbow and help her. To have him touch her thus – with polite consideration, even though he had not even argued when she'd said she should never have come here – took her apart at the fringes again. But she bit back the tears and went out to the washbench and cleaned her face, hands and neck in the dark.

She came back inside and ducked behind the blanket to change into her nightgown. The curtain hung now like a gonfalon, a constant reminder of the night Karl had pulled it down and taken it with them to the barn.

He was waiting for her when she emerged. 'I have made a paste of saleratus and water,' he said. 'It will relieve the itching for tonight.'

She raised her hands to her face self-consciously, touching it, testing it. Even without a mirror, she could tell it was puffed and swollen. 'I'm really a mess.'

'Here, this will help.'

'Thank you, Karl.'

She sat down on the edge of the bed and patted the paste onto her face.

'Take care you do not get it into your eyes,' he warned.

'I'll be careful.'

Karl hovered listlessly, feeling awkward standing there waiting for her to be finished and get into bed so he, too, could lie down.

She covered her face, neck and the backs of her hands. But the paste needed drying to be effective. Sitting there waiting for it, she started twitching. She tried to reach to the centre of her back, but couldn't.

'Karl, they got me all over. Scratch me back there,' she said, wriggling.

He sat down on the edge of the bed behind her. While he scratched her back, she began scratching her ankle, then her arms and soon her chest.

'Ya, they got you good, little one,' he agreed. When he realized what he'd said, his fingers stopped moving.

Suddenly she too fell still, the bites forgotten momentarily, while she let the endearment wash over her.

But the itching started again, so she asked, 'Karl, could you put some paste on my back?'

There followed a long pause while he looked at her shoulder blades, remembering times his palms had run over them while he was carried away by passion. At last he swallowed hard and said, 'Hand me the cup.'

When she had, she unbuttoned the front of her gown and lowered it, exposing her back to him, holding the front over her breasts. It was more skin than she had bared to him since their estrangement had begun. She pictured his eyes scanning her bareness, remembered his hands, gentle in the midst of love, caressing her in the way she now yearned for with daily-increasing fervour. She waited with hammering heart and tingling nerves for his first touch upon her, after all this lonely time. When it came, it was cold, and she flinched, then silently cursed herself, wanting to appear calm before him.

There were welts as big as peas all over her back, white-centred, rimmed with red. When he touched the first one with the clammy paste, her shoulders twitched away.

'Sorry,' he muttered, the sight of her bare back raising old, yearning memories within him. He forced himself calmly to continue his ministrations, keeping his eyes from dropping to the shadow of her spine where the gown sagged, swagged, far enough adroop that he knew there was an inviting shadow there. He dabbed all the bites he could see, then – his stomach went tight and his heart went crazy – he lifted the fringe of hair from her neck and found two more bites beneath it.

She reached an arm back, lifting the hair aside so he could get at the rest hidden there. With racing heart she wondered if he would think her wanton posing so seductively. As if to repudiate his possible thought she clutched the front of her nighty more tightly to her breasts that ached for the sensual way he had touched them so well, days past.

The hair that grew in the hollow of her neck was fine and curly. He had never seen it before, for she always let her hair hang free.

'You must let them dry,' he rasped.

She sat there holding the hair up, feeling his thigh against her buttock on the edge of the bed, wondering if he was experiencing any of the same overwhelming feelings as she – sexual, pulsing, throbbing. But he sat as still as a statue, and finally the hair dropped. Anna reached blindly over her shoulder, saying, 'There are a few more up here. Hand me the cup.'

Wordlessly, he placed it into her hand, carefully avoiding her fingers. He saw her gown drop to her waist, saw her chin lower as she looked down at herself, watched her elbows moving as she touched the paste to her skin. He need not see the front of her to remember. He felt blood surge through his loins, and a tightening contract his chest. He tried to think of her as he had when he was writing letters to her, as his little whiskey-haired Anna. But even as want crept over him, he found himself wondering how many others had seen her brush the back of her hair away from her neck so seductively. No matter how many others there had been, he could not help placing his hand around her neck, squeezing her hair lightly against it.

Anna's eyes drifted closed and she leaned back, lifting her chin, pushing more firmly into his spanning hand. It

255

was warm, even through her hair, speaking of desperation and hope, making her want to turn quickly and be taken into his forgiving arms. But it had to be him beckoning her to return to them.

'Anna,' he whispered in a choked voice, 'there are things we must talk about.'

'I can't go on like this much longer,' she managed, tears in her voice.

'Neither can I.'

'Then why do you?' She could feel her own breath, battling its way up her throat past the heart, which threatened to choke her with its clamour.

'I cannot forget it, Anna,' he despaired.

'You don't want to forget it. You want to keep remembering it and keep me remembering it, too, so I will always know I was once bad.' Her eyes still remained closed.

'Is that what I am doing?'

'I . . . I think so.'

A very long, silent minute eased by, nothing more than crickets, fire and breath speaking.

'Can you blame me?' he asked.

The pain in his question became magnified within her own heart. She leaned yet against his hold, the hair now hot where he enclosed it about her neck. 'No,' she whispered.

'Did you think that if I guessed, I would let it pass?'

'No.'

'I have tried to put it from my mind. But it is there, Anna. Every minute I am awake it is waiting there and I cannot forget it.'

'Do you think I can?'

'I do not know. I do not know you well enough to know such things about you.'

'Well, I can't, Karl. I can't forget it either. But I'd give anything if I could make it so it had never happened.'

'But that cannot be.'

'So will you hold it against me forever?'

'You are my wife, Anna! My wife!' he said intensely, squeezing her neck. 'I took you to me believing you were pure. Do you know what it means to a man to learn that others have gone before him?'

Stung, shamed, she felt his words pierce her heart. So he had thought all this time that her scruples were that low. 'Not *others*, Karl, only one.'

Anger and hurt surged through him. '*Only* one? To me you say *only one*! You might as well say lightning is only fire after it has struck me down. Do you know that is how I felt that day?' His hand tightened painfully for a moment. 'I felt like I was struck by lightning, only it was not kind enough to kill me. It only left me burned and blistered instead.' The hand dropped from her hair as if the sensation were upon him presently.

'Karl, I never meant for you to find out,' she said, ineptly. 'I thought – '

'Don't you think I know that? There is no need for you to say it now. I know what a fool you must have thought me when I did not even guess that night in the barn. Green Karl! Green as the spring grass. I thought we were learning together that night.'

Misery swept through Anna, coupled by her need to have him believe her. 'We were.'

'Do not lie to me any more. I forgave you all the other lies I discovered. But this one I have great trouble forgiving. I do not know if I ever can.'

'Karl, you don't understand – '

'No, I do not understand, Anna.' His voice quivered with intensity. 'I am a person who does not understand the selling of what should only be won with love. I have thought to myself so many times, why did Anna do such a thing? How could she? Do you know that I have even started to think that if you had done this with a man you loved I was wrong not to forgive you? But to do it for money, Anna . . .' His voice trailed away. When it came again, it was heavy with defeat. 'He did pay you, Anna, didn't he?'

She only nodded, then her chin dropped down to her chest.

'A man old enough to be your father . . .' His words had the woeful tune of a lament.

'Don't do this to yourself, Karl,' she whispered at last.

'It is not Karl who does it to himself, it is you who have done it to me.' His agonized voice drove on, killing her, making her bleed with regret. 'How I thought of you as my little whiskey-haired Anna. All those months, waiting for you, thinking of how it would be to have you here, to build the log house and have you here so I would not have to be alone ever again. Do you know how alone I feel now? It was much better – the kind of being alone I felt before you came. This now – some days I do not think I can bear it.'

Dread surged through Anna, but she knew she must ask the question which followed. 'Do you want me to leave, Karl?'

He sighed. 'I do not know what I want any more. I have spoken vows to love and honour you, and have sealed those vows with an act of love. I do not believe this vow can be sidestepped by turning you away. Yet I cannot honour you. I am torn in pieces, Anna.'

As it had the first time she'd heard him pronounce it, her name falling from his lips with that beloved accent, endeared him to her as never before. 'As soon as I met you, that very first day, I knew that this was how you'd feel if you ever learned the truth.'

'Could you not tell by my letters that I am . . .'

'That you are forgiving, Karl?'

They both realized how utterly untrue that sounded right now.

258

'Accepting, Anna. Accepting. Do you understand? If you had told me beforehand I would have accepted.'

'No, you wouldn't have, Karl. Even you aren't that big. You think if I had written to you and told you I was a prostitute's daughter and I had a kid brother I felt responsible for, you'd have brought us here willingly?'

Hearing it put that way, Karl, too, doubted what his reaction would have been.

'Karl, I think it's time I told you about Boston, all about Boston.'

'I do not want to hear it. I have heard enough about Boston to last me a lifetime. I hate the word.'

'If you hate it, imagine what I feel when I talk about it.'

'Then do not!'

'I must. Because if I don't, you'll never understand about my mother.'

'It is not your mother who disappointed me, Anna, it was you.'

'But she's part of it, Karl. You have to know about her to understand me.'

When he sat silently, she took it for assent. Gulping a shaky breath, she began.

'She never had much time for us. We were only two of her miscalculations, two of her mistakes. And in her profession, we were the biggest mistakes she could have made. She never let us forget it. "Where are those two brats of mine now?" she'd holler, until everybody who knew us took to calling us Barbara's Brats.

'We were never told for sure, but it didn't take much figuring to know that it's a pretty slim chance James and I are even full brother and sister. Chances are we had different fathers. But where we came from, that didn't matter to us. We learned early to depend on each other. Nobody else gave us support of any kind, so we got it from just ourselves.

'You were right about something else, Karl. She never

wanted us calling her "mother" for fear it'd scare away her customers. She needed to look young and act young to keep the men interested. Sometimes, we'd forget and call her mom, and she'd fly into a rage. The last time it happened was when I was about ten or eleven, I think. One of the other women had given me a cast-off feather for my hair, and I went running to her to tell her about it.

'That's the first time I ever saw . . . saw Saul. He was with her when I went charging outside as she came home, calling her. Only, I was so excited, I forgot to call her Barbara. When she heard me saying "ma" she tied into me right there in front of that man. Strangely enough, it proved one thing – she wouldn't lose her customers as quick as she thought, once they learned she had two kids.

'Saul was around from that time on, more than I'd have liked him to be. He watched and waited while I grew up, only I never knew he was waiting until I was about fifteen or so. That's when I started staying out of the way. You don't grow up in a place like that without knowing the hungry look on a man's face at too young an age.

'It was about that same time Barbara got the disease all women of her profession fear. She went downhill really fast, and lost her looks, her strength and her customers. After she died, her friends – if you want to call them that – let James and me stay at the place nights. But when the rooms were full, they sent us packing. That's why I knew what the inside of St Mark's looked like. We holed up there when there was no place else to go. At least nobody threw us out of there.

'We did look for work, Karl, honest we did. I used to keep the women's dresses mended at the place – they always had to have their clothes just so, of course – and that's how I learned a little seamwork. They paid me a little to do it, but not nearly enough. When I started writing to you, that's why I told you I was a seamstress. It was the only thing I could think of.

'And you guessed right about the dresses, too. They're cast-offs from the ladies. They were better than nothing, so I took them. I guess you understand now why I'd rather wear James's britches.

'Well, we hung on by our teeth, James and I. Then he started picking pockets and stealing food from the market stalls, and the ladies at the house were starting to encourage me to join their ranks.

'It was about then that James found your advertisement in the paper. It seemed like the first lucky break we'd ever had in our lives. And when you actually answered his first letter, we couldn't believe something had finally gone our way. We knew perfectly well I was no prime candidate for your wife. But all we could think of to do was to lie about my qualifications until I got to you and it was too late for you to do anything but accept.

'Naturally, I was afraid to tell you I had a brother. I had enough strikes against me without saddling you with that fact, too. I was afraid you would say all the things you *did* say that first day when you realized he was with me – he's an extra mouth to feed, an extra body to clothe, but mostly, he's an invasion of your privacy. The men I've seen all my life always liked their privacy. Both James and I knew that from the time we were tykes. When the men came, we went! I only knew I couldn't leave him.

'So James and I set out to get him here to you without your guessing he was coming along. My problem was that you mailed money for only my passage, and I had no way to earn his. He's thirteen and growing like a weed, out of his clothes almost overnight. I managed with my cast-offs, but there was nobody to hand things down to James. He needed boots, britches, shirts and passage money. But the time came for us to leave, and I didn't have it.

'He . . .' Anna took a shuddering breath. 'He was a very rich man, Saul was. He'd hung around after Barbara died, and I knew one of the reasons was me.' All this time Anna

261

had been sitting with her nightgown hugged against her front, draped down at her back. Now, she pulled it up and clutched it protectively closed.

Behind her, Karl put his hand on her shoulder, his fingers folding over into the shallow well in front. 'Don't, Anna.'

But she had to finish. If she wanted Karl to forgive her, he had to know exactly what it was he was forgiving her for.

'I got word to him, and he came in that red leather shay of his, thinking his money made him desirable. But I had hated him for as long as I could remember, and that day was no different, only worse.'

From behind, Karl could tell when she started to cry softly again. 'Don't,' he whispered fiercely, reaching an arm high across the front of her, grasping her upper arm. His forearm rested against her throat, and he felt her swallow. He pulled her back against him, against the lurching pity in his heart, holding her with the steel band of his arm, willing her to stop saying things he did not want to hear.

'He paid for the use of one of the rooms that had been our only home all our lives, James and mine. When he took me into it, I knew all the others knew and I wanted to scream I was not like them, not at all. But there was nothing else I could do. I thought if I was lucky, some last-minute miracle would save me, but there was no miracle. He was big and overweight and his hands were sweaty and he kept saying how long it had been since he'd had a virgin and how much he would pay me and he . . . he – '

'Anna, stop, please stop! Why do you go on?'

'Because you have to know. Even though I agreed to do it, I did it against my will. You have to know how sick it made me feel! You have to know it was horrible and joyless and painful and degrading and when it was done I wanted to die. Instead, I took his money and came to you, bringing my brother along.

'When I got here, even though you seemed a gentle and

kind person, Karl, I went through the whole thing again, worrying about how it would hurt, how awful it would be again. Only it was none of those things, Karl. With you, it was wholesome and good. With you it made . . . it made more of me instead of less. Oh, Karl, with you I *was* learning. You have to believe me. You taught me, you took away my fear, and you made it all beautiful. And when it was all over, I was so relieved you didn't guess the truth about me.'

They allowed silence to settle over them. Thick, unwanted thoughts were their companions, too, as they sat on the edge of the bed with Karl's arm still clasped across Anna's chest.

She felt sapped, overcome by a weariness that made the work of the cabin or the garden pale by comparison. Her head fell forward, and her lips came to rest upon the thick muscle of Karl's forearm, feeling the silken hairs and the firmness beneath them. How long it had been since her lips had touched him.

His voice, when at last it came, was slow, tired, in a way defeated. 'Anna, I understand better now. But I must ask you to understand about me, too, about the way I was raised to believe, and the way my mama and papa were. It was a far different upbringing than yours. The rules I lived by were rules that did not allow for a way of life such as your mother's to exist. I was as old as you are now before I knew about such existence, Anna. Now, I have learned so much so fast about you and James. I must sift it all through and get used to it. To come up against such truths about you puts battles inside me, and I must find my answers. I need some time, Anna. I ask you to give me more time, Anna.' He had the urge to kiss her hair, but could not make himself do it. The pictures she had just drawn were too fresh and hurting. They had opened wounds, which needed healing.

'James kept telling me you were a fair man, that I should

tell you everything at once – all the truth, I mean. But James doesn't know about all this.'

'He is a good lad. I have never been sorry a day that you brought him to me.'

'Whatever it takes, Karl, to make you feel the same about me, I'll do it. I'm not very good at most things around here, but I'll try hard to learn.' Anna could not help thinking of the golden-haired Kerstin, braided and spotless and capable and Swedish. And . . . in all likelihood . . . a virgin. All those things Karl might have had in a wife if only he'd waited another month before bringing Anna here.

He sighed heavily. 'I know you will, Anna. You already have. You have learned much, and you try as hard as the boy does. I can see that for myself.'

'But that's not enough, is it?'

For an answer Karl only squeezed her arm, then removed his own from around her. 'We must get some sleep, Anna. This day has been too long.'

'All right, Karl,' she said meekly.

'Come, get in and try to go to sleep.' He held back the cover, and she slid to her side. Then he slipped his clothes off and lay on his back with a weary sigh. These days, Karl wore his underwear to bed like armour.

For Anna, it was not the bite of the mosquitoes alone that kept her awake. It was also the bite of regret.

16

If Anna and Karl had not reached a reconciliation, they had at least reached a status quo, which they maintained all through the following day. Anna's unvarnished truth about Boston was a laying down of arms after which she waited for full amnesty. But Karl was biding his time, thinking over everything she had said, trying to accept it.

He took Anna and James fishing. It was the perfect activity Karl needed to give himself time to think. They spent a day that was, in Karl's estimation, far from unpleasant, all but for Anna's mosquito bites. He credited her sour mood to her discomforts at the gnawing itch as her body reacted to the toxins it was unaccustomed to, being an Easterner. It didn't help Anna's disposition any when Karl told her the longer she lived here, the greater would be her body's immunity to the bites. But by midday the bites were itching like scabies. She tried saleratus paste again, but it did little good. Finally, by late afternoon when raw spots were beginning to appear on her skin from the continued scratching, Karl took pity on her and announced he would walk over to ask Two Horns's wife what could be done to relieve Anna's bites.

He came back carrying a sheaf of Indian corn, which he shucked, shelled, then ground in a spice quern. He scrubbed a flat spade until it was perfectly clean, then sprinkled the grains of ground corn upon it and laid it in the coals until the kernels were dancing from the heat. Then he took a cold flatiron and pressed the hot corn until it emitted a light, pleasant-smelling oil. When the oil cooled, he in-structed Anna to put it on her skin.

But he didn't volunteer to help her reach the bites on her back. She had to ask him, which annoyed her. He knew darn well she couldn't reach them! Standing with her shirt raised up, holding it behind her neck, she heard Karl say behind her, 'Two Horns's wife said to tell Tonka Woman to soak Indian tobacco in water and wash with it the next time she goes berry picking, then the mosquitoes will not bite her.'

'I hope you told her it won't be necessary because Tonka Woman will not be quite as anxious to pick berries from now on.'

When they went to bed, Anna was sorry for her cutting remark. To make up for it she thanked Karl for going to the Indians and finding out about the corn oil. She thought maybe he would kiss her lightly and say it was no trouble.

He only said, 'The Indians have an answer for everything. Goodnight, Anna.'

She wondered angrily if the Indians had an answer for a husband who was so stubborn he would not bend! She had apologized, explained, appealed, and still he would not forgive her. His polite consideration was killing her!

Damn him and his corn oil! She didn't want his corn oil, she wanted his sweat! And she wanted it on her own skin!

The following day when the Johansons came, as promised, to help with the Lindstroms' cabin, Anna was ripe with irritability. After Karl's dismissive goodnight the evening before, she had alternately hated him and herself. She had worried about what an inept little nincompoop she would seem when it came time to prepare food for the battalion of people. She worried about what a tomboy she looked like next to Kerstin with her impeccable grooming. She worried about how Irish she looked next to Kerstin's blonde Swedishness. She worried about how English she sounded next to all the Johansons.

But Katrene and Kerstin took one look at her the

following day, and the first of her worries was solved. She looked so pitiful with her blotched skin now scabbing in places, her hands still a mess from prairie dig, they said she was to let them prepare the meal and do the work around the kitchen. Watching the pair of Swedish women perform in her kitchen as if they were born to it, Anna felt once again clumsy, stupid and more cranky than ever. She allowed them full sway, taking over the smaller duties.

Katrene suggested that Anna try a mixture of warm beeswax and sweet oil on her hands, making Anna again feel guilty at her irritability with the well-meaning woman. When Anna said she didn't know if Karl had any sweet oil, Kerstin at once said, 'If he does not, you just come to me and I will give you some.' Anna's defences crumbled with her generous offer. Kerstin was a warm lady, thoroughly undeserving of the mental acerbations Anna had been heaping upon her.

'Thank you, Kerstin. You're always helping me out of one scrape or another.'

'This is what neighbours are for.'

After that, Anna and the women spent a more pleasant day in conversation about countless things.

Meanwhile the men laboured outside, completing the work on the shingles and the floors. At the end of the day the fiddle was tuned again, and the dancing christened yet another floor. Even the dancing annoyed Anna, though. Again, she felt second-rate next to the other females. Moreover, when Karl danced with her, he held his distance, as if she would burn him or something. She could only sizzle in silence.

What does he think? That my sinfulness will rub off on him if he gets too close? she thought.

They were catching their breaths between dances when Katrene asked, 'When will you move in, Karl?'

'Not till the windows are installed and the door is on.'

'Windows!' Katrene exclaimed.

'Are you going to have windows?' Nedda asked. 'Glass windows?'

'Of course I will have windows, just as soon as I make the trip to Long Prairie to buy the sashes and panes,' declared Karl.

This was a complete surprise to Anna. She had assumed they would have the same opaque sort as in the sod house. Karl had never mentioned he intended to get glass windows.

'Oh, how lucky you are, Anna,' Kerstin said, obviously impressed.

Of all the luxuries on the frontier, the glass window was the greatest. It was no secret how the Indians could not even believe such a thing as a pane a person could see right through. The Indians spent hours staring into any glass window they came upon with the greatest of awe.

'I should say you are lucky,' Kerstin's mother echoed. 'I would think I was living in a castle if Olaf bought me glass windows.'

'You did not tell me you wanted glass windows when we came through Long Prairie, Mother,' Olaf said.

'I thought they would cost more money than we should spend.'

'But I asked you what it was you wanted when we were there. You should have said, "Glass windows, Olaf." ' He winked at Nedda who winked back. 'If your mother plays her cards right, she could get glass windows yet.'

'Olaf Johanson, you are teasing me! Have you decided we will have glass windows?'

'No, I think I ride along with Karl just to take the air.'

'Olaf Johanson, you are a stubborn Swede if I ever saw one. You know I hinted about windows when I was in Long Prairie.' But she was laughing in her usual merry way.

'But I did not think we would have neighbours to keep up with then.'

She went after him with a fist raised to his head, and

268

when the tussle was over they were dancing again to their son's fiddle.

In bed later Anna said quietly, 'Karl?'

'Hm?'

She imitated Katrene Johanson's Swedish accent as she said, 'You-u-u did not tell me vee vould haff glass vindows.'

'You did not ask me,' he answered. There was a smile in his voice, but still he remained aloof.

Anna's attempt to win him with humour was unsuccessful, and her impatience grew. Once again it came to matter very much that Katrene and Kerstin had done a much better job than Anna could ever dream of doing in her own kitchen.

A trip to town was not made without due planning. The ride was long and was not made often. Summer was drawing to a close. Though they were anxious to have their glass windows, one did not make the trip after them without taking care of all other vital business in Long Prairie at the same time. And so the harvesting must come first.

Karl's wheat crop was ripe and needed cradling so he could take it to the mill to have their winter supply of flour ground while he was in town. Wild rice and cranberries were cash crops readily available on Karl's land. Cranberries in particular were in demand in the East and brought a dollar a bushel, compared to the fourteen cents a bushel brought in by potatoes. Potatoes, therefore, were kept for the family's own winter use, along with turnips and rutabagas, all of which could be dug up later. The cash crops and table grains must be harvested first.

They cradled and raked the wheat field first, Karl, James and Anna. It was a backbreaking chore even though they had only a few acres in wheat. Karl handled the cradle, crossing and recrossing the plot with its giant, curved fingers sweeping out before him while his shoulders swayed rhythmically in the sun. The rake's fingers were fashioned of weighty steel. Its handle was shaped from sturdy green ash and was abominably heavy, too.

Again, Anna marvelled at the stamina of her husband. The massive cradle seemingly became an extension of the man. Like a switch that turned his power on, once it touched his hands he could wield it uncomplainingly in that unbreaking rhythm for endless hours.

The bundling of the grain was done by gathering it in clusters and using loose hanks of it as a self-tie. *Self*-tie? thought Anna tiredly – if only it would. This required much bending and stooping, though not as much muscle as cradling or raking.

If cradling and bundling were backbreaking, flailing was soulbreaking. Flogging the grains on smooth, cloth-covered earth in the clearing, Anna vowed that henceforth she would eat bread only once every other day to save on flour, if it took all this to produce it! Never had she experienced such aching shoulders as the day after flailing.

But at last the gunny sacks were filled, ready for loading, and Karl announced that all they had left was to gather wild cranberries, then he could make the trip to town.

The cranberry bog was deep in the woods where no trails had yet been cut. Karl fashioned a travois, which a single horse could pull easily through the woods with the baskets of berries loaded on it. Karl and his two helpers picked cranberries by hand and had many inquisitive visitors during the days they spent at the chore. The bogs, it seemed, were the favourite feeding grounds of many wild creatures who were perhaps put out at having their dinner table usurped by the marauding humans. Karl kept his gun close at his side while they garnered the berries, ever on the lookout for the black bears that considered this territory their own.

The group was busily picking the cranberries one day

270

when James asked, 'Why don't we move into the cabin, Karl?'

'Because it is not yet finished.'

'It is, too! All but the windows and door.'

'We cannot live in a house without a door, and I have been too busy to make one yet. And without windows it is too dark inside. We would use too many tallow dips.'

'The windows in the sod house are so thick not much light comes through them. Besides, we use tallow dips there, too.'

'It is customary to make the door last,' Karl said adamantly, 'and I cannot make the door last if I must yet make windows.'

'Well, I'd move into the cabin all by myself even without windows and a door. I can't wait!'

Karl threw a look at Anna, but she was picking cranberries as if she didn't hear anything. 'When the door closes on us for the first time, it will be on a finished house. I have promised Anna a dresser for her kitchen, which I have not yet made.'

Anna glanced up sharply.

'Well, I wish you'd hurry so we can move in,' James went on. 'I wish I could sleep in there tonight.'

'Without a door the wild animals could come right in and sleep with you.'

'Not in the loft! They couldn't get up there!' James was suddenly excited by the idea, thinking he was only a few hours away from using his loft for the first time. But Karl remained firmly opposed to the idea.

'You will wait until we have a proper door fashioned, and windows and furniture. Then we will all move into the log house together.' Karl's face now felt as red as the cranberries. Actually, he wanted James to stay in the sod house in his place on the floor for other reasons, too. Whether or not he admitted them to himself, he had spoken more harshly to the boy than he'd intended. The boy looked

271

aside while Anna, too, turned her attention back to the berries.

'It won't be long now,' Karl said in a more kindly tone. 'We have only to finish the cranberries and Olaf and I can make the trip to town.'

'Can I go with you?' James asked.

Anna longed to ask the same thing.

'No, you will stay here with your sister. Olaf and I will have a wagonful by the time we buy windows and bring back our winter flour. There are things you and Anna can do here that will be more useful than riding to town.'

Anna was so disappointed she had to turn her back on Karl to hide the glint in her eyes. Karl had treated her kindly since their talk, but now she felt he was eager to get away from her for a couple of days. She turned to peek at Karl again, but froze. Across the clearing, at the edge of the willow bushes stood a massive black bear. He was standing on his hind legs, sniffing the air as if it had flavour.

'Karl,' Anna whispered.

He looked up to find her startled eyes riveted on something behind him. Instinctively, Karl knew what he'd find. But he had worked his way several feet from his gun, and there was a basket of berries between him and it.

James, unaware, was picking away. 'How long will it take you to get your flour milled?'

'Pass me the rifle, boy,' Karl said, his voice silken, unequivocal.

James looked up, then glanced to where the other two were already staring. The blood dropped from his face.

'Pass me the rifle, boy. Now!' Karl snapped in strained, hushed tones.

But James stood stricken by the sight before him. The bear caught sight of them and dropped down on all fours and lumbered off into the pressing thicket of willows with a grumble that raised shivers up Anna's arms.

'Boy, when I tell you to pass me the rifle, I don't mean

next Tuesday!' Karl snapped in a tone such as neither James nor Anna had ever heard from him before.

'I . . . I'm sorry, Karl.'

'There might come a day when sorry will not be good enough!' Karl went on in the same dissecting voice that somehow made his Swedish accent far more pronounced than usual.

James stood defenceless before the big man, frozen, a palmful of cranberries forgotten in his hand.

'Do you know how fast a bear can run?' The question was rifled at the boy unmercifully.

'N . . . nossir.'

'The first lesson I ever taught you was that when I give the order to get the rifle you do not tie your shoelaces first! Your life and your sister's life might depend on how quick you move! If that bear had decided he did not like us helping ourselves to his cranberry patch he would not have stopped to tie his shoelaces! Besides that, you have just watched our entire winter's supply of candles and meat run off into the brush!'

'I . . . I'm sorry, Karl,' James quavered. The blood that had earlier fallen from his countenance now scorched it to a deep, burning red. In his stomach burned a molten trail of shame.

But still Karl continued his attack. 'I warned you the bears come to this spot, so if this happened you would be prepared!'

James stared at Karl's knees, speechless before this barrage that had flared up so quickly out of nowhere. It was doubly effective in cutting the boy because from Karl, who was normally so patient, so understanding, it was totally unprecedented. Defenceless, James turned to pick up his heels and run.

'Come back here, boy!' Karl shouted. 'Where do you think you will go? To find that bear again?'

James stopped, brought up sharp by Karl's command,

yet unwilling to turn around and be chastised in this unfair manner before his sister. Karl's unnecessary wrath brought tears to his eyes.

'He said he was sorry!' Anna snapped.

'Sorry is not enough, I said!'

Suddenly, the dam broke in Anna and she was answering Karl with venomous indignation of her own. 'No, it never is for you, is it, Karl? What is enough? Do you want him to take the gun and go after the bear singlehanded? Would that be enough for you, Karl?'

His face was redder than Anna had ever seen it. 'I expect him to do no such thing. I expect him to act like a man when it is necessary, not to freeze into his boots on the spot!'

'Well, he's not a man,' Anna shouted, defying her husband with hands on her hips. 'He's a boy of thirteen and he's never seen a bear in his life. How did you expect him to act?'

'Do not tell me how to teach the boy, Anna! This is a job for a man!'

'Oh, sure, this is a job for a man all right. If you had your way you'd stand there and yell at him about your stupid bear until he was in tears, but I won't let you! He's my brother and if I don't defend him nobody will. He won't talk back to you and you know it!'

'I said keep out of this, Anna.'

'Like *hell* I will!' she spit, glaring at Karl, defying him. 'He's trailed after you all summer, doing everything you ever asked him to do, and now when he does the first little thing wrong, you jump on him as if he was an ignorant fool. How do you think he feels? How could he possibly know how fast a bear could run? How could he possibly be thinking about your precious tallow candles when all he sees is a black monster standing on his hind legs, for the first time in his life?'

'It would have been the last time in his life, if that bear

274

had decided to run in our direction instead of into the woods. You do not seem to realize that, Anna!'

'And you don't seem to realize that you're treating him like he committed the biggest crime of the century when he only reacted like any thirteen-year-old boy would.'

'He has cost us enough meat to feed us and the Johansons for the entire winter!'

'Ah, the Johansons! Naturally, you'd have to bring them into this!'

'It is true! That meat was enough for them, too.'

'And I just bet you'd love to haul a bear carcass over there and present it to Kerstin with some little pink ribbons tied on its head!'

'What is that supposed to mean, Anna? Just what are you saying?' His fists were clenched and he glowered menacingly.

'It means exactly what you think it means! That you're more concerned with running over to fawn over Kerstin than you are about staying here with us. Of course, who could blame you when Kerstin does all that lovely cooking, and has those lovely yellow Swedish braids?'

Karl raised his nose to the sky and let out a solid snort. 'At least when I am at the Johansons I do not have a senseless woman chewing on me when I take a boy in hand for what he deserves!'

'He doesn't deserve it and you know it, Karl Lindstrom!'

'How would you know? Just how would you know? He came to me as green as these cranberry leaves and I have taught him well all summer. So far he has not done too bad listening to me!'

'So far! But not now. He doesn't have to listen to you now! Why should he when you're being an *unreasonable, stubborn, bullheaded fool!*'

Karl threw his hands up in the air. Both had forgotten that James stood by listening to them, watching them face each other like fighting cocks with their necks arched. 'Ya, you can call me a fool and know what you are talking about. You are good at finding a fool, aren't you, Anna? An eager, blushing fool!'

Her mouth was pinched and her eyes slitted as she spit, 'You can go straight to hell, Karl Lindstrom!'

'Is that the way they teach you to talk in that place you come from? Some lady I married, with a mouth like a sailor. Well, let me tell you something, Anna. I have been in hell. I have been in hell for weeks now! You think Boston was hell for you – '

'You leave Boston out of this! It's got nothing to do with it!'

'It has everything to do with it!'

'You just can't forget it, can you? I can work until I get dizzy around here. I can cook over your . . . your stupid smoky fireplace and flail your *damn* wheat till I can't straighten my shoulders, and scrub clothes with your rotten lye soap and pick blueberries till I'd like to die, and it doesn't matter one bit to you! I'm still the same fallen Anna, isn't that right? No matter what I do you want to punish me because you can't admit to yourself that maybe . . . just maybe . . . I was justified. Maybe, just maybe you are wrong to hold it against me all this time. But you can't back down and admit maybe the holier-than-thou, self-righteous Karl Lindstrom should lower himself! Well, let me tell you something! You're just a big, stubborn, *stupid* Swede, and I don't know for one minute why I slave my britches off to try to please you!'

'What kind of wife thinks she pleases her man in britches. Ya, you have britches all – '

'You leave my britches out of this!' she hissed. 'You know why I wear these britches. I'll wear them until they fall off my bones before I'll put one of those dresses on! I remember a time when you didn't exactly cry over the way I look in britches!'

'That was a long time ago, Anna,' he said more quietly.

276

'Ya-a-a, you-u-u bet it vas!' she retorted, using the exaggerated Swedish accent now as a hurting weapon. 'It vuz before the *beau-u-u*-tifful Kerstin *mu-u-uves* in next door vitt her *blu-u-u*-berry cobbler and her big *bu-u-u*-som.' Anna put a hand on her hip and swayed it provocatively while she drew out the vowel sounds, taunting Karl until his rage became fury.

'Anna, you go too far!' he shouted.

'Me?' she shouted back. 'I go too far?' Then she kicked viciously at a basket of cranberries, upsetting it so the berries rolled around Karl's feet. 'I can't go far enough to get away from you! But you just watch me try, Karl! You just watch me try!'

She swung around and strode across the lumpy earth and grabbed James by the arm. 'Come on, James, we don't have to stay here and take any more of this!'

Karl stood in his mound of cranberries, shouting at their backs. 'Anna, you come back here!'

But Anna only pulled James along, forcing him to walk faster.

'Anna, that bear is out there! Get back here!'

'No bear would want to touch a paw to me any more than you would!' she threw back over her shoulders.

'Anna . . . get – Dammit! Get back here!' swore Karl, who had never sworn at a woman in his life. But she only swooped away, riding on her wave of anger.

He tore his hat from his head and threw it on the ground, but knew nothing would make Anna turn around now. He bent to scoop the spilled berries back into the basket, glancing up at the diminishing figures disappearing across the bog. If he left the cranberries the bear would surely return and eat up Karl's most valuable cash crop, and all his richest earnings along with it. Karl could hardly leave the horse either, with the travois attached behind and loaded with the day's pick. The best he could do was hastily take what he could slap into the basket, load it as fast as possible and follow the wilful wife who was striding away with her britched backside defying him with every step.

Anger and concern turned Karl's face a mottled red. The woman had no idea of the danger she'd just put herself and the boy into by running off through the woods with that bear around! Karl finally got the baskets somewhat secured and led poor Belle off across the bog at such a pace that the horse resisted on the precarious footing and got herself unjustly yelled at for the first time in her life.

By the time he reached the clearing James and Anna had been there for some time. Relieved to find them safe when he arrived, everything exploded inside Karl's head as he strode into the sod house like a war lord.

'Woman, don't you ever do a thing like that again!' he shouted, pointing a finger at Anna.

'I'm not deaf!' she spit back at him.

'You are not deaf, but you are certainly *dumb*! Do you know what that bear could have done to you? You put not only yourself in danger but the boy, too. It was a stupid, senseless thing you did, Anna!'

'Well, what do you expect from a stupid, senseless woman?'

'That bear could have torn you to ribbons!' he exploded.

Hands on hips, defiance in eyes, sneer on lips, Anna flung words at him she didn't mean. 'And would you have cared, Karl?'

His face looked like he'd been slapped with a dirty rag for offering to wipe dishes. Anna knew immediately she had gone too far, but there was too much anger and pride and pain built up inside of her to pull back the words. Karl's blue eyes opened in surprise, then the lids lowered in hurt. The golden cheeks became mottled beneath his expression of disbelief.

They stared at each other across the rough-hewn table and it seemed like a lifetime passed in those few strained moments. Certainly, an entire marriage did. Anna saw the forced relaxing of muscles as one by one they eased from the tight hold Karl had upon himself. And by the time he turned to grab a canvas bag and stuff it with some food, too much time had passed for Anna to apologize gracefully. She watched as Karl silently went to the trunk, raised its lid and found a couple pieces of clean clothing and jammed them into the sack as well. He brushed around Anna to reach the spot above the fireplace where he kept his extra shot. He grabbed a handful of lead balls, thrust them into a leather pouch that lay on the mantel. Then he shouldered his way around Anna, picked up his gun, which he'd braced beside the door as he entered, and resolutely left the house.

Anna watched his back as he strode angrily across the clearing. Then, halfway across, he stopped, did an abrupt about-face and marched back into the hut, slammed the gun onto its hooks above the fireplace, slapped the bag of balls onto the mantel again and once more strode outside.

She continued watching him from the deep shadows of the dwelling. He disappeared into the barn, then came out with Bill and Belle, hitched the team to the wagon, loaded up all the sacks of grain, the hops, then all the baskets of cranberries – and left the yard without as much as a backward glance.

It was nearly evening. There was no question in Anna's mind where Karl would spend the night before starting out for town. That realization finally made Anna collapse onto the cornhusks and sob her heart out.

Poor James stood with his hands dangling at his sides until finally he couldn't stand listening to her and watching her any more. Helplessly, he went out to climb the ladder to his loft. There he, too, cried at last.

17

Karl left his home, glad to be doing so for the first time since he'd built it. He watched the broad rumps of Belle and Bill, time and again forcing himself to loosen his hold on the reins. He tried to put Anna's harsh words from his mind, then tried even harder to remember them exactly as she'd said them. He tried to put his own angry responses from his mind. Then, in the most human of ways, thought of sharper, wittier, truer retorts he might have made that would have put her in her place far better.

He wondered what her place was. He told himself he had made a mistake bringing her here. Thinking of the boy, he told himself he was wrong. The cruel words he had spoken to James made Karl ache in a way he had not remembered aching for a long, long time. How unfair he had been to the boy when it was the thing between himself and Anna that was what he railed against. About that much Anna had been right. He had treated her brother unforgivably.

Karl admitted that he loved the boy as much as any father might. Throughout the summer it had been a sweet thing to have the lad working beside him, following him with those wide eyes that always said how anxious he was to learn, to please. And how well the lad had done. There was not a thing for which Karl could fault James.

But when he thought about Anna, Karl found he could more readily place the brunt of the blame on her instead of himself. The cutting things she had said burned his innards. She had called him a big, *stupid* Swede, taunting him with an imitation of his dialect.

I am Swede, he thought. Is this wrong, to speak my native

language with the Johansons? To bring back only a little bit of the place I loved, still love – the place where I was born? Is it wrong for me to sit at their table and eat foods which bring back the picture of Mama cooking, putting food on our table, slapping lightly any hand that reached for a bowl before Papa had come to his seat?

He longed for the solace of his deep-seeing father, who was a teacher such as Karl never thought to be. If his papa was here, he would make Karl see things clearer. His papa would puff on his pipe and think long and hard, weighing one side against the other before offering any advice. Papa had taught him this was the wisest way. Yet, today Anna had taunted him for this very deliberate slowness, had called him dumb.

But most painful of all had been the last thing Anna had said about the bear, intimating he cared so little about her that such a thing would not bother him. Her words were weapons, he knew, weapons wielded by instinct, not by premeditation. Still, like all people when they are hurt by the tongue of another, Karl flayed himself with her words instead of admitting why she had spoken them.

At the Johansons', candles were burning in the new log house and everyone was at the supper table. When they heard Karl's wagon pull in, the entire family left its meal to come outside and gather him in.

'Why, Karl, this is a surprise,' Olaf greeted.

'I thought we would get an earlier start in the morning if I came up this way and maybe slept in your wagon tonight.'

'Why, sure, Karl, sure! But you will sleep in no wagon, you will sleep in the cabin you helped us build!'

'No, I do not want to put nobody out,' he assured them.

'You want to see somebody put out, you try sleeping in our wagon, Karl Lindstrom!' Katrene scolded, shaking a finger at him as if he were a naughty child.

Their table was like his own family's table had been in

Sweden. There was much laughter, much food, many smiles, big hands reaching this way and that, the fire glowing, and all around Karl's ears, his beloved Swedish.

Karl found himself more aware of Kerstin than he had ever been before. He had never singled her out any more than the others. But Anna's unfair accusation now made him do so. Kerstin laughed while fetching more food from the ledge of the fireplace, tweaking Charles's hair when he scolded her for letting the bowls grow empty. The firelight reflected off the gold coronet of her braids, and Karl found himself wondering if Anna had been right and he had been conscious of Kerstin's femininity all along. When she stretched between two broad shoulders to place the wooden bowl on the table, he caught the outline of her full breast against the firelight. But Kerstin caught his eye as she swung back, and he put his thoughts in order where they belonged.

When the meal was over, there came the supreme joy of sharing pipes together, man to man. The fragrant smoke drifted through the cabin – postlude to mealtime, prelude to evening, while the women put the cabin in order, washing dishes, sweeping the wood floor with willow broom. Talk slowed. Katrene, Kerstin and Nedda removed their aprons for the night, a thing Karl remembered so well his mother and sisters doing. Always they had worn a copious apron such as Kerstin had just removed.

'Papa,' she said now, 'you have filled Karl's nose with smoke long enough. I want to take him outside in the fresh air for a little while.'

Karl looked up at Kerstin, startled. Never before had the two of them been alone together. To be so tonight, after he had been thinking what he had been thinking, during supper, was not a good idea, he thought.

'Come, Karl. I want to show you the new pen we have made for the geese,' she said casually, and grabbed up her shawl and walked out of the cabin, leaving Karl little choice but to follow.

What could he do but excuse himself and trail behind her down where the new split rails showed white in the blueing evening. Yes, there was a new pen all right, but it was not about it which they spoke.

'How is Anna?' Kerstin opened, without preamble.

'Anna?' Karl said. 'Oh, Anna is just fine.'

'Anna is just fine?' Kerstin repeated, but her inflection made her meaning clear. 'Karl, your place is no more than a half-hour's ride up the road. There was no need for you to save a half hour by staying at our house tonight.'

'No, there was not,' he admitted.

'So,' Kerstin said quietly, 'I was right. Anna is not so fine as you would have me believe.'

Karl nodded. The geese were making soft clucks, settling down with their plump breasts looking plumper as they squatted to the ground. They were a pair, a goose and a gander. Karl watched as they wriggled themselves into comfort, closely nestled beside each other before the goose tucked her head beneath her wing.

'Karl, I must ask you something,' Kerstin said in a matter-of-fact tone.

'Ya,' he said, absently studying the fowl.

'Do you like me?'

Karl could feel the red creeping up his collar even before he turned to look squarely at Kerstin. 'Well . . . ya, of course I like you,' he answered, not knowing what else to say.

'And now I am going to ask you something else,' she said, meeting his eyes with a steadiness that unsteadied him. 'Do you love me?'

Karl swallowed. Never in his experience had any woman been so bold with him. He didn't know what to say without hurting her feelings.

Kerstin smiled, unchagrined, turning her palms up. 'There, you have given me your answer. You have given yourself your answer. You do not love me.' She turned aside and leaned her arms on the top of the fence. 'Forgive me, Karl, if I speak to you in a straightforward manner. But I think it is time. Tonight at the supper table I thought I saw you looking at me in a way a woman senses is – let me say *different*. But I think it is because of something between you and Anna, not something between you and me.'

'I . . . I am sorry, Kerstin, if I offended you.'

'Oh, for heaven's sake, Karl, do not be so foolish. I was not offended. If things were different, I would be outright proud. But I do not bring it up to make you feel uncomfortable. I bring it up to get you to talk about whatever is wrong between you and Anna.'

'We have had terrible words,' he admitted.

'I thought as much. And, forgive me again, Karl. I do not mean to sound as if I think so much of myself. It is not that. But as soon as I met Anna, I knew this fight was coming. I felt a kind of jealousy from her. Between women this is something that can be felt almost immediately. I thought right away it might bring about disagreements between you and her. Tonight when you rode in, I thought to myself, it has happened. Anna has said something to Karl at last. Am I right, Karl?'

'Ya,' he said, looking down again at the geese.

'And you have stomped off like a stubborn Swede and come here to pout?'

It was all right for Kerstin to call him a stubborn Swede, because she was one, too. She was proving it right now by not letting up on him. He found enough goodwill in him to laugh lightly at her badgering. Then he sighed and said, 'I am a little mixed up about Anna right now. I needed to get away to think.'

'It is all right to think, as long as you think things that are true. What I believe you were thinking inside our house at the supper table, that was not true, Karl.'

'I did not know that what I was thinking showed so much, and I am sorry, Kerstin. It was wrong of me. It was Anna who put those things in my head.' But suddenly he stopped, contrite, a little embarrassed. 'Oh, it is not like it sounds ... not that I do not admire you, Kerstin, but – '

'I know what it is you are saying, Karl. I understand. Go on about Anna.'

'What Anna and I fought about ...' But Karl's words trailed away.

'You do not need to tell me. I think some of the things that bother Anna, I have already guessed. I guessed them when you came here with her the first time. But, Karl, you must look at us with her eyes. I could tell how she felt that day, coming in here and all of us so excited we were talking in Swedish, and she not understanding a word of it. All that talk about the homeland, and things we all loved back there. When we talk in English, this is what she hears. And then, when we came to your place I learned even more things about your Anna. She feels like she does not please you because things around her house come hard for her. I could tell when Mama and I worked in her kitchen she wished to feel comfortable in it, like we did. Something tells me Anna has not had much experience at the things I have been taught since I was a little girl.'

'She has had a much different bringing up than us.'

'I guessed that. The way she dresses tells that and more.'

'She grew up in Boston and did not have a mother that was like yours and mine.' Even the word Boston was hard for him to say now.

'Boston is far from here. How did you meet her?'

'This is part of our trouble. Anna and I did not meet before we got married. I ... we agreed to get married through letters we wrote to each other. Here in America they would call Anna my mail-order bride.'

'I have heard of such things, but I did not know this about you two.'

'We were only married at the beginning of this summer.'

'Why, Karl, you are newlyweds!'

Karl thought that over a moment. 'I guess this is true,'

he said, though it seemed like the strain between Anna and himself was years old.

'And you are having some troubles like all newlyweds have, getting used to each other, is all.'

'There seems to be much that neither of us will ever get used to in each other.'

'Oh, Karl, I think you are looking on the dark side. So you have had your first fight. You are being too hard on both Anna and yourself. Things take time, Karl. You and Anna have not had much of that yet.'

'Why would she say such a thing about . . . about . . . well, about you and me?'

Kerstin was a girl who met things head-on. 'What was it she said, Karl? I do not know.'

'That I – ' He leaned on the fence rail, too, rubbing one big hand in the palm of the other. 'That I would rather be here with you and your blueberry cobbler and your braids than with her.'

Kerstin laughed, surprising Karl. 'Oh, Karl, it is so plain! You are just a little bit foolish, I think. She sees you coming here to everything that is familiar, and I can do all the things and be all the things you have left behind in Sweden. Naturally, Anna is going to think you want those things when she sees how happy and gay you are here with us. She does not see that it is all of us who make you happy instead of just me. Do you know what she asked me to do when we were at your house?'

'No, but I hope it was to teach her how to make decent bread, though.'

'There, Karl! You see! She tries very much to please you, but things like that come hard for her. No, it was not that which she asked me. It was to teach her how to put her hair up in braids.'

Karl turned to Kerstin genuinely startled. 'Braids?' he repeated. 'On my Anna?'

'Yes, braids, Karl. Now why do you think a woman with

286

such lovely curling hair as Anna would want to put it up in these awful braids?'

He remained silent.

'Karl, why do you think she went out picking blueberries for you?'

But he was busy trying to imagine Anna in braids, which would certainly not suit her at all.

'Do not be a fool,' Kerstin went on. 'Anna loves you very much. An Irish girl who tries so hard to be a Swede because she thinks it is what her man wants . . . Why, Karl, don't you see?'

'But I never told her she needed to pick blueberries or wear her hair in braids to please me. Once, a long time ago, I even told her braids were not important.'

'A long time ago, Karl? How long ago? Before I came here?'

'Why, sure, but what does that matter?'

'What matters is that she sees you happier at our place than at your own. Even I see that. It should be the other way around.'

'There are things you do not know, Kerstin.'

'There always are, Karl. There always are. But I know a woman in love when I see one, and I know she tries very hard to please you. But I also know you hold yourself back from being pleased by her for some reason. This is why Anna accused you of liking me more than you do.'

Karl lowered his face and covered it with callused hands, his elbows braced upon the fence rail.

'Anna should know better,' he admitted raggedly.

'Why? When you have left her in anger? It is she who is maybe suffering more than you right now, wondering where you are and when you will come back. You need to go back and make things right with her, Karl.'

He knew she was right. Knowing this, he admitted the rest of his day's transgressions. 'I shouted at the boy today, too. I fixed it real good with both of them, I think.'

'So, what is wrong with saying you are sorry when you get back, Karl? James needs to learn that people make mistakes. People do not always use good sense in everything they do. Surely the boy . . . and Anna, too . . . will see that and forgive you.'

'She said she could not get far enough away from me and said I would not care if she was killed by a bear.'

'Sure, I'll bet she did. But that is only part of the story. The part you left out is what went before. I do not even need to hear all of it to know you both said things you did not mean. But, Karl, you must remember Anna is human, too. She makes mistakes. She is probably sorry right now she made that one.'

Yes, she is sorry for that one and the other one she cannot live with until I forgive her. Karl leaned his face in his hands, remembering Anna the night they had found her treed by the wolves. He remembered her sobbing in his arms, saying over and over again, 'I'm sorry, Karl, I'm sorry.'

He had known then it was not the getting lost, not that alone, for which she was sorry. She was telling him how sorry she was for everything, all the lies, all the things she saw as failures in herself, but mostly, for the thing he could not – no, now Karl knew the fact was that he *would* not – forgive.

And he, stubborn Swede that he was, had deliberately rejected her apology and held himself higher than her by doing so. How well he'd been taught by his mama that self-praise stinks. By refusing to accept Anna's honest efforts to please him, he had made himself better than her. And he'd clung to his stubbornness because of something she had done in desperation long before he had even met her.

'You know, Karl,' Kerstin was saying, 'I have reconsidered, and I think you could not go to buy windows at a better time. I think that a couple days away from Anna is going to do you both a world of good.'

288

18

James could build a beautiful fire by now. He could curl shavings off a piece of wood and make them as thin as paper, just like Karl. He could get a spark off his flint with the very first stroke. He could lay on the kindling without smothering the first flame, and add split logs until there was a hearty blaze. And through all this, not so much as a wisp of smoke backed up into the sod house.

But he caught himself squatting on his haunches, gazing into his freshly built fire as he'd so often seen Karl do, and immediately he arose and turned his back on it.

'Why'd he do it, Anna?' he asked defeatedly at last.

'Oh, James, it had nothing to do with you,' she said in a soft, sorry voice. 'It's something between Karl and me. Something we need to get straightened out, is all.'

'But he was so mad at me, Anna.' The hurt was intense, tangible in his voice.

'No, he wasn't. He was mad at me.' Anna gazed ruminatively into the fire, seeing Karl's angry back as he drove out of the clearing, wishing she could call him back and apologize for her words which had hurt him cruelly when he deserved her love and respect instead.

'For what?'

'I can't tell you everything about it. Come and eat your supper.'

Brother and sister sat in dismal companionship unable to eat, each of them at once angry at yet longing for the presence of the man who made this . . . who *undeniably* made this . . . *home*.

'It's got something to do with Barbara being what she was, doesn't it?'

'In a way, yes.'

'I never would've guessed it about Karl. I mean . . .' James paused, confused, then went on. 'Well, he's just about . . . he's just about the most perfect person I ever knew. He just doesn't seem like he'd blame us for what she was.'

Anna reached to touch his hand. 'Oh, James, he doesn't. Honest, he doesn't. It's not because of that, really. It's mostly me. I can't – well, I can't do much of anything around this place. I can't cook right or dress right or wear my hair right or any of the stuff that a wife oughta be able to do. Barbara didn't teach me much of that and every time I try to do something for him, it turns out bad.' She stared into the fire and tears glimmered on her lids as she remembered all the disasters resulting from her attempts to please Karl.

'Like the blueberries.' She raised her palms in a gesture of futility, then dropped them back between her knees. 'I mean, I wanted to pick him those blueberries so bad, James. I just wanted to do that for him. So what do I end up doing but getting lost, and he's got to come searching for me and carry me all the way home and put stuff on my mosquito bites like I was some baby.'

'But that wasn't your fault, Anna,' James put in loyally. 'He wasn't mad about that.'

She shrugged and sighed. 'It's not that he is really mad at me, James. It's more that he's disappointed with me. He thought he could get over all the disappointments he found in me when he learned about all the lies from those letters. But he can't. I'm nothing like he really needs a wife to be.'

'But we had lots of fun in the beginning and he didn't seem to mind if it took you time to learn to do things around here.'

'That was before the Johansons moved in up the road.

Ever since Kerstin came he'd rather be up at her place than at home.'

'That ain't true, Anna. I don't think that's true.'

'Well, Kerstin can do everything. She can cook blueberry cobbler and she's not skinny and she's got braids and blonde hair and talks Swedish.'

'Is that what's got you all hot under the collar, Anna?' James said, wide-eyed. 'Why, shoot, that day we were up at their place without you, Karl hardly paid her any attention at all. They asked us to stay for supper and he said no, he thought he'd better get back here for supper.'

'He did?' She brightened a little.

'Well, of course he did.'

But then her face fell again. 'See? I didn't have anything ready for him the very first time he goes away and comes home expecting a hot meal. Instead, he finds me sitting up in some godforsaken maple tree with a pack of wolves at my heels.' It made her want to cry again at the thought of her failure. 'He never even got any supper that night,' she chastised herself.

'Supper was the last thing on his mind. I know that for sure. When we came home and you weren't here, why, I never saw Karl so upset. He pretended he wasn't, but I could tell. He ran all over, out to the log house and into the barn and everywhere, looking for you. When you didn't turn up and it was getting dark, I thought for a while Karl was gonna cry again.'

'Again?' Anna interrupted, big-eyed now, disbelieving.

'Oh, forget it.' James suddenly became engrossed in scratching a dab of dry gravy from the knee of his britches.

'You saw Karl cry once?'

'It don't matter, Anna.' He scratched all the harder, keeping his eyes carefully lowered.

'When?' she insisted, and James threw her a look of appeal.

'Anna, he doesn't know I saw him and I don't think I should be telling you about it.'

'James, you've got to tell me. There are so many things Karl and I need to straighten out between us that can't be straightened out until we know things like . . . like how we've made each other cry.'

James still looked doubtful, but after considering what Anna had said he decided it would be all right to tell her. 'It was the night after he came stomping out to the barn and asked me point-blank if Barbara was a seamstress. Then, when I said no, he asked me if I knew what she did to earn a living. All I said was yes, and I thought he'd make me say what it was. But he just told me I did a good job on Belle's hooves, and walked out. I never told him, Anna. Honest, I didn't. Later on I went outside when I heard him get up in the middle of the night. I'd made up my mind I was gonna tell him, and explain to him how you hated what Barbara was, and how you only lied because of me. But I never got a chance to tell him because I come on him out by the garden. He was just standing there by the horses and when I got up behind him I heard him crying. He . . . he was holding onto Bill's mane . . . and . . .' James's voice had softened until it was a pale whisper. He scratched at something on the tabletop with his thumbnail. 'Anna, I never seen a man cry before that. I didn't know men cried. Don't tell him I said so, okay?'

'No, James, I won't. Promise.' She reached out and patted his hand.

'Anna, I know Karl likes you more than Kerstin. Otherwise, why would he cry?'

'I don't know.' She thought about it for a while. 'Kerstin's sure pretty though,' Anna admitted wistfully. 'And she's got some meat on her bones like Karl likes.'

'Nothin's wrong with you, and if Karl thinks so, he's the one that's got somethin' wrong with him!'

There it was, what she'd thought she'd lost from her

brother. She realized she had been silly to think that just because he admired Karl with increasing fervour, his feeling for her had waned. But when it came down to the wire, when it came to Karl finding fault with her, there was James, ready to stand up and fight for her, just as he'd always done.

'Oh, James, thank you, baby,' she said, using the name she used to call him when he was a runny-nosed toddler tagging after her dresstails through the Boston streets.

'Anna?' James asked, after studying the fire intently to avoid the confusing rush of feelings that had made him feel so much like a man when she called him *baby*, 'do you think he'll come back?'

'Of course he'll come back. This is his home.'

'He didn't take the rifle, Anna. He left it here for us.'

'Oh, don't be silly. If you're worrying about that . . . that *cougar* out there in the pines, you know perfectly well Olaf will be with him and Olaf will have his gun.'

'Well, you're one to call me silly, since it looks like the same thing's been on your mind, too, or you wouldn't have brought it up.'

'Karl is the most careful person I've ever met in my life. And one of the most cautious woodsmen, too. Now, believe me, that cougar is the last thing we have to worry about.'

Yet after Anna went to bed, she lay in the dark for long hours imagining the very scent of those pines, her nostrils pricking as if searching here in the dark cabin for the musk of cat, as if she could warn Karl should she detect it. His pillow lay beside her, puffed and empty. She punched it and made a hollow in the centre of it and pretended that he had only gone outside for a minute. For the thousandth time since he had learned the truth, she cried out silently, from her aching throat, 'I'm sorry, Karl. I'm sorry. Forgive me.' Tonight, she added, 'Please don't go to her, Karl. Please come back to me.'

* * *

She slept. She awakened, thinking of Karl crying into a horse's mane, knowing he had cried because of her. I'm sorry, Karl, she thought, tortured.

She'd been sound asleep again, but sat up as if she were attached to the ceiling by a spring. Something was wrong! No sooner had she coherently thought it than James's voice came to her, strident, panicked.

'Anna, are you awake? There's something out there! Listen!'

She sat stone still, listening to the scraping and thumping that came from beyond the door. It sounded like something was trying to eat the panel itself.

'James, come here!' she begged in a whisper, wanting him near enough so she could put her arms around him and know he was with her in the dark.

'I gotta get the rifle,' he whispered back. 'I gotta get it like Karl said to.'

She heard him kick against a bowl or bucket on the hearth. She heard him pick up the bag of shot Karl had slapped down when he'd come wheeling back in the house this afternoon.

'James, it's already loaded!' she warned. 'Karl always keeps it loaded and he didn't shoot at that bear today!'

'I know, but I gotta be ready to load fast if I need to take a second shot.'

'Oh, James,' she wailed, 'do you think you'll even have to take a first one?'

'I don't know, Anna, but I gotta be ready. Karl said.'

Outside the door they heard a grunt, like when a man lifts something heavy.

'Do you think it's a man, James?'

'No. Shhh!'

But when she sat quiet, she could hear the intruder scraping around again on the puncheons.

'James, is the latchstring in?' Panic hit her afresh. If the latchstring were hanging outside, all the intruder needed to do was pull it to lift the heavy bar that secured the door. She heard James make his way carefully through the dark to the door while she held her breath at the mere thought of his being so near whatever was on the opposite side of it.

'It's in,' he whispered, and backed away from the door again.

Relieved somewhat, she swung her feet to the earthen floor and said, 'I'm coming, James, don't point the gun this way.'

'Don't worry, it's pointed straight at the door.'

'But you can't see anything. What are you gonna do?'

'What I can't see, I can hear. I'll know if he breaks it down.'

'B . . . breaks it down? How big – what do you think it is?'

'I think it's that bear, Anna.'

'But . . . but there's never been a bear here before. Why would he come now?'

'I don't know, but it sounded like something big.'

'Shhh! Listen, it sounds like he's going away.'

They heard thumping sounds again, then the unmistakable loud grunt and whine of a bruin. There was some clattering, then the sound of earthenware crashing, then a louder groan.

'He's in the springhouse, Anna. He's eating stuff in the springhouse!'

'Well, let him eat. Who cares? At least he's not eating us!'

'Anna, I gotta go out and shoot him.'

'For God's sake, don't be stupid! Let him take anything he wants, but don't go out there.'

'Karl says once a bear finds food he'll come back and raid you time after time as long as he knows where it is. He'll come back unless I shoot him.'

'James, please don't go out there. Forget what Karl said

about you not getting the gun fast enough today. He didn't mean it. It was me he was upset with. I told you that.'

'I gotta go. It's got nothin' to do with Karl today. That's darn sure a bear out there. What if he decides to come back some day when we're not safe inside the house?'

From outside came the sound of splintering wood.

'No, James, don't go. It's so dark you won't be able to see him anyway.'

'There's enough moonlight.'

'No, there isn't.'

'Then get the torches, Anna. Get the torches that Karl made when you were lost. They're leaning in the corner behind the ash bucket. Get one and light it and when I say the word, you're gonna have to do just what I tell you to. You're gonna have to lift the latchstring and take the torch outside a little bit ahead of me, so the bear won't be able to see anything behind it. As soon as I get the first shot off, you drop it and run, though, Anna!'

'No, I won't! We're not goin' outside with any torches and I'm not dropping it and running. We're staying right here.'

'I'll do it without you if I have to, Anna,' her baby brother said. The steel determination in his voice made her realize that he meant every word.

'Okay, I'll get the torch, but, James, if you miss him the first time, you gotta run with me!'

'Okay, Anna, I promise. Now hurry and light the torch before he goes away!'

She struck the flint and steel, and the sparl grew to orange flame upon the cattails while the two big-eyed nightwalkers stared momentarily into each other's faces.

'We can do it, Anna,' James said. 'We got the rifle, not him.'

'Be . . . be careful, James. Promise you'll run the minute the shot goes off?'

'I promise. But, Anna?'

'What?'

'We ain't gonna need to. I promise that, too.'

She raised the heavy latch with every fibre of her body trembling so violently she thought it would rattle the door in spite of her efforts at silence. The door squeaked softly once. She nudged it open and thrust the torch out before her.

The bear was slurping watermelon syrup as if he was in bear heaven. When the light caught his eyes, he sluggishly nodded his head and looked quite human, as if torn between finishing this delightful drink or being put off by the intrusion. He made the wrong choice; his long tongue snaked out into the pink drink one more time, and the gun exploded and knocked James clear off his feet. He was up and running for the door of the sod house before the stunning reaction had truly registered, keeping up step-for-step with Anna, who had completely forgotten to drop the torch. They slammed the door, barred it and leaned against it, chests heaving, hugging, trying to hold perfectly still, listening . . . listening . . . listening.

All they heard was silence.

'I think you got him,' Anna whispered.

'He could be just stunned. Wait awhile longer.'

They hugged for what seemed an hour.

'Anna?' James whispered at last.

'What?'

'Don't burn my hair with that thing!'

They'd been standing there for so long the torch had burned down. James's remark broke their tension somewhat, and they agreed to light another torch and go outside to check and see if the bear was really dead. Anna got the torch and James reloaded the gun before they crept back out.

When they saw what they had done, they both broke into relieved laughter. The bear lay half in and half out of what used to be the springhouse. The massive black body was sprawled across the little pool where they'd always gotten their water. The blood from the hole in his head

297

flowed downstream with the current. The crocks and pots were lying in pieces all around. The bear had made mincemeat of some wooden pails, too. What walls of the springhouse had not been splintered by the animal had been blown to kingdom come by the blast from the gun, which Karl had 'loaded for bear.'

'James, you did it!'

'I did it,' he repeated, now quite breathless at the realization. 'I did it?'

'You did it, baby brother!' Anna squealed, throwing her arms around him again.

'By golly, I did!' he exclaimed.

'And you know what?'

'Ya, I know what. My backside hurts. That gun kicks like a mule.' James rubbed himself back there while they both giggled.

'No, that's not what I was going to say. I was going to say, there lies our winter supply of tallow dips and enough to feed our family and the Johansons all winter long.'

James beamed and couldn't resist slapping his knee like Olaf was fond of doing.

'Guess what else?' Anna went on.

'What else?'

'We got no horses to budge this monster with and he's laying in our spring and he's gonna start rotting before Karl gets back and both him and our spring will never be the same again.'

James started laughing. Then Anna started laughing at James because he was out of control. Then James started laughing at Anna out of control and before long they were on their knees, tired from the vast relief after their petrifying fright, and the fact that it was somewhere around four o'clock in the morning.

After some time Anna said, 'Tomorrow we'll have to walk over to Olaf's house and see if one of the boys can come over and help us gut this big fellow and get his carcass strung up and tell us what else we have to do with him.'

'I'm not sure, Anna, but I don't think we can wait till then. I think we have to gut him now or the meat will foul.'

'Now?' Anna exclaimed with disgust in her expression.

'I think so, Anna.'

'But, James, he's laying in that cold spring water. Won't that keep him fresh?'

'The meat's got to be bled right away. I know that much because Karl told me. He says what you do in the first half hour after an animal is shot makes the difference between good meat and bad meat.'

'Oh, James! *Ish!* Do we really have to get our hands in that thing?'

'I don't see how else we're gonna get him gutted. If we don't, Karl will just come home to another mess we've made.'

That finally convinced Anna what must be done, must be done. 'There are still some torches left in the corner. I'll get them.'

'And bring some knives, too, and I'll go get Karl's oilstone that he uses for sharpening his axe. I think we're gonna need it.'

Anna turned back before she was at the doorway of the house and called to her brother, 'Karl's gonna be so proud of you, James.' She was proud herself in a way she'd never dreamed she could be of her baby brother.

'Of you too, Anna. I just know it.'

For some inexplicable reason, Anna remembered she had forgotten to water her hop bines that day, and promised herself she'd do it first thing in the morning. Soon as that bear was gutted and she got a little sleep and they'd gone over to get one of the boys to help hoist that bear up and they'd taken care of digging the potatoes and the turnips and the rutabagas and . . .

No, she thought, the hop bines will come first. First thing when I get up. Those hop bines *will not* fail!

19

Three days later Karl Lindstrom rode northward along the trail that was now showing evidence of autumn coming on. The first sumac glowed brilliantly in startling scarlet from the edges of the forest trail. The hazelnuts were brown and thick. Karl remembered he'd promised Anna he would show them to her. As soon as the cabin was finished, he would bring her back here and do just that. In the meantime, he pulled the team up and picked a stem of the nuts and put it in his pocket. Once again on his way, he passed through the place of the wide heartpine, which he knew would make thick planks for Anna's kitchen dresser. He must come back here and fell it and split it as soon as he had a free day, and begin making the piece of furniture, which, too, he had promised Anna.

A pheasant lifted itself, disturbed from its dust bath at the edge of the road as Karl's team came clopping. The bird flashed in brilliant bars of rust and black, and iridescent green head, as it scaled quickly up toward cover in a graceful swoop, scolding, 'C-a-a-a!'

I would shoot it and take it home for supper, Karl thought, but I do not have my gun. The pheasant can wait for James to bring it down.

No, Karl did not have his own rifle. He had a gun all right, but when it was shot for the first time, it would be shot by James. It was a Henry repeater that made Karl smile in anticipation. He had much to make up for with the lad. The gun would be a start. Karl thought about himself and the boy walking out in the amber autumn mornings, their guns slung on their arms, companionably silent as they stalked pheasants, brought them down and carried them home to Anna.

Then he would teach Anna how to stuff it with bread stuffing enhanced by their own wild hazelnuts. Karl supposed he would have to teach her to make bread all over again, now that she would be doing it in the cast-iron stove.

Karl smiled. He flicked the reins. But Belle and Bill each turned a blinder in his direction, as if asking him what the hurry was. They were already cutting a good pace toward home, and they were as anxious as he was.

When the team turned into their own lane a short time later, Karl wanted to slow them instead of hurrying them. But now they obstinately refused to be slowed. Karl saw the familiar opening in the trees up ahead, then his skid trail, and at its base, the beautiful log house he and Anna and James had built together. Leaning beside it were neatly placed sacks of potatoes. Out on the grass by the garden were willow baskets with grapes drying in them, shrivelling themselves into raisins. There was smoke coming from the chimney of the sod house.

But there was something missing. Karl scanned the clearing again and realized with a start that it was the springhouse! His springhouse was gone! There were two pails sitting where it had been before, and some rutabagas that looked half-washed. Some crocks were submerged in the sand, as usual. But the building itself had disappeared into thin air. There was a smell in the air that made Karl's nostrils twitch, but he couldn't figure out what it could be that smelled so much like bear. The horses seemed to smell it, too, for they threw their heads and flicked their manes until Karl had to say, 'Eaaasy. We are home. You know home when you see it.'

Neither Anna nor James was in sight as Karl drove the team up near the log house. There it stood – the house of his dreams. While he reined in his team before it, he wondered once more if he had shattered those dreams beyond repair or if he and the boy and Anna could patch them up. He forced a calm into his limbs as he tied the reins to the wooden brake handle, and spoke to Belle and Bill.

'You will have to wait a while till I get these things unloaded.'

The horses told him in no uncertain terms they were impatient to get to their barn.

Coming around the rear of the wagon, Karl glanced toward the sod house. James stood just outside its door, his hands in his pockets, staring at Karl. Karl stopped short and looked back at the boy. A sudden stinging burned the back of Karl's eyes, seeing how James just stood there, making no move to come forward or greet him in any way. Karl tried to speak, but his tongue felt like it was stuck to the roof of his mouth. Finally, he just raised his hand in a silent gesture of hello. His heart beat high in his throat as he waited for a return greeting from the boy. At last James removed a hand from his pocket and raised it silently, too.

'I could use a little help unloading this wagon, boy,' Karl called.

Without a word, James came toward him, watching his feet scuff up puffs of dust on his way. At the rear of the wagon he stopped, looked up at Karl, silent as before.

Inanely, Karl managed to get out, 'I got the wheat ground.'

'Good,' said James. But the note escaped him in a high contralto. 'Good,' he repeated, deeper this time.

'We will have plenty flour for winter.' Karl remembered how he had once told the boy he was an extra mouth to feed.

'Good.'

'Got those windows for the log house.'

James nodded his head as if to say, yes, so I see.

302

'Everything all right here?' Karl's eyes flickered toward the cabin, then back to the boy's face.

'Ya.' After a pause, he went on. 'We thought you'd be back yesterday.'

'It took a day to get the flour milled. They were busy at the mill and we had to wait our turn.' Did they think I wouldn't come back, Karl wondered. Is that what they thought?

'Oh.'

Tentatively they hovered, brawny man and gangly boy, hearts surging with remorse and love, neither of them yet having said what he wanted so desperately to say.

'Well, we'd best get it unloaded,' Karl said.

'Ya.'

Karl stepped to the wagon to remove the backboard, but when his hands were upon it he did not pull it loose. He stood instead braced that way, gripping the rough wood as if it were his security. He closed his eyes. The boy stood unmoving, near Karl's elbow.

'Boy, I . . . I'm sorry,' Karl croaked. Then he leaned his head back and looked up at the autumn sky. The sharp edges of the clouds were blurry.

'Me, too, Karl,' James said. And for once in his life his voice came out strong and masculine.

'You got nothing to be sorry for, boy. It was all me. Me! Karl!'

'No, Karl. I shoulda got that gun like you said.'

'The gun had nothing to do with it.'

'Yes it did. It was the first lesson you taught me. Move for the gun like your life depends on it, cause it probably does.'

'I was wrong that day. I was mad . . . I had things on my mind about Anna and we weren't getting along, so I took it out on you.'

'It don't matter, really.'

'Ya. It matters, boy. It matters.'

303

'Not to me, not any more. I learned a lesson that day. I figure I needed it.'

'I learned a lesson, too,' Karl said.

Karl looked up then, found the boy's wide green eyes filled to the brim and understood how his own father had felt when he waved to him for the last time.

'I missed you, boy. I missed you these last three days.'

James blinked and a tear rolled down, unchecked, for his hands were still stuffed in his pockets. 'We mi – we missed you, too.'

Karl took the plunge, loosening his hold on the wagon and turning in one heart-filling motion to sweep the boy into his arms and hug him to his chest. James's arms came clinging to Karl. Karl took James by the sides of his hair, holding him back to look into his face, saying, 'I'm sorry, boy. Your sister was right. You did everything right that I ever asked you to learn. A man couldn't ask for anything better than a boy like you.'

James pitched roughly against Karl's chest, releasing all his pent-up anguish in a torrent of words that came muffled against Karl's shirt. 'We didn't think you were coming back. We looked for you all day yesterday, and then night-time came, and you didn't have your rifle and we knew about the cougar.'

Karl thought his heart would explode. 'Olaf was with me, boy, you knew that.' But he was rocking James, feeling the boy's heart beat against his own. 'And he had his gun. Besides . . . a man would be a fool not to come back to a place like this, with all this plenty.'

'Oh, Karl, don't ever go away again. I was so scared. I . . .' Standing there against the big man's chest, against the smell of him, that mixture of horses and tobacco and security, the words that ached in James's throat could be denied no longer. 'I love you, Karl,' he said, then backed away, his eyes cast earthward, and dried them sheepishly on his sleeve.

Karl pushed James's arm down and held him by the shoulders, forcing him to look square into his face as he said, 'When you say to a man that you love him, there is no need to hide behind your sleeve. I love you, too, boy, and don't you ever forget it.'

At last they both smiled. Then Karl swiped his own sleeve across his eyes and turned to the wagon again. 'Now are you going to help me unload this wagon or do I need to get your sister to help me?'

'I'll help you, Karl.'

'Can you lift a sack of flour?' Karl asked.

'Just watch me!'

They unloaded the flour and the windows, which were protectively couched between the sacks. Lifting a precious glass pane, Karl said, 'I bought five of them. One for each side of the door and one for each of the other walls. A man should be able to look out and see his land all around him,' he said, entering the log cabin.

Coming back outside, Karl said, 'I see you picked potatoes while I was gone.'

'Ya. Me and Anna.'

'Where is she?' Karl inquired while his heart danced against his rib cage.

'She's getting some supper.'

Now it was Karl's turn to say, 'Oh.' Then he jumped onto the wagonbed again and said, 'Help me move these last couple sacks, boy. We will take them to the sod house for Anna.'

James pulled a sack away, revealing a long wooden box. He could see the words, 'New Haven Arms Company' stamped on the front of it. He pulled the second sack away, and the words 'Norwich, Connecticut' became visible. His hands fell loose upon the sack, and it would have tipped over sideways if Karl hadn't caught it. James's green eyes flashed up to Karl's blue ones.

'A man does best with his own gun,' Karl said simply.

305

'His own gun?' James repeated doubtfully.

'Do you not agree?'

'Su . . . sure, Karl.' James looked back down, wanting to touch the box, afraid to. He looked up again.

'I picked one with a stock of hand-shaped walnut that will fit your grip like your pants fit your seat. It is just right for a boy of your size.'

'Really, Karl?' James asked disbelievingly, still not pulling the crate out. 'Is it really for me?'

'I have taught you everything except how to be a hunter. It is time we got started. Winter is coming on.'

James had the carton slipped free and in his arms. He leaped from the wagon and was running across the clearing, long legs bounding toward the sod house as he bellered, 'Anna! Anna! Karl bought me a gun! Of my own, Anna, my own!'

Karl waited for her to appear in the doorway of the sod house, but she didn't. He shouldered a sack of flour and headed that way, for James had disappeared inside.

James was going crazy, talking far too loud, repeating that Karl had bought the gun to be his own. Anna was overjoyed for her brother.

'Oh, James, I told you, didn't I?' She had seen from the depths of the cabin how Karl and James had made their peace out there. It was not necessary for her to know what they had said. To see the two of them hugging that way in broad daylight had filled her heart to bursting.

Anna glanced up now as Karl's form filled the doorway, shutting out the daylight behind his wide shoulders. A queer, weak sensation flooded through her. He looked like a blond Nordic god, bigger than life, with that sack of flour on his shoulder and the muscles of his chest bulging as he paused uncertainly before coming all the way in. Sudden shyness overwhelmed her. She longed to rush to him and say, 'Hold me, Karl,' to feel his strong, tan arms take her against his chest.

'Hello, Anna,' he said quietly. He had not thought he'd missed her this much, but the things his heart was doing told him how empty the last two days had been. He could tell she, too, was very tense and nervous.

When she spoke, her voice trembled. 'Hello, Karl.'

She wondered if he would stand in the doorway all evening.

'You're home,' she at last thought to say. It sounded inane.

'Ya. I am home.'

'And James says you've brought the gun for him?'

'Ya. A boy needs his own gun, so I bought him the best – a Henry repeater. But he had better not be thinking of using that hatchet to open the crate. Go out to the tack room and get a clawhammer, boy, like I taught you.'

'Yessir!' James obeyed, and nearly knocked Karl back out the door.

There was a fire and something was cooking. Anna turned to stir it. The sack on Karl's shoulder grew heavy, and he passed just behind her to set it on a free spot on the floor.

His very nearness made her pulse throb faster, but she stirred the pot in order to appear busy, then clapped the cover on, saying, 'I'll get some sticks from the woodpile to put under that sack.'

'It can wait,' Karl said, straightening.

'But the bugs will get it.' She headed for the door.

'Not that fast.'

His words and their boyish note of appeal stopped her halfway to the door. She turned to face Karl, then stood looking at him, and he at her, while time roared backward to the last time they had faced each other across this confined space.

'I have some small things in the wagon you could carry in for me.' He glanced apologetically at the simmering pot. 'It wouldn't take but a minute.'

She nodded dumbly, then whirled toward the door, leaving him with his heart in a turmoil.

Is she afraid of me? thought Karl with fading hope. Have I fixed it so she wants nothing but to run from me like a brown-eyed chipmunk every time I come near her? Does she think I ran off to Kerstin to spite her?

When he came within inches of her to climb on the wagonbed, she skittered sideways to give him wide berth. He picked up a parcel from behind the seat, walked back to the open end of the wagon and stood above her, looking down at the top of her whiskey-hair.

'Here,' he said, waiting for her to look up so he could toss the parcel down to her, 'these are some things I thought you would need.' Finally, she lifted her eyes, and he dropped it.

'What is it?' she asked as she caught it.

'Necessities,' was all he would say.

Her eyes became wide with surprise, while he turned away with the picture of her undisguised delight in his mind.

Anna tried not to feel giddy, but it was hard. Nobody had ever given her a gift before. But Karl did not say it was a gift, she thought. Perhaps it's only some spices or things for the new kitchen. But it's soft, she thought. It bends and there is a lump in the middle of it!

An iron clank interrupted her notions as Karl dragged something black and heavy from the front of the wagon. It made another metallic clink as it scraped on the other pieces resting against it. One by one he pulled all the black iron sections of the stove to the tail of the wagon, before leaping lightly down and heisting up the largest.

Anna gawked.

James came out of the barn then, polishing the stock of his new rifle with the sleeve of his shirt. He stopped long enough to watch Karl disappearing into the new cabin with his burden.

'What's that?' James called.

Karl swung around slowly, the iron sheet turning with him until his face appeared from behind it. 'It is Anna's new stove,' he answered. Then, without another word, he disappeared into the log cabin with the first of it.

Anna's new stove? thought Anna.

Anna's new stove!

Anna's new stove!

Had Karl answered, 'It is Anna's new diamond tiara,' he could not have surprised his wife more. Her eyes followed Karl's every step, back and forth, as he carried the pieces into the new house. Gladness filled her chest until she felt she would pop the seams of her shirt! She fought the urge to follow along at Karl's heels each step of the way to see where he was setting the pieces, if he was putting them up, connecting them together. Instead, she just stood in the yard while Karl marched to and fro, carefully attending to his stove-carrying and keeping his eyes from his wife. At last came the pipe from under the wagon seat. It was silvery black, shiny, clean. Anna could stand it no longer.

'Could I carry those for you, Karl?' she asked. Could I touch my stove? Could I touch this gift? Even this much of it – to make sure my eyes are not playing tricks on me?

'You do not need to help with this. It was only that little package I wanted you to carry.'

'Oh, but I want to!'

He stopped, understood, handed her the sections of the stovepipe, pleasure growing in him at sight of her pleasure. Her freckles looked delightful beneath her excited brown eyes.

'There is more, Anna,' he said.

'More?'

'More. When you buy a new stove, it seems they give you these newfangled kettles with it. They say they cook even better than cast-iron ones and they are lighter to lift. They are in the carton.'

309

'Newfangled kettles?' Anna asked, incredulous.

'In the carton,' he repeated, enjoying her disbelief.

'Are they copper?'

'No. Something called japanned ware.'

'Japanned ware?'

'They say things don't burn in it as easy as copper, and it does not rust like iron because it is covered with lacquer.'

At the mention of burned food, Anna's eyes skittered down to the package. She picked at the wrapping absently with a fingernail, remembering all those times she had charred poor Karl's dinners. He saw her eyes drop and wondered what he had said to disappoint her.

Then James intervened. 'Wow, Karl! Anna gets a stove and all them kettles, and I get a gun! I wish you'd go to town more often!'

Karl forced a laugh. 'The kettles are no good without food to cook in them.'

'When can we go hunting?'

'When the cabin is done and the vegetables are all dug.'

'The vegetables are all dug, Karl. Me and Anna did it while you were gone.'

'The turnips, too?' Karl asked, amazed.

'Of course, the turnips, too. We already got 'em washed and down in the root cellar and Anna's cooking some for supper.'

'She is, huh?' Karl eyed his wife again, finding a pleasing blush creeping upon her cheeks. 'My Anna is cooking turnips?'

Always, when Karl called her 'my *Onnuh*' that way, it made the blood beat at her cheeks. But James was still babbling away.

'You were sure right about the turnips. I never saw such big ones in my life!'

'What did I tell you?' Karl chided James good-naturedly. Then, lowering his voice, turning away, he repeated, 'Turnips, huh?'

But while Karl went to the cabin with the box of japanned ware on his shoulder, Anna turned quickly to James and ordered in a feisty whisper, 'James Reardon, you just keep your nose out of my turnip-cooking, do you hear!'

'What did *I* say?' he asked, stunned by her sudden attack on his innocent comment.

'You never mind!' she whispered back. 'My turnips are my business!'

Just then Karl returned. He hitched his britches up at the waist a little, then turned toward the empty place where the springhouse used to be.

'I have been waiting to be told where my springhouse is, but since nobody tells me, I guess I must ask.'

Turnips were forgotten as Anna and James smirked at each other conspiratorially.

'The springhouse got wrecked, Karl,' James said in a masterpiece of simplicity.

'How does a springhouse get wrecked, just sitting there holding pails?'

'I blasted 'er to kingdom come when I shot the bear.'

Should he live to be as old as Karl's virgin maples and their abundance of nectar, James would never forget the sweet nectar of that moment – the look on Karl's face, the jawfall of disbelief, James's own billowing pride, his self-pleasure at dropping the comment so casually, so manfully.

And if Karl lived to be as old as his maples, he would clearly remember forever the shock of that moment – the way the boy stood holding the new Henry lever action repeater, trying to look nonchalant when the pride was beaming from his face in shafts, when his knuckly hands squared the rifle before him as if to say, 'nothing to it, Karl.'

'A bear?'

'That's right.'

311

'You shot a bear?'

'Well, not alone. Anna and me, we shot him together,' James confirmed. There was no pretended nonchalance now. The words came tumbling from behind his widely smiling lips in a grand rush. 'Didn't we, Anna? We were sleeping and we heard all these scraping noises and it sounded like something was trying to eat our door down, so we tried to figure out what it was, and pretty soon it moved to the springhouse and you shoulda heard all that racket, Karl. I think he had trouble gettin' through the doorway and by the time he did, why, he had it splintered five ways from Sunday and then we heard all this crashing and cracking and he got busy eatin' watermelon syrup after he broke most of the crocks and stuff, so I told Anna to light one of them torches that was left over from when she got lost, and she did and took it out in front of us to blind the bear so I could get off one good shot before he had a chance to think twice. 'Cause once you said that when a bear knows where to find free food he never fails to come back time after time and the only way to stop him is to kill him, so that's just what I did, Karl. I beaned 'im right between the eyes and there wasn't much left of his head when I was done, either!'

At last James stopped, breathless.

Karl was flabbergasted. He hunched his head and shoulders forward. 'You and Anna did that?'

'We sure did, but you loaded that shot a little heavy and it blew the back wall clear off the springhouse. Blew me clear off my feet, too, didn't it, Anna?' But before she could even nod, James hurried on, 'But Anna, she made me promise that as soon as I fired that first shot I'd run back in the sod house fast as my feet would carry me! I swear, Karl, I hardly knew if I had any feet left after that gun smacked me over, though. You said she'd kick, but I wasn't expecting 'er to kick like a mule!'

The import of all this was beginning to register on Karl.

Suppose James had missed? Suppose the gun hadn't fired? Countless dire probabilities gripped Karl's gut.

'Boy, you knew it was just my temper out in the bog that day when I got on you for being slow to the gun. You could have let that bear eat everything on the place and I would not have scolded, just so I come home and find you and Anna safe.'

'But we *are* safe,' the boy reasoned.

'Ya, you are safe, but because of my silly scolding I make you take such a risk to prove yourself when you have proved yourself all along.'

'It wasn't cause of what happened in the bog, Karl, honest. It was . . . well . . . I don't know how to say it. It was kinda like when you say to Anna, "A person keeps clean," or when you say to me, "A door faces east." All I could think of was "A man protects his home." ' Once said, the adultness of his simple statement struck James fully. He had taken his first steps across the threshold of manhood.

'Karl,' James said now, suddenly very sure of the truth in what he was about to say, 'I'd have done it anyway, even if I'd never seen a cranberry bog in my life before.'

Anna watched the only two men she had ever loved coming to terms with each other, setting their tack toward a course of future respect and sharing. Joyful though she was for them, her heart ached to reach a similar plane of understanding with Karl. But their private truce would have to be put off for a while yet, for Karl was saying with an appealing half grin, 'So show me this bear with his head shot off, who only bargained for a little watermelon syrup.'

James broke into a grin and a jog at the same time. 'He's out here behind the sod house. We wanted to put him where you couldn't see him at first, and spring the surprise on you when we were good and ready.'

Karl began to follow him, but realized that Anna hung back. He turned, asking, 'Aren't you coming, Anna?' She hesitated a moment, until he added, 'The fireman must come along, too. If it had not been for you there would have been no torches in the house.'

Was he teasing her? Anna wondered with a little skip of her heart. Oh, he was teasing her about getting lost in the blueberry patch! How long had it been since Karl had teased her?

He turned to follow James, and she studied his high boots, remembering the first day they'd met, how she'd wanted to look up at his face but had only walked along, like now, with her eyes on his boots, wondering what he thought of her.

Coming around the sod house, Karl was confronted not only by the carcass of the black bear hoisted into a tree. Beside it, hanging from its heel tendons, hung a twelve-point buck whitetail deer. Karl stopped dead in his tracks. He stared incredulously while Anna and James shared another conspiratorial pair of smiles. Karl's reaction was exactly what they'd hoped it would be. 'But where did the deer come from?'

'Oh, that's Anna's,' James said offhandedly, stifling a smirk.

'You two are just full of surprises today.'

'Well, the deer was a surprise to us, too,' James revealed.

Anna was poking around in the dirt with the toe of her shoe.

'Do you want to tell me about it?' He levelled his eyes on his wife.

'You tell him, James.'

'Somebody tell me. I do not care who.'

'The reason Anna doesn't want to tell you is 'cause she's scared you'll be mad at her about the potatoes.'

'What potatoes?'

'The ones the Indians stole.'

Karl was getting more confused by the minute. Still, Anna kept poking her shoe in the dirt, and he knew he wasn't going to get anything out of her.

'I see I must ask again,' Karl said, playing their game. 'What potatoes did the Indians steal?'

James completed the story. 'The ones from the garden. We dug up all the potatoes and got them all washed and in gunny sacks, but we forgot how you always said the Indians would steal anything that wasn't tacked down if they wanted it. I guess, to tell the truth, we never really believed you. So we got all those sacks of potatoes lined up against the wall of the log house, but we figured there was no hurry getting them into the root cellar. We left 'em there overnight and when we got up yesterday morning, one of the sacks was gone. All we could figure out was that the Indians took it. Anna was pretty sure you'd be mad because you said we need all the potatoes we can raise for the winter ahead. Anyway, she was really upset about it and we didn't know how to get them potatoes back. Then, this morning when we got up, here hangs this deer in the tree next to the bear. I guess the Indians are pretty much like you had 'em pegged, Karl. They have the strangest sense of honesty I ever heard of. The deer has to be their way of paying us back for the potatoes they stole.'

'I'm sure it is. I guess we will just have to eat more meat than potatoes this winter, that's all. Could I ask one question?'

'Sure,' James answered.

'If Anna was so scared about the sack of potatoes that was gone, why are the rest still sitting there?'

'Because neither one of us could lift them down the steps of the root cellar. We figured we'd bruise them all up if we dragged 'em down and dropped 'em over the side. We had all we could do to get 'em this far. So Anna took a chunk of wood from the woodpile and leaned it against each sack during the night. She said that if the Indians want the potatoes that bad, let them take 'em and she'd eat turnips!'

'But I thought Anna hates turnips,' Karl said, eyeing her.

Relieved that Karl didn't seem too upset about the stolen

spuds, Anna finally braved a glance at him, but stubbornly didn't answer.

Karl again turned his attention to the pair of trees. 'So, that takes care of the deer. But how did you get this other monster up?'

Warming to the game now, James answered, 'Oh, we had a hard time pulling him up there, didn't we, Anna?' He had been around Karl long enough that he was unable to resist such an opportunity for teasing!

'Now do not try to tell me that you strung that bear up there, not two skinny little – ' But Karl quickly amended, 'Not two young pups like you!'

James couldn't wait to finish his story. As before, the words came bubbling out like the spring bubbled out of the earth near them. There was no stopping either.

'When we shot him he fell back into the springhouse and we knew we were in a terrible fix. He'd lay there and foul up the water in no time, I figured, so I took your axe and knocked away the walls that were left standing and Anna and me we gutted him right then and there. Anna, she got pretty queasy, but I told her if we didn't do it that meat'd be pure spoiled by morning. We washed the carcass out real good and let it lay, then first thing in the morning we walked up to Olaf's place and Erik come back with the team and got him hung up here with the block and tackle. Erik says he thinks this fellow would go three hunnert fifty pounds anyway. What do you think, Karl?'

But what Karl was thinking was, *Anna* gutted that bear? In the middle of the night, by torchlight, probably dressed in her nighty? My *Anna* gutted that bear? Anna, who retched at the sight of a prairie chicken being dressed? 'I would say closer to four hundred, myself,' Karl finally answered James.

'He mighta gone four hunnert with his head on. Course, Erik never saw him with his head on. We all had a pretty good laugh when he come down here to the spring and sees that headless bear. All the while we were stringin' him up, Erik keeps sayin', 'Yup! You two sure fixed one mighty beautiful bear rug!'

Pleased as punch, getting into his story better all the time, James rambled on. It was 'Erik this' and 'Erik that' until Karl got quite peeved at hearing the man's name so much. Then, when Karl learned that Erik had stayed for dinner, he couldn't help but remember the way Anna had clung to Erik's neck the night he'd rescued her from the wolves. But just about the time James began telling about Erik staying to supper, Anna remembered she had those turnips cooking and took off for the sod house.

Damn you, James! she thought as she scurried away, do you have to go on and on and make it sound like Erik stayed here all day!

All through supper Karl and James talked bears and guns. They dissected the Henry forty-four calibre lever-action repeater and how she could hold fifteen rounds in her tubular magazine, and how she had a breech so tight she never leaked gas and how she would soon put Karl's own single-shot Sharps out to graze in obsolescence. When the meal was done, the Henry came to take the place of the dishes. The two of them took the gun apart, piece by piece, then put it back together, while Anna listened to foreign words again and was left out of the conversation: chamber, breechblock, wedge bar, finger lever, magazine spring. She grew fidgety.

Night came on, and Anna wondered what was in the package Karl had brought for her. In all the excitement over the stove and the kettles and the gun and the bear and the deer, the package had been eclipsed, and by the time they were all in the house for supper, Anna decided she wanted to open it when she was alone. Meanwhile, the package lay on the bed unopened.

At last Karl arose in his customary way and stretched,

twisting at the waist with elbows raised. He picked up his tobacco pouch from the table. Now, Anna thought, while he is out there in the barn, and when James is already in bed, I will open the package.

But Karl startled her by saying, 'I must check the horses. Will you come with me, Anna?'

She took a jacket. Nights were getting cooler now. It helped to have some place to stick her useless hands. She jammed them into the pockets and folded the jacket fronts deeply across one another. Karl lit his pipe and they sauntered toward the barn. Halfway there he noted, 'You were very busy while I was gone.'

'It just happened that way.'

'I thought I would have to come home and dig potatoes and turnips.'

'Oh, that was James's idea, to dig them. He said you told him they were ready for digging or I never would've known. I'm sorry about the potatoes the Indians took, Karl.'

'I can see we will not be in need of them. I can tell just how busy you were when I look around and see how good the crops were. There will be plenty for winter. Plenty.'

'Well, that's a relief. I really wasn't sure how much one sack of potatoes meant. But James forgot to tell you that we still have a few rutabagas and carrots left to take up. We didn't quite finish them.'

'Ya, I see them out there, but they will keep. Carrots like to be in the earth to sweeten after the first frosts, my papa always used to say. We have plenty of time yet.'

They swerved, nearing the barn. Anna's feet quite refused to take her into it. She turned and began sauntering with careless steps toward the vegetable garden, which was washed in moonlight, the carrot tops and rutabaga leaves and pumpkin vines clearly defined in the blue-white beams.

'That was something to come home and find that bear hanging in the tree. You were just as brave as the boy.

318

Anna, to go outside not knowing for sure what was out there.'

'I didn't feel very brave at all. If it had been up to me, we would've stayed right where we were and kept wondering what was out there. It wasn't my idea to open the door.'

'But you did, Anna. The point is, you did.'

She shrugged her narrow shoulders. 'Well, what else could I do? Let James go out there by himself? I tell you, he's got a stubborn streak in him a mile long. You didn't see him, Karl. He was bound and determined to go out there alone if I refused to go along. I told him to let the bear eat everything in the place for all I cared, but he was determined. He kept saying "Karl says this" and "Karl says that," and there was no way I was going to change his mind.'

Karl's heart warmed, realizing the extent of his influence over the boy, just how fully James respected his teachings.

'He is something,' Karl said ruminatively.

'Yes, he's something.'

'Anna, if something had gone wrong and that bear had harmed either one of you, I could not live with myself.'

The bitter, thoughtless words she'd thrown at Karl about the bear came back to plague her. They hurt her now more than they had hurt him at the time they were spoken. She struggled for the right words, needing so badly for things to be set right between them again.

'Karl . . . what I said before you left . . . about the bear – '

'Listen to me, Anna. It was my own stupidity that brought it here. I have thought about it and wondered why a bear would come nosing around when I have never been bothered by one before. It is because I was so angry when I left the cranberry bog that I did not use good sense. I think I must have left a trail of cranberries straight to our door. When a man loses his head that way, he uses bad sense. I think this is what I did that day. I even put my own good horse in danger by making her hurry where the

319

footing was bad. And when I make her hurry, I spill cranberries. I should have covered the baskets, but I didn't. Instead, I foolishly led that bear to the door by inviting him with cranberries. Then I ran away and left you two to take care of him.'

'That's not true, Karl. I think you say it now because of what I said before you left. I never should have said that and I knew it as soon as the words were out of my mouth. I didn't mean it, Karl.' She glanced up at him penitently.

'That is what Kerstin said.'

'Kerstin?' Anna's eyebrows shot up irritatedly. 'You told Kerstin what I said?' Already Anna's face felt like it would glow in the dark.

'We had a talk, Kerstin and I, and she said you were only human and spoke without thinking, like we all do sometimes.'

The idea of Karl exchanging confidences with Kerstin wounded Anna so fiercely that she climbed up on the top fence rail and sat down, facing away from Karl so he couldn't see her face in the moonlight. He must be closer to Kerstin than I guessed, she thought, to speak with her about our private affairs.

'You spent the night at Johansons, Erik said.'

Erik said, thought Karl dismally.

'Ya. They were only too glad to take me in.'

I'll bet! Anna thought sourly, *especially one.*

'Karl,' Anna began, wanting the subject of Kerstin dropped once and for all so they could get on to mending their differences, 'thank you for the stove.'

'There is no need to thank me, Anna. Kerstin called me a stubborn Swede, and I guess I have been, saying all the time that we do not need a stove. We talked a long time, Kerstin and I, and she made me see that we should have a stove.'

Something inside Anna turned to stone with those words. She was hurt beyond words to think that Karl came around to buying a stove only when the delectable Kerstin thought he should! Not because his own wife wanted one. All the joy went out of her at the thought of the stove now. She found herself wanting to lash out and hurt Karl in return, in any little way she could.

'You really gutted that bear, Anna?' Karl asked in admiration.

'I hated every minute of it!' she snapped coldly. 'I never want to smell another bear as long as I live!'

Confused by her abrupt chilling, he went on, 'You will have to smell this one a little longer. Tomorrow James and I will have to take care of the meat. Then there is still the melting down of tallow to be done before we can make winter candles.'

'I guess that means you won't get to making the door for the cabin yet for a couple days. How long will it be, Karl?'

'Tomorrow I will work with the meat. It will take a day to put the windows in. And perhaps another day to make the door and put up the stove. And we have to move things out of the sod house, too, and I will have to make the new rope beds, and I promised you that dresser for the kitchen.'

Anna had climbed down from the fence and was brushing off her seat as she curtly stated, 'Well, you can skip the dresser. Just get me out of that sod house as fast as you can. I'm sick to death of that stinkin' fireplace and living like a badger in a burrow!'

Bewildered, Karl could only stand wondering what had so suddenly changed Anna while she sat on that fence. She had been almost too sweet to resist when they had first come outside. And she hadn't mentioned anything about the package he'd brought her.

When he went in to bed she was already there. He wanted desperately to turn and take her in his arms and put an end to their enmity. But she lay far over on her side. Seeking

321

to soften her, he whispered, 'Anna, how did you like what I brought you in the little package?'

'Oh, I haven't had time to open it yet,' she said brusquely. And Karl withdrew the hand that had been planning to touch her back.

Anna could smell the aroma of Karl's pipe still in his hair. She lay miserably beside him, listening to the long-eared owl who sat with his yellow eyes and rusty face, on a limb above the woodpile, calling in a slurred whistle, 'Whee-you, whee-you.'

When Anna could no longer stand pretending she was asleep, she fluffed over onto her back like Karl.

It was then that the question came.

'You made dinner for Erik, then?' he asked.

Anna's heart kicked up its pace, pattered in double time like the owl's.

'Well, Erik had helped with that bear. What else could I do?'

But some new welling of hope was reborn in Anna. Karl, it seemed, was jealous.

20

The next morning Karl and James left the house to set up a butchering slab near the spring. As soon as they were gone, Anna took the package and pulled it open with anxious fingers. Inside was what she had hoped for. She found a length of delightful pink gingham, several hanks of thread and a bar of camomile soap. The material was wrapped around the bar, and when it dropped out Anna caught it in a surprised hand. She raised it to her nose. It smelled of flowers and freshness and femininity. She raised the gingham to her nose and it, too, smelled of these things.

She looked down at her britches. She glanced out the door at the new log house. She thought of the new glass windows and wondered if Karl meant the material for curtains when he said *necessities*. Who was there to look into the windows out here in the wilderness except an occasional raccoon or a passing swallow?

Anna was honestly torn by what Karl had meant the material to be used for. She wanted very badly to think the fabric was intended for something personal. Remembering Karl's last comment last night, the way he'd asked about Erik staying for supper, she could have sworn Karl was jealous. Yet, why was he so all-fired taken with Kerstin if he could be jealous of Erik? It didn't make any sense.

There was no denying the personal implication of the scented soap. And, after all, Karl had given her the material without putting any restrictions on it. Maybe she could put them both to use to end this breach between herself and Karl once and for all. She was the one who had coldly snubbed his gift, and thereby snubbed him. Could it be possible he waited for her to make the first move?

A plan formed in Anna's head.

Excitedly, she flipped the length of gingham out across the bed and began measuring it by scant yards – nose to outstretched hand equalling one yard. She found there were more yards of the stuff than she'd guessed. Enough for both curtains and a dress? Smiling to herself, she thought: Goodness! If there is, I will look like my windows!

Karl saw Anna cross the clearing and go into the log house. He wondered what she was doing in there. Maybe admiring the stove, he thought hopefully. He had been so proud of the fact he bought her that stove. With it he sought to win her favour back again, to tell her he accepted her. At first she had seemed very gratified by it. But later, out there by the garden, something had happened. He remembered Anna's eyes, as big and round as a cocker spaniel's when she'd first seen him unloading the stove. He remembered the hard edge on her voice later and knew his gift had not done the trick.

He turned back to his butchering but kept an eye on the log house to see when Anna left it again.

Inside, Anna was measuring the glass panes as they leaned against the fireplace wall. Marching back across the clearing, she saw Karl stop his meat-cutting to look her way. She braved a little wave of hello and continued on into the sod house to begin cutting curtain lengths. When Karl and James came in for lunch there was gingham all over everything. She had two lengths cut for each window and was busy with needle and thread.

'Thank you for the necessities, Karl,' she said with renewed sweetness. 'They will make lovely curtains.'

Karl felt his heart fall. Curtains? Out here in the middle of nowhere? But he could not say to Anna that he'd meant her to have the gingham to use for dresses. If he said so, she would only feel like she'd disappointed him again by

324

already cutting the fabric into pieces for the windows. He returned to his afternoon's work gravely disheartened. Would he have to look at her in those britches for the remainder of the winter then? Or could he find time for another trip to town before the snow flew?

As soon as Karl and James were gone, Anna found the pieces of the dress she'd been tearing apart to use as a pattern. She would follow it loosely, adding to the height of the neckline, making the sleeves looser, more serviceable, making the skirt less clinging, more like the dresses Kerstin and Katrene wore. During the afternoon she got the pieces of the new dress all cut out. But whenever Karl entered the house during the next few days, all he saw was his wife stitching curtains. She hid the dress pieces, easily camouflaged, beneath the plain panels on her lap.

For Karl and James there was not only the butchering to be done, but also the processing of the two hides. Karl showed James how to flesh out the hide, draping it over a felled tree, lying at an angle, still attached to its stump. Together they removed all the fat and sinew. They scraped away with their fleshing tools while Karl warned James not to puncture or score the hide, nor to expose the hair roots. It was a malodorous and tiring job. By the time the hides were placed in a lye solution to soak for two days, both Karl and James were well ready for a bath in the pond.

Anna refused their invitation to go along. She said she'd stay behind and get their supper ready. Karl, with disappointment threading his veins, wondered how to get her to do any of the things they used to so enjoy. He wanted to ask Anna if she had found the soap in the gingham, but was afraid she might think he was intimating she needed it. So Karl said nothing about camomile soap, and neither did Anna. But he detected the smell of their homemade lye soap, and figured she spurned the scented bar and used the stuff she still adamantly called 'lardy' just to spite him.

Still, the next day, Karl thought he detected something about Anna, which he chose to think of as 'saucy.' It was as if she was teasing him about something he didn't quite catch. She walked around with an undeniable air of self-satisfaction. About what, he could not guess.

That day he began inserting the windows. It was a delicate job, requiring great accuracy when Karl cut each hole. If the openings were cut too large, it meant losing tightness when the weather caused the frames to expand. But if they were cut too small, it meant broken panes when the frames contracted. After Karl cut the first opening, he went to where the yellow poplar billets were stacked on the skid trail. Although the autumn air was crisping, Karl loosened his shirt, for it was warm in the sun. Finding his axe needed sharpening, he took out his oilstone and was working the steel upon it when Anna came out of the springhouse with a dipper and started up the hill toward him. He watched her approach, paying only cursory attention to the honing of the blade. He wondered what it was that made Anna tick these days. At times she seemed to be artfully flirting with him. Yet when she hit the bed last night, she'd been first to turn on her side away from him. He was terribly confused about what she wanted out of him. Now here she came, up the hill with a dipperful of water, wearing those abominable britches again. Karl was getting mighty tired of those pants.

When she neared, she handed him the dipper, saying, 'Here, Karl, I thought you might be thirsty out here in the sun.' She raised her wide eyes coyly to assess his beaded brow and the damp tendrils of hair across it.

'Thank you, Anna, I am.' He took the dipper, studying her across the lip of it as he raised his head and drank. 'How are your curtains coming?' He handed the dipper back to her.

'Fine.' She hooked the dipper over her index finger and swung it like the pendulum of a clock, with her other hand still resting on her cocked hip. 'So how are your windows coming?'

'Fine.' He had all he could do to keep from smiling.

She looked around innocently, glancing at the billets, his axe, the pile of chips. 'What are you working on up here?'

'I am splitting window edgings from yellow poplar.'

She glanced around, spied the pile of rocks nearby, then asked, 'Do you mind if I watch for a while?'

For the life of him he couldn't figure out why she would want to, but he nodded. He used two wedges and a small wooden sledge. She sat on the rock pile left over from their chimney, watching as Karl worked. It was disconcerting having her sitting there with that innocent look plastered all over her face. He wished that he knew what she was up to.

He picked up his axe, drove it into the edge of a billet, inserted the wedge, watching carefully for knots, which could make the cleavage go awry. When the first board fell free, Karl picked it up, looked at Anna and said, 'Yellow poplar splits smooth as anything. The only thing you must remember is to watch for knots where branches grew before.'

Anna lounged casually upon her rock, knees crossed, one foot swinging. 'I'm not James, Karl,' she said in a voice as smooth as warm honey. 'I won't be needing to learn the art of board-making. I just came out to watch, that's all. I like to watch you work with the wood.'

'You do?' Karl asked, his eyebrows lifting in astonishment.

She swung a foot, and let her eyes wander over him in a most suggestive fashion. 'Yes, I do. It seems there's nothing you can't do with wood. I like to watch your hands on a piece that way. You sometimes look like you're caressing it.'

Karl dropped his hand from the newly hewn plank as if it had suddenly developed nipples. Anna laughed lightly and settled more comfortably onto the rock pile, leaning her elbows back so her breasts thrust forward.

'Don't your shoulders ever get tired, Karl?'

'My shoulders?' he parroted.

'Sometimes I watch you and I can't believe how long you can work with an axe without tiring.' Somehow she was toying with her hair, lifting it off the back of her neck and letting it flop back down repeatedly.

'A man does what must be done,' Karl said, trying to concentrate on his board-making.

'But you never complain.'

'What good would complaining do? A job takes so many hours of work, complaining will not shorten those hours.'

Her eyes followed his every flex of muscle as he worked – every movement sinuous and inviting as her voice rippled on provocatively. 'But with you, Karl, I think there's no complaining because you like what you're doing so much.'

He kept his eyes and hands busy with the poplar, but a giddy sensation was tingling his nerve endings. He knew now that she was playing him like a northern pike on a long, strong line. He had avoided being caught by her for some time now, but this was the first she had ever retaliated with such obvious flirting.

She leaned back and studied him from behind half-closed lids awhile longer before murmuring in a low tone, 'It's like watching a dancer when I watch you with your axe. From the first day I saw you with it, I thought so. You make every motion smooth and graceful.'

The only thing Karl could think of to say was, 'That's how my papa taught me. That is how I teach the boy.' He wondered if his face was as red as it felt. He continued working while she just sat there, stretching in the sun, lazing, eyeing him up and down until he thought he'd lose control of his own axe.

At last she sighed. Then she clenched both fists and stretched her arms straight out at her sides in one last sinuous pose. 'Ooops!' she squeaked with a little giggle, for she'd knocked one of the rocks off the pile behind her and it went tumbling, taking a couple others with it. She stood up, bracing hands on knees and thrusting out her breasts and derrière, sighing, 'Well, I guess I'd better get back down to – '

'Don't move, Anna!' he whispered, a fierce warning in his voice. His eyes had veered down to the base of the rock pile. They remained glued to the spot while he reached blindly, feeling for his axe.

The rattler had not made a sound, had given no indication it was sunning itself on the rock pile. But when the stones became dislodged and went rolling, the snake was suddenly exposed. Startled, the reptile curled into its fighting coil, raised its neck into the sharply oblique bow that warned of an imminent strike.

Anna looked down, following the path of Karl's gaze just as the stout tail began its warning buzz. Her stomach tightened and her limbs tensed as she confronted the snake's sulphur yellow eyes with their demonic elliptical pupils.

It happened so fast Anna scarcely had time to become mesmerized by shock. Karl's blind hand found the axe handle, and the next second the timber rattler was in two pieces, each leaping and coiling while Anna screamed, unable to take her eyes from the streaks of dark brown and yellow that writhed through the air in grotesque death twirls. Before the severed snake fell lifelessly to the earth, Karl's arms were around Anna, one of his big hands cupping the back of her head as he picked her up that way and set her away from the rock pile.

'Anna . . . Oh my God, Anna,' he spoke into her hair.

She sobbed, followed by frightful spasms of quaking.

'It is all right, Anna. I have killed it.'

'Your axe, Karl,' she wailed senselessly.

'Yes, I killed it with my axe. Don't cry, Anna.'

James was running up the hill by this time, alerted by

Anna's scream, which had carried through the still air over the clearing like the shriek of a screech owl.

'Karl, what's wrong?' he called.

'There was a timber rattler, but it is all right now. I killed it.'

'Is she okay?' James asked, frightened instantly.

'Ya, she is safe.' But Karl did not relinquish his hold on her.

Anna continued to mutter senselessly something about Karl's axe while he attempted to soothe her. He tried to take her over to the woodpile and set her down, but she was too panicked to go near it.

'Your axe,' she cried again.

'Anna, the snake is dead now. You are all right.'

'But, K . . . Karl . . .' she sobbed, 'your axe is . . . is in the dirt . . . your axe is in the d . . . dirt.'

It was. Karl's precious honed steel, which never touched anything but worthy wood, had half of its poll buried in the earth. He looked at it over Anna's head, then squeezed his eyes shut and held her trembling body against his chest.

'Shh, Anna, it does not matter,' he whispered.

'But you . . . s . . . said – '

'Anna, please,' he entreated, 'shut up and let me hold you.'

There was no question of trying anything intimate with Anna that night. She was in such a shaken state when Karl tucked her into bed, he would have felt guilty even to lay a hand on her.

He and James sat up examining the rattles the boy had cut off the carcass. When James asked why a rattler would show up this late in the season, Karl explained that contrary to popular belief, they could not stand the hot sun. During the height of the summer they hid beneath their stone piles. But when the autumn sun grew less fierce, they came out once again to warm themselves, as if storing up heat before hibernating.

'They are getting ready for winter, too,' he ended, glancing at the bed where Anna tossed fitfully.

'Like us, Karl, huh?'

'Ya. Like us, boy.'

James looked at Anna, too, then asked, 'Karl? When will we move into the cabin?'

'How about tomorrow? I must put up the stove and finish putting in one more window and make the door. But I can do that if you will wash the hides and get them ready for stretching. I think it is time we get Anna into a wooden house.'

But they did not get everything finished the next day, though each worked like a dynamo.

Something told Karl that tonight was not the right night to make his final peace with Anna. One more night . . . one more night and they would be in the cabin for the first time. Then, then he would do what he now longed more than ever to do.

During that day and the next, he looked up often to find Anna watching him, whether from across the clearing, or from across the cabin, it was always the same. He knew that she, too, was waiting for the first night they would sleep in the house they had built together.

She brought him a drink again while he sat in the sun of the cabin door, smoothing the planks for the door. She stepped inside and after she'd been in there quietly for some time, Karl turned around to find her standing there, unmoving, studying the new floor of the loft above her, white and sweet-smelling and with its own ladder that rose to the hatchway across the way.

During that last day Karl put the stove up. It fitted together like pieces of a jigsaw puzzle, but Anna did not rejoice over it as he thought she would. She remained almost timid now since he had killed that rattler and held her while she cried and trembled.

James worked at stringing the ropes for his own bed while Anna worked on those for her and Karl's bed. Karl showed them how to weave and splice the tough fibres of the prairie grass into tough, thick-gauged rope.

Once when James's fingers got tangled up and his weaving slipped loose, he asked Anna how she could do it so smoothly.

'Don't ask me,' she answered. 'Ask Karl. If anyone knows his way around a bed rope it's Karl.' But she never glanced up, just kept weaving away at her own rope, sitting cross-legged in those britches in the middle of the cabin floor. Even James might have suspected a play on words had Anna looked amused or sprightly. But she only pulled her lip between her teeth, concentrating hard on her chore.

Meanwhile, Karl finished the door. He used the undauntable oak, which took more work splitting than any other wood because of its hardness. Karl worked away patiently, shaping and rubbing the panels smooth, then fashioning cross braces onto which the panels would be pegged.

In the early afternoon James and Anna began carrying their belongings from the sod house into the log house. They lugged dishes and bowls and barrels that were half empty, leaving the full flour barrels for Karl to fetch. Karl watched them parade past him, while he hinged the door, then tightened the final wooden pins. Then he set about tying the loosely placed ropes that needed only fastening to become beds.

Anna, a little withdrawn, sometimes almost shy, continued carrying their goods to the log cabin. Once, as she paused across the way to stretch her back after a heavy load, Karl watched her tuck her shirt into her britches, pulling in a deep breath and thrusting her breasts forward, standing that way, unaware that he watched her. Then she looked as if she sighed, though he heard no sigh from this distance, and she ran her hand deeply into the recesses of those pants, both front and back, ostensibly tucking in her shirttails again. She did all this in full profile to Karl. Just when he began to ask himself if Anna knew that he watched her, she looked up and discovered him with his hands idle upon his work, his eyes busy on her silhouette. She snapped almost guiltily away and fled into the sod house.

After she was gone, Karl contemplated what he had seen. When had her sharp-boned thinness mellowed and moulded? How long had this contoured woman been hiding in boy's britches? Karl smiled, thinking of Anna's cooking, realizing she'd done all right eating it herself, in spite of all the self-criticism she heaped upon it.

Anna watched James taking down the blanket that had served as her dressing room ever since they'd lived here. He stepped off the trunk and she offered, 'Here, I'll help you fold that.'

'All right,' he said. They each took two corners and stretched them out; there was scarcely room to do so in the cramped sod hut.

'James, I have a favour to ask you.'

'Sure. What is it, Anna?'

'It's a very selfish one,' she warned.

'Don't kid *me*, Anna. I know you better than that.' He angled her a knowing smile.

'Oh, but it is! Especially because I ask it today, of all days.'

'Well, ask!' he demanded brightly.

'I want you to ask Karl if you can take the team and ride over to the Johansons as soon as all the work is finished.'

'You mean tonight?'

'No, this afternoon,' Anna declared, feeling uncomfortable at this suggestion, for surely James would guess her intentions.

'What do you need from over there?'

They came nearly chest to chest, folding the blanket.

'I don't need anything from over there.'

'Well then, what am I going for?'

'Just to get away from the house for a while.' Her face went pink.

'But, Anna – '

'I know, I know. Today we're moving into the log cabin and everything. I told you it was selfish. You'd have to miss our first supper on the new stove and our first meal in the cabin together.'

'But why?' James balked, and Anna despaired of ever enlightening him without drawing pictures.

'James, things have been – I need some time alone with Karl.'

'Oh,' he said shortly, the light suddenly dawning. 'Well . . . in that case, sure. I'll be gone just as soon as I can.'

'Listen, little brother,' she said, reaching out to touch his arm, 'I know it's unfair of me to ask it tonight, but believe me, it's got to be tonight. Karl and I have to straighten out some differences between us that have been festering for too long already. I'm afraid that if we don't get things ironed out now, they may drag on forever, and I couldn't stand – oh, James, I feel just awful asking you tonight.' She suddenly plopped down on the bare rope bed and looked at the floor dejectedly. 'I know you've been looking forward to moving in just as much as we have. Believe me, I wouldn't ask if it wasn't absolutely necessary. I can't explain it all, James . . .' She looked up beseechingly. 'But it's got to be today, tonight.'

'What should I tell Karl? I mean, I never asked to take the team out alone before.'

'Tell him you want to go calling on Nedda.'

'Nedda?' James's Adam's apple did monkeyshines.

'Am I too far wrong in thinking you won't mind?'

'Go calling on Nedda?' James seemed thunderstruck by

the idea, even though he, himself, had been toying with it ever since Nedda suggested it herself. 'No! No, I won't mind a bit. But do you think Karl will let me?'

'Why not? He made you a teamster himself. He trusts you with Belle and Bill. Anyway, you went to Johansons the night I got lost in the woods, and made it just fine.'

'I did, didn't I?' He remembered how proud Nedda had been of him then.

'That's not all I need you to do, James.'

'What else?'

'I need for you to get Karl away from the house first, for at least an hour, longer if you can.'

'How can I do that? He won't want to leave the log house.'

'Make him go to the pond with you for a bath. Try to get him playing like we used to do all together, remember? That should keep him there a while.'

'What are you going to do while we're gone?'

Anna arose with the blanket folded over her arm. She ran her hand over it with a little look of slyness. Then she smiled at her brother in a way he was soon to learn meant some fellow was going to meet his match. 'James, that is a woman's secret. If you're old enough to go calling on Nedda, you're old enough to know a man doesn't ask a woman to tell all her secrets.'

James coloured a little, but he was unsure of something and didn't know what to do but ask about it.

'Anna, do I – should I ask the Johansons if I can stay all night?'

'No, James, I wouldn't ask that of you. I know how you've been waiting to sleep in your own loft for the first time. There's no need for you to stay out long past mid-evening. We'll be looking for you to come back then.'

'Okay, Anna.'

'You'll do it?' she asked breathlessly.

' 'Course, I'll do it. I'm sorry I didn't think of it myself.

From now on, if Karl lets me go this once, I'll go more often. I like visiting at their place. Besides,' James added, hooking a thumb in his back pocket, gazing down at the floor almost guiltily, 'I'd do darn near anything to see you and Karl the way you were before. I know things've been sour between you for a long time and I hate it. I just . . . I just want us all to be happy like before.'

Anna smiled and reached to lay her hand on the long hard forearm and force him to take his hand from his back pocket so she could hold it. 'Listen, baby brother, if I haven't said it for a long time, it's been my fault, not yours . . . but, I love you.'

'Gosh, I know that,' he said with a sideways smile lining his face. 'Same goes for you.'

Anna put her arms around him, taking the blanket into her hug as she pressed him to her. She had to reach up now to get her arm around his neck, he was so tall. She could sense James's having grown up not only physically but also emotionally this summer, for he made no attempt to pull away in embarrassment. He allowed himself to be hugged, and returned the pressure with a silent wish that whatever Anna had planned for tonight, it would work.

She pulled away. 'Thanks, baby brother.'

'Good luck, Anna,' replied James.

'You, too. That's one stubborn Swede out there, and if he decides he doesn't want to go to the pond, you'll have your work cut out for you getting him away from the clearing.'

The hanging of the freshly hewn door was symbolic to all of them, but mostly to Karl. When it swung on its wooden hinges at last, he stood in its opening, looking first into the cabin, and then out of it.

'Due east,' he said, glancing contentedly off across his cleared grainfields to the rim of the woods, which waited yet to be cleared.

'Just like you always said,' James confirmed.

Karl turned to rub his hand over the panels of the door. 'Oak,' he said, 'good, tough oak.' And he gave the door a slap.

'Just like you said, too.'

'Just like I said, boy, and do not ever forget it.'

'I won't, Karl.'

Karl now looked at Anna. 'And you have not forgotten you made me promise to let you be the first to pull the latchstring in.'

Pleased he had remembered this from the days of early summer when they had lain in the dark whispering of such dreams to each other, Anna beamed and turned pleasantly rosy. But she hung back yet, wondering if this meant a reconciliation. The way he gazed at her, the way he stood with the light from the doorway behind him making his hair into a golden halo, the way he reminded her of those whispered secrets from long ago . . .

'So, Mrs Lindstrom,' Karl said, 'why do you not try out your new door?'

Flustered now, she hastened to do so, saying, 'Well, come on in, both of you. I'm certainly not going to take the latchstring in against my two favourite men, leaving them on the doorstep for the first time!'

Karl and James went inside to join her. James closed the door. Karl raised the bar and dropped it in place. Anna pulled at the latchstring, finger over finger, until a little round ball filled the hole and dropped inside.

'Did you carve this?' she asked Karl, holding the small wooden ball in her fingers. It was so perfectly round!

'No! It is a hazelnut. I promised I would show you a hazelnut.'

She smiled mischievously. 'But the squirrels will eat it right off the string.'

'The squirrels must eat, too. So, let them. I will get another. I have plenty.'

She looked up into Karl's face, keeping her own carefully expressionless, yet sincere, as she said, 'Yes, Mr Lindstrom, I believe you do.'

James observed the way both Karl and Anna seemed to have forgotten he was there. Suddenly, with high heart, he believed he *would* have trouble getting Karl away from the clearing, but not for the reason Anna had predicted. He broke into their reverie, suggesting, 'Karl, why don't you get that stove stoked up and then we'll go down and have a swim?'

'A swim? When we only just got into the log cabin? A man needs time to get acquainted here first.'

'But I'm in kind of a hurry, Karl.'

Karl was reluctant to tug his eyes away from Anna, but the boy was persistent. 'You are in a hurry? What is it that makes you hurry? All these days we rush to finish the cabin. Now it is done and it is the time to ease up and enjoy it.'

'Well, I want to – I got something I need to ask you.'

'Ya, well ask then.' Anna had turned away and had started fiddling with the stove lids. She'd probably never built a fire in a stove either, Karl thought, seeing what she was doing. So he went to do it.

'Could I take the team down to Johansons by myself?' James asked.

Karl turned around from the stove, genuine surprise on his face. 'The team?'

'Yeah . . . I . . . I wanna go calling on Nedda.'

'Today?'

'Well, yeah . . . what's the matter with today?' James had his thumbs hooked in his rear pockets again.

'But this is the day we are going to have our first supper in the cabin. Anna's going to cook on the new stove.'

'Today's the first chance you give me to set down, too. We've been working on this cabin practically all summer. And when it wasn't the cabin keeping us busy, it was harvesting or trimming hooves or something else. What else have you got for me to do today?' James sounded genuinely irked.

Anna turned away, smiling at her brother's ingenuity, thinking, good for you, James! You can be a little shyster if you want!

Karl was truly surprised. He hadn't realized the boy had been hankering to get away from the place. If there was one thing Karl was gullible about, it was about James's deserving some time away. Without realizing it, James had tripped upon the weakest spot in the big Swede.

'Why nothing,' Karl admitted. 'There's nothing for you to do here. We are finished with everything.'

'Then why can't I go?' James actually managed to sound persecuted.

'I did not say you could not go.'

'Is it the team, Karl? Don't you trust me to take 'em out alone?'

'Sure, I trust you with the team.'

'Well, can I take 'em, then?'

'Ya, I suppose you can. But what about supper?'

'I'd just as soon eat with the Johansons if it's all the same to you. That way I can get an early start over there.'

'But, Anna was maybe planning something on the new stove.'

'No offence, Anna, but if it takes you as long to get used to cooking on the new stove as it did to get used to the fireplace, I'd just as soon eat at Katrene's. Do you mind?'

Anna almost giggled out loud. Here all this time she'd thought her brother had forgotten how to be a little con man, but James was a genius at it!

'No, I don't mind. There'll be other meals at home.'

'I don't think Katrene will mind either, and I sure do like her cooking.'

To herself, Anna thought, all right, *brother*, enough is enough!

'I'd like to go as soon as possible, Karl, but first I need

339

to talk to you. I thought maybe you'd come down to the pond with me. I want to clean up before I go, anyway.'

'I was not planning on going down to the pond. Could we talk here?'

'I . . . I wanted to sort of . . . you know, talk man to man.'

Bravo! thought Anna.

'Well . . . well, sure.' Karl looked hesitantly at Anna.

At the look Karl gave her, Anna encouraged, 'Listen, you two go. The water is too much for me now. I don't think I could stand getting into it when it's that cold. I'll stay here and play with my new toy,' she said, indicating the stove.

Karl could only go along with the boy's request. 'Get your clean things, James. We'll go now and you can get to their place before supper, like you want.'

James climbed the ladder to the loft where his articles were neatly laid out, next to his own rope bed with its new tick of cornhusks.

Downstairs, Karl turned his eyes again to Anna. 'I wish you would come with us today, but I think the boy has something on his mind.'

He's not the only one, Karl, thought Anna, before she said, 'It's his first time going to call on a girl. He's probably nervous and the swim will calm him down a bit. You remember your first time, Karl.'

There was something different about Anna today. Something almost provocative as she laid that seemingly innocent reminder on her husband. She merely continued doing little things around the stove while she said it, but at her words Karl certainly did remember his first time, quite vividly. His first time with Anna. The incredible wonder of his first time with Anna.

'Ya, I remember,' he said. 'I was plenty nervous.'

'Tell him that then, Karl, so he'll know he's not the only one to feel that way,' Anna said.

At last she looked at him. Was it a challenge in her eye now? The words were spoken in simplicity, but what ulterior meaning was behind them? She was talking about herself and her first time with him, Karl was sure of it. She had kindling in her hands, a look of utter artlessness upon her face. With all this talk, that fire had never been built. That first fire in the stove had never been built.

'I will build the fire before we go,' Karl said, breaking the invisible grip that had him clutched by his windpipe. He reached out, and she placed the pieces of kindling in his hand. He turned to build the fire in the stove which he had brought home for his Anna, thinking to her, I will build my fire always for you, Anna. What a fool I have been to keep it banked for so long.

James came clattering down the ladder and crossed to Anna. He put an arm loosely around her shoulders, casually, in a grown-up brotherly way.

'So, you have your stove at last. I just hope it does the trick.'

Anna thought, don't you worry, baby brother, it will. I'm sure of it!

When the fire was going strong, the two left the cabin. Karl had carefully refrained from eyeing his wife too much in the presence of the boy. Things had suddenly kindled in himself, things that he was sure would show if he wasn't careful.

She watched them walk across the clearing. When they reached the far side, Anna called, 'Karl?'

He turned to see her standing in the open cabin door with a hand shading her eyes.

'Ya, Anna?'

'Would you take a little water with you and water my hop bines as you pass them in the woods?'

He raised his hand – a silent salute of consent – and went to the spring for a pail. Anna knew that the hop bines had already taken root out there in the woods.

21

Anna sprang into action the minute their backs disappeared up the trail to the pond. Her stomach hurt with the old familiar ache of unsureness. Every nerve in her body, every muscle, every fibre wanted this to work. All she could think about was pleasing Karl. How much time did she have? Enough to wait for the water to warm on the stove?

She listened for the first sizzle of the kettle while she put their house in order. She hurried to hang the curtains at the windows on arching willow withes. Next she laid a matching gingham cloth upon the table, then their dishes, knives, mugs. She used precious minutes to pick the wildflowers, running all the way out to the edge of the field where they grew. These she placed in the centre of the table in a thick pottery milk pitcher: clusters of Karl's beloved Minnesota. There were the late-blooming lavender asters, brown-eyed susans, lacy white northern bedstraw, feathery goldenrod, rich purple loosestrife, brilliant pink blazing star and lastly ... most importantly ... she interspersed the bouquet with fragrant stalks of yellow sweet clover. Standing back, she took a moment to assess her handiwork, wondering what Karl would say when he walked in and saw it.

But time was fleet-footed; the water was warmed now. She bathed, using the fragrant camomile soap for the first time. Then she hurried to don the new dress. Her stubborn hair thwarted her fingers, its wilful curls resisting her efforts to bend it to her will. But she persisted with trembling fingers.

When at last both she and the cabin were in order, she

gave herself one last look in their tiny mirror. Peeping into it critically, she closed her eyes, feeling the blood raddle her cheeks. She put the mirror down. She pressed both hands upon her stomach, fighting for calm, for reassurance that what she was doing was the right thing. Again doubt assailed her. Suppose Karl was not wooed by her efforts? How could she ever face him again? Suddenly, she thought about James entering the cabin and seeing the evidence of her attempted seduction, and knew she couldn't face him while he took in the curtains, the table, her dress.

When she heard them returning, she hid behind the curtain in the corner. She sat down on the trunk and pulled her feet up off the floor so they wouldn't know she was back there. Agonized, she hugged her knees to her chest, waiting with closed eyes to hear what was said when they first walked in.

James was speaking as they entered. '. . . because it gets dark earlier these nights, so I'll be sure to start back – ' She didn't need to see him to know that James came up short at the sight of that table. The silence spoke volumes before James said in an awed tone, 'Gosh, Karl, look at that!'

Not a word came from Karl. She imagined him, stopped in the doorway, holding his dirty clothes, maybe with a hand on the edge of the new door.

'Flowers, Karl,' James said almost reverently, while Anna's heart threatened to choke her. 'And the curtains. She hung the curtains.'

Still not a word from Karl.

'I thought she was kind of silly to spend all that time on curtains, but they sure look good, don't they?'

'Ya. They sure look good,' Karl said at last.

Anna leaned her head against the wall in her little corner, breathing as shallowly as possible so they wouldn't suspect she was there.

'I wonder where she is,' James said.

'I . . . I guess she is around somewhere.'

'I . . . I guess she is. Well, I better get my hair combed before I leave.'

'Ya, you do that. I will get Belle and Bill harnessed for you.'

'You don't need to, Karl. I can do it myself.'

'It is all right, boy. I have nothing else to do until Anna gets back from wherever she is.'

'Okay, I sure appreciate it.'

An eternity passed while James whistled softly through his teeth, going up the ladder, coming back down. When Anna thought she couldn't stand it a minute longer, she heard his footsteps echo across the floor toward the door, then disappear. From outside came their voices again.

'Thanks, Karl.'

'Ya, it was nothing. You have harnessed them plenty times for me. It was nothing.'

'Well, this might be, too, but here goes.'

They laughed together, then Anna heard Karl say, 'Just remember what I said.' She smiled to herself.

'Now you say hello to Olaf and everybody for Anna and me.'

'I will. And don't worry, I'll take good care of Belle and Bill.'

'That is one thing I do not worry about. Not any more.'

'See you later then, Karl.'

'Ya. Have a good time.'

'I will. Bye.'

Now is the time, thought Anna, Now, while Karl is still outside, I should go out and maybe be waiting by the stove when he comes in. But she couldn't make her limbs move. I've wrinkled my skirt by sitting here hugging my knees too tight, she thought wildly. I should have an apron like Katrene's. Oh, why didn't I think of making an apron?

She waited too long and heard Karl's heels on the floor. A few steps, then he paused. Was he studying the table? Is he wondering where I am? Will he think me stupidly

344

childish when he discovers I have been hiding behind the curtain all this time? She pressed her hands to her cheeks again, but her palms seemed as hot as her face. She swung her feet to the floor and pulled the curtain open. In the pit of her stomach things were jumping and twitching like there were live frogs in there.

He was standing with his hands in his pockets, studying the table. The movement of the blanket as it was drawn aside caught his eye, and he looked up. Slowly, he withdrew his hands. Slowly, he lowered them to his sides.

Anna paused, holding onto the blanket.

The right thing to say eluded both of them, especially Karl.

Upon what should he make comment? Her table, set beguilingly with that crisp flowered cloth and the fresh blossoms she had gathered and placed in the homespun way his own mother used to do? Or should he mention the curtains she'd hung at the windows; they charmed him when at first he'd been so disappointed she was wasting the pink gingham on such things? Or the dress she had stitched as a surprise for him – simple, long-sleeved, full-skirted, matching those crisp, pink curtains? Or maybe her hair, her lovely, curling, Irish, whiskey-hair drawn severely into braids and wound into a coronet at the top of her head.

Karl searched his mind for the proper word. But, much like the first time he had ever laid eyes on her there was only one word he could say. It came out, as it had so often, questioning, wondering, telling, a response to all he saw before him, a question about all he saw before him. All he had, all he was, all he hoped to be was wrapped up in that single word: 'Onnuh?'

She swallowed but her eyes stayed wide and unsure. She dropped the curtain, then clutched her hands behind her back.

'How was your swim, Karl?' she asked.

Unbelievably, he didn't answer.

'Was the water cold?' she tried again nervously.

Thankfully, he spoke, at last. 'Not too cold.' His cheeks and forehead were shiny clean, lean and tanned. His hair was freshly combed. The late afternoon sunlight came slanting in one of their precious glass windows, reflecting off his clean skin and hair, turning it even more golden. From clear across the room she thought she could smell his freshness.

'I see James got off all right.'

'Ya. He is gone.'

Her hands hurt. She suddenly realized her hands hurt. With a conscious effort she loosed them and brought them out of hiding. 'Well . . .' she said, flipping them palms up in a nervous, little gesture.

Karl swallowed. 'You have been busy while the boy and I were at the pond.'

'A little,' she said stupidly.

'More than a little, I think.'

'Well, it's our first meal and all.'

'Ya.'

Silence again.

'So, did you and James get things talked over?'

'Ya. I don't know what good I did him, though. I am not so good at courting myself.' He stuffed his hands into his pockets again.

Anna felt as if her tongue were paralysed.

They stood there with only the sound of the fire snapping in the new wood stove, until finally Karl added, 'He seemed to be a little less nervous by the time he left. The talk must have done him good.'

'I thought it would.'

'Ya.'

Anna searched frantically for something to say. 'Well, he sure didn't seem to mind missing supper with us.'

'No, he didn't.'

'Thank heavens for Nedda.' Once she said it, she could have pinched her tongue!

'Well . . .' Karl said, much like she had a moment ago.

'Are you hungry, Karl?' she asked.

Hunger was the farthest thing from his mind, but he answered, 'Ya, I am always hungry.'

'I have supper started, but I need to do some last-minute things.'

'There is no hurry.'

'We could have some tea, though, while we wait.'

'That would be good.'

'Rose hip?' She saw Karl's Adam's apple lunge as he swallowed.

'Ya. Rose hip is fine.'

'Well, sit down and I'll make it.' She flapped one clumsy hand toward the ostentatious table and finally forced her feet to carry her to the stove.

Karl pulled out his chair, but stood next to it, watching as she reached for the container from the makeshift shelf on the wall next to the stove. 'I wanted to have that dresser done for the kitchen by the time we moved in,' he said.

'Oh, it doesn't matter. There's plenty of time to get it made when the weather turns cold and there's not much else to do. I think I'd enjoy the smell of the wood while you're working in the house.'

'I have a tree picked out for it.'

'Oh? What kind?'

'I decided on knotty pine. The knots look like jewels when they are polished up. Unless you would rather have oak or maple, Anna. I could use oak or maple.'

He watched the sway of her skirts as she took the kettle and filled the pot with steaming water. She whirled around then, saying, 'Oh, no, Karl, pine will be fine.' But she whirled too fast and had to slap quickly at the lid of the teapot to keep it from flying off. He flinched as if to catch it if it came his way.

'Sit down, Karl, and I'll try not to scald you with the tea.'

He thought about pulling her chair out for her, but she didn't go over to it. She stood beside his, waiting for him to roost. When he did, she bent to pour his tea, and he caught the distinct drift of camomile about her.

While she poured his tea, she apologized, 'I'm sorry it's not comfrey. I know you like comfrey best. But I have a feeling you wouldn't have asked for it anyway, just because we don't have much left.'

'It doesn't matter that the comfrey died. We can find more of it wild in the woods and transplant it in the spring.'

'But you told me comfrey is your favourite.'

'I like rose hip just as much.'

She poured her own tea, then sat down opposite him. 'The first drink you taught me to make,' she said, raising her mug. 'Here is to rose hips,' she toasted, waiting with her mug aloft.

He followed her lead and clicked his mug against hers, remembering the first night. He'd made her rose hip tea to calm her down before bedtime. 'Here is to rose hips,' he seconded.

They lifted the cups to their lips, looking first at each other, then sharply away, over the rims of their mugs.

'When did you get all this done?' he asked, scanning the cabin.

She shrugged her shoulders, limp yet from the hurrying.

'The flowers are . . . I like the flowers in the milk pitcher that way.'

'Thank you.'

'And the cloth on the table, too.'

'Thank you,' she repeated.

'And the curtains. You match the curtains, Anna,' he said with a smile.

She too smiled. Funny, how they thought alike.

'I am a little camouflaged at that. You might have to search to find me.'

'I do not think so, Anna,' he said. 'The gingham does not look the same on the windows and on the table as it does on you.'

Damn my hands! she thought as one of them went up to brush down her collar like a simpering school girl.

'I was beginning to think I would have to make another trip to town for gingham if I did not want to see you in britches all winter.'

'You did mean it for dresses, then?'

'I guess I was a litle disappointed to see you using it all for curtains.'

'Not quite all.'

He lifted his cup toward her as a fencer might touch the tip of his sword to his fencing master. She lifted the tea pot to refill.

'The dress is lovely, Anna.' The tea jiggled a bit on its way to his cup.

'It is?' she asked, as if she'd only now discovered it.

'Much better than the britches.'

She couldn't help badgering him some more. 'I kind of got used to those britches, though.'

'I kind of did, too.'

'Don't tease me, Karl,' she said.

'Was I teasing?' he asked.

'I don't know. I think so.'

'And you do not want me to tease you any more?'

Oh yes, her heart cried, like you used to do. But she had to say, 'Not tonight,' hoping he would read the rest in her eyes.

He nodded silently.

'I have some things to do. You sit here and enjoy your tea while I get things . . .' But her words trailed off. She got up self-consciously, knowing he would be watching everything she did. She took down the new japanned frying pan and placed it on the stove. She took up the bowl and the whisk and began breaking eggs, cracking them against the edge of the crock.

'Where did you get the eggs?' he asked.

'From Katrene, the other day when we went over there to fetch Erik to help with the bear. But I was saving them for tonight.'

Again he fell silent, watching her as she whisked the eggs, then added them to the other dry things she had gotten ready in another bowl beforehand. She added milk, feeling his eyes on her back. When the batter was ready, she almost forgot and poured it into the pan without grease. But at the last minute she remembered, put a knob in the pan and sneaked a peek behind her to find Karl, indeed, watching her every move. The batter went sizzling into the pan, and she suddenly stamped her foot, remembering the jar of lingonberry jam still hidden in the root cellar.

'Oh! I forgot something. I'll be right back!' She ran at a most unladylike clip out the door, around the corner, and struggled with the ground-level door of the cellar. Down the steps she went, her skirts hindering her, worrying all the way how long it took Swedish pancakes to fry. The jar of jam was there, and she hurried back with it, dropped the cellar door in place and flew into the house to be greeted by the smell of scorching batter. She forgot to take up a pot holder, so the handle of the frying pan burned her hand when she reached to slide it to a cooler part of the stove.

Karl watched all this happening, not knowing if he should get up and flip the pancake over or let her do this her own way. It took every effort to stay where he was and let the pancake burn.

But when the japanned pan sang out in the quiet house, it echoed into too deep a silence. Anna's chin dropped down onto her chest, and from behind he saw the tender curls in the nape of her neck fighting to be free of the braids. Karl

350

saw her pull up a forearm and swipe it across her eyes, realizing she was crying.

He got up from his chair and picked up the pot holders, took the frying pan and flipped the pancakes out the door. He came back and set the pan down on the stove, then stood behind Anna and placed both of his hands on her upper arms, squeezing lightly.

'I make a mess of everything I do,' she wailed pitifully.

'No, Anna,' he said encouragingly. 'You have not made a mess of the curtains or the table or your dress, have you?'

'But look at this. Katrene showed me just how to do it, and I did everything like she said, but still, for me it's a disaster.

'You worry too much, Anna. You try too hard, and things upset you. Is there more batter you can fry?'

She nodded her head, dismally trying not to sniffle.

'Then put more on and start again.'

'What for? They'll just be another disaster. Nothing I do ever turns out right.'

He hated seeing her so defeated. If he could not get her to succeed at this attempt, which was so vital for both of them, he was afraid the beautiful beginning she had created would lead to nothing but defeat. He had to get her to smile a bit and try again. So, even though she had said she did not want to be teased tonight, he had to tease anyway.

'Perhaps the first ones were not such a disaster as you think. Nanna ate them this time.'

She turned to look out the door, and sure enough! There stood Nanna, her happy face turned their way while she ground her teeth against the last of the burned pancakes. Anna gave a sorry little snuffle of laughter, wiped her eyes with the back of her wrists and resolutely picked up the batter and began pouring cakes again while Karl took his chair at the table.

This batch turned out perfectly, but Karl didn't know it until she brought the plate to him.

'I would like to wait until yours are done, then we will both eat together,' he said.

'But these are all hot.'

'Use the warming oven of your new stove to keep them that way while you cook yours.'

'All right, Karl, if you say so.'

Her failure to produce perfection immediately lost some of its sting as she placed the lovely cakes into the oven, then poured more. While she did this, she heard Karl get up and light tallow dips flanking the pitcher of flowers. She turned with the two plates again. The sun had gone away; the candles were welcome now as dusk settled.

'There now . . . see?' he said sensibly when she was seated across from him again, 'these are beautiful pancakes you have made.'

'Oh, Karl, you don't have to say that. The biggest dolt in the world can make pancakes.'

'You are not the biggest dolt in the world, Anna,' he said, so painfully sorry he'd called her dumb the day of their fight, realizing how those stinging words must have added to her sense of inadequacy.

'Well, almost,' she said, staring at her plate.

'No,' he insisted, 'not even almost.' They gazed at each other for some time before Karl asked, 'Is that lingonberry jam you have there, or are you not going to let me find out?'

'Oh! Sure . . . here!' She handed it to him. 'But I didn't make it. Katrene did. She gave it to me.'

'Quit apologizing, Anna,' he ordered gently.

Unconcernedly, he garnished his pancakes with lingonberry jam and began eating, looking at her across the table with his shining face as placid as the surface of the pond. Never in his life had Karl had to force himself to eat like he did now. For all he cared, the goat could come in and eat up pancakes, jam and all, right off the plates, and it would not concern him one bit. But for Anna, he knew he must eat these pancakes, and ask for more.

She picked at her food with pitiful interest; Karl was much better at acting than she was. She jumped up gratefully to fry more, when he asked for them. By the time she brought the second batch, the candlelight was intimate and disconcerting, limning as it did every expression that passed their faces as they stared – silently, most of the time now – at each other, across the pancakes and lingonberries, the cups and rose hips, the asters and loosestrife, the gingham and sweet clover.

When he finished, he leaned back and slung one arm around the backpost of his chair. 'You never told me, Anna, what you thought of my gifts.' Those blue eyes studied her in a way that turned her calves to the texture of Katrene's jam.

'I thanked you for the stove, Karl. I love the stove, you know that.'

'I am not talking about the stove.'

'The gingham?'

'Ya. The gingham.'

'The gingham ... I love the gingham. It's really made the place cheerful.'

'I wanted to buy you a hat with a pink ribbon, but Morisette did not have any at this time of year.'

'You did?' She was surprised and warmed by his even wanting to.

'Ya, I did. But I had to get you the soap instead.'

She studied the tablecloth, picked at the edge of it absently with her thumbnail.

'I do like the soap, Karl. It's ... it's very special.'

'It took some doing to get that out of you.'

'It took some doing to get that soap out of you,' she said softly, thinking of all those bitter words they'd said the day he ran off in such anger.

'The night I brought it home, you did not seem to care much about it.'

'I was saving it.'

'For tonight?'

'Yes.' She looked down at her lap.

'Like the eggs for the pancakes?'

She made no reply.

'How long have you been planning tonight?'

She only shrugged her shoulders.

'How long?' he repeated.

Her tear-filled eyes flashed in the candlelight as she looked beseechingly at him. 'Oh, Karl, you came home that night and all you could talk about was Kerstin.'

'And I will perhaps talk about Kerstin often. She is our friend, Anna. Do you understand that? She made me see things, made me talk about things that only a true friend could make me see.'

Anna put her forehead in her hand and fought the tears. 'I don't want to talk about Kerstin,' she said wearily.

'But to talk about us, I must talk about Kerstin.'

'Why, Karl?' She looked him squarely in the face again. 'Because she's the one between us? Because she's the one you want?'

'Is that what you think, Anna?'

'Well, what am I supposed to think when ever since she came you have everything down the road you could have had if you'd only waited a few more weeks before bringing me here and marrying me?'

'Those are your words, Anna, not mine.'

'Well, they're true,' she accused with a touch of petulance. 'Do you think I don't know how you feel when you're at their place? It shows, Karl. You . . . you're happy and smiling and talking Swedish and eating Swedish pancakes like you were back in Skäne again!'

Karl leaned forward, placing his forearms against the table edge, looking deep into her eyes. 'Listen to me, Anna, and listen to yourself. You just said *their* place. That is what Kerstin made me see. It is *their* place that makes me happy. Yes, I am happy there, but it has nothing to do with

Kerstin any more than the others there. But she made me see how it must look to you. That is why I must talk of her.'

She sat across from him with her narrow shoulders pulled forward as she clasped her hands tightly between her knees. 'Karl,' she said plaintively, 'I can never be Kerstin, not if I try for a thousand years.'

His heart seemed broken and healed at once, broken for all the insecurity he had made her feel, but healed by the love that had driven her so far as to try to become what she thought he wanted. 'Anna, Anna,' he said with deep feeling, 'I do not want you to be.'

Suddenly she seemed confused. 'But you said – '

'I have said many things that were better left unsaid, Anna.'

'But Karl, she is everything you wanted for yourself, everything I lied about being . . . and more! She is twenty-four years old, and she can cook and keep house and raise gardens and talk Swedish and – '

'And wear her hair in braids?' Karl finished smilingly, raising his eyes briefly to her hair.

'Yes!' Anna answered wretchedly, 'and wear braids.'

'And so you thought you would try to be like her and it did not work?'

'Yes! I didn't know what else to do anymore.' She sounded utterly miserable, felt utterly miserable. Karl was so tempting, sitting there in the candleglow talking all nice that way. Every time she met his eyes, she wanted to fly around the table and kiss him. Instead, she looked at her lap, clenching her hands tightly in bonds of pink gingham to keep them from reaching out to him.

'Did you think, Anna, that maybe it was not you who needed to change, but me?' he asked now, so softly.

'You?' Her head snapped up and she laughed a little too harshly. 'Why, you're so perfect, Karl, any woman would be a fool to want you to change. There's not a single thing on this earth that you can't do or won't try or can't learn. You're patient, and you have a ... a grand sense of humour, and you care about things so much, and you're honest and ... and I have yet to see you defeated by anything. Why, I haven't found a single thing you don't know how to do.'

'Except forgive, Anna,' he admitted before the dusky room grew silent.

Flustered, she reached for her cup only to find it empty. But Karl captured her hand for a moment, then she pulled it away, clutched it between her knees again while she said, 'Even that, Karl, you would not have had to do if you had waited for Kerstin. I'm sure of it.'

'But I did not wait for Kerstin. That is the point. I had you, and I could not look past the one and only thing you could not change and try to forgive it. I have held onto my stubborn Swedish pride all these weeks, long after I could see that until I forgave you that one thing, you would not find pride in anything else you did.'

'Karl, I can't change what I did.' Her luminous eyes looked to him in supplication, which he knew she should not need to be feeling.

'I know that, Anna. It is something that Kerstin made me see. She made me see that I was wrong to hold it against you all this time.'

'You ... you talked with Kerstin about that, too?' she asked, aghast.

'No, Anna, no,' he assured her. 'It was about other things that we talked. About things like blueberry cobbler and an Irish girl who wants to have Swedish braids. She made me see you were trying to make up for things that did not need making up for, you were trying to be things you do not need to be. She made me see you were trying so hard to please me, you even try to be Swedish for me.'

He arose from his chair and came to bend on one knee beside hers. 'Anna,' he said, putting both hands on her knees, 'Anna, look at me.' When she wouldn't, he put a finger beneath her chin and raised it. He saw into the wide, brown eyes with the luminous teardrops quivering on their rims.

'Tonight you have done all this to please me. All the pretty gingham curtains and the flowers and this dress.' His hand rose to her collar, and he took it between two fingers. His eyes rose to her hair, and an infinitely tender tone crept into his voice. 'And these terrible braids that do not suit you at all because you have beautiful whiskey-hair that wants to curl its own way, flying free like it should be. All of this you do to win what was yours by rights from the first. Only I was too stubborn to give it to you. Do you know what that is, Anna?'

She thought he meant the right to his body, his love-making, but could hardly answer either of those. Instead, she remained silent.

'It is your pride, Anna,' he went on. 'Do you understand what I am saying?'

She shrugged her shoulders in a childish way.

'I am saying that when I walked into this cabin today I felt small and guilty at what I have made you do here. You have tried in all the good ways that make you my special little own Anna, to please me. All these weeks you have tried. But I make you do a thing like this.'

'Don't . . . don't you like it, Karl?'

'Oh, Anna, my little Anna, I like it so much that it makes me want to cry. But I do not deserve it.'

'Oh, Karl, you're wrong. You deserve so mu – '

He reached to cover her lips with his fingertips, stopping her words. 'You are the one who deserves, Anna. More than I have given. It is not enough that I have taken up my axe and cut trees to build you a home and that I have cleared land and raised food for its table and bought you a stove and a bar of soap. A home is only a home because of the people in it. A home is only a home when it has love.

357

And so if I give you all these things, what does it matter when I withhold myself?'

In his own fiercely honourable way, Karl kept his eyes glued to her face while he said all this. *When a man speaks of things which mean much to him, he does not hide it from showing in his face.* There, before Anna, all the pain and longing and want of Karl Lindstrom lay naked in the expression of his eyes upon hers, of his lips as he spoke, even in the hands that now stroked her hair, her collarbone, then the gingham skirt draped upon her knees.

'All these months, Anna, while I have planned this log house, I have dreamed about this first night in it and how it would be. I have thought of having you here and sitting with you at our table, and talking about things the way we would do after our supper was done. And always I dream of a fire in my hearth, and of loving you before it. Now, Anna, I find I have, by my own foolishness, almost lost all those things I worked so hard for. But I want them, Anna. I want them all, just like it is tonight. This beautiful table you have set, and you in your starchy little dress, and – '

But this time it was Anna who placed her trembling fingers over his lips, stilling them. 'Then, why do you talk so long, Karl?' she whispered, her voice soft and quavering and yearning.

The hunger in his eyes spoke passionately, even before he reached to take her face between his two hands and bring it slowly toward his own. Lips parted, eyes closing, he touched her mouth hesitantly with his own while she sat too stunned to move.

'Forgive me, Anna,' he whispered hoarsely, 'forgive me for all these weeks.'

Into his azure eyes Anna gazed wonderingly, wanting this moment to draw on into the forever of their years. 'Oh, Karl, there is nothing to forgive. I'm the one who should be asking.'

'No,' he uttered, 'you asked long ago, on the night you picked blueberries for me.'

Still kneeling, he took her hands apart and lowered his face into them where they lay on her lap. He needed so badly to be touched by her, to be assured of her forgiveness now. She looked down at the back of his head, at the blond wisps that waved into the shadowed hollow of his neck. Her love surged in devastating swells that overflowed from her eyes, blurring Karl's image before her.

To Anna came the intrinsic understanding that he must have the words she alone could give. Karl. Karl who in all ways was good and loving and kind. Karl needed her absolution from a transgression of her own making. She felt his flesh upon her palm and moved her other hand to twine her fingers in his hair. 'I forgive you, Karl,' she said softly, knowing utter fullness at the words, at the look in his eyes as he raised them to her face again.

Then the expression on his countenance changed, beautified, intensified. He rose to his feet and grasped her upper arms to draw her inexorably up, up, too. He pulled her to his chest, leaning to kiss her, clutching her arms like they were his salvation. Then, suddenly he freed them, placed them around his neck, hungry for the clinging to start.

She came against him in a grasping, wild, tumultuous kiss that touched his body from nose to knees. Within her open mouth his tongue tasted salt tears mingling with the kiss, and he took them from her, stroking her tongue with his, swallowing the salt of her sadness, taking it into himself, that she should never again know tears because of him.

'Don't cry, Anna,' he crooned, covering her face with kisses, holding the back of her head in both hands, as if she might slip away. 'Never again, Anna,' he promised, wiping away tears with his lips, then seeking the warmth of her neck, bending to her again, his face in the hollow of her gingham breasts now. Downward he kissed until he knelt on one knee with his face pressed to her stomach, drowning in the fragrance of camomile.

'Anna,' he said against her, 'I have loved you longer than you know.'

She leaned her head back and her eyes slid closed as he cradled his head against her and held her with one arm while he ran a hand warmly, firmly, possessively, from the hollow of her back to the hollows behind her knees, then up again.

'How long, Karl?' she asked greedily, drifting in sensuousness while his hands played over her. 'Tell me . . . Tell me everything you dreamed of telling me long before I came to you.' Her voice was a joy-wracked whisper as his hands continued their reacquaintance with her curves.

'I have loved you when I did not know you existed, Anna. I have loved the dream of you. I have begun loving you before I left my mother's arms. I have loved you while I find this land to which I would bring you and while I cut its timbers to build this home for you and while I reap my grains for you and build my fire for you . . . I know all my life you are waiting somewhere for me.'

'Karl, stand up,' she whispered, she begged. 'I have been waiting so long to feel you against me again.'

He rose to his full height, running his hands up her legs, up her hips, up her ribs. She was waiting with seeking mouth for his return.

Together they clung and touched: faces, hair, shoulders, breasts, tongues, hips. Even the hollow of his spine was hers at last as she ran her hand down inside the back of his pants. 'I can't believe you are letting me touch you at last,' she said breathily, her voice a strange thing in both their ears: aroused, eager, throaty.

'Never ask. You never have to . . . Never, Anna.' His eyes were closed, his breathing strained.

'Karl, how I used to watch you when you would lean to

build the fire, and think of running my hands over you this way.'

'And I watched you in those britches and wanted to put my hands here . . .' He fondled her breast, her stomach, 'and here . . . and here . . .'

'You never have to ask either, Karl,' she whispered, while his hands made free with her.

'Anna, I want to build a fire now. Do you want to watch me lean to build a fire?'

'Yes,' she whispered.

'Always have I dreamed of a fire.'

'Yes . . . yes . . .' she whispered, the waiting now a joyous agony.

'But I do not want you to ask anything while I do it.'

'I won't ask, Karl,' she whispered against his lips. 'Go build your fire for me, but if I cannot ask, you cannot either.'

'Only one thing, Anna, but now . . .'

Instead of asking what, she moved sinuously against him, blending her curves against his while her body promised what her words did not.

'Pull in our latchstring, Anna, and close our curtains that I did not think we needed.'

He had to put her from him, turning her toward the door while he went to the fireplace and knelt before it. He shaved golden curls from the hardwood logs. And he heard the swish of one curtain after another whispering upon their willow withe curtain rods. He leaned to touch steel to flint and heard the gentle rap of the hazelnut swinging upon its string against the sturdy oak panels of his door. Keeping his face to the hearth he laid kindling to the growing flame, hearing the rustle of cornhusks behind him, then a strange brushing sound that whispered along the floor. But he gazed into the fire, kneeling upon one knee until her hand slid slowly down from his neck onto his shoulder, then down, down across his back and into the back of his pants to pull his shirttail up. She caressed his warm skin there, fanning her fingers upon him until he closed his eyes to the fire, basking instead in the heat of her touch.

'How I watched these shoulders in the sun,' she whispered, raising his shirt as high as it would go, riding her hands up his back, then lowering her lips to the warm skin near a shoulder blade. Hunkered there on one knee, an arm cast out loosely, he dropped his forehead onto his biceps as she touched her tongue to his exposed back. 'How I watched them, you'll never know.'

He pivoted to face her then, finding her on both knees behind him, kneeling upon the heavy buffalo robe she had dragged over from the bed.

His hands moved onto her hips, pressing seductively. 'Did you watch them like I watched these hips, bending over in those britches?' Now his hands swam upward along her ribs to her breasts again. 'And how I wondered if I was mistaken about what was inside that shirt of your brother's.'

She pressed against his palm, heat rising everywhere through her body now. 'Were you mistaken?' she asked.

He had a handful of her firm breast, yet he answered, 'There is only one way to find out when memory is dim.'

He teased her buttons while she took lipfuls of his mouth, nipping gently at his lower lip.

'Memory can't recall what the eyes haven't seen, Karl,' she whispered, braving a hand upon the inside of his knee as he knelt before her.

'But you have worked so hard on your pretty gingham dress. It is a shame it got so little use.' Buttons came open one by breathtaking one.

'It would rather lie peacefully on the floor than get wrinkled and crushed,' she whispered against his lips.

'Would it?' he asked through his kiss.

'You said no questions, Karl.'

'These are not questions, Anna, these are answers.'

362

Then Karl's hand found the warmth of her breast and followed the valley between her ribs to the warm, low place that hungered for his touch.

Her eyes blinked once, slowly, as the contact of his hand swept the breath from her. Open-eyed again, she moved her hand to cup him, taking her turn at answers.

They leaned into each other's hands. Karl's moved exploringly. Anna's followed suit. They kissed, touching, learning each other, asking questions with only their hands.

'Warm . . .' Karl murmured in her ear.

'Hard . . .' Anna murmured in answer.

'Beautiful . . .' he said, knowing before he saw.

'Beautiful . . .' she answered, knowing, too.

They lost their balance and clung. They regained it and separated, looking deeply into each other's faces by the fire that blazed. And then there were only vivid sensations.

Light and heat accompanying his hands as they moved down the remaining dress buttons, then fell away in invitation as he knelt with knees slightly apart before her. Heat and light on the movement of her fingers as they opened the line of his shirt buttons, then dropped obediently to her sides to wait. Gilded shoulder as he pushed the dress back and the fireplay danced along one side of her body. Golden skin as she answered by taking his shirt in her hands and wresting it from his shrug. Adoring eyes as he took the hem of her shift in both hands and pulled it upward until she raised her arms. Roving glances as they knelt, resplendent in the fire's light, letting the goodness build. Time holding its breath as he slowly plied her last barrier, curving his palms to the shape of her hips as he rustled her naked. Time beating at her breast as he dropped his hands to his thighs again, kneeling before her expectantly, waiting in the gold hue of the burning logs. The force of a long summer's love, moving her to reach out to this man and free him from the last restraint of woven threads.

And then there were only two lovers, kneeling in the glow that limned their bodies in fireshine, that splashed a half of each with orange, that picked the radiance from one pair of eyes and sent it dancing to another, eyes that wandered and worshipped, widened and wondered.

When Karl at last raised his eyes to Anna's, he beheld there a breathless wonder to match his own. Moved by it he forgot himself and spoke to her in Swedish. The lilting mellifluousness fell from his tongue as a song in Anna's ears, although she did not know what he said.

How ever could she have taunted him for this mellow, musical richness? It was, she knew now, a part of Karl she loved as much as his muscled body, his golden face, his patience and inherent goodness. She suddenly wished to understand the songful words he spoke to her in such a reverent tone.

'What did you say, Karl?' she asked, her misty eyes lifting to his.

Running a finger beneath her jaw, down the rim of light that gilded her chin, neck, breast, stomach, thigh and knee, he spoke this time in English. 'Anna, you are beautiful.'

'No, say it in Swedish. Teach me to say it in Swedish.'

She watched his lips form the strange sounds. He had beautiful, bowed lips, a little full, very sensual now as he repeated, *'Du ar vacker, Anna.'*

Touching his lips, searching his face, she repeated, *'Du ar vacker, Karl.'*

With her fingertips still touching his skin, he said, *'Jag älskar dig.'* The way his eyes closed when the words were gone, the way he pursed his lips and cupped her palm hard against his mouth, she knew even before he repeated it, what it meant.

'Jag älskar dig, Anna,' he said, the beautiful pronunciation, *Onnuh,* making her heart dance crazily.

'Jag älskar dig,' Anna said softly, her Swedish sounding Yankee, but the meaning ringing forth, no matter what the

language. 'What did I say, Karl?' she asked in a whisper.

'You said that you love me.'

She took his face between her hands to kiss it. '*Jag älskar dig,*' she repeated, '*Jag älskar dig, Jag älskar dig, Karl,*' planting fevered kisses across his skin until she again forced his eyes closed.

Their warm flesh met. He took her tumbling down and over, until she felt soft fur below, firm flesh above, sandwiched between the two textures.

He clasped her, caressed her, kissing, learning what pleasured her when she smiled and nuzzled, then arched and moaned. With hands and tongue he brought her to a precipice where she trembled, waiting for the plunge that would carry her over. But the low sounds from her throat told him then to play her more slowly, extending the pleasure they found, each in the other.

He rolled over onto his back and stretched, taking every touch she gave, savouring the feel of her hands and lips becoming intimate with his honed body.

And then Anna slipped down and lay atop him, pressing warm and firm against him with breasts, belly, hips. Her braids had fallen down, the strands of her hair like filaments of the fire itself, surrounding her girlish face. He found a loose end, his fingers working it looser while she lay above him, kissing his neck and chest, meandering downward, downward. Soon he forgot her braids.

The two of them curled their bodies together, changed directions, kissing, tasting, trying to get enough, unable to. They gave each part of themselves freely, letting their senses expand beneath the joy. And when they hovered near their climaxes, righted again, shivering with anticipation, he made her say it one more time to compound his joy.

'Tell me again, Anna,' he uttered fiercely, one hand twined in her hair, the other touching her depths as she moved rhythmically against it. 'Tell me you love me like I love you.'

'*Jag älskar dig*. I love you, Karl,' she said, almost savagely, underlining the meaning of this act they now shared.

Once again they found the remembered magnificence from their first time, the grace in the blending of their bodies as he entered her, the litheness of movement as they flowed into a rhythm of mutual thrust and ebb.

They passed the bounds of language, creating a new one of their own, built of lovesounds – wordless murmurs, racked breathing, throbbing silences, pleasured moans. When their strength and suppleness brought them to the limits of fulfilment, they spoke the universal language: the deep, masculine shudder and groan, the strangled female response. Then together they collapsed, spent, in sated silence, with only the pop and titter of the fire sharing their communion.

He rested in her, at peace after all this time. She stroked the damp hair at the nape of his neck. His shoulders were drying now, beneath the touch of her fingers and the fire. His mouth rested in the depth of her neck.

When they had rested so for a long time, she spoke to the ceiling where the shadows danced. 'Karl, do you know what you are like?'

He spoke to her neck. 'What am I like?'

She wondered if she dared tell him, yet it was there on her mind, had been there since she first touched him, since before she had first touched him.

'You're like your axe handle when you have just laid it down.'

He braced himself up to look into her face. 'Like my axe handle?' he asked, puzzled.

'Smooth, warm, long, hard, curved . . . and like you once said, springy.'

'Not any more, I am not,' he said smiling.

'I knew you would tease me if I told you.'

'Yes,' he said, kissing her nose. 'From now on I shall

366

tease my Anna so she will never forget the feel of an axe handle.'

'Oh, Karl . . .' But her laugh came splashing.

'How I have missed that laugh,' he said.

'How I've missed your teasing.'

They smiled into each other's faces.

'Oh, Anna, you are something,' he said, gloriously happy. He let his eyes wander all over her face and hair.

'What am I?' she probed.

But he could not liken her to anything he knew. Nothing else was as good as she. 'I do not know what you are. I only know what you are not. You are not Swedish, and so you must not put these awful braids in that Irish hair of yours ever again. I tried to get them out, but I have only made them worse.' Then seeing her concern, soothed it. 'No, not now, Anna. You are a tempting little mess, so just leave it. And you are not fat and you are not the best cook and you are not the best gardener, but I do not care, Anna. I want you just as you are.'

'All right, Karl,' she said, looping her arms about his neck. 'I promise I won't ever change.'

'Good,' he said.

'But, Karl?'

'Ya?'

'If you're going to the trouble of teaching me to read and write this winter, you might as well teach me in both languages, right off the bat.'

He could only laugh and kiss her again, saying, 'Oh, Anna, you are something.'

When the night sounds were hushed and even the nocturnal creatures seemed abed, Anna and Karl joined them.

'Put the latchstring out for the boy, Anna,' Karl said, while he lifted the heavy buffalo robe and took it to their rope bed in the corner.

Anna opened the door and stood gazing out at the night

for a moment. 'Karl, I really never felt what you did about this place and all its plenty until I thought I had lost you. But I know now. I really know.'

'Come to bed, Anna.'

She smiled over her shoulder, then closed the door and padded across the newly hewn boards of the floor to the candlelight at their bedside.

Karl stood waiting there for her.

And in the centre of the bed, between their two pillows, lay a single shaft of sweet clover, plucked from the bouquet that had graced their dinner table, where lingonberry jam now dried on two forgotten plates.